Praise for THE SWINGING BRIDGE

"It is [Espinet's] unique combination of scholarship, poetic vision and childlike guilelessness that holds the reader captive. A moving island voice." *—The Gazette* (Montreal)

"*The Swinging Bridge* is a piece of activist fiction that offers . . . a forum for imagining, admission and healing. Espinet writes . . . in language that sings and stings with intellectual accuracy."*—The Globe and Mail*

"Innovative, searing and trail-blazing." *—Trinidad and Tobago Review*

"[Espinet's] writing swings and sing-songs with Trinidadian beats and rhythms. [She] allows . . . her lush, lore-soaked prose to take over . . . making this first novel one of promise and passion." *—Quill & Quire*

"Ramabai Espinet is a gifted writer who makes you feel like you are . . . a part of the 'history [that is] like a spider's web in which we were all caught fast.'" *—The Lethbridge Herald*

THE SWINGING BRIDGE

Ramabai Espinet

The
Swinging
Bridge

HarperPerennial Canada   *A Phyllis Bruce Book*

A Phyllis Bruce Book, published by Harper-
*Perennial*Canada, an imprint of HarperCollins
Publishers Ltd

Gabriela Mistral, "Doors" (excerpt), translated
by Doris Dana, from *Selected Poems of Gabriela
Mistral: A Bilingual Edition* (Baltimore: The Johns
Hopkins University Press, 1971). Copyright
© 1961, 1964, 1970, 1971 by Doris Dana.
Reprinted with the permission of Joan Daves
Agency/Writer's House, Inc., New York, on
behalf of the proprietors. Excerpts from Lord
Kitchener's calypsoes reprinted with the per-
mission of Mrs. Valarie Green Roberts. Parts of
this novel have been published as "Cane in
Arrow" in *Aurat Durbar,* ed. Fauzia Rafiq
(Toronto: Second Story, 1995) and as "Rain" in
Small Axe, Number 7, March 2000.

First published in hardcover by Phyllis Bruce
Books and Harper*Flamingo*Canada, imprints of
HarperCollins Publishers Ltd, 2003. This paper-
back edition 2004.

HarperCollins books may be purchased for
educational, business, or sales promotional use
through our Special Markets Department.

HarperCollins Publishers Ltd
2 Bloor Street East, 20th Floor
Toronto, Ontario, Canada
M4W 1A8

www.harpercollins.ca

National Library of Canada Cataloguing in
Publication

Espinet, Ramabai
The swinging bridge / Ramabai Espinet. –
1st HarperPerennialCanada ed.

"A Phyllis Bruce book".
ISBN 0-00-648595-2

I. Title.

PS8559.S68S894 2004   C813'.54
C2004-900351-8

RRD 9 8 7 6 5 4 3

Printed and bound in the United States
Set in Monotype Perpetua

For my parents,
Grace and Winston

THE SWINGING BRIDGE

I enter as one who raises
a cloth from a covered face,
not knowing what the narrow
almond husk of my house holds for me—
my salvation or my ruin.

Gabriela Mistral
1954

PART ONE

BORROWED TIME

KALA PANI

It is an untold story. Lines of women, veils pulled over their heads, seeking refuge at the shrine of Shiva in the holy city of Benares, walking round and round the sacred space, saying their secret prayers. Their burdens, their tragedies, their reasons for being here, lie hidden deep inside the layers of cloth that cover them—their orhnis, their dupattas and saris and cholis, the still fertile lines of belly exposed between subtle twists of diaphanous cloth. They are mainly rands, *widows who have escaped the funeral pyre by means of the laws forbidding sati laid down by British administrators in 1829. With no husbands to support them, many of these women face destitution. Those who have not given birth to sons are particularly vulnerable to abandonment by their in-laws. These unfortunates have swelled the ranks of women who sing in groups at street corners, in marketplaces, gardens, and at weddings, many of them belonging to the sect known as Vaishnavites, followers of Vishnu. The records of indentureship to the Caribbean show that Brahmin widows formed an inordinate number of the females who migrated.*

The year is 1879, and the women have been brought by train from Benares to the port city of Calcutta. Small boats ferry them to a ship, the Artist, anchored in the mighty Hooghly River. The gangplank clacks and swings precariously as the women scramble up onto the deck. Once aboard, those who are unattached keep their heads cast down as their names are checked. Those who are married, some of them quickly in the immigration depots as a means of finding male protection, stay one step behind their husbands. There are bold ones among them, proud women with fierce eyes, but many are insecure and frightened. At the Garden Reach Depot they have been registered as indentured immigrants and have been assured of safekeeping until they arrive in Trinidad—Chinidad, land of sugar. They will make plenty of money and the work will be easy because they will chinny chalay, sift sugar, all day long.

It takes a day to load the ship: whole families, single men, and this crowd· of women who cling together. On the Artist in 1879 there are 285 women and 159 men—unusual on these early voyages of lonely labouring men. Single men sleep in one large area near the prow of the ship, families occupy the middle area, and the single women are consigned to the far end.

Finally, once they are all on board—men, women, a few children, some topazes for cleaning the decks, sirdars, cooks, some of them Madrassis who travel with the ships and speak both Hindi and English, a doctor and two nurses, one of them Indian—the rickety bridge swings up and the ship is on its way, towed by tugboat down a treacherous channel to the island of Saugor. Dockside voices grow faint and then cease altogether. The evening darkens as they head out of the Bay of Bengal, India receding before the immensity of ocean billows, and now there is no horizon but water, nothing but pani, pani, pani . . .

My foremothers, my own great-grandmother Gainder, crossing the unknown of the kala pani, the black waters that lie between India and the Caribbean.

ONE

January 15, 1995.

Lately, words have been assailing me. Words like *ashes, cocoyea brooms, sem, chataigne, roti, chunkaying, lepaying, washing wares.* Everyday domestic words from long ago, a far-off time and place. Other words fly past me like spectres and they want something—words like *gloaming, lovevine, lianas, poisdoux, zaboca, mango vere, pomme-cythère, Manzanilla, calypso, j'ouvert morning, ginga, carilee, googoonie, chuntah, calchul.* Patois words and Hindi words.

Words are ghosts, ancestors on this side. They are not symbols. They are alive and sensate—full of flesh and stone and jagged edges. Word jumbies.

Mona Singh. That's me. I live in the eye of a storm. My whole life arches backwards and forwards according to the speed of the gust around me. In the centre, near the eye, in the place where I live, it is still. A small mercy.

Those were the words I was writing in my notebook early one morning in January when the phone rang and everything in my life turned around. Those old-time words were calling out to me, words like *carilee, sem, macajuel, mammy-sepote,* arising unbidden out of parts of my life no longer in use. Signals, beckoning me into the past.

The telephone rang and it was Muddie at the other end. Her voice was brisk but I heard something else, something like death stalking through the lines, she in Toronto and I in Montreal, and my brother Kello lying in a hospital bed, his lanky figure stretched between us like a hammock.

"Is Kello." She talked rapidly, sharply, as if giving instructions. "What happen is he collapse yesterday in his apartment and we had to call an ambulance. They take him to the hospital and we still don't know what it is. They doing tests now. We should know by next week. But they keep him there—no question about it, he was too sick to come back home. Mona, I so worried, I don't know what to do. What could be happening to Kello? He is the one always so strong, so capable, so fit . . . I don't understand what is happening."

What could be happening to Kello? Put like that, I felt certain that something was happening, something terrible. After trying to reassure Muddie I hung up the telephone and stared numbly through the window down at the empty street. Dirty snow drifts closed in on me. My flat was on the third floor, and the bare branches of an oak tree outside were so close that they would rattle menacingly against my windows when the wind was high. But the day was still, the silence unnerving, and I welcomed the flash of a creamy white squirrel, the kind I had seen nowhere but in Montreal, leaping through the air on its busy way to yet another, higher branch. Muddie's panic hung in the air; I hadn't even spoken to Da-Da or my sister Babs, but I knew the smell and sound of urgency. I would have to do something, make rapid decisions, move quickly. Kello was in danger, one of us was in peril, and maybe moving quickly would make a difference. I dialed Babs's cellphone but got only her chirpy message. *Oh my God, oh my God!* The words beat dully at the back of my mind. Muddie was enlisting my help, the way she had in old times, the kind of old times I had fled from years ago. I shut the notebook and jumped up to kickstart the day.

By the time I left the flat, the weather had turned blustery, and I fought my way to the metro against a fearsome wind. It was a day full of mindless trivia, all the tiresome details of tying up the research on a film project. The weather promised to get worse, so I bundled up my notes from the office, thankful that I was free to work at home. I was at the end of amassing data for a film on the lives of Haitian women in Montreal. Films Canadiana, a small innovative outfit, had provided my friend Carene with a base for her work over the last five years. In that time we had worked on several films together, mostly documentaries on immigrant life in Canada. She was beginning to earn a respected reputation as a filmmaker and I was happy for her—God knows, she had struggled long enough. Carene had come from St. Lucia in her twenties to attend university but somehow found herself still in Montreal, still talking about going back and making films in her own place, on her own terms.

I had been Carene's researcher for all of her projects, initially taking on the job simply to make money but continuing in spite of hectic plans to do my own film. I had in mind an experimental piece, *Rhapsody on a Windy Night*, using the T.S. Eliot poem in combination with live jazz, shot in the streets of Montreal. I wanted the frantic rhythm of the city, street scenes in stark black and white, the feel of grit under people's feet, hundreds of feet crunching the dirty sidewalks, the desperation of yet another mean day in the city. I imagined a film, or a photographic essay, but was never able to secure the means for devoting myself to my own project.

Later that evening I telephoned the hospital in Toronto and found out that Kello was still in intensive care and sedated. Another day passed before I could speak to him, and even then it wasn't really Kello. His thin voice jangled absurdly through the wires as if someone was shaking one of those cheap alabaster dolls of our childhood, a doll, with a defective voice box. Kello had never been sickly as a child, but in the past few years he had been ravaged twice by severe colds that had turned into pneumonia. He had made light of these illnesses; once, in fact, we had not known until afterwards, and his jokes about overwork and old age had stilled my anxiety. But something sharper was in the air now, and I was truly worried. Kello was still so young, only forty-four, and in great health. Or so we all thought.

I walked through the flat feeling haunted and wanting to call somebody over——Roddy maybe, but he was out of town on assignment, not due back until the weekend. I left a message at his hotel, drew the blinds, and lit some candles, trying to fight a feeling of doom. It was a relief when Carene dropped in unexpectedly, just back from a weekend of skiing. How she had taken to snow sports was a mystery to me; snow and ice and blizzards I respected from afar. But I was glad of her company, glad to distract myself from my own anxiety.

"How de spice?" she greeted me, sinking into a pile of cushions on the floor. Carene loved the casualness of my style of living, which had not really changed since my student days. My place was so different from her own beautifully laid-out flat, West Indian style, complete with crocheted doilies and elegant silk flowers on her low coffee table. My makeshift bookshelves, painted wooden furniture, posters, and wall hangings made my apartment look like an artist's studio, a great workshop space, she thought, though her own conventional nature would not allow her such surroundings. She started to tease about Roddy, whom she insisted on calling my spouse since we had been inseparable for the last few months. We should live together and save on rent was her practical take on the situation. But her banter ceased abruptly at the sight of my face. When I told her about Kello, whom she knew, her distress calmed me, helped me to put my fear aside for the moment.

"God, this country! It will kill all of us in the end, watch and see. Every day some little piece of nastiness eating away at your soul until you drop dead. Sometimes I think I can't take it for another minute. I know what is happening to Kello, Mona. Stress, stress, and more stress! That is what is happening."

"Well," I said, composed for the moment, "the tests won't be back until next week. If it's something serious, I'll have to go right away. Do you think it'll be okay—the research, I mean?"

I was turning into the old Muddie, brisk and in charge, concerned only with the practical aspects of the situation.

Carene nodded firmly. "Mona, if it's serious, of course you'll have to go. Poor, poor Kello. I hope it's nothing, though. Maybe it's only chronic fatigue or mono or something like that." Her voice was hopeful; just the sound of another human voice was comfort enough. "And don't worry about the research. It's practically done anyway."

True. But what remained was the final selection of the data, and I usually collaborated with her on that, my talent for picking out oddities and quirky correspondences something that she depended on. When she suggested brainstorming about film titles, I welcomed the distraction of playing with Haitian *kweyol* sayings and proverbs. *Ou bwa seche?* was the title that resonated with me. It was a taunt to an opponent in a riddling contest who could not solve the riddle thrown to him. "You give up?" was a poor substitute for its meaning. The question invoked the whole array of Haitian Creole proverbs, sayings, taunts, and mock competitions that always ended with the threat of the loser being forced to eat dry wood, *bois seche*. I loved the way these word contests threw up unexpected puns and double entendres.

Ou bwa seche? I insisted for the title, but Carene thought it was too obscure.

In the end, though, she humoured me and added *Ou bwa seche?* to her already long list of possibilities such as *Les Suivantes* and *Les Mesdames Saras*. We reminisced for a while about the Haitian women we had interviewed together. They had been eager to respond, eager to share their hardship and their warmth with us, two Caribbean women—one from St. Lucia, one from Trinidad—in front of whom they could talk freely. I will always remember the meals we ate from those fragrant soup pots in NDG, the bad jokes and ole talk, their lyrical Creole speech now proclaimed as a language, *kweyol*, with its own orthography, its nuanced lexicon asserting what they had become since the Haitian Revolution at the beginning of the nineteenth century. Poverty notwithstanding they had established the first Black Republic in the world, only a few short years after the French Revolution, and had shown the mighty Napoleon a thing or two about pride and courage. "Rid me of these gilded Africans, and I shall want nothing else!" he had cried. But Napoleon's famous words on dispatching LeClerc's battalion to Haiti had come, like other efforts at routing the Black Jacobins, to nothing. These Haitian mothers and grandmothers spoke to us freely, full of story, full of history, full of the proverbs and riddles of *libète*, the liberty they continued to pursue, the liberty that had brought them here to the shores of Montreal. Like us they lived as strangers among the Québécois people. Over the weeks we moved from interviewers to friends, the different strands of our fragmented Caribbean roots entwining us together.

The historical research was a revelation. My schoolgirl history books had mentioned heroes such as Toussaint L'Ouverture, Dessalines, and Henri Christophe, but nothing had prepared me for the explosion of scholarly ideas since those books had been published. I had begun with what I thought was the classic text on the subject, *The Black Jacobins* by Trinidadian C.L.R. James. But in no time I found myself rethinking everything about Haiti, its poverty, the Western propaganda about its role as the crucible of the AIDS virus, and especially the recent redefinitions of *voodoo*, now corrected to *vodou*.

Part One: Borrowed Time

At a small vodou exhibition I encountered for the first time the part played by a priestess, a *manbo* named Cecile Fatiman, in the Bois Caiman ritual, which Haitians acknowledge as the act that launched the revolution. It was hard to find more information on this woman; the standard histories I consulted mentioned the priest's name only, the *houngan*, Boukman Dutty. He had sacrificed a black pig in a grove at Bois Caiman while lightning and thunder rent the skies. Our women friends in NDG, however, knew of Cecile Fatiman and described her variously as an old black woman, well known and respected as a priestess, and as a young mulatto woman with green eyes. They took for granted her part in the sacrifice; she was the one who had slit the pig's throat and offered the blood. But even to them her role had remained secondary.

"I still think we should include Cecile Fatiman," I said stubbornly, finishing the bottle of Spanish red, but Carene and I could not agree. Our argument had been going on for days and I continued to hold out, even though it was her film. The thought of yet another woman edited out of history made me angry. And I saw an obvious connection between Fatiman's act that stormy night and the lives of these Haitian women who had found their way to Montreal, by hook or by crook, carrying whole families on their backs. A connection as well between them and the Madame Saras in Haiti, who carried food for market on their backs, uphill and downhill, keeping the sluggish economy boiling like the pots of bone soup they dished out in stalls at the roadside. Carene agreed with all of that; her problem was that this film offered no good place to explain Cecile Fatiman.

She stayed until after midnight. At the door she hugged me and kissed me gently on both cheeks, then held me at arm's length. "Mona, nothing is more important right now than Kello's good health. Don't worry about the film. Let Cecile Fatiman and me fight up with it, and you go and see about your brother. Yuh hear mih? Don't worry bout nutten."

When she left I went to bed exhausted and slept at once. As Grandma Lil would say, Que sera, sera. I stayed in for the next few days, anxious and irritable, worrying about Kello, talking to Muddie daily, grappling with my research notes, waiting for news. Babs called too, trying to reassure me, but I heard the panic in her voice.

Roddy's return was a relief. I was intent on taking my mind off Kello, and we spent the weekend doing simple things together: going to cafés, listening to jazz, eating in an all-night restaurant on St. Denis, making love for endless hours. I walked through the deep winter streets with him, happy, safe for the time being, holding on to his arm, taking comfort in the feel of his biceps under the roughness of his jacket. Roddy was a complex person, sometimes stubborn and difficult, but never boring except when he escaped into one of his deep sulks. His sulks drove me crazy; days would pass and he would not let up. I respected his dedication to his work, however. He could be a real hound when running down a news story, but afterwards he would abandon all discipline, smoke a joint, relax over drinks, let everything down. Not like me, never knowing the meaning of downtime.

I was in love with Roddy but adamant about not living with him, one of the many disagreements that we had. I couldn't see why a domestic arrangement was necessary in this or any relationship. Living together would only tie me up in knots from which I would have to break loose. For Roddy the equation was far simpler—he wanted to go to sleep together and wake up together, holding hands. I would sometimes awaken in the morning to find him poring over my face, ardent, smiling. He would run a crooked finger along my cheek, and once he whispered, "Mona, you're a child in sleep. So open, so vulnerable."

And I suppose that was one of the things I distrusted—I had always slept soundly, with full abandon, and I did not want soul and spirit pried out of me in an unwary moment, benign though such prying might be.

When Kello's tests finally came back, the news was bad. Muddie called to say that he had been diagnosed with lymphoma. It was advanced and he had already made his choice. He had refused chemotherapy. He would be discharged in a few days and would be going to a hospice. Why a hospice? She didn't know, she knew nothing. How long? She didn't know, she had no idea what would happen to his business matters, his job, his life. She didn't know much about this illness, lymphoma. She had looked it up in her medical encyclopedia but the information was so general that she could make no sense of it.

Babs was more forthright. "He's dying, Mona. The doctors have told him he has only a couple of months, maybe less. We have to be there for him. I talked to Johnnie tonight and he'll come when he can, I suppose." She sighed deeply. "Mona, when are you coming? I need you, you must come right away. And let me know when so I can meet you. You'll know everything when you get here. Muddie and Da-Da suddenly seem so old. God, sometimes I feel I can't cope with a single thing more."

That Babs should fall apart shocked me. A nurse by profession, she had seen it all, and her black humour about sickness and death would often appall me. It appealed to Roddy, though. He would listen with relish to Babsie's scandalous accounts about what went down on emergency wards on weekends. Friday night sexual antics ending in Emerg at one in the morning, giant-sized dill pickles stuffed into vaginas, glass in ass (Babs's favourite mishap), transplanted collagen leaking out of busted lips. All of us laughing together at easy times, like Christmas and New Year's and Easter. Not like now.

I walked the five blocks to Roddy's apartment on Aylmer Street, thinking about all the chaos that had suddenly turned my life upside down. The words rushed out as soon as he opened the door. "Babs says that Kello is dying and that I'll know everything when I get there. But I already know it's lymphoma—I don't know why Babsie is sounding so mysterious. Anyhow, I'm taking the train in the morning. I'll stay for a while, Rod. I really don't know what I can do. It's all so sudden."

He held me close and stroked my cheek gently. His face was grave but unsurprised, and for a moment I wondered whether he already knew that Kello had cancer.

He and Kello had never taken to each other. It was Babs whom Roddy teased and cajoled and flirted with, and it occurred to me that she might have talked more directly to him. When he spoke, his voice was firm. "Those are not words Babs would say lightly, Mona. You have to prepare yourself for the worst. Kello is his own person. Don't be too surprised if he had some intimation of his illness and kept it to himself. Just keep a grip on yourself, sweetheart. You'll get through it, no matter how bad."

He knew something more, I sensed; he and Babs were chums, and she must have confided in him. A jealous possessiveness came over me, and my passion for him was sudden and overwhelming. Forgetting about wine and supper and candles, we fell into bed and stayed there until near midnight.

Our meal later on was quiet and relaxed. He had cooked a supper of fish and potatoes and green beans. He fussed over me, pouring wine, touching my hair as he lit the candles. The solid wooden furniture of his apartment, its ordered outlines, provided relief. I had to blink away the tears when I left him, wanting nothing more than to stay there safe and warm, safe from the encroaching present.

Early the next morning I packed a bag, left notes for Carene dotted with Post-its, and took the train to Toronto. The trip was a little over five hours, and with seclusion in mind I bought a first-class ticket. I've always loved trains and was glad of the length of the journey, preparing myself for what lay ahead. How could Kello have cancer? Nobody in our family had ever had cancer. And why was he going to a hospice? Kello had always been so independent. I couldn't imagine him sick, bedridden, dying.

In our own separate ways, I suppose, we all stayed in that place of silence about Kello's illness, never really discussing it as a family, taking refuge in not understanding and cursing the cruel randomness of fate, letting it hover at the back of our minds like one of those near-hurricane clouds that was black and blue at the same time, threatening to break into fury but always passing over the island of Trinidad and waiting until we were out of the way before lashing at smaller, rockier islands and inlets.

If you happen to be born into an Indian family, an Indian family from the Caribbean, migratory, never certain of the terrain, that's how life falls down around you. It's close and thick and sheltering, its ugly and violent secrets locked inside the family walls. The outside encroaches, but the ramparts are strong, and once you leave it you have no shelter and no ready skills for finding a different one. I found that out after years of trying.

In a strange way Kello was the glue that held our family together. He had left home a long time ago, long before 1970 when we emigrated from Trinidad to Canada. He had never returned to the island, as far as I know, even though I remembered vaguely some talk a few months ago about his buying back our land on Manahambre Road in Princes Town. Now I wondered whether he had already done so; he conducted all his business in such secrecy. Kello was an engineer and worked for a construction company, but that was all any of us knew about his professional life. That and the fact that he was well off, had invested wisely, and was a seasoned deal-maker.

Kello had always left his own stamp on the world. It was he who had given our parents the odd names of Muddie and Da-Da as soon as he had begun to talk. Everyone else, all our cousins, most of our friends, used Mommy and Daddy in their families, occasionally Ma and Pa or Mammy and Pappy, but in our home Muddie and Da-Da were Kello's doing and they stuck. Our parents tried in vain to shake off these outlandish names until they too forgot that they had once protested.

My brother was so different from me, built like Muddie's family, lanky and straight as a pole, with dark ochre skin and a sombre face. Family legend had it that he looked exactly like Old Man Jagdeo, Muddie's grandfather, who had come from India on one of the earliest immigrant ships. But Muddie's father, Grandpa Jamesie, never liked Kello much. From the beginning my brother belonged to his other grandfather, Pappy. Kello's good looks were not extraordinary in any way, but he became ravishingly beautiful when he flung his head back and laughed, throwing everything away for a few seconds before recovering his composure. In a world that called for constant vigilance he could be absolutely contained. Even as a boy he had had this composure, I remember that well, although we had no close-ups to prove it; we hardly ever took photographs except for family group shots. If I had got the camera I wanted that Christmas long ago instead of a silly old pair of field glasses, we would have had lots of photographs. The year I did not get my camera was also the year of the big row. Everything changed after the big row. Everything.

Kello was the most affected, I think; the big row made him a man, even though he was only nine years old at the time. Much later, in one of his rare moments of intimacy with me, he summed it up.

"That was the day I really left. Da-Da always said that two bo-rat can't live in the same hole. That is why I had to leave. Either he would have killed me or I would have killed him."

He made no comment about me, but I knew that if I had been a butterfly like my sister Babsie instead of an old boar-rat just like Kello and Da-Da, my own life would have been very different.

The big row happened around Christmas. The year was 1958. It was some months after my grandmother's death and everyone had gotten over it; they all said so. But I hadn't. Da-Da was Mama's only surviving child after the death of his brother, Junior, in the Maracaibo oil fields in Venezuela five years before. Mama had been a force in all our lives, but in my world she had been everything and I could not imagine life without her. I was hers and Kello was Pappy's. By the time my younger brother Johnnie came along, the space had been taken and he never knew that special thrill of ownership. As for Babs, born that same year, the question never arose except when she chose to assert her place as everybody's favourite baby girl; no wonder she remained a butterfly. I knew now that Da-Da had never gotten over Mama's death. And neither had I.

The big row had to do with the sale of our family property in Princes Town. We lived in a rambling board house set back from busy Manahambre Road. Facing the traffic was Muddie's flower garden, which she had lovingly planted as a new bride and which, years later, continued to reseed itself into a spectacular array of zinnias and sunflowers. On one side of the house was a massive celamen tree and a chenette tree with spreading branches. At the back the land sloped downwards, and the structure rose on high pillars, leaving a clean dirt area underneath where we played, with a washtub at one end and a little tin bathroom standing next to it. Those pillars, pilotries they were called, had to be constantly strengthened and propped up as the land threatened to slip farther down the hill. The landslides were frequent but small, and the pillars always managed to contain them. Way up the hill, leading from the ochro grove beyond the trees, was Pappy's low wooden house where he and Mama lived. Various country relatives and visitors had stayed there over the years, but when Da-Da got married, Mama and Pappy fixed up the low house and moved into it, leaving the bigger dwelling to Da-Da and his new bride. We grew up in an enchanted forest between two houses, surrounded by mango and plum and mammy-sepote trees. There was even a small patch of sugar cane behind the pigpen; Pappy would painstakingly peel the cane for us and cut it into little strips. We would sit in the grass and suck the sweetness out, each of us with a personal pile of bagasse beside us.

But the big row changed everything, not just the enchanted land we roamed in, but everything. It had started on a Sunday, a few days before Christmas, when we were getting ready for church. The washing had piled up for a couple of weeks and Johnnie was wearing a pair of socks with visible holes, salvaged from the bottom of the drawer. Muddie had been beside herself coping with the pressure of the funeral, the parade of visitors from town and country who had to be fed, the grief and the never-ending work, so when Da-Da pointed to Johnnie's footwear, her retort was quick and sarcastic. "What, those 'holy' socks? Well, Christ say to render thy heart and not thy garments."

Da-Da steupsed loudly but said nothing in return. He was vexed, though; we knew it by the way he flung his shoes down, slammed his feet into them, and pulled the laces so taut that if they had come away in his hands, no one would have been surprised. We walked to church in near silence, our feet sinking slightly into the melting bitumen. The Sunday road was empty; the Sunday houses cool, comfortable inside, shaded by trees and bushes. Through open doorways I could see lace curtains blowing gently, tables being set for meals, vases of crepe flowers set on doilies. Outside on the road the sun beat down with a fury, and my broad-brimmed straw hat with the smart blue ribbons made my scalp itch at the back. I wanted to tear it off, throw it onto the ground, and jump up and down on it. I wanted to cry. The road looked different today. A sprinkle of sudden rain on the hot pitch brought up the smell I hated, the smell they said was that of the devil and his wife fighting for a bone. I had to walk fast because the big people were behind me. I had always walked slowly behind the group, holding Mama's hand. We had missed a couple of Sundays after the funeral and this was the first time I was going to church without Mama.

In church I noticed Da-Da's voice breaking and cracking a few times, especially when they sang, "Shall we gather at the river / the beautiful, the beautiful river / shall we gather at the river / that flows from the throne of God." It was Mama's favourite hymn, the one we had sung at her graveside. Did they choose it for us, for our first day back into the congregation? My heart filled with joy and I sang it loudly, singing with Mama by my side again.

Lunch at home was awkwardly silent, and afterwards Da-Da rose abruptly, put on his felt hat, and left. I helped Muddie clear the table while the boys ran out to play, then I looked after Babsie while Muddie went to lie down. It was the Sunday of the candlelight service and Christmas cantata at church. I was looking forward to it. Muddie's relatives were coming from San Fernando and Curepe, and after her rest she spent the afternoon making little sandwiches and icing cupcakes for the snack she would serve them after the service. Princes Town was the nearest big town to Iere Village, where Muddie's family came from, and the three sisters had kept the tradition of going to the cantata together at Christmas. Maybe Sonia would come too, but usually my aunts didn't bring the children on these late night outings. Muddie was going to wear her silver moonlight dress that Auntie Vannie had sewn out of a fabric Da-Da had bought in Port of Spain. I would wear blue organdy, the same as on Christmas morning.

Da-Da came back as it was getting dark. I went into the bedroom to get dressed. I was thinking of the old ballads and love songs that Muddie and her sisters, all the big people, would sit around and sing: "In the gloaming, oh my darling," and "When the deep purple falls." The big people were such limers and always had such good times together; when I grew up I wanted to be exactly like them. Happy and singing, laughing and making jokes about everything. Not all the songs were romantic, though. They used to sing Stephen Foster songs about lonely Old Black Joe: "Gone are the days when my heart was young and gay / Gone are my friends from the cotton fields away / I hear their gentle voices calling Old Black Joe / I'm coming, I'm coming / Though my head is bending low." That one reminded me of Mama and of gathering by the river. And the heart-breaking one that I knew only two lines of: "Come home, Mother, cries the little baby coon / The night is dark and I am so alone." The house was dark and very quiet. Suddenly I was afraid and wanted to know where everybody had gone. It was then the big row started.

The quarrelling quickly became nasty and Da-Da was soon cursing in a way I knew he never would have dared had Mama been alive. The curses were wild and frightening, and Muddie looked dazed and shocked. I had never seen Da-Da looking like this; his face was red, and every few minutes he would pull his hand through his thick hair so that wild tufts stood up on his head. Our house was shaking as he stamped around it.

After he had tramped through the house and smashed many valuable pieces from the dinner wagon, even Mama's precious glass decanters, Muddie was terrified that he would come after us. When Johnnie began screaming loudly, she hid us both in the bathing place underneath the steps and tried to reason with Da-Da, who had raced down the stairs after us. We listened fearfully to the voices ricocheting off the patchy galvanized siding. Then we heard Kello telling Da-Da to shut up and stop being a disgrace to us. Suddenly Muddie was beating down the thin shaky door of the bathhouse to get in. I heard her panic as she pleaded with me to open it—the latch was rusty and difficult to manage but I opened the door and she flung herself in, pulling Kello behind her. But Kello could not be stilled and shouted his rage at Da-Da from behind the flimsy walls.

"You want to kill your family! You is a nasty nasty man! I shame to call you my father! You is a beast—you is not my father! Is all the rum you drinking have you so! And why we must suffer? Why Muddie must suffer so? You think I too small but I not small, you hear? I know my mind. You can't sell all we own, this house and Pappy house and all the land and leave everybody with nothing! You don't care about we, all you care about is yuh stupid friends! You old drunkard, you!"

Da-Da's sounds outside the flimsy door were not human; I had never heard any noises like them before. He growled and grunted and every few minutes he burst into a new string of curses. He was not my Da-Da. He had left the house with his felt hat but a stranger had returned in his place. We were locked behind the tin walls of the bathing place and a stranger outside was cursing his enemies. Inside Kello was shrieking for Pappy at the top of his lungs, while Da-Da's rage continued unabated: "Is all yuh who have me in this trap! All yuh have me in a vise, yuh hear? I must be kill priest to have all yuh like a blasted millstone around mih neck! Every fucking day, sun or shine, is pressure in mih blasted arse because of all ah all yuh! Who put me in dis trap, eh? Who? Is all yuh! All yuh bitches think all yuh could squeeze my neck, eh? Well, this is the end, is the end of de fucking line! Is the end of the fucking line!"

With this Da-Da burst into a wild howl and began to kick the tin door so viciously that the whole structure would have come down on us if Kello had not rushed out the door before Muddie could stop him.

"Close the door, Muddie, close the door!" he had the presence of mind to shout as he hurled himself outside with such force that he winded Da-Da temporarily, throwing him down on the dirt near the end of the house where the pilotrie held the floating land together. The central beam of the pilotrie held firm, but the extra reinforcing posts fanning out erratically from the centre quivered. When Da-Da fell, one of these posts caught the side of his head. The galvanized siding of the bathing place was riddled with tiny holes, and when I peeped through one of these, my heart caught in my throat. Kello had killed Da-Da. He was lying still on the ground while Kello watched him warily.

But in seconds Da-Da had recovered, had sprung to his feet and was advancing towards Kello. We saw his back; then we heard nothing. Muddie peeped through a pinhole, gasped, and moved closer to the door as, with a great roar, Da-Da knocked Kello to the ground. He was almost sitting on him.

"Yuh little bugger, you, playing man for me! I go show you who is man today!"

Silence again. Then *whack*, and Muddie opened the door cautiously. Peeping around the side of her dress, her lovely moonlight dress that she had put on to go to the Christmas cantata at church, I saw the shadow of a stick coming down on Da-Da's back. It was Pappy, who had heard his grandson's cries from his verandah way up on the hill, at the Pierre Street end of the land. The stick flew again and again; the sound of its whacks cut through the stillness with dull thuds. It took a number of blows before Da-Da, the murderer, loosened his hands from Kello's throat. When he did, he collapsed on the ground, face flung upwards, eyes closed, hair rising up from his forehead in unruly bursts.

Pappy stood for a minute looking down at his son, shaking his head and saying nothing. Then Kello stood up, rubbing his red throat, a small boy now, and fell on Pappy's shoulder. We all came out and held on to Pappy as if he was Jesus, his head covered with snow white hair, his grey-brown eyes full of tears now, his frail body leaning heavily on his walking stick. How fast did he have to run across the ochro field and down the hill, hurrying towards the sounds of a wild animal? When did he hear the sounds? If Kello had not shouted and screamed for Pappy, what would have happened? Da-Da had been on the rampage for a long time, for hours, it seemed to me. Pappy must have been sitting quietly on the verandah of the low house, sitting in the hammock, enjoying the evening. It must have taken time for the sounds of violence to reach Pappy.

Da-Da lay on the ground and nobody moved to touch him. Muddie leaned against a pillar, crying helplessly. Pappy gathered up Kello and Johnnie and me and took us up the back steps, rickety even then, and into the vast kitchen. Everything remained still as death, as at the end of something terrible for which no words could ever come. Babsie lay in her crib against the window, still asleep. Hours had passed, it seemed, but Babs had not woken up from her nap. Pappy put the big black kettle on to boil and I brought down the enamel teapot and started to mix the cocoa for dinner. After I swizzled the mixture I sat down at the window and looked at the outlines of the trees in the distance——chataigne, breadfruit, mammy-sepote——and beyond them the pigpen. Everything was different and Mama would never come back.

The big row had flared up because Da-Da wanted to sell our property and move to San Fernando, a rapidly growing commercial centre on the southwestern coast, soon to be dubbed the industrial capital of the country. He had grown up in Princes Town, but times were changing and he wanted his children to live in a city, with a more modern way of life. His argument had been reasonable at first. "Look, Mudds," he had said as he sat down to talk the matter through, "we don't even have electric lights here. Look at this radio. Is months since I win it in a raffle and we can't even play it. Yuh want us to live in backwardness for the rest of our days?"

And, in truth, I didn't understand Muddie's objections. She kept referring to the mortgage and how we wouldn't get much after paying it out. I always found the word *moggage* enticing and imagined it wrapping the house tightly with strong threads that would keep it safe even through earthquake and hurricane. Our house was a safe place, wrapped like a cocoon with moggage threads, built securely on "pillow-trees" that cushioned us as we slept. We had no lights because the electric lines hadn't reached us yet, but the lamps with their "Home Sweet Home" lampshades cast a perfect glow throughout the house at night. Muddie would sit in the bentwood rocker, putting Babsie to sleep and singing "Love's old sweet song": "Once in the dear dead days beyond recall / When on the world the mists began to fall." Home was soft and full of flickering shadows. But the big row changed that. The shaking that day burst the moggage threads. I will never forget the big row, how the cloying smell of rain on hot pitch lingered throughout the day and into the evening while the devil and his wife fought for a scraggy little bone.

In the end nobody went to the Christmas cantata that year. When the carload of relatives including Auntie Vannie and Aunt Alice arrived, they saw at once that something was wrong. The uncles stayed in the drawing room while Muddie's sisters whispered in the kitchen with Pappy. Then Muddie and Da-Da came slowly up through the darkness of the back steps. My aunts made tea and set the table while Muddie got us ready for bed. No one asked anything or mentioned the big row, even though the whole house was like the funeral night all over again. I tried to stay awake to hear the talk that I knew would come as soon as they had put us to bed. The relatives stayed for a long time. Falling asleep in the darkness I could hear the murmuring cadences of their voices dipping in and out of a deep, deep well. I woke up in alarm more than once to hear Muddie sobbing and saying that she was "going home." Home was Grandma Lil's house in Iere Village. I knew that nothing would be the same again. My eyes remained dry, and I stared and stared through the darkness, but no outlines of any objects appeared and at last the pillow-trees claimed me.

TWO

The train entered Ontario and the landscape changed to bare trees standing in uneven patches of snow. I strained to hear the comforting *clack-clack* of the train's wheels, but this carriage was more tightly insulated from the noise outside and almost silent. The waiter served drinks and the straight Scotch warmed my insides. I stretched out my legs and began to look around, listening to empty snatches of conversation. In first class on a full train I felt far less protected from the encroachment of other passengers. Everybody was relaxed, everybody the same—all Anglo in appearance except for me and a little Chinese man who nodded and smiled to himself at intervals. Us and a black waiter, exceptionally courteous and getting on in years. In the place he came from he might have been a village schoolmaster—perhaps he was in fact a village schoolmaster who had ventured forth to seek his fortune and had landed here, on the trains, the place for black men in earlier times in this country. Why did people leave the place they were born for an illusion of a better life? I wondered. All of us migrants, the Chinese man, the black waiter, Da-Da never finding a place here, Babs turning into a brittle magazine girl, Kello dying—why did anyone leave? And Roddy, leaving the countryside of Scotland but finding a home here more readily than any of us, inventing a home, wanting so much to drag me into a home of his invention when I have invented none. Nothing. I have spent my life just getting by.

Ever since that morning when Muddie phoned about Kello, I had found myself thinking over and over about our life—all our lives—that had become so different from our expectations during those early times in Trinidad. Sometimes I felt that we had lived then in a curious state of suspension, as if caught in a gigantic bubble, waiting for the real times to come.

Da-Da had to leave Trinidad, I could see that now. I could understand how life must have been closing in on him—wife, children, work, respectability, and the mortgage on his country property draining his lifeblood. To keep the land. Everything for the land. Old-fashioned thinking, completely out of step with progress and modernization. The entire property had become Da-Da's because of Junior's death. Uncle Junior had made money, but had no will and no children, and his Venezuelan wife had inherited everything. Da-Da's only sister Babsie had died at fourteen of typhoid fever. Mama and Pappy had deeded everything to Da-Da with the proviso that they would live in the little house on the hill until they died. The land had been everything to Mama and Pappy. They had fought to keep it through thick and thin, even fighting off a moneylender and mortgaging the house to pay a debt that rightfully belonged to the previous owner. But Da-Da was a modern man, sure that he could not have been as easily fooled, and that his decision to sell and move to the city was a sound one.

Da-Da's dream, we all knew, had been to become a lawyer, and throughout his youth Mama and Pappy had encouraged him to pursue this ambition. Every night they would get the newspapers out after dinner and he would read aloud the published transcripts of the cases of the day. Most of the time they had already read the papers, but they never minded this exercise. They were proud of his enunciation and his strong delivery, and they would all turn the evidence this way and that, scrutinizing the arguments presented. Even Junior would join in sometimes, although he was not the studying kind.

Da-Da's missed chances had to do with Mama's early illness and his own marriage. He would have remortgaged the house, used all their savings, wheedled a loan out of Uncle Junior, anything, to get the passage to England. Once there, he would say later, come hell or high water, he would find a way to put himself through law school. But he could not bear the thought of leaving Mama, and then when his brother died, his fate was sealed. He got married and soon found himself with us, his personal millstones.

My parents married after the Second World War. Da-Da was an adventurer, a rogue, a good-looking, good-time guy. Muddie, whose real name was Myrtle, was the opposite—a serious, studious girl. Her prettiness was quiet, even shy. They had met earlier at school. Later they met again and united in their fearlessness. He loved her for her fidelity to any position she decided to take. She loved him for his daring qualities—the same qualities that would later doom them to a state of perpetual uncertainty.

By the time my parents were born, many Indians in Trinidad had become Christian converts, and those who had not still took advantage of the church schools set up by Presbyterian missionaries from Canada. A precarious middle class had begun to spring up among those formerly doomed to indentured servitude. But in the growing gentility of this little Presbyterian world my father Mackie was a bad boy. He smoked and drank and partied. He was a great dancer. Myrtle danced quietly and well. They danced to their favourite song: "Ramona, when day is done you hear my call, Ramona, meet me beside the waterfall," even though there was no waterfall in their lives, only miles of pitch road (the famous Pitch Lake where the Elizabethan adventurer Sir Walter Raleigh had caulked his ships), their occasional excursions to the beach at Mayaro, and the big big life on the Hollywood screen.

Muddie and all her friends permed their hair in cascading shoulder-length waves like Jeanette MacDonald. Mackie slicked his curly hair back with green Palmolive brilliantine, looking like a cross between Clark Gable in *Gone with the Wind* and Nelson Eddy in *Rose Marie*. Their song "Ramona" told the sentimental tale of an American Indian girl's seduction. Fancy naming me after this girl, destroyed and abandoned! I'm Mona now, I've always been Mona.

My parents, stylish and cool, keeping in step with the fashion of those far-off times in cosmopolitan Trinidad, once dubbed nothing less than "the Paris of the West Indies." They had a real courtship, their parents more enlightened than they themselves were to become with me. I imagine they wooed each other in simple Hollywood pastiche. Their glamour they got from the movies of the day; their noble ideals they got from the book-club memberships that brought Lloyd C. Douglas, Pearl Buck, and Émile Zola into our home. Their moral rectitude, though, they got from the Bible and the evangelical enterprise of the Canadian Mission. Indentureship was over; it had ended in 1917, before they were born, and denial had set in. All that backward stuff was best forgotten.

When Myrtle and Mackie walked hand in hand at the edges of the cane fields, they were already several levels removed from anything resembling bonded labour. It was a time when newly educated people would throw out almost everything Indian at first, and would slowly gather back into their lives only those relics that were essential for survival. Eating sada roti and tomato chokha, wearing gold churias at weddings, drying mangoes for achar and kuchela, treating nara with a special massage, rubbing down the limbs of babies with coconut oil: all seeping gradually back into Indian life in the towns and all well hidden except at home.

Like their parents before them, abandoning Hindu and Muslim traditions in favour of education, Muddie and Da-Da anchored themselves inside their Presbyterian community, building a slow, deadly respectability. They lifted themselves into a space free as air through the hymns they sang at church on Sundays, those old hymns wrought out of the stoicism required for life in a frozen land, peopled by hymn writers with eyes of cold blue steel. Inside the armour of those hymns they found repose: *O God, our help in ages past / our hope for years to come / our shelter from the stormy blast / and our eternal home*. The Canadian missionaries and their wives sat in special pews at the front of the beautiful Savana Grande church, one of the first buildings of their mission. The orchids near the altar were magnificent—purple and white with gold centres—and the choir carried the congregation to unexpected heights of harmony while the organist accompanied them on the new organ with its resonant chimes. Our hearts flew up to heaven, and all the soot and flying dust of burning cane vanished into the smoke fires of hell while we ascended skywards, washed in the blood of the lamb.

I would be wearing my new white lace dress and a wide-brimmed hat with grosgrain around the band, my two brothers seated on either side of me, all of us singing: *Eternal ruler of the ceaseless round / of circling planets singing on their way*. My favourite hymn, my favourite time—I would be swinging my short legs over the side of the pew, Mackie's deep Nelson Eddy baritone creating a comfortable chaos in the air, me perched at the edge of one of the circling spheres, riding as securely as I ever would. The hymns swallowed us, embraced us, promised us neutrality and a bigger place in which to live. Somehow I always stayed at the edge of that circling sphere, never making my way to its centre.

In Cornwall a large party boarded the train and their chatter began to grate on my nerves. I walked over to the dining car and sat for a while. On my way back to my seat the Chinese man nodded and smiled, his face creasing into thousands of tiny lines. A warm smile, vanishing abruptly as he resettled into his own reverie, once more nodding occasionally to himself.

I wanted the trip to end. I wanted to see Kello, to find out what was happening from Babs. What the hell did Roddy mean, asking me whether I knew everything about Kello? Did I know everything about Roddy? The last time I had seen Kello was at Christmas when we had all teased him about losing weight and working too hard. He had borne our teasing with good humour, saying little. But then Kello never said much about what was going on inside. Had I ever known Kello? Roddy's words forced themselves on me again and again.

After the big row everything changed in our family. Even the Christmas after the big row was different. We posted our silly letters to Santa Claus and Kello painted the dry branch white in preparation for our White Christmas, Uncle Sweetie's brainchild. Uncle Sweetie was our craziest uncle, the most fun, and we all adored him.

"Sweetie is a creative genius," Da-Da would say fondly of his favourite brother-in-law, "with no damn outlet. That's why he like batty-mamselle all over the place and can't settle down."

Most people made Christmas trees out of unravelled rope dyed bright green with little red stoppers at the tips of the strands. But one year the forestry department spotted a potential windfall and began to experiment with dwarf conifers for the few who could afford them. Naturally we couldn't, but Uncle Sweetie decided that rope trees were passé, so he selected a well-shaped dry branch, painted it white, and presented it to Muddie as her "personal white Xmas." Muddie was delighted and relieved because our old rope tree had become frayed and shapeless. Sweetieboy added hunks of white cotton for snow and small patches of red "snowberries." Our old decorations and lights followed, and our tree was not only stunning but one of a kind, and Sweetie was happy. After that a white Christmas was established as the family tradition, and we still kept the painted branch, absurd though it was. Muddie would always put up the tree the day before Christmas Eve. Later in the evening Uncle Sweetie would drop by with a wild bunch of friends, singing Christmas carols, drinking poncha crema, and hugging up everybody, and he would hang the lights just so. He would arrive so late that my brothers, Babs, and I would never see the decorated tree until Christmas Eve morning when it would be resplendent but bare underneath, waiting for Christmas morning when the space would be filled with presents.

Kello put the tree in a pot early that morning and Muddie fixed it up, but even though we waited until late, Uncle Sweetie never came. We woke up the next morning without the Christmas Eve transformation and Johnnie began to cry, sure that Santa would never find the house. I had asked for a camera but I knew, I just knew, that I would never get it. Later that evening after Kello hung the lights and plugged them in, we all stood around the branch and clapped, but it was not Uncle Sweetie's wonderful drunken wizardry and our tree looked ordinary.

During the night I woke up to shrieks and shouts of "Fire! Oh God, fire!" I rushed out of the bedroom to see the Christmas tree in flames and Da-Da shouting in panic, standing immobile next to the blaze. It was Muddie who unplugged the lights and smothered the flames with a blanket. And afterwards, when the dried branch still showed some embers, Da-Da appeared with a bucket and doused the tree, wetting down everything, cotton wool, Christmas paper, everything. I saw then that he was drunk.

Muddie sat heavily on a chair, her face in her hands. "Why you had to touch the lights?" she whispered. "Why? Kello fix them so good and look at everything now. Everything just mash up."

Da-Da said nothing and then left the room. I started sopping up the water and wadding the cotton wool back around the sodden tree. Kello didn't wake up, and after a while Muddie sent me back to sleep.

Miraculously the next morning the tree looked as if nothing had happened to it. Muddie had fiddled with the wires, everything had dried out and the lights were working. Some of the fragile ornaments had broken and the gilded dome at the top had a deep hole at the side, but there were presents everywhere. We couldn't open the presents for a while because Da-Da was still asleep, but when he joined us everything fell into place again. I was so happy that I walked around saying over and over, "I so happy! Happy, happy, happy!"

I left my big present for last, hoping that it would be a camera.. When I opened it, the box said Field Glasses, and as I turned it over, two racetrack tickets fell out. The camera looked kind of long and narrow, but I adjusted the sights and walked around looking at everybody. I wondered where the clicker was but decided to figure that out later. No one remarked on my peculiar activity, but later that evening Kello caught me alone and said meanly, "Da-Da must be get them binoculars free when he went to races. Or he must be win them. Why he didn't keep them to watch horse and buy a real camera for you, eh?" Only then did I admit that I had received no camera for Christmas, exactly as I had known beforehand. I continued to look through the field glasses, though, and kept them through all my moves and uprootings. They hang now over my desk, suspended in a corner from a rusting nail, one lens worn loose and unfocused, the other tight as a drum.

Everything looked clearer and bigger when I looked through the field glasses, and I liked that. I liked to look through the window to Pierre Street and see children playing or watch Miss Lady tying up her head before balancing her tray of pone and sweetbread and setting out. I loved those Creole pastries that we would never make at home—rock cakes, coconut drops, and paimies steamed in banana leaves. Before she even reached our house, I would be out at the roadside waiting, marking her progress through my lenses. But the field glasses were not a camera, and all the snapshots I wanted of objects and places and people came and went in my head in a never-ending kaleidoscope, folding and unfolding in crazy sequence.

In the end the big row didn't change Da-Da's plans, and he sold our house and land and everything we had ever owned. There were dreams and signs and portents, and Mama came from the other side to warn Da-Da about the perils in store for him. Pappy was asleep in the hammock one day when her voice came to him clear and strong, saying, "Dear, don't let Mackie sell the house." But two years after Mama died the house was sold, and though I never heard Muddie voice her disapproval about the sale, she often said that was when our pitching about from pillar to post started.

I was heartbroken to leave our house on Manahambre Road. One of my pet black pigs was buried near the mammy-sepote tree. Pappy's sweet potato hill was on the other side; the iron contraption he had rigged up for roasting sweet potatoes freshly dug out of that hill—the best sweet potatoes in the world—was left behind. John-nie didn't talk about the sale but one day I caught him playing horse and rocking frenziedly on the zaboca tree, singing "Ride a cockhorse to Banbury Cross," the tears running down his face. But when I asked what was wrong, he just shook his head and wouldn't say.

Da-Da had purchased land in La Plata, a new suburb that was being established in San Fernando, Trinidad's second largest city. At the time San Fernando was enjoying the beginnings of a booming oil industry. While the house was going up, we pitched about madly and spent a whole year sharing Grandma Lil's big old house in Iere Village with Auntie Vannie and Uncle Baddall. This was when Muddie's parents had gone on what the whole family described as a world tour. They had never left the island before, and the trip was quite an event. They went to Europe first, visiting

Grandpa Jamesie's nephew and his family before joining a short organized tour to the Continent. Apparently, when they landed in England, a porter picked up their luggage and Grandma Lil was alarmed, remonstrating with poor feeble Grandpa to take the suitcase from the white man's hands. She couldn't accept the reverse order of the world, in which they tipped and gave menial tasks to white people, even though her very own money had bought the trip. Muddie's elder brother, Uncle Tristram, had already migrated to Canada and they had an extended stay with him, his Canadian wife, and their new family. Everybody was talking about how Canada was beginning to open up. Church missionaries were helping people in all sorts of ways to migrate to Canada and to get settled once they arrived. Grandpa Jamesie wrote a letter to Auntie Vannie, saying how Indian people from good families should think about settling in Canada because it was such a nice place, with such nice polite people.

Uncle Baddall was planning to migrate with Auntie Vannie, after he had paid back his church scholarship. He had combined his degree in theological studies with comparative literature, and had managed to get a certificate in public relations on the side while being fully supported by the church. He considered this accomplishment a coup. He described himself as versatile. Da-Da described him as a "damn scamp" and declared that the church was wasting its time behind con men like Baddall, but you would never know this by the civil way both men spoke to each other. They laughed, cracked jokes all the time, and argued only about politics. Da-Da thought that the new nationalist party had a vision for the future, while Baddall was certain that the Indian-only politics of Apanjaat was the way to go. "Your own people first," he would declare. "Others after."

• • •

35

Some of my permanent memories from that time are made up of the snapshots I took by fixing my eye to a hole in the floor just above the kitchen. Grandma Lil's house was built in many different time periods; pieces of the old lay side by side with renovations, modern touches. The hole itself was caused by a small area of rotting floor-board between the bed and the wall behind it. Lying down there, I was completely invisible, completely happy as I watched a play whose scenes changed constantly. The play cheered me up because the house had a deserted feeling. It was so big that even with all of us living there, we could not fill it up without Grandma Lil's presence. And the house felt temporary; our belongings were still in boxes and some rooms were out of bounds.

Peering through the hole one day I watched Uncle Baddall trying to turn Muddie around, his arms holding her waist in a clinch from behind, rotating her with an iron lock until her head faced his squarely. Her petite frame was pulled up to meet his brawny chest; he was close to six feet in height and powerfully built. When she dressed up for church or for a dance, Muddie looked really pretty—"classy" was how people described her, with her neatly permed hair, her high-heeled shoes, and her slim figure. But right now she looked wild, desperate, squirming and wriggling in his grasp as Baddall bent and tried to kiss her. I heard her small animal cries, saw her eyes darting around frantically, even up towards the ceiling, and for a moment I was sure that she was signalling me.

A zigzag feeling came over me, and I felt as if all my thoughts and movements were racing together at the speed of light, doing something, anything, to help Muddie. I was running down the stairs, grabbing the kitchen knife, the big one with metal rivets and a broad ridged handle, and stabbing Baddall in his back. The blade was broad, it would go right through his shirt, the blade was dull, it might not go through his shirt, then he would snatch the knife from my hand and slash my face, or slash Muddie's face, both our faces.

He would know how to use it, I was certain. All of this happened, I felt the speed with which I hurtled down the stairs, the air rushing past my face. But the zigzag feeling passed and I was still lying between the bed and the wall, my eye fixed to the hole, watching.

Muddie was making the cries of a small caught animal, Uncle Baddall was trying to bend his head to kiss her, and why didn't she take the pot of hot water off the stove and dash it in his face? His smiling face, he was smiling, he knew that he would get what he was after. Then Muddie's eyes flashed to the ceiling again and her flailing hands caught Baddall's thumb and twisted it back as far as it could go. From above I watched as his thumb almost reached the back of his hand. He screamed in pain and shouted, "Yuh bitch, you!" He let go of Muddie so roughly that she rocked back against the stove, and the whole pot of boiling water shook dangerously but somehow did not spill. Baddall turned and stamped out of the kitchen.

The sunlight from the window was pure liquid gold falling in rivers of tears down Muddie's smooth heart-shaped face and running freely onto her blouse. I wanted to run down the steps into the kitchen, hug her, and dance around because she had beaten Uncle Baddall, whom I already knew too well. I wanted to dance in the sunlight with her, kiss her . . . But again the zigzag feeling passed and I was still lying flat, my eye fixed to the hole in the floor.

The zigzag feeling was like those electric shocks in comic books, travelling from somewhere around the middle of my back down to my toes and up to my head at lightning speed. I felt mad. Vex too. Madvex. And I wondered whether all the weird thoughts I could not explain and that kept hurtling through my head would one day form a zigzag that I could not control. That zigzag could turn into lightning or burst into flames, depending on how madvex I really was that day. The deadly zigzag would find Uncle Baddall and *pouf*! That would be the end of him.

I lay on the floor as my murderous rage towards Uncle Baddall abated. And then sudden feelings of shame rushed over me. I felt confused and angry and resentful towards everybody. I hated everybody. I hated Muddie for letting Uncle Baddall touch her. Would she tell Da-Da? She should tell Da-Da, and he should curse Uncle Baddall upside down. Then he would leave us alone, all of us. But I knew that Muddie would say nothing; nobody in our family ever said anything about anything.

After a while I came down to the kitchen. I offered to help, but Muddie was brusque, waving her hand vaguely and telling me to go and play outside. Kello and Johnnie were nowhere in sight and Babsie was napping as usual. The question came out before I could stop myself.

"Where Uncle Baddall?"

And instantly I regretted it. A shadow passed over Muddie's face and I knew she was wondering how much I had seen. I realized that she was already behaving as if nothing had happened and was going about her work as usual. She began to clean a cupboard, moving so fast that a tin of Koo guava jam slipped out of her hands and crashed to the floor, denting in several places. She snatched it up and flung it into the rubbish bin with a look of satisfaction.

The table was full that evening at dinnertime. Auntie Vannie and Uncle Baddall usually came home later and ate together, but today the dining room was crowded and everyone was enjoying Muddie's cooking. She had made stewed beef with heavy Creole dumplings instead of rice, an innovation that everybody liked. Da-Da looked around afterwards for dessert but there wasn't any. Uncle Baddall, getting into the spirit of the evening, suggested gaily that even biscuits and jam would do. He brought out a tin of Koo jam and started opening it. It was then that Muddie lashed out with such savagery that everyone fell silent.

"Why you bring that jam on my table? Why you buy that jam at all? You don't read the papers? You didn't hear about the boycott?

You know what they doing people in South Africa? Just because all the Koo jam in the grocery gone on sale, you had to pack up the cupboards with all them nasty tins of Koo jam? Vannie, why you don't talk to yuh husband? He don't have no conscience at all. Everybody joining the boycott and he looking for bargain. Look, let me get up from this table before . . . !" With that Muddie gave a loud steups and began to clear the table with a vengeance.

Da-Da had been silent throughout her outburst, but now he shook his head and looked over at Baddall, trying to inject some humour into the evening. "So you see who is the real politician in this house, eh, Baddall? When Myrtle set her mind on something, nobody can't budge her, yuh hear? Is boycott in yuh tail, whether you agree or not!"

Baddall smiled lamely and excused himself from the table shortly afterwards. Kello looked questioningly at me but I averted my eyes swiftly. I didn't know how to explain Muddie's anger to Kello.

In all our lives Muddie had been the force holding together the fragments, creating something out of nothing each time. And this skill she had taught me so well that I often felt I wanted for nothing and I wanted nothing at the same time. The one thing I did not want was domestic life. I would not marry Roddy and become his little wife. All I wanted was to be his love. And Muddie—what did she want? She must have wanted love but hardly the labour and pain of countless years of toiling beside Da-Da, the man without a place. She seemed to love him and resent him with equal ferocity. She loved Kello purely. Me, I was her creature totally. Sometimes I was sure that she did not love me very much and would never like me. But that did not matter. I was still her creature, her female child, her right hand. It seemed to me that she had room in her heart for two people only: Da-Da and Kello, her personal bad boys. They occupied all her loving, and she would have killed without thinking to defend either of them, as they both would have killed to defend her.

As for me, I was consumed with the thought of escape. I dreamed of ways that it would happen, and sometimes I sat for hours planning fantastical getaways. One of my favourites was escaping with a gypsy caravan and roaming the world:

> I wish I lived in a caravan
> With a horse to drive like the pedlar-man
> Where he comes from nobody knows
> Where he goes to but he goes

I never talked about these escapes to anyone, but I was sure that most people wanted some kind of escape from the place they lived, from their ordinary lives. As soon as people got old enough, if they could manage it, they left for England or America or somewhere else. A few people received scholarships to study in India. But I never wanted to go to India, a place our ancestors had left more than a century ago, where we heard that poverty was the way of life. I was glad they had left and I too planned to leave Trinidad for somewhere better.

The day I really knew I had to escape (and not in a gypsy caravan either) was when I was eleven. I was sure because Muddie herself confirmed it. It was the day I escaped from rape and probably murder, although Muddie never used those words about the incident. I knew now though—as the train rushed past the winter trees, cutting a swath through the frozen land—I knew now that it was rape or murder or probably both.

No camera could have recorded that day with the detail that was engraved on my memory. I could see the crackling blue of the afternoon sky and feel the heaviness in the air. The heat, the dry season, the smell of the car seat grimed with the sweat of a hundred thousand bottoms resting on it day after living day, the one gold tooth of the driver floating in a vacant brownish-black face, the red eyes of Sonny whom I listened to in spite of the warning I had received a short half-hour before from Muddie. There had been recent reports about attacks on young girls by unscrupulous taxi drivers. The most frequently heard was that of a young girl who had been abducted for a whole day and was then flung out of a speeding car at a busy intersection in San Fernando, her clothing torn, her underwear missing. She was dazed and frightened, and the way the rough men drinking in a nearby rumshop had wrapped her in shirts and jackets and had comforted her while they waited for the police was the talk of the town for weeks. "Is a good thing that taxi driver speed off, you hear?" one of the drinkers would remark at intervals. "If ah could only get mih hands on him, I would string him up now for now." Worse threats were uttered, but the villain had not been found and young girls were warned constantly about being careful.

Muddie had taken a chance in sending me downtown to buy ric-rac braid, buttons, and thread for some clothes she was making for us. We had recently moved to the La Plata house and I had never made the trip downtown alone. It was the August holidays just before I started at La Pastora Girls' High School.

I had to take a taxi from La Plata into the downtown area. The trip was only fifteen minutes, but Muddie cautioned me against talking to strange men or boys and told me to come straight home afterwards. As soon as I got out of the taxi and approached the ric-rac store, I heard a man's voice behind me. He was an ordinary working man, the kind who would come to fix the house or dig the drain, not somebody who would come to visit us. But he spoke pleasantly and politely.

"Miss, excuse mih, but how yuh mother keeping today?"

"My mother? Fine, thank you," and I moved to walk on.

"Miss, I asking for a reason, yuh know. Yuh mother was very kind to me. She lend mih some money when ah was real hard up and ah want to pay she back. Is a long time now so ah want to send back a nice piece of watermelon for she too."

The man was an ordinary, simple man. He did not look like a bad person. Muddie did not lend people money, but suppose she had? Suppose he had come to fix something at the house and had asked to borrow a few dollars, and now wanted to pay her back? He would easily recognize me, but I had never paid any attention to the workmen who came to our home sometimes or repaired the road nearby. I suddenly remembered Muddie's admonishing words after I had passed my big exam at the end of last term.

"You feel you too great now that you going to start high school. Because you win free books and free school you feel you reach. You feel you too great suddenly. But you can't stop having respect for ordinary people, not while yuh living in this house. You not greater than everybody, yuh hear?"

The poor man just wanted to repay a few dollars. I decided to question him; my keen eleven-year-old intelligence would tell me what to do.

"How much money you owe my mother?"

"Twenty dollars but I only have twelve with me. Here, hold it." He thrust some dirty-looking dollars into my hand. "I name Sonny. I living just down the road, near Cedars Trace. It lil far to walk. Come, leh we take a taxi and you could get the rest of the money. My wife will give yuh a nice piece of watermelon and then yuh could take the rest home for yuh mammy. Come, it won't take long. What yuh come to buy downtown?"

I told him about the ric-rac but he didn't know what that was. He talked for a few minutes to the driver after we entered the taxi and then fell silent. I was silent too. Then the taxi rounded a corner near an open field leading to a side road. Sonny stopped the taxi and we got out. The sign by the road said Cedars Trace.

We walked just past the field to a place where the line of cocoa trees began, short and stubby. Their curving branches bent themselves near the road into a sheltered arbour. Underneath, the leaves looked crisp and clean. It was a hot dry day, without the usual August rains. Sonny explained that we were taking a shortcut and we had to go into the cocoa to connect with the track to his house. On the way we would pass the watermelon field and I could pick out a good one for my mammy. I stood there watching him, not saying a word. He folded his arms and looked at me, an untroubled look on his face. I walked away nearer to the open field and looked around me. At the other end of the field the sugar cane started, and at the top was a big plantation house. I looked up at it and the door magically opened. As if in a play a maid in uniform and cap stepped out and stood on the narrow landing at the top of the stairs, shaking out a tablecloth. Suddenly I was aware that Sonny was gripping my arm urgently. "Yuh see, yuh waiting so long to make up yuh mind, yuh even make the maid come out to see we. Now yuh go get the two a we in trouble."

A car passed and the driver popped his horn inquiringly at us, even though he already had five people in the car. It was a pirate taxi; the PH on its licence plate was all I could remember afterwards, no numbers. The passengers stared out of the window at us. One even turned his head around and continued looking as the car swooshed past. He was a bearded young man in a clean white shirt. I thought he looked Muslim.

They were all seeing a burly man and a young girl locked in combat at the side of the road. *Locked in mortal combat* were the words that flashed through my mind, and I knew for certain then that I was not stooping under any cocoa branches to take a shortcut anywhere. I stood still. More cars passed but none stopped. A bullying red-eyed man, probably the girl's father or uncle, was trying to make her do something. The girl's legs were curved inwards at the knees, a sign of her unwillingness. Something in the scene must have seemed odd to the Muslim man who had craned his head around for a second look.

The maid would have seen more from the landing as she shook out the white people's lunch tablecloth. She shook and watched, and then she stopped shaking and continued to watch down past the cedar and samaan trees and the horses, staring fixedly at the curve of cocoa road where a man and a girl stood at its edge. The man held the girl's arm and attempted to pull her down the slight slope under the cocoa trees. But the small girl did not budge. The man was heavy-set and ignorant looking, waving both hands and talking in a frantic manner. The girl had turned away from him and was facing the road in the direction of the oncoming cars. The maid's eyes would have held the whole scene together for one long minute after the lunch crumbs had fallen off the soiled table linen. When I turned and looked again, she had already gone inside.

The eye of the world was on that scene in a far corner of a cocoa plantation, centred on the stretch of road winding like the body of a macajuel snake around the wealth of cocoa almost ready for cutting. I stood at the edge of the grass verge, rooted to the spot. Another car passed and my arm raised itself in rapid movement. The car stopped and Sonny got in too, squeezing me against the two other people already in the back seat. He smelled strongly now of stale saffron powder and stinking ram-goat sweat. His breathing was hard and I sat in silence again, this time feeling as if I would vomit.

We rounded the corner where Canaan Village began and suddenly, as the San Fernando Hill came into view, Sonny started
berating me with real anger in his voice. "Yuh see how yuh harden?
All now so yuh coulda have de piece a watermelon for yuh mudder
and all the money she lend mih too. Now yuh have to go back with
yuh hand swinging. To beside, give mih back the twelve dollars ah
gie yuh. And tell yuh mudder if she want the money to come and
collect it sheself. Me eh dealing with no lil gyul again. All ah allyuh
so damn harden." A loud steups followed.

The passengers made no comment, but the lady next to me
pulled her orhni aside so that I could see her face, smiled, and patted my hand gently. That was all. As the car approached the library
corner Sonny snarled, "Driver!" The driver slowed down and
Sonny jumped out, the echo of a second loud steups ringing
through the air for several moments afterwards.

Trembling, I made my way back to the ric-rac store and bought
the items Muddie had sent me for. I still felt like vomiting. I took a
La Plata taxi and arrived home more than an hour later than Muddie
had expected. She was worried. She pounced on me and demanded
to know what had happened. She suspected the worst and was
determined to get to the bottom of it. The worst was that I had met
a boy and had spent a stolen hour with him. I did not know how to
start. I wanted to cry but instead I found myself standing before her
dry-eyed, telling her everything, from the man's first approach to
the maid to the return of the twelve dollars. She was livid. Before I
had finished speaking she started to shake me.

"You ever see me even talking to a man like that? I would ever
lend money to a man like that? Where I would even go to meet that
kind of man?"

I stared at her dumbly. Then a deeper suspicion filled her mind
and she turned to me frantically. "Anything happen? He touch you
anywhere? He kiss you?" The thought of that was too much and I

burst into tears, bawling so loudly that Kello and Johnnie ran into the house from outside. Muddie sent them out without answering any questions and shut the door to her room. She sat next to me on the bed and spoke in a low voice.

"We can't tell your father. Promise me that you will never talk to anybody about this. It too disgraceful. What yuh think people will say about this, eh? Answer me." She shook me roughly and then stopped, talking almost to herself. "Nobody will believe you didn't go with that man under that bush. You hear me now. Never say anything about this. You is such a fool, such a damn little fool. How you could think that I would know a man like that? You making me lie to your father. You know I don't do that kind of thing."

Her anger was too much for me. I lay face down on the pillows and wept as if the world had ended. In a daze I heard Muddie muttering, almost to herself, "I can't tell him anything. If I tell him anything, Mona will never escape. Mona will never escape . . ."

Abruptly I was back on the train. My thoughts had been rudely interrupted by the sound of a radio two seats down. The music was loud and unappetizing, the announcer's voice grating. I turned and caught the eye of the middle-aged offender. Politely, I asked whether he could turn the radio down or perhaps wear earphones. He acted surprised. "Is it disturbing you?" he said, in a voice of apparent concern. I nodded, and the car fell silent until two university types boarded at Kingston. They were confident, hearty, established, and they discoursed heavily about budgets, appointments, and the administration of places of higher learning. I was more irritated than ever and wanted to steups loudly. Suddenly I felt a tap on my left shoulder. I half-turned and saw the radio owner's face leaning down solicitously. Bending closer he asked softly, "Are you hearing that conversation?" I nodded. Then without warning he put his lips directly to my ear and in a piercing whisper hissed, "Then you must be listening too hard! If you don't like it, why don't you go back to where you came from?" Nothing in his manner had prepared me for this assault. And the ease and finesse of its execution had rendered it invisible; no one else in that car full of people had witnessed it. I had no words, nothing but shock. I kept my head up, my back straight, but I was shaken, suddenly close to tears at the unkindness of life, of the racism of this place that was always ready to crack you across your back when you least expected it.

Finally I fell into a blessed doze. The sounds of luggage being pulled off overhead racks roused me; the train was pulling into Union Station. Babsie was there alone, waiting to meet me. As soon as she saw me, she ran up, held me tightly, and would not let go. She buried her face in my hair and kissed my cheek over and over, her sobs deep and racking. When we were seated in the car, she turned to me and held both my hands together, looking directly into my face.

"Mona, you have to help me. We have to help Kello. You and I and Kello—we're in this together. It's just us." She paused, then everything rushed out rapidly. "Kello is dying. He swore me to secrecy and you have to keep it secret too. He has AIDS, has had it for a while now. That's why he's in a hospice. He probably told me because I'm a nurse. Muddie and Da-Da, Johnnie and the rest of the family must never know—this is what he wants, all he wants. You must help me Mona, promise me that. We have to do this for Kello."

I promised, nodding dumbly, my tears frozen somewhere inside. A thousand questions rushed through my mind but only one word came out: "How?"

Babs shrugged, and even before she spoke I knew the answer. "I don't really know. It's not a question I can ask and he gives up nothing. You know Kello."

There was nothing more to say. Why would he want to keep it secret? Muddie and Da-Da were not ignorant people—they were forward-thinking and they deserved to know the truth. And how did he get AIDS? Promiscuous sex? Needles? Was Kello gay? So what if he had AIDS? Surely we weren't such creeping, crawling hypocrites, inching along, looking over our shoulders every second for fear of what people would say? God!

Babs was impatient and anticipated my thoughts. "Mona, listen to me and listen hard. Kello asked me to meet you and talk to you alone. Mon, you must help. This is what Kello wants. Never mind your own ideas about truth and digging up skeletons. This is Kello's business. Kello is dying. He may be bisexual—I don't know how he describes himself, but his present relationship is with a man. I've met him a couple of times—his name is Matthew. A nice man. That's all I know because Kello does not share. But he wants this passage to be his, without Muddie or Da-Da or Johnnie knowing and especially without the whole tribe of relatives whispering and shooshooing about him in the way that they will if they know any of this. You can just imagine the ole talk, God!" Babsie shuddered. "Taking man and battyman this and that, and heaven knows what other nastiness and bacchanal. Kello wants quietness, peace, and some comfort. He wants to be left alone and to answer to no one. And he is asking his sisters to guarantee that. We owe him this much, Mona."

But I had other, more pressing questions. What treatments had been used? Had the doctors offered Kello any drug cocktails that could prolong his life? Babsie was very tired, but she struggled to be gentle with me. "Everything has been tried. Kello has known for years that he was HIV-positive. There comes a time when it's the end-game and this is it. He is fully in charge still, but he knows that he is on his way out. What he wants from us is help to make sure that he dies the way he wants. That's all he asks."

Babs was incredibly nervous, I could see that. She turned on the radio and her hands shook as she lit a cigarette. Someone was singing "Moon River." Kello and I had been two drifters searching for the same rainbow's end—and one of us had reached it. I was suddenly overwhelmed by the finality of it all and broke down. I hadn't wept like this in years. It was too much, all of it was too much, something was being pulled from under my feet and I was landing on ground that I could not feel, not with my toes, not with any part of my body. When did Kello become gay or bisexual? He was married and divorced and had two kids. And the lymphoma . . . Roddy's words came back to haunt me. "What do you know of Kello's life, Mona?" What did Roddy know that I didn't?

We drove through the city, heading north through a mess of construction debris and ugly high-rise buildings erupting without warning out of the sidewalk. Not a pretty place, I muttered to Babs, who managed a weak smile.

The day was cold and windy. Muddie and Da-Da lived in a North Toronto suburb where all the houses were identical. In summer Muddie's gardening magic would transform their miniature front yard into a field of rhododendrons, peonies, day lilies, clematis vines, and climbing rose bushes, but now it was winter, and the line of ugly grey-toned warrens stretched into the distance. The stand of evergreens was splendid, though, pines and junipers shielding the windward side in a protective arc.

I kissed Muddie and she held on to me, sobbing uncontrollably. "Why? Why Kello?" I could see that Da-Da was trying to be stoic, but when I hugged him tightly, he sank into my arms as if they offered shelter from unspeakable dangers. I stood there, holding my father, our roles temporarily reversed. Dying hung in the air; Kello was dying. And he couldn't be. Whatever had happened in my own life, however rough the passage, I had always known that Kello was there, would always be there. I could not imagine life without my big brother.

49

The Swinging Bridge

I looked at Muddie and Da-Da, standing in their living room with its comfortable deep chairs, the warm russet tones of throws and cushions signalling coziness and refuge from the white avalanche outside, and they seemed stripped down, bereft. Their frailty as they stood side by side, looking towards their children, waiting for guidance almost, gave me a powerful sensation of vertigo. Life had gone into reverse. The harsh Canadian winter held the earth around their house in its unyielding vise, while my parents stood firm, trying to be resilient, bravely contemplating the lymphoma that was about to kill their eldest child in mid-stride. How could I keep the truth from them? I hated to be part of such a lie; it was all wrong but I had no choice. Somehow I would have to hide what I knew.

THREE

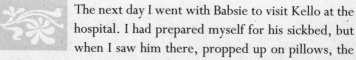The next day I went with Babsie to visit Kello at the hospital. I had prepared myself for his sickbed, but when I saw him there, propped up on pillows, the drapes over the window pulled shut, the drab artificial lights puckering his skin in greyish patches, I lost all thought of restraint. I held on to him and wept, Babs patting my back in an awkward manner. I stopped only when Kello said in his old teasing way, "Stop bawling like a cow, Mona. I ain't dead yet." For a moment our hysterical laughter was so loud that a couple of nursing students popped their heads in to see if anything was the matter.

I had last seen Kello at Christmas. It was hard to believe that in one month so much change could have taken place. His breathing was laboured and he had a constant dry, rattling cough. He looked thinner too, although when he held me I found that his arms had not lost their wiry strength. But the biggest change was in his sallow complexion, that and his glittering, slightly mad eyes. All my life I had admired Kello's ruddy dark brown skin, wishing that my own was not so light. His arms were always the strongest and he could lift anything. Even as a child he could open the tightest jar, hang from a branch the longest, and beat everybody at tic-tac-toe. When he laughed out loud his whole face broke open. This I loved especially because it happened so rarely. I was always watching and listening for it. I loved Kello in a way I hardly understood, almost as if he were my second self.

Babs left us together and we talked. I did ask him how he had contracted the disease. Not unexpectedly, he said that he was not sure. He had discovered, however, that two casual lovers were also

HIV-positive and one of them was sick. "Casual lovers" flowed easily from his lips, and once more I felt my foundations rocking. I had never thought of myself as homophobic and found my inability to take in Kello's unknown life surprising. "What about now? Are you in a relationship?" He nodded briefly. He knew our ways, of course, knew that Babs would have already disgorged everything she knew, and I read his impatience accurately.

An awkward silence sprang up between us. I sensed that he was at ease with his sexuality but unwilling to be drawn into confidences with me. I had never felt a guardedness between us before and resented this Matthew, whoever he was, for causing it. My own relationships had never closed a door between us, and neither had his, not even his marriage to Irene.

We talked about his preference for a hospice. I couldn't see how his wish to keep his illness a secret fitted into the equation. He was at pains to explain. "Mon, I've lived with this for many years. I've thought about how I would handle it. I am involved in a leave-taking. I've already left, in a way. Right now I want to be among other dying people. I've arranged everything, automatic payments for my care, funeral and cremation arrangements, a will. Everything is set, and I'll be transferred in two days." I wondered at his preparedness, feeling small and ignorant in the face of such complicated undertakings. I found myself saying words I had never dreamed that I, the family rebel, could utter. "But Kell, what will people say?"

The irony did not escape him. He threw back his head and laughed before answering.

"I don't know, Mona. And I really don't care. But I explained to Muddie and Da-Da that the acute strain of lymphoma that I have can mimic many of the symptoms associated with AIDS. So the hospice is the most appropriate place for me because I'll get the care I need. I told them that at this stage we can't spend time worrying about what people will say, and Da-Da said, 'Is true. I mean you seeing about yourself. The same people who ready to run their mouth, they ain't rice-ing you. You just do what you have to do.' Mona, don't worry, there's something else you have to help me with."

It turned out that the land rumours were true. Kello had been negotiating to buy back Pappy's land in Trinidad. The whole property, he said, the land on Manahambre Road, with Pappy and Mama's house on the Pierre Street end and our big wooden structure smack in the middle. My memories on the train about this early childhood home of ours came back sharply, and I was about to remind him of the big row but stopped myself short. Kello mentioned that our cousin Bess in Trinidad, Uncle Sweetie's daughter, was a realtor and was handling matters on that end. But Kello's unexpected request was that he wanted me to be his proxy for the land business.

"Mona," he said, and his tone was sharp, "I want you to go and act on my behalf. Go to Trinidad, inspect the land, and confirm that the transaction takes place. Be my right arm. Bess says that the whole Southland is booming because of oil revenues. She is suggesting a development—terraced townhouses, something like that. I'm asking you to go look at the property, get a feel for things on that end. Even if I wasn't sick, I've been away for so long that I wouldn't know how to read the scene. You can do it better than I can, you always researching Trini ting, you're the best one to go. Do this for me, Mon. I want this land, Pappy's land."

He was intent on purchasing land from his deathbed, yet the decision did not strike him as unusual. Now I understood the manic look in his eyes, the incendiary quality to his energy. God, this could not be happening. Kello was losing his mind; he would have to be monitored more closely. I tried to make light of his request.

"Me? You must be mad! What the hell I know about real estate and terraced townhouses and that kind of stuff? I don't know what advice I could possibly give about a land deal. Kello, I would do anything you asked me to, really, but real estate is not my strong suit. I'm the wrong person for this. I wouldn't know where to start."

He ignored my protests and said quietly, "Could you go, though? I mean, could you take the time now from your work? What about your new boyfriend . . . ?"

"Roddy. No, I'm not worried about him or even my research for the film. I'm worried about me and my hopelessness about matters like this. Finance and upset price and land values—what the hell do I know about those matters?"

He interrupted triumphantly. "You see how much you know? Upset price, eh? Well, Bess advised me to hold out, said most likely we would be able to get the land at the upset price. You had the whole deal figured out before I told you. You see? Mona, do this for me, please. It's Pappy's land and I want it. Think about it, please."

I left, agreeing to think about it but cursing myself even for that. It was a wild idea and what use would the land be to us? And if he was so set on buying back Pappy's land, how could I advise him not to? Kello's deathbed folly, I thought, suddenly blinded by tears.

Kello soon moved to the hospice, located on a quiet treelined street in downtown Toronto. The neighbourhood conveyed an atmosphere of settled values, Victorian chic, and elaborately concealed Anglo-Saxon attitudes. I'm not fooled by all of this fake gentility, I thought savagely, as I wheeled Babsie's hatchback into a tight spot between two other vehicles while a householder paused in his driveway, leaning on his snow shovel and waiting for me to hit the car at the back which, I was certain, had fuck-all to do with him. Thank God I can park, I thought, as I entered the accursed hospice in which my brother had elected to die, surrounded by people schooled in prissiness and low-keyed voices.

The hospice, however, turned out to be a beautiful Victorian house with a regal entranceway and ornately carved doorposts. An indoor garden, well-placed lighting, and deep wicker furniture in the large hallway reinforced the patrician atmosphere. Kello's room was on the second floor, a bright airy space completely unlike the hospital room. The furniture was old dark wood and the curtains were country style. There was a small deck overlooking what was probably a garden. It would be pretty in springtime, I thought. He was obviously comfortable in this place. I didn't see any other patients, but the staff were friendly and several young volunteers introduced themselves. On my way out, somewhat mollified now, I saw the neighbour staring at me again, but this time he nodded in recognition. I wondered what he thought of an AIDS hospice being planted in his solid neighbourhood.

The days settled into a routine where Muddie and Da-Da, together at first and then singly, visited Kello in the morning and I in the mid-afternoon. Babsie flitted in and out between shifts at her own hospital, checking this or that solution or his drips, not caring to talk much. She had a concentration at these times that was astounding, in complete contradiction to her butterfly personality. And Johnnie called from Vancouver often but seemed unable to visit. His was a remoteness that remained whether he was in our presence or not, and I suspected that Kello's illness did not seem real to him.

As for Kello, all his talk was about my going to Trinidad as his proxy for the land deal. He was bent on buying, but I couldn't help trying to tell him how ownership meant nothing to me. I wondered to myself about the men of the family and their very different responses to land. Pappy had felt all along that our land should never have been sold, while Da-Da, always reaching for the big kill, had seen that country property as an impediment to his mobility upwards and townwards. Of course, the land was no longer in the countryside, so Kello was showing good business sense. But beyond that, I thought, he was manifesting a powerful masculine drive to possess, to control, even in the face of a terminal illness.

I began to say as much but stopped when I saw the look of resignation on his face. For a moment he could only stare at me tiredly, and then he gently spoke. "Mona, Da-Da and I could never see eye to eye. The difference between us is complete. Pappy told me when I was small, 'Yuh Da-Da hand open wide and he will never learn to close it. Everything will slip through. Son, you must close yours. You must start now.' And every month he gave me two dollars in small change from the fourteen he received as a government pension."

Laughing, I reminded him of the used cocoa tins he would save the money in and how stingy he always was with those few cents. He would make a hole at the base for the coins and nail down the lid. Nobody could break into his savings. Everybody, even Da-Da on occasion, would ask to borrow, but he never lent a black cent. Kello, however, was not laughing. He had accumulated twenty-four of those little cocoa tins by the time he left home, he said. He was convinced that these savings gave him his start.

"It wasn't the money, Mona. Because Da-Da went and beg, borrow, or steal, I don't know what he did, but he put three hundred pounds sterling, just so, in my hand when I was leaving Trinidad, when I was on the wharf with Uncle Samuel about to go up the steps into the ship. He pushed it in my hand. He didn't say anything. Where he got it, I don't know. But it was Pappy's hope for me, his little pension money that started me up, the cocoa tins . . ."

He broke down and I put my arms around him. Then, looking straight ahead, not at me, Kello began to recall Pappy's journey to Petitbourg to secure a mortgage for the land in Manahambre Road.

"I was not there, I wasn't even born yet, but I know what happened. I know from Pappy. One night Pappy had to walk to Petitbourg because by then the bigshots from Port of Spain had stopped the mule train from Princes Town. It was an Indian man who was running the mule train and doing very well. But when the off-white bigshots in Port of Spain heard about it, they sent the government vet to test the mules. The vet ordered all the man's mules to be slaughtered because he discovered that they were infected with a deadly disease. An epidemic—but only for the mules in Princes Town! Other people in the area lost their mules too. So people without their own horse-drawn carriages had to walk.

"The land was the reason why Pappy had to walk to Petitbourg. All the lawyers were in Petitbourg. The land had a lien on it. Mama and Pappy knew they could lose everything. They scrimped and saved to buy that land and it took two whole years for the gossip about the debt to reach them. They ignored the gossip, but one day the moneylender himself came to their door, claiming the land. He had a set of court papers in his hand. The previous owner had borrowed money from him, sold the land, and left. The moneylender demanded his money, but there was no money and no owner, only their land, the surety on his loan. Pappy begged for a month's grace to come up with the money. But the man held out for fourteen days.

"Mona, I can see it now. Pappy and Mama sitting down at the long table in the kitchen in Manahambre Road, you remember? The one where you nearly burned me with the kettle." He chucked my chin and smiled. I would never have burned him with the kettle, but I let the comment pass. This gentleness was new to Kello, new and touching in its simplicity.

But his mind was fixed on the land, its history, its future. "They would be sitting there, discussing the details, because they did everything together, studying what to do because they had no money and four little children. Uncle Junior would be playing somewhere, Da-Da toddling around, the first Babsie a small child, and the little baby boy too, the one they say died of maljo soon after they got the mortgage. It was the time when Pappy wasn't working."

Kello reached for the pitcher of water on the bedside table. His hand trembled as he poured it. I watched in silence. How did he know all of these details? It was as if he had been there himself.

"A little while before the moneylender appeared, Pappy had lost his job in the sugar factory. He used to do the weighing when the canes came in. He was fired because he cussed up a young white overseer. The man horked and spat near Pappy's foot and called him a stupid bong coolie. For nothing, just because he was white and could do it. You know Pappy, how quiet he was, how polite. Well, not this time. Pappy cussed the man upside down, and afterwards everybody remembered that cussing. He cursed the overseer in Hindi, in patois, in Chinee, he cursed the man's mother and all his generations to come. The overseer turned red and started to stammer out something, but by then Pappy had finished and knew that his days at the factory were over. He had reached the gate already by the time the young white man found his voice and shouted, 'You're fired! You're fired, you coolie bitch!' But Pappy was out of the gate already.

"When the moneylender appeared, they had to find the money somewhere. The only way was through a mortgage, but they decided to try a lawyer rather than go straight to another money-lender who would skin them alive. Pappy sold the two horses they had, Sailor and Jumna, to get the money for that lawyer."

I was listening now in amazement. Kello knew everything, even the names of those horses. The grief of losing that land must have cut Pappy's heart in two. Da-Da's ears had been closed to his father's pleas; Pappy could lay out his grief only to his little grandson, the boy whose fingers he had closed over the pennies and cents that came out of his meagre government pension.

Kello's eyes blazed out of his thin face. He hardly stopped to draw breath. "Pappy left in the night because it was cooler. By the time he reached Petitbourg it was daylight. He asked people for directions and some of them jeered openly at him, a coolie man from the country who couldn't find his way around town. When he reached the law office, he pulled out the papers and started to explain the whole situation to the red-skinned lawyer, about how unfair it was and how it wasn't really his debt. The lawyer cut through and asked how much money he had. When Pappy took out the roll, the lawyer said, 'We in business. Sign here. Now sign there and there and there . . . Awright. Yuh have back yuh land as long as yuh keep up the payments, Mr. Singh.' He took all the money at first. But Pappy told me that suddenly, without explanation, the lawyer stripped off some bills and handed them back to him. 'Buy a donkey with that and start up again,' he said.

"Mona, it was that donkey that saved them. Pappy and Mama had owned a cart and two horses. When they sold the horses, they still had the cart. Pappy started to load canes and transport them from the fields to the weigh scale. And that is what helped them to get their second start. But soon afterwards the little baby boy died of maljo. Mama and Pappy knelt down after that and prayed every night that bad would leave them and get flung back to whoever it was that put the bad-eye on them. But they survived and they kept the land. And that land will be ours again, Mona. All is not lost."

I was moved to tears by his grasp of the sheer endurance, the courage, and the wiliness that early Indians like our own grandparents, ignorant in the ways of the Creole culture, needed to work out a means of survival in the face of so much hostility. And so I found myself agreeing to go to Trinidad as Kello's proxy, clutching to my chest the power of attorney he had given me. He was signing his life away, I couldn't help thinking, and forcing me to accept all of his intentions, his and Pappy's, all of the plans that he had set into motion and which were gathering their own momentum, heedless of whatever fragile little freedom from possessions I was trying to maintain for myself. I said yes but I wondered if I was up to it, not the land deal itself, but the opening up of a vast sea of responsibility, something I had spent my adult life trying to shake off my heels.

FOUR

Having agreed to go to Trinidad I found myself eager to see the land again, to finalize the deal. Now that I understood Kello's stake, I wanted to complete the repossession before it was too late. But Bess insisted on holding out for the upset price if Kello could wait, and Kello said that he could. He wanted the land, but he was still reluctant to spend a bad cent.

I went back to Montreal twice. On both occasions I travelled by air; the comfort of trains and their *clackety-clack* had vanished for the time being. Carene and I made final decisions about the research. She finished the script, leaving out all the information about Cecile Fatiman. And so even in a liberating film about the lives of contemporary Haitian women, poor women scratching out a life on the snowbound streets of Montreal, a film made by a woman of the Caribbean, researched by another Caribbean woman, the only woman's name connected with the Haitian Revolution had no place. Toussaint, Christophe, Dessalines, Boukman. No mention of Fatiman.

Roddy was travelling a lot and I saw him only infrequently, but on those occasions our relationship was marked by a hunger that consumed me. I waited for the times we spent alone, sheltered from the outside, living in a time warp where we held each other close and talked and talked about everything. His settled Scottish Canadian sense of order calmed me down, was a relief from the turbulence of my own life. But Roddy was a journalist and had seen much of the world's underside. It disturbed him deeply to think that the order of his world depended on a deeper disorder elsewhere. Once he told me, "Peace in Europe; no peace beyond the line. That hasn't changed, Mona, not since the beginning of this century and long before that. " And for no good reason those words gave me a sudden pang of uncertainty at our separateness, the distance between our two worlds. It was only a passing cloud though, and I linked my arm in his, living in the moment.

In the long periods I spent in Toronto, staying in my parents' home, I was preoccupied with memories of Trinidad and found myself raking over certain events, wondering at the inevitability of Kello's illness, at my own unfulfilled ambitions. I undertook to clean the attic, a job Muddie disliked and had been trying to get me to do for years. I had steadfastly resisted the task because I knew that she wanted me to make the decisions about what to keep and what to jettison, and I had been determined to reject the role of family custodian, family caretaker. But something had changed now, and I found myself approaching the job with interest, wanting to handle the evidence of our passage—the mementos, the letters and prizes from a past time.

In that attic I found a bulky little parcel wrapped in old brown paper and labelled Love Letters. The penmanship on the outside was my own, as uneven and clear as it still is, *crapaud foot* they used to call it at school. The whimsical nature of the labelling struck me only after I had unwrapped the parcel and chuckled at the odd assortment of letters, among them one addressed to Mr. Ganga Singh. The wrinkled official-looking envelope looked familiar. It turned out to be a love letter written to my grandfather by his "bamboo wife." That incident had happened after Mama's death and was still vivid to me. The day the postman brought the letter to the house on Manahambre Road I was bunched up with Pappy in the hammock slung in the long verandah, and I looked curiously at the typewritten label as he turned the letter over without opening it.

"But ay, ay," he said musingly, "this is a lawyer letter or what?"

It was addressed simply to Mr. Ganga Singh, Princes Town.

Everybody knew Pappy by his Christian name, Stephen, so it was a mystery how the letter had found its destination. When he finally opened it, he jumped up so swiftly that the hammock did a sudden flip, depositing me on the wooden floor. Pappy had a habit of reasoning aloud and I waited to hear what was what. After reading the letter again he shook his head and said, "Ay, ay, Etwaria? Whey yuh sending letter now for?"

That evening the house was full of loud talk and discussion, and Da-Da got Muddie totally fed up by his references to Etwaria as "the bold-face bamboo wife." Although I had heard the term bamboo wife several times that was the day I truly understood it. Pappy had been married before but the marriage was a Hindu ceremony conducted "under bamboo," in the bamboo and tarpaulin tents that Indians in villages built for their lavish wedding ceremonies. These weddings were not recorded legally.

Once before Mama died, Kello and I had gone to a ceremony under bamboo, the wedding of Pappy's niece. We left early in the morning and came back very late at night. We were given special seats at the front of the open bamboo tent and watched the ceremony with Mama. The pundit went on for a long time and Kello grew restless, whispering in my ear nonsense Hindi words and sending me into fits of giggles. Mama took us outside after a while and talked sternly about how we must have respect for other religions. When it was time for the bridegroom, the doolaha, to start eating, Kello rushed in to see and I followed him. The doolaha took his time while a few more dollars were added to the brass plate in front of him, and some of the older men on the doolahin's side began to suck their teeth loudly. He ate then, grinning at everybody over his dish of sweet rice as if it had all been a game. We ate too. The food was served on fresh sohari leaves and eaten with our fingers: rice and dhal and curried chataigne, curried channa and aloo, pumpkin, curried mango, achar, kuchela, phoulouries, and roti.

Indian food, but different somehow from what we cooked at home and much better. It was better too to eat off a fresh-cut leaf without bothering about knives and forks. I enjoyed myself at that wedding.

The groom wore a tall pink hat and a bright pink dhoti. The bride wore a beautiful red sari embroidered with gold thread. They looked like a fairytale prince and princess, and I told Mama so on the way home. But Kello kept jeering at the whole celebration and said that if he was the doolaha, they would have to put gold on that plate before he would eat. Pappy smiled at this but Mama remonstrated with him, saying that they were our family too and that we should understand that not everybody was Christian like us. But Kello had just one question for Mama: "They poor?" She nodded, and he looked wise and nodded too, as if the case were closed. The day Etwaria's letter came, I found it impossible to imagine that Pappy had been such a bridegroom once and had then turned his back on his wedding vows.

That evening was full of angry discussion and the kind of palaver everybody called ole talk. Opinions had to be stated even though decisions hung in the air, already made. Da-Da's talk was fierce; Muddie's was soothing and full of recollections of several other men of Pappy's generation who had done the same thing, persuaded by missionary interventions. These church people from Canada interfered so much with our lives; to me it was very puzzling. Big strong men like Pappy and Mr. Bhim up the road, allowing a few white men to rule their lives and tell them who to marry and who to leave. And what about love? Did Pappy love Mama or was the bamboo wife his one true love, like in love songs?

Now in the attic I held Etwaria's letter in my hands, bundled up with the other bits and pieces in the parcel. I thought of how our whole family might never have existed. Or how, if we were Etwaria's grandchildren, born out of bamboo, we would all be illegitimate. Pappy's land could never have been ours. For the first time as well, I thought of Etwaria's longing, her hopes as she had waited in her hut alone, waiting day after day for a reply that only came much later.

After two months of waiting Etwaria sent a man from her village to find out what Pappy's answer was. The man found Pappy alone at home, and they talked and talked. Then Pappy walked up the road with the man and they sat together at a rough table in front of a rumshop in the heart of Princes Town, a bottle of rum between them, continuing the talking. On his way home that night Da-Da saw them. He tried to get Pappy to leave, but my grandfather refused outright. After midnight we heard noises of stumbling and falling in Pappy's house at the top of the hill, and Da-Da went to check. I never found out what happened between them that night. But the ole talk had ended.

I opened the letter. It was written in a bold cursive style, even and well rounded, the voice emanating from it as clear and direct as a child's.

> My dear Ganga,
>
> I wait all these years for you. Now your wife die you can come back with me. I live in my house all this time. The house still empty. I alone live here. I plant a little bodi and bhaji and sem to eat. I work weeding in the field the same as before. Mr. Baxter (the young one) let me stay here but now I have the deed. I still waiting for you. Now everything settle you could come back soon.
>
> I remain,
> Your living wife,
> Etwaria

Out of Pappy's earshot Muddie and Da-Da continued to puzzle out the letter's true meaning. The letter writer had to be a person of some standing in the village, they reasoned, typed address and all, so "living" instead of "loving" must be an act of spite. But on whose part? Muddie was inclined to believe that Etwaria had meant no harm. She was touched by the letter. She saw romance and waiting and longing and fidelity over all these years. She warmed to Etwaria right away.

But Da-Da's unbridled anger was raw, and without a shade of remorse he shot down any chance of such a reunion. "Disrespecting my mother memory? And so soon too? Nah, nah, that can't happen."

The letter had come early in the new year, after the big row at Christmas. The memory of that row was the only brake on Da-Da's behaviour the day he learned that Pappy was thinking of taking up Etwaria's offer. Kello and I stayed in the background, fearful, not wanting Pappy to go, but knowing that this decision was all big people's business.

Etwaria had come from India as a young girl, already widowed. Her marriage to Pappy lasted for two years. She had no legal hold on him when he accepted the Christian minister's suggestion of Mama's hand in marriage. Mama was a fine young Christian girl, educated; her own mother was a widow too. Pappy had had a good life with Mama. But I heard him explaining to Da-Da and Muddie that he would not be a burden to anyone if he went back to Etwaria. Kello could come and visit him often. "Not so, son?" He looked at Kello, and my brother, knowing what was expected of him, nodded in vigorous assent.

The row smouldered for days without really exploding. But after Etwaria's messenger had been sent away, there was no further mention of her. I imagine that she died alone in her tapia hut, childless, still faithful to Ganga, the husband who had rescued her from loneliness in the strangeness of Trinidad.

There were more than love letters in that pile. I scrutinized a

torn slip of paper before throwing it out and found the words to the
Canboulay song that La Rosette, the dancer and folklorist, had
taught us at La Pastora High School during her three-week stay in
the south of Trinidad, touring several schools and teaching us about
our culture.

Cannes brulées, cannes brulées
Ah la la . . .
Captain Baker . . .
L'arrivé Tamana
Cannes brulées, cannes brulées
Ah la la . . .

The words were incomplete and I had never filled them in. Sitting in the attic I still could not summon them, even though the
melody that we chanted lingered at the back of my consciousness,
hypnotic and strong. It was 1963, the year after we got Independence from England. "De Doctah," Dr. Hector James, was our
prime minister, a highly educated son of the soil, a black man walking proudly through the land, now that "Massa day done" and we
could all come into our own. Coming into our own meant celebrating our own culture and not some washed-out white people song
and dance sent from England. It was real, this culture of ours, a
Creole bacchanal, multiracial, multicultural, cosmopolitan. De
Doctah had used wonderful words like these to describe the promise of our new nation when he visited us as part of the nationwide
tour of schools.

La Rosette was sent to La Pastora directly after De Doctah had
visited, as part of the Ministry of Culture's new program. In
appearance she was an ordinary-looking, mixed-race, brown-
skinned woman until she took to the floor and transformed herself,
before our dazzled eyes, into La Petite Rosette, the legendary

dancer and choreographer from Port of Spain. On her first day with us she opened her arms wide, throwing her low voice effortlessly to the back wall:

"Come, my darlings, come. Show me your worth. Come, follow me, my darlings."

And with one graceful lift of her long skirt à la Belle Créole, she moved in a light two-step around the school auditorium. The dance was not as easy as she made it look, and after a while she stepped out to observe us.

"I want to create something from the Southland, something with your natural movements. Your movements, my darlings, are exquisite, and exquisitely different from anything I have ever worked with. Now follow me." Her voice cracked sharply through the air. "Cut cane! Like this! Now bend, now walk with a bucket of water on your head, walk with a bundle on your back, a child, a bag of cocoa, walk with your heads up, proudly, proudly, peasant women, country women, cut cane!"

But the cane-cutter image did not work at all; we were stiff and unresponsive and all her appeals to ancestral pride ("This is you, my darlings! The Indian South!") met with nothing. Obviously we at La Pastora were done with cane cutting. She spoke about the incredible mixture of races in our country—African, Indian, Chinese, Portuguese—but especially in the Southland she discerned a unique ambience. "Oh, my darlings, if you could only see your beauty. You are distinct, you know."

It was an impossible task, and in the end La Rosette gave up her vision of creating something that echoed this ambience. She took her famous "Canboulay" piece and reworked it for us. She tied traditional Indian bells around our ankles and dressed us in full skirts made of sari cloth and the customary Creole white blouses with off-the-shoulder necklines. Sequins in our hair and tikkas for our foreheads completed the ensemble. A few girls played Indian men in dhotis or Creole men in plain black pants.

"Imagine, my darlings, caneland burning, men with Canboulay sticks held high above their heads, bright skirts swishing, saris shimmering, Indian bells tinkling at first, then clashing, clanking, crashing, and the resolve, the resolve of the people! People in the Canboulay riots, the Hosay riots, people, our people, all our different races coming together, imagine the beauty, my darlings . . ."

We danced that resolve on the stage of La Pastora at Speech Day, with Dr. Hector James and La Rosette flanking our principal, Miss Boodram, everyone smiling and nodding brightly. The dance opened with the gaudy flare of skirts, moving into the slow undulation of stick movements turning and turning, the underplayed melody merging with our chants of "Cannes brulées . . . ah la la!" and picking up the rhythm of cane ash flying, the mad clanging of hundreds of ankle bells, the blaze in our eyes, on our cheeks, the crescendo building to the grand finale:

FIRE IN DE CANE! FIRE IN DE CANE!

The melody stays but those missing words of the song remain beyond reach.

In the love letters parcel I had also thrust a set of newspaper clippings from the time Da-Da spent a year and a half writing letters to the editor in the Trinidad papers. He signed the letters with the unlikely name of Nizam Maharaj because he wanted to speak for all Indians. "For all a we, Hindu and Muslim, Indian is Indian," he burst out one night to Muddie. Da-Da was so unexpected, so full of logical argument, so full of inexplicable bursts of fury. Full of Indian pride too when it suited him. Yet he was a Creole to his heart, as Mama used to say, a real throwback to his wild grandfather on her side. Drinking, smoking, gambling, loving calypso, steelband, and Carnival—"a Creole to yuh heart, mih dear," she would chuckle.

Uncertainty, apprehension, and fear of change characterized that period leading to the end of colonial rule. I read later about the historic meetings in 1956 in Port of Spain's square and San Fernando's town hall when Dr. Hector James was hailed as our new leader. He had returned only recently from abroad and was described as a Negro man of genius, a man with a vision for his people, a man who would lead us out of the wilderness. He held out the promise of self-government, when the white man's foot would be off our throats. He had lots of catchy phrases such as "Massa day done" and "all ah we is one." It was a time of promise and excitement.

At the town hall meeting there was a reception, and Da-Da had come to De Doctah's attention. Da-Da's quick wit, his popularity with his friends, and his gift of the gab were evident to the man who was intent on becoming our new leader. He sent word two days later that Mackie should come to see him and his partner, an Indian doctor named Ishwar Khan. He wanted Mackie to join the party; he said that he saw in him "a devil of an Indian." Da-Da's friends promptly dubbed my father "The Indian Devil," a drinking name that endured years after its source had faded from their memories.

De Doctah painted an attractive picture of what could lie ahead. "Think of the possibility, man. The possibilities are endless." And Da-Da did think carefully about the possibilities. A seat in the Legislative Council, honours, recognition throughout the land, speech-making, toasts, a chauffeur, responsibility, wealth, the good life.

"You will be an important person," De Doctah had said, clapping Da-Da on the back. And Da-Da thought it over for a week, walking around in a daze as he imagined himself surrounded by hordes of people, friends and foes. At the end of the week he declined. Afterwards he still wrote speeches for his friends on both sides of the

House and he would listen to the delivery of his words as the government program came over the radio at night, sputtering in rage when
they made a miss, when "Gird your loins, my countrymen!" turned
into "Grid your lions!" and the speaker's voice rose to a mighty roar.

Da-Da did not trust the situation. When his opposition to Dr.
Hector James became more vocal, he declared that his intuition had
been right. He spoke rarely of De Doctah's invitation, but when he
did, he stressed his point that to survive he would have had to sell
Indians down the river. He couldn't advance himself at the expense
of his own people, he said. And why couldn't we make a place
where every creed and race had an equal place, as the new anthem
proposed? Somehow Da-Da refused to believe in racial divisions,
even when they were all around him. He held fast to the romantic
idea of a body politic that would accept people of every creed,
every race. He saw himself as an Indian man and a Trinidadian, neither cancelling out the other, a natural inheritor of the Creole culture he loved.

But in the end he had found nothing. Nothing but the same routine rising up to confront him day after day, sitting at his desk, a
nondescript government officer like thousands of others, watching
for an opening that would not strangle him, refusing to rise through
the system by making deals. All the deals were corrupt, he told
Muddie, and in a small vicious place with little opportunity it was to
be expected. He wanted no part of it. He would leave, he said.

Da-Da could not make deals. He only knew how to give everything to something he believed in or to turn away from what he did
not like. In another place he might have found his calling as a writer.
He thought so himself, and had the titles of the books he would
write one day already in his head. I knew them all. Names like *Paradise Isle*, *Iere: Land of the Hummingbird* and *Coral and Quicksand*. The
new books by the up-and-coming West Indian writers offended

him. He thought they had one purpose only: to make us look bad. All of these new writers in England were making it, he said, on the backs of the poor people they had left behind.

"What the arse they know? All them bitches come from riches, they ain't know a blasted thing bout real people life. Why they have to make us sound so, man? We could talk better than that any time."

Da-Da's letters to the editors of both daily newspapers were full of outrage and a growing sense of despair. De Doctah was in power, but to my father and many others the prime minister's partisan display of power for the benefit of the black population had destroyed any vision of oneness and equality. "Indians don't stand a chance. Massa day was better than this. We go eat grass here, wait and see!" I heard these discussions at home, in taxis, in shops, and even at school. In Da-Da's letters I read the map of our departure from that early island home into a Canadian migrant existence. About our new land all he could say was "Well, yes!" and shrug noncommittally. Or at other times, "Look at me, eh? Look what I come to. Living in a country where they so racist they could just take it for granted that is so people have to live. But what the arse these people know anyhow? No class, man, no class at all. And they ain't even know they arse from they elbow."

Over the years Da-Da perfected this kind of non-communication when people asked whether he had made the right decision in leaving Trinidad. His letters, however, were anything but noncommittal, written at a time when the young Da-Da was still wrestling with everything.

January 3rd, 1964

Dear Sir,

      I write this letter as a true patriot of this country. My love for this land where generations of my forebears have toiled and struggled, wept and loved, is a pure one. I write not for myself but for my countrymen.

Sir, the leader of our land, fondly regarded by everyone, even myself, as De Doctah, has labelled my people, the Indians of this land, as a "hostile and recalcitrant minority." In so doing he consigns us to the dungheap of history. How can we contribute to the enterprise of nationhood, trapped as we are by this perception of ourselves which is lodged in the hearts and minds of our fellow countrymen of other races? I say other races, but let us honour plain speaking and be more blunt. The two chief races in this land are Negro and Indian. I say that our leader is setting us up, one against the other. I say that this is wrong.

My countrymen, when will you wake up and see the light? Our only hope for the future is unity! We must unite!

Think, I beg you.

> I remain, sir,
> Yours sincerely,
> Nizam Maharaj

March 6th, 1964

Dear Sir,

I was in the Square on that momentous occasion when our esteemed leader, De Doctah, let his bucket down. I walked every mile with him, literally and figuratively. I was on the march to Chaguaramas. How well I know the arrogance of Americans on the military base from personal experience! Our winning that battle was a step forward. My hope in the vision put forward by that multiracial team of men that day in '56 is matched today only by my deep feelings of betrayal.

Sir, I want to express my outrage at anybody, anybody at all, telling me how to live my life. The principles of democracy are such that we hold these truths to be self-evident. Our forefathers left behind in India a backward system of arranged marriage and suttee. We strode forward on a path to freedom and enlightenment in the few decades since we arrived on these blessed shores.

Now I hear that we are to form a new nation and there is to be no more Mother Africa or Mother India and that "all ah we is one." Sir, I speak as a very broad-minded person. I do not wish to restrict anyone's choice of a mate. I myself, in my day, have had girlfriends of different races too. But I object deeply to the kind of brainwashing contained in your remarks. Is this a declaration of war upon our Indian population? If there is to be no more Mother India, where do we stand? Is our right to exist as Indians, with a distinct way of life, now threatened?

My comments may seem like over-reaction to you. But I can assure you that I have my ear to the ground in the south of this land, in San Fernando, Princes Town, Penal, Siparia, and Debe, and in every rumshop, on every street corner, this is the talk. As a group we Indians are worried. You cannot expect us to be happy with the threat of extinction. Mother India, with all of its many faults, is still our homeland. We reject coercive efforts to force us to become a mixed race of people. If this happens naturally, over time, all well and good. But national rhetoric that seeks to obliterate Indians—our ways, our appearance, our religion—is an act of racialism, and we must reject such ideas at all costs.

> I remain, sir,
> Yours sincerely,
> Nizam Maharaj

I had never read these letters carefully before. I recalled how Indian men were enraged at what they perceived to be a coercive drive to intermarriage between Indians and Africans in the Trinidad of the fifties and sixties. That deep-rooted fear had never gone away. I had heard only recently about protests from the Indian community in Trinidad about forced *douglarization*. But *dougla* was such an old term for a person of mixed African/Indian ancestry.

Once when we were driving back home with Uncle Baddall and Auntie Vannie, who had taken us to Kiddies' Carnival, we saw a countryish-looking Indian woman, middle-aged, walking with an African man of similar dress and station. But for their racial difference they would have been unremarkable as a country couple come to town for the Carnival celebrations and now scouting around for transportation to return home. It was shocking the way Uncle Baddall steupsed loudly and exclaimed in a voice that could cut glass, "Huh! Indian with she Creole man!" Everyone was silent in the car.

Da-Da's letters wept not only with disappointment and anger but with heartbreak, pure and simple.

September 22nd, 1964

Dear Sir,

   I write this letter as a citizen and a son of the soil. My navel string is buried in the south of this island. The south of this island, sir, is the Indian heartland. I write to say that the leadership on both sides is dividing this country by race, and if this continues, a wedge will be driven that may take generations to heal.

  Where is the idealism that unfolded before us that night on the Promenade two short years ago when our leaders spoke as a united force? Where did that dream disappear? All around me I see envy and disunity; I hear talk of racial hatred. The day is coming when right-thinking citizens like myself will not want their children to grow up in this country, when citizens of conscience will move out rather than have a hand in the kind of racial politics being practised here. The leader says that Indians help each other, so his people must be helped too and the government must do it. Is this an example of fair play?

I have been passed over recently for my fourth promotion while a less qualified, less experienced person of another racial group received the promotion in each instance. The same has been true of training opportunities. Scholarships are advertised in the national newspapers daily. I have applied for several, but I have never made it even to the interview stage. Friends on the government side (and I have many) have insisted that all I have to do is get a party card. Sir, I cannot in all conscience join a party that is bent on keeping my people in second-class positions.

People like me will be passed over because we refuse to toe the line, or if our beliefs are strong, we refuse to be hypocrites. I want to state categorically here that I am not racial myself. I believe in equal rights for all. Is it unusual to think that these equal rights also include me? I firmly believe that I have a right to the patrimony of this country. My ancestors toiled here. They put their blood, sweat, and tears into building this place. The time, my brothers, is now. Justice and fairness can only prevail when we all stand up and demand it.

I am, sir,

Yours sincerely,

Nizam Maharaj

When Da-Da left Trinidad, he left with many other Indians who had also felt themselves at a standstill. The bloody racial riots in British Guiana had fuelled their growing sense of despair about the future. I heard the emphatic conversations about how that kind of violence could never happen in Trinidad because we knew how to live together, every creed and race, they said. But all the same many teachers, doctors, accountants, and middle-of-the-road professionals left. Skilled artisans left too. Those with business interests tended to stay. Our family divided.

People of other races left as well, at different times, to pursue opportunities not available in the country. But the late sixties migration seemed to all of us to be an Indian exodus. Indians who stayed regarded the migrants with scorn. After all, here was not like B.G., and any fool could and should learn to deal with what fate threw up for him. Uncle Samuel had joined De Doctah's party and was a highly placed civil servant by this time. He was full of contempt for people who were leaving for a place where you couldn't even fart freely, he said, where the white man was in total control.

The talk on the island was that Canada's doors were opening. Professionals were needed and there was a big push for teachers. A few years before there had been a big push for domestics throughout the Caribbean, but people in Trinidad had not responded the way they were responding this time. Da-Da did not like the idea of migrating and starting all over, but in the end he decided to leave, even though it meant that his separation from the earth that had made him, the earth where his navel string was buried, was now complete.

It is true that navel strings mean something. Tiny Daisy's navel string under the caimite tree in Iere Village is marked by a yellow croton bush, planted by Grandma Lil so many years ago to mark the birth and death of her firstborn. All our navel strings are buried in that Manahambre land. I remember Da-Da digging the hole in the back of the house the night Babsie was born, sweating because of the unaccustomed labour. At the time Kello was studying the stars, and after the excitement of seeing the new baby had died down, he and Johnnie and I had gone out into the yard so that he could show us the Little Dipper. "Look for the frying pan in the sky," he said, but Johnnie insisted it wasn't there. When we opened the back door Da-Da had paused, leaning for a moment on the garden fork, turning his wet face towards the light. His face was haggard, tortured.

Remembering that face as I sat in my parents' attic, scrolling down the years, hearing their voices echo in my head and holding these clippings of a young man's futile rage in my hands, I saw the Da-Da that I had never understood then. At that time he was only in his mid-thirties. No money, a dead-end job, dreams enough to create another galaxy of stars and nowhere to put them. Da-Da, a young gifted man, full of love for Myrtle, for his generations to come, full of rage for us, the ever-present millstones around his neck. Da-Da, burying his infant's navel string, a man lifting his tortured face to the light, forever haunted by God only knows what demons.

FIVE

On one of those rare winter days of brilliant sunshine I drove to the hospice to pick up Da-Da, who was waiting outside. I watched the sunlight catching the red glints in his wavy iron grey hair, his still handsome face upturned and thoughtful, and I realized with a sudden fearful pang that my father was old. He was leaning slightly forward on his walking stick, waiting for me.

Da-Da had been a sharp dresser in his youth; a striking figure in any gathering. But against the Canadian landscape I saw only a brown Indian man, his impeccable sense of style unnoticed, his appearance ordinary. An elderly South Asian man, I thought, that's all this country can ever make of him. I saw his strong squarish chin, his face with its high cheekbones and round cheeks, his body grown heavy over many winters of inactivity, and all at once my tenderness for my father was overpowering. His face showed gravity, patience, even tolerance for my lateness. When did this happen? When did his great lashing impatience disappear, when did he begin to accept the hand dealt him, when did he grow old? Da-Da was old, Kello was dying, and what about me, my whole life still hanging suspended in mid-air, waiting and watching for some twist of fortune.

Bewildered, I waited for him to get into the car. I had lost something, but what was it and how would I begin to replace it? At age forty-two I was still reluctant to join the ranks of adults in the family, the big people. I couldn't see myself functioning the way they did in family matters. They had not told me enough. I needed more legends, more stories, more knowledge of the past to sustain me.

When we were growing up, there were lots of stories, funny, sad, cautionary ones, repeated over and over until we knew them by heart. Now I found these tales fading from my memory, in spite of my own drive to document history, to capture these stories somehow. And what if Da-Da had forgotten his own stories?

Weaving through the traffic on Yonge Street, I tried to draw him out about the Waller Field story. It was one of my favourites, and he told it so well and so differently each time, revelling in the piquancy of his Trini language. But not this time. Instead he turned to me for the story, waiting with an eagerness that made me uncomfortable to hear my version of the events.

All of it happened during the war. Overnight North Trinidad became a place full of American soldiers, their pockets bulging with cash. The island was strategically located at the bottom of the Caribbean Basin, hugging the curving tip of the South American land mass. A military base was established at Chaguaramas in the northwest and out of it spewed loud music, green army jeeps, and soldier boys. Local girls from respectable families were "dating, necking, and petting" with Yankee boys, sometimes even "going all the way," while their behaviour with local boys was different. With local boys they used to go out, kiss, feel up, but then hold out and not "give nutten till they get de ring." Da-Da's cousin was working for the Yankee boys. He was high up in the military order because he drove one of the big shots around and would sometimes get to bring the jeep home. Then Da-Da got a job at the base too and learned to talk fast fast. It was the speed, man, he used to say. I never knew it had so much speed in life.

Speed was in everything the Yankee boys touched. One day Da-Da was liming with friends in a rumshop near Arima. Some Yankee boys pulled up in a jeep and came in, drank a few beers, and started a fight. Before the hour was over they had wrecked the rumshop and broken two chairs over the bar as a matter of course. That hurdle over, as Da-Da would relate it, they moved into the little Spanish town of Arima to look for girls. Two girls from good families were snatched and taken to Waller Field, but ·all ended well because one of the soldiers fell in love with the younger girl and later married her. At this point in the story Da-Da would always register disgust. I waited for his familiar snort, usually followed by a loud steups and comments about selling out and how advantage could never end. But he remained silent and thoughtful, and after a few moments I realized that he had nodded off. He had let go; the story was now mine.

We had reproduced our very early life here in many ways; being in my parents' house again brought this truth home to me. We, and others like us, were living in our own insular world, oblivious of how we appeared to the rest of the society around us. However protected we had been in our little Presbyterian world in San Fernando, one shove into the bustle of Port of Spain would put us squarely back into our places as country Indians, nothing more. All it took then in Trinidad was looking Indian; all it took now in Canada was skin colour. We had not moved one inch.

The Canadian missionaries had brought sweetness and light to us on their terms, wrapping us in a tight cocoon while they enjoyed the privileges of whiteness in a colonial society. New converts were not allowed to smoke or drink, a rule probably established to rein in the estate drunkenness of Indian labourers on payday and to quiet the night-time cries of beaten wives. But Da-Da and his friends scoffed at such absurd attempts at control. The business interests of key church figures were no longer hidden. An early missionary had become a director of one of the biggest chocolate manufacturing companies in Britain, where Trinidad's cocoa was prized for its intense flavour; another missionary's family had set up a prosperous import trading house. All the while we were being schooled to value sacrifice and throw away worldly possessions and follow the one true saviour, Jesus Christ, our Lord. Young men like Da-Da felt a reckless need to break out of these constraints, but where could they go? They drank and smoked and gambled, embracing the Creole culture with a vengeance, as stylish and cool as any other saga boys, as if those now-distant cane fields had had no part in their history. Drunkenness they treated with contempt. The mark of a real man was how well he could hold his liquor.

The way to have a good time was to get a little drunk, to party, and to dance. Uncle Sweetie got a little drunk once and took a chicken drumstick to Grandpa Jamesie's bald pate, dancing around him and drumming furiously. Grandma Lil was a great wine drinker on festive occasions; at these times, her wonderful loud laugh would echo through the teak trees, rising and falling and rising again.

It was at Grandma Lil's house in Iere Village that my cousin Sonia and I first invented drunk pies, refining the recipe over several August holidays that we spent together. It was the first real secret we had, and we held it close to our chests—a phrase we had only recently learned. Whenever we whispered, "We have to keep this recipe close to our chests," we would puff out our button breasts and collapse into fits of giggles. The recipe was two parts fine sand, one part finely crushed dirt, one part crushed cigarette bush leaves. We added water to make a firm mixture. The firm mixture was then shaped into little cakes and baked in the sun on flat stones. Later on, we continued to make drunk pies at Sonia's house, adding sawdust collected from the sawmill on the main road. The smell of wood shavings and the roar of the big round saw as it sliced through the wood, the traffic roaring past and the apprehension of danger—

all of these sensations mixed together perfectly in those tiny drunk pies.

We would not touch the pies until early afternoon when we always had biscuit and jam sandwiches and juice or tea. Then we would set out our extravagant repast, also made up of odds and ends found in Auntie Alice's kitchen. At the centre would be the drunk pies, which we would have at the end of the meal, holding them up to our mouths with dramatic gestures, surreptitiously stashing them behind the patch of aloes.

The magic of drunk pies was that they gave us unlimited licence to do anything we wanted because they made us drunk. We would stagger around or insult each other or tell secrets. The first time we ever swore, we were under the influence of those drunk pies. My favourite response was to stagger for a while and pretend to fall asleep. On one of these occasions I kept my eyes closed and started to talk nonsense. This activity soon got boring and I inserted a few words such as *damn it in hell* and *bottom*. I heard Sonia's stifled giggles and continued to improvise. When I awoke, I said that I remembered nothing. A few days later Sonia beat me to it and began the cusswords. She was way ahead of me, using words I had never dreamed of, such as *yuh mudder milk* and *yuh must wash yuh shame in water and drink it*. The drunk pie during the day was always a prelude to those frantic whispered cussing sessions.

One day Sonia, who knew much more about sex than I did, whispered that drunk pies helped us to practise cussing.

"For what?" We were alone but all our conversations about sex were conducted in these loud whispers.

"For the real thing, man-and-woman thing. When you have yuh husband and all yuh doing the thing every night. Yuh does have to cuss too bad."

Doing the "thing," something big people did while cursing each other, while using their own separate "things," was linked in some way to Sylvan at school, whom I liked, and to nice things like eating drunk pie and practising cussing, but to ugly things too like Gokool, the yard man, and his young wife, whom he beat often. Nothing about the man-and-woman thing made any sense.

Spending holidays with Sonia was the best. Her family lived in an expansive compound in the North of the island along with other officials who all worked at an institute devoted to the study of tropical agriculture. Only later did I realize how such colonial projects served as nurseries for some of the most famous gardens and conservatories in Europe. The land in that area was set aside for an experimental farm, and there were trees and plants from all over the world. Uncle Samuel had remarked at dinner one day that we children didn't know how lucky we were, wandering freely in a living lab. "Just yesterday," he said, "Indian people and black people couldn't set foot here. Was pure white people from away."

A "living lab"—the phrase enchanted me. The idea of "tropical agriculture" was grand too. The trees were so different from those in San Fernando, where houses and yards were smaller and more contained. Here everything was abundant and left to itself, as in storybooks. Sonia's family had a big purple jacaranda tree in the yard and a smaller one with an incredible smell labelled ylang-ylang. We called it lang-a-lang for short.

It was under the lang-a-lang tree that Uncle Samuel had found a pile of hot love letters that Sonia and I had written to our absent husbands, the singers Pat Boone and Elvis Presley, who were off on yet another whirlwind tour. That must have been the year we were ten. We fancied that practice was necessary so that we would be ready for the unceasing lovemaking that would occur when the starving husbands returned, and this was when we first started to touch each other. Our experiments grew bolder, mixed in with peppery mango chow in the afternoon, the fragrance of ylang-ylang, an old blanket, and several old sugar bags. Sonia was the first to have a climax, which we had heard vague talk about. She shivered. "Just like when you pee-pee" was all she said. My climax was more engulfing than that, or maybe Sonia's fingers were more enterprising.

For a while we became consumed by our afternoon adventures, but Uncle Samuel's rage upon finding our love letters stopped all of that. He slapped Sonia's face hard, one slap on each side, and gave her such a clout at the back of her head that she went spinning into the centre of the drawing room before she skidded on the polished wooden floor and fell. Me, he gave a hard look, but said nothing and stamped into the kitchen clutching the offending scraps of paper. We heard Auntie Alice's voice rising and falling and his persistent steupsing. That was all.

Still, those holidays were times of incomparable freedom. Auntie Alice would say, waving her hands with their long red fingernails, "Roam freely but remember not to go further than the swingbridge." The swingbridge hung over the river, suspended by delicate filaments above the water rushing downstream. It reminded me of a spider's web—as transparent and as fragile. Every morning we walked down to the swingbridge, collecting playmates on our way from the other houses, all separated by wide orchards and landscaped gardens. There was a gate at the driveway into the compound, and beyond the bridge, just out of sight, was another gate with a watchman.

I was the country girl from the South, even though I lived in La Plata now, a modern, fast-growing new suburb in San Fernando, even though these acres of forest and wild savannah looked much more like "the country" to me. When I met Kenny La Fortune, he established without delay that I was a country girl. He was keen to put me in my place. Kenny was a skinny brown curly-haired boy, mixed-up like callaloo, Sonia explained sideways to me, and bad like hell.

He was waiting for us at the swingbridge. Kenny and Sonia were attracted to each other, that was clear, and as soon as I appeared the lines of battle were drawn. He spoke to me only through Sonia: "Tell that young tess I dare she to go to the end of the swing-bridge and come back here." He jerked his head at me. "The country girl there. Tell she to do it if she name man." I hated him on the spot and was determined not to back down. In any case I couldn't because the whole band, ranging in age from seven to ten, was now watching.

I made for the bridge and ran smoothly along until suddenly the spiderweb began to rock violently from side to side. The ropes at the side picked up speed and swung high in the air—exactly like a swing. A swinging bridge. I turned and saw Kenny and two other boys hard at work swinging. I was terrified. I heard myself scream-ing loudly, but I continued to run the length of the bridge until I touched the end and then I scampered back to the other side. At any minute, I feared, the fine silk threads would break and I would be flung into the roaring river below.

I vaulted off the bridge and collapsed in a heap on the grass, feel-ing utterly disgraced and panting to get my breath back. Then I heard Sonia yelling, "She do it! She do it! My cousin is a hero!" A cry went up from the band, and as I breathed once more I realized that indeed I had done it! I had taken Kenny's dare and I had done it.

I stood up then with new courage, my chest still heaving, marched up to Kenny, and nudged his shoulder roughly with my own. "Now I dare you to cross. Cross now, nah!" I flung the words in his face like a real badjohn. All my fright had turned into a rage that would have broken that bridge, had I been given the opportunity to swing it. "Don't call me young tess! And I not from the country either. I from La Plata, in San Fernando. Cross the bridge yuhself!"

Now the whole band had begun to taunt: "Cross, Kenny, cross! Cross, Kenny, cross!"

Kenny had no choice. I tasted victory, marking the fear on his face as he approached the bridge, all of us behind him. Then out of nowhere the watchman appeared at the other end. My earlier screams must have prompted him to investigate. Kenny seized his opportunity, walked briskly up to the end, said good morning to the watchie, and sauntered back, taking his time on the return. The bridge stayed solid and I never got the chance I wanted to swing my enemy up into the air, much higher than he had flung me. It wasn't just his swinging of the bridge that enraged me; it was his little mannish attitude, as if he was sure that he was better than I was and would always be.

Auntie Alice was a famous cook and she often gave recipes to friends on the telephone—so many cups of sugar and flour, equal parts of syrup and lime juice. She was always being asked to do favours for people, to make wedding or Christmas cakes or special dishes for parties. Once some of Uncle Samuel's country relatives journeyed from D'Abadie to get help in preparing an excursion basket. One of the daughters was attending the government training college for teachers and an excursion had been planned to Maracas. She wanted to take "good food" instead of roti and a little curry this or curry that. So they arrived early on the day before the excursion and Aunt Alice set to work. I remember that the young woman wanted baked chicken with stuffing. Auntie Alice lectured in vain about the perishability of a stuffed bird after a day in the heat. In the end she prepared the chicken as requested, but for days afterwards she made comments about nutrition and food poisoning.

Every day Auntie Alice's kitchen turned out surprises. For her parties she would make all kinds of ordinary food into tiny morsels that she called cocktail bites. Accras, phoulouries, even mini-dhal puris stuffed with deboned curried chicken—she thought up the most unusual concoctions. In the evenings she would throw off her cooking dress and wear pretty clothes. She would sit on her front porch, looking glamorous, smoking a cigarette, wearing a pair of old high-heeled shoes.

Esau, Sonia's brother, slept in these cooking dresses night after night. Everybody teased him about it, but I understood why he did the night I too received the incredible comfort of Auntie Alice's dress. It was the time a hurricane had hit the northeastern tip of Trinidad and some of Tobago—an unusual event for us because we were out of the path of hurricanes and that was why, together with the oil, that was why, Uncle Samuel used to say, Trinidad was so prosperous.

We went to sleep with thunder and lightning and pouring rain outside. In the middle of the night I awoke to find myself alone in Sonia's big room, the window flung open and banging dangerously against the outer wall, the wind howling and circling, while ghoul-ish light played in and out of strange patterns on the wall facing me. I ran out of that nightmare straight into Bella's room where Sonia was already on Bella's little cot, hugging her big sister tightly. "Go and sleep with Esau," Bella commanded. Out on the windy upper gallery I ran, down to Esau's room at the other end. I jumped into bed with him, and without waking up he opened his arms and folded me into a space in Aunt Alice's huge cooking dress, its daily smells intact, where we both slept snug and safe till morning.

Sonia and I would break away often to visit Gokool's young wife,

Jasmine. She was from the country too, but unlike Uncle Samuel's niece she had no feelings of shame about Indian food. Jasmine always greeted us fondly, offering us roti and whatever kind of curried vegetable she had made, together with chalta or tamarind achar. After we ate, she would quickly wash the wares with dry coconut fibres and ashes from her chulhah. She showed us how to make curried mango and ginghee talkari, chatting with us as if age did not matter. She worked all day long. Gokool beat her regularly, she said, and most times, even after the beating, he would force her. Force? The question in my mind was fleeting; even as I was framing it, I knew the answer. Sonia and I exchanged glances. We discussed it afterwards and shuddered.

Auntie Alice disapproved of Jasmine because Gokool had put away his first bamboo wife for her, and she herself had been married to another man whom she had left for Gokool. None of it made sense to me, especially the way Jasmine complained daily about his beatings and about being forced at night while she continued to look so pretty and so happy.

At Uncle Samuel's house I first heard about *kala pani*, the crossing of the ocean from India to the islands of the Caribbean. Uncle Samuel had one brother whose Christian name was Peter. I found out that their real names were Samraj and Patraj and that their late father had been a pundit in Chaguanas. Unlike our family who never mentioned such matters, my cousins knew everything about the background of their family in India. Uncle Peter was a big shot. He was in the diplomatic corps and had only recently returned from India. All the talk at the dinner table the night before he visited was of tracing the family's roots. Uncle Samuel spoke of the journey made by their people long ago from Uttar Pradesh to Trinidad. "We come far," he kept shaking his head and saying, "from U.P. to here. We come far."

Uncle Peter arrived the next day in a light blue imported sedan.

It was lunchtime and he had driven down alone, leaving his wife Kitty and his two children at home. The table was spread with a fresh white tablecloth, there were cut flowers, everything was ready. But instead of having lunch the big people sat in the drawing room after the maid had served the rum cocktails, talking heatedly about something.

From our vantage point near the bedroom door Sonia and I could make out only bits and pieces of that conversation, but we heard enough to know that a terrible tale was being told.

Uncle Peter talked about tracing his family's roots in India. The village small small. The dust white and blinding. It was a crime to cross the black water, the *kala pani*. One of several brothers went to town one day and he never returned. Just so, he vanished off the face of the earth. A family legend. A circle broken. Someone in the village saw him talking to a white man that evening. Late at night a message came that he had gone away on a ship.

In the little house in the village everyone surrounded Uncle Peter and spoke at once. Then the oldest male present motioned for silence. He walked out of the house, beckoning Uncle Peter to follow him. The whole group went outside as well and watched. The old man sat cross-legged on the earth underneath a neem tree. Uncle Peter squatted opposite him. The man took a stick and traced a circle in the dust; then inside the circle he drew a smaller circle with a question mark. He directed his interrogation at the translator who accompanied Uncle Peter, never looking directly at Peter himself. Peter responded in like fashion. The old man listened to his answers, nodding his head and considering. After a short while he stood up. Only then did he turn to Uncle Peter and embrace him formally. Now we can close the circle, he said, rubbing out the tracings in the dirt with his foot. Uncle Peter was beside himself with emotion. The women offered him tea, chapatis, kulfi. He took nothing; he only wanted to cry, to hold them close. But no one moved to hold him or touch him. Nor did they ask questions about his home or his family. In a rush Uncle Peter told them that he had been posted to Delhi, that he would be there with his wife and children for three months. But no invitation to return was offered, nor did they ask to see his children. They were satisfied. The circle had been closed.

The reunion was emotionally wrenching, Uncle Peter said, cataclysmic. Like him they had displayed anxious anticipation at first. But then nothing. They simply wanted their lives to continue as usual. Maybe, Uncle Samuel said soothingly, they acted like that because they were simple village people.

"Peter, boy, I don't think people like that would mean any offence. They don't have it in them to offer no insult. How many times they would have a chance to meet a man like you? They would see you as a big man in the city, coming from overseas. They wouldn't think you would want to see them again. Don't mind, nah. Ain't they close the circle? That was their way of accepting you."

But Uncle Peter, he of the proud and erect bearing, whom I had never seen without a suit and a tie, was sobbing uncontrollably, like a child, mumbling about his family, his own family who had treated him like that, all because of *kala pani*. Uncle Samuel held his brother awkwardly, rubbing his back. Auntie Alice turned and saw us spying from the bedroom doorway.

She said very gently, "Go and start eating. Sonia, tell Gemma to give you all lunch. Go now." We sat down in the kitchen and ate the special meal Auntie Alice and Gemma had cooked to welcome Uncle Samuel's brother back. They had made all of Uncle Peter's favourite dishes: the stewed beef, the macaroni pie and red beans with pound plantain, rice, and tomatoes, cucumbers, and watercress. They had run out of time or we would have had crab and callaloo as well. A real Sunday lunch. And Uncle Peter never tasted any of it because he left soon after, still crying. Uncle Samuel walked to the car with him. They were brothers, but until that day I had not noticed how much they resembled each other.

My holidays with my cousins—how much I remember! The swingbridge, the springbridge—the swinging bridge. The flower garden with phlox and lang-a-lang. Eating mango chow in the jacaranda tree, catching a fish right out of the river—a tata fish, a bottom feeder—and burying it like Shango Baptist people. Esau playing preacher in the rain, shouting at the top of his lungs, and all of us teasing Sonia: "Here lies Kenny La Fortune Tata Fish, who was chopped to death by his wife, Sonia." And Sonia, the murderess, dressed in a blue cotton sari brought from India by Uncle Peter, holding her head and wailing. Wailing and dancing in the rain with a cutlass, digging a hole and burying Kenny the Fish, snug in his matchbox coffin. From the kitchen window Aunt Alice glanced at our antics from time to time, amused at first, then alarmed at our mock funeral. She called us in and lectured us sternly. If you make fun of other people's religions, bad things will happen to you, she told us. Bad bad things. You might break your foot and not know why. Or get sick or fall down and cut yourself. As it happened two days later I fell down and bruised my upper thigh quite badly. Even though I knew how the accident had happened, I wondered about vexing Shango for a long time afterwards.

One day the sawmill caught fire and burned to the ground. Gokool ran up to the house excitedly, shrieking and gesticulating. The whole main road was burning and the fire was spreading fast. He set off on his old bike, pedalling like mad, and we kept up easily, running behind him the whole way. The fire spread to the Chinese shop and the dry goods store. People were shouting about water and the direction of the wind. Others were running for the fire brigade. But by the time the fire brigade arrived it was too late. They saved the adjacent stores but the sawmill was destroyed.

"Never mind," Auntie Alice said. "You must take life as it comes."

SIX

Evenings were the hardest. Babs was rarely home then because of her shifts at the hospital. I found myself longing to talk with Da-Da and Muddie, confirming, perhaps, my own memories of past events. But Da-Da had aged so much in the last few years that he was now only a shadow of the rambunctious man I had grown up with. A heart condition was one of his many ailments, and he was often too worn out at the end of the day to listen to my chatter. His voice had not changed, however, and sometimes all I wanted was to hear that Caribbean lilt, still deeply resonant underneath the cracks and warps that the years had brought him. The special timbre of his voice was identical to Kello's, even though their accents were so different, Kello's purged of any Creole talk except in moments of high excitement.

Kello was dying; in a few months he would be gone. I would never see him or hear him again. I faced that fact daily, and it brought sharply into focus all of my questions about myself. Kello's life would be over, but who was Mona? Had I even made a life for myself? Drifting had always been my style, even from an early age. I had embraced the idea of holding on to few possessions and leaving everything to fortune's whim. Yet whenever I forced myself to think of the years to come, without Kello, without Da-Da or Muddie, the familiars whose simple existence held my chaotic universe together, I was overcome by terror. My parents had occupied the background, but Kello was an immediate presence, separate though his life and mine had been. He had always been part of my life, a small boy flying out of a rickety tin bathhouse to fight a big man who was threatening his family, a young man meeting every obstacle head-on and finding a way to survive and even win, finding comfort in the end, paying a steep price for that comfort.

Muddie's grief seemed to need distance from all of us and I felt the distance keenly. I wanted her closeness of years past, our old conversations on nights when she would iron for hours while I struggled over Latin translations on the rough wooden desk made for me from boards left over from repairing the kitchen. I would take a break, make tea for both of us, and sit mesmerized while she told stories about her childhood, about the family closet full of rattling skeletons, giggling like a girl at all the well-hidden follies and scandals that had been managed so successfully over the years. What lessons I had learned then (and Babs too) were now needed to protect us as a family, to shield our brother; whatever happened our house must not fall down.

I asked Da-Da one night about leaving Trinidad.

"Do you think that coming to Canada was worthwhile? Giving up everything in Trinidad, I mean? On balance, you would do it again?"

Da-Da answered with a great deal more heat than I had anticipated. "Never! It wasn't worth it at all, at all. I shoulda never leave! Look at us here, not one single bit more advanced than when we left, and every damn thing you have to fight so hard to get. Every blasted little thing. I feel in my heart that if we had stayed there, Kello wouldn't be sick like this today. The stress on Kello would be different there, not like this. Lymphoma, huh? How he could have lymphoma?" Da-Da snorted so derisively that for a moment I wondered whether he knew the truth.

He seemed to have forgotten that Kello had left early of his own volition and that nobody could have changed his mind. I said nothing. But then he fixed on me.

"Look at you, eh, Mona! So brilliant, so much promise. I say by now you would be working for some big science outfit, even for NASA, pottering around in some old lab, doing space research, experimenting with this or that, dress up in some old dragging lab coat. Life is a hell of a thing, you understand? And look here, Mona, things didn't work out as I expected, but don't think I complaining, you know? The old man upstairs know what he doing. You could never tell what woulda happen if you had gone in that direction. In life the good does often come mix up with the bad, yuh hear?"

He gestured expansively, turning his palms towards his chest. "Look at me, now. All my schooling, all my hopes, and not only me, all my parents' hopes too, you know how they wanted me to be a lawyer. Look at how all a that come to nothing. But God don't sleep and I have a lot to be thankful for."

Me too. I had become their child again, locked with them into the tightness of yet another fragile shelter. Later, as I drifted off to sleep, I was thankful for the thick warm blanket that covered their house and sent me into a sleep as deep as when the world began, when I had slept safely, tucked in between pillow-trees. I could touch that night-blanket and feel its texture, falling asleep in the house our parents had built in this foreign land, as impregnable as any other shelter they had provided, even those precarious ones we had pitched about in, the spanking new building in La Plata, the borrowed house in Ramgoolie Trace, and the first one, Pappy's house, the old board frame in Manahambre Road.

Some nights I would go to sleep in that old board house, with carlights from the street only occasionally filtering through the cracks, feeling myself falling into a place of dreaming, falling into a sea of words rhyming and twisting, piped straight into my brain from the calypso tents in Port of Spain. These nights would begin in the weeks before Carnival when Da-Da would stay up late to hear the new crop of calypsos. When my father's drinking friends came to our house, he would entertain them with obscure gems that nobody knew. If he forgot a line or a chorus, he would summon me and I never failed to deliver. He took pride in his friends' remarks: "What! A lil' girl so, and she know so much kaiso!"

"Is pure poetry, man," Da-Da would exclaim. "Is we poetry, that's why she know it."

I was the only one with Da-Da's passion for calypso; the others were indifferent, only humming a stray bar now and then, and Muddie cared not at all. One of Da-Da's favourites was a little ditty sung for a local competition by a former unknown who had become one of our most famous calypsonians. Da-Da would sing this one to illustrate how sticking to your guns, fool that you might seem to others, was the only true road to success:

> *Oh bargain store*
> *Why yuh doh shut yuh door*
> *Every time yuh open*
> *Another customer broken*

And there were others like this one:

> *Nora Nora Nora*
> *Ah beg yuh doh leave Lord Kitchener*

One of my own favourites was about a mango tree:

> *Ah wish ah was a mango tree*
> *Planted in Laventille . . .*
> *Bric bric bric rico*

The Swinging Bridge

See dem schoolchildren run below
But when dey run, dey hold dey head and bawl
Cause when dey think is mango is mih branches fall

The night sky over Manahambre Road was clear for miles around. Nothing but the stars high above and the moon sailing cleanly over the celamen tree. Falling into sleep hearing the minor key dipping and falling and making music out of our daily lives, I was a happy child. I lived in this magical world until I was seven.

The new calypsos would hit the island right after Christmas. Throughout the weeks before Carnival people would listen keenly, picking their favourites, calling to request them on radio programs, improvising different arrangements for steelband competitions, until by Carnival Day you could almost predict the road march, the one played by the most bands. Carne Vale, the festival that heralded the start of the Lenten season, took over the country on the two days before Ash Wednesday.

J'ouvert was the real start of Carnival, breaking open the Monday morning while it was still dark, turning upside down the order of the world we knew. Everything was reversed: man turning into woman with rude-looking false bottom and breast, and woman turning into man in waistcoat and moustache and high high voice. Men wore diapers smeared on the outside with mustard, while drinking rum out of bumper baby bottles with giant nipples. Devils, soucouyants, ladies of the night, women in old dresses and men's pants—everybody on the road jumping up in bands to calypso music beaten by steelbands. There was parody, burlesque, satire, and placards with lewd messages, punning on politics and dirty tricks. J'ouvert morning possessed a wonderful temporariness, a reckless space without boundaries.

Da-Da and I shared a passion for J'ouvert, like our passion for calypso. We would wake up in the dark, Da-Da conspiratorial, whispering and tiptoeing around so as not to disturb Muddie, making strong coffee sweetened with condensed milk for us to drink quickly before we left, buying peeled oranges on the street and afterwards going to Blizzards for beef pies. The smell of those mornings will never leave me. The raw, fresh smell in the air. The pitch road so clean, I had to resist the temptation to sit down right in the middle of it. The grass wet with dew, fowls still asleep in the trees, madcap roosters crowing, our life moving with a symmetry that I was certain existed nowhere else. And my father, excitement all over his face, cracking jokes, humming calypsos, anticipating the J'ouvert bacchanal.

Kello used to accompany us, but after the big row everything changed. In fact, he began to hate J'ouvert. The Carnival before the big row, a Jab Malassie masquerader, a molasses devil glistening with tar and car grease, had cornered Kello and rubbed his body rudely against my brother's, smearing him from top to toe. He had rubbed his devil's tail around Kello's legs, his wicked red trident stabbing the air as he writhed around my brother, shouting, "Play de devil! Jab! Jab!" The chorus was a signal to hand over some coins, but in spite of Da-Da's promptings Kello refused to give a cent to the molasses devil. He swore off J'ouvert after that, calling it a nasty, stinking parade of fools. One year later, after he and Da-Da had drawn their swords, Kello never went with us again.

Those years with Da-Da on J'ouvert morning blur in my mind into a single procession of events: steelband and old iron and feet chipping on the dark pitch road, San Fernando showing its motion without shame, people who kept everything hidden the whole year not giving a damn if things leaked out, woman jumping up with woman, big big panty covering broad male backside, old bra upside down on big-belly man chest, woman gone wild wining up on man, political scandals and personal secrets broadcast on every corner.

The year of the body in the bag murder everybody was jumping up and down in sugar bags. A white woman's body had been found sewn up in burlap bags in a marshy area on the outskirts of Port of Spain. She was the foreign wife of an Indian doctor and the body had been jointed, people said, just like meat, so the murderer had to be either a doctor or a butcher. Suspicion might have fallen on the husband anyway, but his conversation with his butler, part of his imported style in keeping with his medical credentials and blonde wife, led to his instant arrest. The doctor had rung the little bell in his sitting room, where he was reading alone. When the butler arrived, he received the evening's instructions. They became the most repeated words that Carnival: "Dinner for one, James. Madam will not be dining."

On the streets that year some masqueraders presented an improvised tableau: a butler in full uniform pouring tea graciously out of a child's plastic tea service and handing it to an Indian doctor, he dressed to kill in waistcoat and watch-chain. The masquerader delivered the doctor's line with exaggerated urbanity and sangfroid before he and the crowd collapsed into laughter. The murder was inexplicable, absurd. Not part of our real lives. Yet it had happened in Trinidad and one of us had done it.

Another year the road march was "Hang up Boland and Boysie," a kaiso written about two men, also Indian, also accused of murder. One of them was a flamboyant and well-known gangster in Port of Spain. People danced all day to the music's incantatory beat, but Da-Da came home sickened by the revelry. The dancing crowds were urging the hanging of the two men because they were Indians, of that he was convinced. I listened to his voice, flat with despair, telling Muddie how he would choke and strangle in this blasted place if he stayed.

"It ain't have no place here for Indians. All ah them think we less than them. I have to get out a here. By hook or by crook I go get out, yuh hear mih?"

The question was rhetorical and she made no answer. But his ranting did not cease, and he continued with his hook and crook talk until Muddie's own impatience got the better of her and she erupted into a fit of giggles. "By crook, I sure is by crook! Is only by crook you could get out!" They both began to laugh then; I heard their whispers and giggles for a long time while I was falling asleep. They were both crazy, I thought.

Lord Kitchener's "My Pussin" was the road march. We were standing at the top of the hill near the hospital when a stunning black woman, her eyes glazed with the night's rum, danced out of the band and up to Da-Da, singing, *Is my pussin / Is my pussin / Is my pussin / Is my pussin / I bathe her, feed her, clothe her from small / Man take way yuh hand from she / Doh touch my pussin at all.*

The woman was middle-aged, voluptuous, dressed in tight pants and a short jersey top. She sang before Da-Da in a trance, her closed fists positioned at crotch level, both thumbs making scooping movements, while he stared straight ahead, not a flicker crossing his face. As I watched avidly, she stuck out a rude tongue at me, flung her head back, and danced out of sight in seconds. I glanced at Da-Da; there was still no expression on his face.

And another time, just as we hopped out of the taxi on the once-elegant walkway called the Promenade, a stout dark-skinned man, drunk and staggering, walked up to an electric light pole and began to rub his genital area on it in desperate circling motions. A young man—I saw his face, contorted in the half-light. I looked down his body and observed that the whole area being rubbed was swollen. Underneath his protruding belly the outline of his penis was visible, almost bursting out of his tight gun-mouth pants. Again Da-Da looked straight ahead as if he had seen nothing, but other passersby commented loudly: "But how he so ridiculous? Look, man, go home, yuh hear? Yuh ain't have a wife or what?"

Only one old lady, selling peeled oranges at the side of the road, her head tied up against the dew, shook her head over and over and whispered, "Poor thing. Poor, poor thing." Exactly as if it was the sight of a stray dog just mashed by a car.

A montage of images—Carnival, J'ouvert, the burlesque of life in the old San Fernando I knew—bisects my life at odd moments. Sometimes the memories slough off all colour and become precise black-and-white shots, unreeling in slow motion while those early calypsos, mine and Da-Da's, sung in the minor key, wail plaintively in the background.

San Fernando. An ordinary little city, hardly more than a town when I grew up in it, though it possessed a mayor, a cathedral, its own general hospital. Driving along the southern highway into San Fernando you can easily miss its quiet, distinct charm. The beat is its own, not frenzied or hustling like Port of Spain, a city that hits you over the head with its rushing intensity, its goods, its people, its kaiso music hawked continuously in the streets. No, not that percussive beat, but a steadier, more monotonous rhythm, anchored perhaps to a securer slate of values, shored up by habit, by persistence, by the flow of unchanging time.

San Fernando. A mean city, hard-eyed, unforgiving. Go against its grain and wait to find out. And then there is its large-heartedness, its warmth and open arms, its heaping plates of rice and dhal and curried plenty, ochro-and-rice, bhaji-and-rice, pumpkin-and-rice, blessed plates of kitcheree, won by hard hands out of hard seeds cracking open in rock-hard dirt, slits of soil offering themselves up for random harvest, gongs sounding, butter yellow marigolds curling on brass plates, incense, orchids, hymn singing and white dresses in church, imams holding lessons in mosques, children learning Arabic, steelbands tinkling out the darkness dropping slowly over fields of cane in arrow, Carnival around the corner, women's eyes overcast with pain, shadowing the long stretches of tomorrow, nothing in the house to cook, while down the road, men's voices rise in strident rumshop arguments—the right or wrong opinions of men in rumshops, no exchange or in-between there, only man better man, big mouth versus long-windedness and who gives a damn anyway, but mano a mano, man is man, and if he is not man then he is nothing but a damn ooman.

The city of San Fernando housing its twin but separate populations, African and Indian, each lacerating the other, each tolerating the other's crossovers, the strayaways, the inveterate mixers seduced by curiosity and a taste for difference, whose blood and semen and juices would solidify and form the rickety bridge across which others might begin to cross the rapids that they feared would wash them out into the open sea. My place, this fertile, exuberant, wounded city. Its lovely shadowed hill; its stinking wharf.

My flying visits to Toronto for Christmas and family gatherings had never really given me a chance to explore the city. Every August Babsie would urge me to come for Caribana and play mas in the parade, but I always thought of the one-day event as a watered-down affair, nothing like the real Carnival I knew. Now I was surprised at the extent to which Toronto had become almost a Caribbean city in North America. Roti shops, patty shops, dasheen bush and ochroes and Scotch bonnet peppers in the supermarkets, West Indian accents everywhere—it was not the city I had left in the seventies. The Montreal I lived in did not exude the same sensibility.

The migration of many families like ours took place with a rush in the sixties and the early seventies. After Enoch Powell and the British anti-immigration policies of 1968, England had closed down. We could no longer see it as the mother country. Many families like ours came to Canada, the natural home, perhaps, for Indian/Presbyterian people. We arrived in 1970. There was a preponderance of teachers among our ranks because Canada had opened its doors to people from the Caribbean while actively recruiting teachers and domestic servants. Many people came here trained and ready to launch into a comfortable existence, inching their way along the narrow course set out for them. If you persevered, you did well—look at Uncle Tristram in the Prairies. But Da-Da had big plans, and inching along was never his intention. He jumped into every chance venture available, including sales jobs on commission. His glibness even earned him the position of manager in one company before racist attitudes caught up with him.

As Da-Da walked through the streets of Toronto in a state of high expectancy the day after he arrived, he saw walls and fences scrawled with graffiti that read Keep Canada White. At first he scoffed at this ominous message until it began to measure itself out in his own life.

He was at the liquor store one day when an ugly incident erupted. His anger was so loud and uncontrollable that he was almost arrested on the spot. He had been waiting at the counter while behind the cash register the clerk fiddled with the tape, completely immersed in his task. But when a blonde woman came and stood in line behind Da-Da, the clerk looked up at once and said brightly to her, "Sorry, this cash register is closed. Would you please go to the next one?"

Da-Da exploded. He shouted, "So you didn't see me here all the time? I look invisible to you? You don't have the manners, the simple courtesy to treat all the customers here the same way? What kinda people you all are, man? What kinda service is this?"

Alarm bells began to go off all over the store, and a huge stockroom guy with an apron emerged from the back, hands on his hips as he surveyed the scene. But the cash-register clerk looked so bewildered and alarmed that Da-Da was nonplussed. The man obviously thought that he had done nothing amiss. All the staff and customers in the store were looking at my father expectantly, prepared for the worst, but he could see that they were utterly surprised by his outburst. How could Da-Da begin to explain what had just happened to people who saw this incident as normal?

"This place so deep in race," he had raged to Muddie afterwards, "people don't even know they doing it. Is automatic. Like how they always putting your change on the counter just out of reach of your hand. And what for? What thrill it could give them to watch your hand groping and fumbling to pick up one or two dimes from a counter top? How so much people could think and act in the same lowdown way? They have a course that they take in this kinda behaviour? They must be born so. It must be a inborn nastiness inside them, generations upon generations of them."

Babsie visited Kello often on her own, and divided the rest of her free time between an old boyfriend and a new one, claiming to be serious about neither. She found the time, though, to talk to me more intensely than we had ever talked before. I had left home the first year we arrived in Toronto, welcoming my acceptance at a university in Montreal as a chance to escape from what I had come to see as a hothouse. I had stayed on in Montreal after my degree, and even though I remained in close touch with the family, I was never really a big sister to Babsie. She had grown up with my parents as if she was an only child, and we teased her all the time about how spoilt she was. I know for certain that Da-Da had never laid the restrictions on her that he had on me. Dating, boyfriends, sleep-overs at girlfriends' homes—she had embraced a wholly North American lifestyle, and if my parents objected, I heard nothing about it.

She also ate badly, I thought, though it never showed in her figure or her beautiful satin skin. In the kitchen one day we began talking about nutrition and the food we ate when we were growing up in Trinidad. It was my opinion that our diet there was healthier than that of people here, especially those who subsisted on take-out fare. We ended up talking about times Babsie hardly remembered, when Muddie's creative flair in the kitchen had produced magic out of nothing at all. How to make something out of nothing was my mother's greatest gift to me. Babs was almost sorry that she had never lived through those hard years. "That's your strength, Mona. Your toughness." She hugged me. I told her as well about the time we lived in La Plata when my eavesdropping had convinced me that Da-Da's occupation was gambler. Muddie heard us laughing and came into the kitchen. When I reminded her of the time I had filled in an official form at school with *gambler* in the space for father's occupation, we all collapsed into hysterics.

That evening we cooked a magnificent meal together, the three of us. The food was purely the Trinidad of my youth—the dhal chonkayed with geera and garlic, the bhaji perfectly cooked, the carilee bitter and crisp, the fried fish peppered to perfection. But the bhaat was different, the flawless white Basmati rice that we had never seen in Trinidad. The aroma of that meal pervaded my life for weeks to come because Cousin Bess phoned while we were at the table, and only a few days later I was in Trinidad.

Part One: Borrowed Time

It turned out that Bess's negotiation behind the scenes had paid off. The land was being auctioned off, as she had predicted, at the upset price. A decision had to be made quickly and I would be the one to make it.

SEVEN

 On the Sunday night before I left for Trinidad I went to bed very late, having exhausted myself playing interminable rounds of cards with Babs and one of her boyfriends. Wet snow turned to freezing rain and ice pellets. The wind howled in the pine trees outside with the fury of a hurricane as I lay in bed listening.

I fell asleep but woke during the night to the sound of rainwater pouring down the galvanized spouting at the back of the house into the drain at the side. But it couldn't be, there was no spouting, no drain to catch the rainwater, nothing like that. Still the sound persisted, then I heard that familiar dissonant singing at the back of rushing water, exactly like the first time so long ago.

The first time, I was lying in bed, sleeping in borrowed time (a phrase I had heard my parents use about the brief period we spent in Ramgoolie Trace), on a borrowed bed, in a borrowed village. The village itself was strung along a roadway between somewhere and somewhere. Later I learned that it was situated on a side road between Penal and Siparia. I didn't know the place before we moved and I didn't like it at all. None of us did. The little wooden house was set back from the road by an enormous drain, over which was built a shaky bridge of rotting boards. The two months that we lived in Ramgoolie Trace fell in the school holidays, July and August, and it rained every day. The drain at the front of the house swelled and the water roared through like a rushing river.

The boys of the village played roughly in this drain, and Kello was always out with them. Little Johnnie joined whenever he could or

just sat on the steps and watched. We stayed indoors, Muddie and I.
It was a village where women knew their place and all I ever did was
help look after Babsie. While no one ever stopped me from going
outdoors and running wild with the boys, I simply never considered
doing it in Ramgoolie Trace.

Lying in that borrowed bed (in borrowed time) after Muddie
had placed tin cans and buckets underneath all the leaks, after she
had shone a candle in every crack and crevice of the house searching for scorpions and chenilles and had killed all the mosquitoes
that had flattened themselves along the walls, waiting for blood
until the lights were out, I drifted into sleep with the torrent of
water only a few feet from my bed, knowing that I was in the safest
spot on earth.

Later I woke to hear Muddie and Da-Da arguing furiously. He
was insisting that the nasty old beggar woman who had come to our
house that morning should not cross his doorstep again, while my
mother, equally insistent, demanded to know why. When he could
give no good reason, she used her never-failing weapon: her tears
and accusations.

"You just want me to slave whole day and end up just like
Baboonie. Like that old beggar woman. And when I could get a little bit of help to do the real hard work in the house, you don't even
want to pay for it."

I recognized Baboonie's name immediately. She had appeared
that morning at the front door, a scarecrow of a woman. "I name
Baboonie," she said, brushing past Muddie and entering the house.

At school we had seen National Geographic pictures of the starving millions in India, and she looked exactly like that. Her head was
hooded rather than veiled with an orhni, her skirt reached her
ankles, her wrists were bare and stuck out prominently from the
rest of her clothes, which were swaddled around her.

Muddie had opened the front door only a crack to peer out, confirming my view that she was as afraid as I was of the villagers. They all seemed to be tall, swarthy men striding about with wicked-looking brushing cutlasses, lashed around the handles with cloth to make them easier for grasping, or big, stout women with loud voices. The women called out to each other as they walked along the road and made rude jokes about men's lolos and totis and each other's doonkas as they carried pails of water. Not my mother's style at all. She told them "Good morning," formally and from a distance, whenever she had to.

"I name Baboonie," the figure repeated decisively, walking straight through our house into the kitchen. "I come to find out if you have lil work for we to do. We old but we could work hard hard. We could scrub the floor and scrub down everything." Her gesture was expansive, taking in all of the house and the empty yard, neatly lepayed with mud.

Muddie was relieved, I could see that, because we had moved in a hurry and she had not had time to scrub the house with disinfectant and lye as she had done with every house we had ever lived in. When she nodded, Baboonie got up and began to leave. She was surprisingly agile for a bundle of rags, but Muddie caught her arm before she reached the door.

"Yuh don't want a cup of tea, a lil food, stay and take something, nuh?"

But Baboonie only shook her head and left as swiftly and invisibly as she had appeared.

Listening to my parents' quarrel that night in the darkness of the small house, I wondered at Da-Da's dislike of the beggar woman. I never felt even slightly guilty for eavesdropping on my parents' discussions, and I always took sides, constructing and reconstructing the best arguments for each of them. When they didn't follow my script, which was most of the time, I felt cheated and wished that I could intervene. Now as I listened to Muddie complain about my father's stinginess, I thought that she was being unfair because Da-Da had never once mentioned money. Under pressure, Da-Da caved in and began a kind of explanation that made no sense to me.

"Look, Mudds, is not the beggar woman fault but she does live alone, she don't have nobody . . . she don't have nobody. The fellers in the village does use she. She living in the back of Toolsie house and he tell me so heself."

I knew that Toolsie was the big contractor who had given Da-Da the place rent-free for two months while we waited for the house in La Plata to be finished. Da-Da used to do endless favours for people, and he had written so many letters to agents and officials for Toolsie over the years that no repayment would have been too great. But Da-Da took pride in never accepting the gifts offered and would not have taken this one either except that we had to find somewhere to live.

"Toolsie say that in the night he does hear footsteps running and people beating down the door. He say, 'Everybody around here does beat that.' That is what he say. She used to scream at first and try to chase them away by cussing real nasty but that didn't stop them. Then Toolsie himself try to help her but it was no use. Them fellers around here worthless too bad." He sighed. "They used to wait in the bush till Toolsie drop asleep again and come back. Toolsie say in the end he couldn't be no nightwatch for a old beggar woman so he give up. I can't have no woman like that coming in my house."

I waited full of fear. Silent deadly figures stalking through the night intent on one thing. At nine I knew what that one thing was, and it was terrifying. Baboonie, huddled in a corner, waiting for her assailants, cursing to protect herself. Baboonie, subjected to the inevitable, a grunting, groaning man, a whole procession of them, I imagined, a procession of villagers walking strong and tall in the morning dew holding their brushing cutlasses firmly, ready for the day. A grunting, groaning man, doing what big men do. Baboonie, a bundle of sticks and stones, whose bones remained unbroken.

There was a long silence or maybe they talked but I didn't hear, locked as I was in the terror that was Baboonie's as the long string of villagers crashed into her hut and did what they had come to do. Her cursing. I wished that I could hear her, that I could listen to her words cursing them. "She could really cuss you know," was what Da-Da had said.

Then I heard Muddie's voice, low and controlled: "Toolsie could say what he want. Baboonie coming tomorrow to scrub the floor, I will pay her and she will go her way and I will go mine."

There was no answer from Da-Da and I fell asleep. Much, much later I awoke to hear the rain pouring down on the galvanized roof. I heard it in a sleepy haze and I snuggled down under the blanket, enjoying the night, the rain, the river racing just past my head, and the slow driftiness of sleep. Then I heard a sound above the rain. At first I thought it was the river, catching some tin cans or rusting iron in its flow, because the sound was hoarse and clanging, yet high and sweet at the same time. The sound came from the other side of the culvert river, just where Toolsie's house curved into wilderness. In that back bush was Baboonie's shack, hidden from view but facing us across the water.

As I listened, I realized that the sound was a voice, singing with the rain yet high above rain and river at the same time, the notes discordant but clear, beating out a rhythm that I recognized. It was the rise and fall of women singing Ramayana at kathas. The words were in Hindi and I knew only a few of them—*dhuniya*, *popo*, *beti*, *kala pani*. And there were others that I heard night after night and will never forget, their harshness ripping through earth and water and tearing up the air around me so that even breathing became fearful—*kangaal*, *parishan*, *triskaar*, *thokna*, *parishan*, *parishan*, *paris-*

han . . . pani, pani. The voice rose and fell in harmony with rain and river and wetness, *pani, pani, pani . . .* the whole world grieving in unison, crying tears into the river that flowed inches from my head, threatening to carry me in its rushing waters down to the sea, the sea near the belly of the map of Trinidad, just near the part where the mouth of the Serpent opens, swallowing me into the rain of everything the jaw of night had opened up and revealed while Baboonie fought off intruders upon her body with curses and threats and words sung from the holy books, while bundles and bundles of rags walked upright in the early morning, following the strong men of the village as they walked with proud brushing cutlasses, lashed with cloth by wives and daughters, walking to work, walking to do task work, to earn the dollars that made homes and families and life. Dreaming of voices, high and sweet, singing in the rain of grass and fields and butterflies, of playing and laughing and dancing in the forest, freer than the water making its wayward journey to the sea, singing the wetness and dislodging stones from the hard hearts, the hard sinews of strong men, singing . . .

I listened to music and a story, till then unknown to me, coming through the wailing voice of an old beggar woman, crying through the rain, breaking up the classical words of the Ramayana with her own tale of exile and banishment, and in broken chords and unexpected riffs telling the story of a race. Of racial and tribal grief, of banishment, of the test of purity.

The words had scant meaning to me at the time, solidly implanted as I was in my own family, for whom Hinduism had already become a relic. Save for the snatches gleaned from the kathas and bhagwats held sometimes on the hillside behind Grandma Lil's house, I knew the Ramayana in name only. But I remembered the voices of women who sang Ramayana in Iere Village and in neighbouring Mt. Stewart; how respected they were and how famous. For miles around people would come to invite them to sing at their kathas.

But now, lying in the darkness of the sleeping house, pieces of the puzzle began to fall into place. How Baboonie must have had no real name, and how much cruelty must have gone into naming her Baboonie, meaning young girl. How she was singing Ramayana alone in Toolsie's hut, singing of such abandonment that words lost their power and only raw sound could capture it, pelting the broken shards of that holy text into the night, singing her grief. And I listened again, as though to a blessing, hearing Baboonie's strong voice, washed in rain.

PART TWO

*MANAHAMBRE
ROAD*

*A*cross the kala pani, *the fearful black waters, leaving the Indian Ocean, sailing past Madagascar, skirting the Southern African coastline, meeting the murderous ocean billows around the Cape of Good Hope, named by indentures the* Pagal Samundar, *the Mad Sea. Here the ship's steam engines are shut down, prayers and lamentations reach the skies as the deck and even the sleeping places become slippery and yellow, stinking with vomited rice and dhal and pumpkin curry as the* Artist *drifts slowly into calmer seas. Moving northward up the western coast of Africa, the ship stops for a day at St. Helena, a narrow, rocky little island on which Napoleon Bonaparte died, exiled from his native land.*

Napoleon died here, on a rocky promontory facing the Atlantic Ocean, facing the coastline from which millions of Africans were driven westward to provide labour for the sugar and cotton plantations that fattened the purses of Europe. That forced marriage of Africa with Europe occurred on Caribbean soil, creating Creole plant and animal hybrids of astonishing beauty and hardiness, beauties such as Josephine of Martinique——Marie-Josephe-Rose Taschez de la Pagerie de Beauharnais, Napoleon's own doomed empress, a Creole girl for whom his desire never waned. The defeat of Napoleon's army in 1803 under his brother-in-law, General Jacques Leclerc, in San Domingue, the Pearl of the Antilles, had set in motion the chain of events that brought this shipload of seasick travellers from the Indian subcontinent——a girl of thirteen named Gainder among them——to dock at St. Helena, watching from the deck its masses of red geraniums sprouting from black rock crevasses, its clumps of white arum lilies, while the captain and crew go ashore to take the fresh air and exercise their stiffened sea legs. The captain is intent on visiting Napoleon's first burial site at a place called Longwood.

The Swinging Bridge

The Artist with its cargo of coolies docks at Jamestown, and the captain attends to urgent business before setting out. A prisoner must be handed over to the authorities and jailed. Crew members lead an Indian man, handcuffed and in leg irons, out of a dark corner of the ship's hold. He is dirty, unkempt, with hair tufting untidily about his face. He shuffles as he is led off, and as he reaches the gangplank, the leg irons are removed. He turns then, searching the crowd of shipmates on deck until he meets her eyes. A fire leaps between them. He is led off the ship, and in her last sight of him he is being roughly bundled up the hill to the town, staggering between two white men.

His name is Jeevan; his village is Baraiepur, from Uttar Pradesh. He is skilled in the practice of gatka, one of the martial arts from the Indo-Gangetic plain. Jeevan had killed a white sailor who grabbed Gainder and tried to fondle her breasts as she was making her way one night from the upper deck to the women's quarters on the aft side of the ship. Jeevan heard her screams and grabbed an oar from the pile bolted to the side of the deck. The white man drew a knife, but the Indian's stick would show no mercy and in the end, the curved knife remained gripped in the buckling sailor's hand, only falling to the deck as he slumped and stayed still. The girl the sailor tried to fondle had screamed and shouted for help and some of the men ran up from their beds on the lower deck. But nothing could prevail upon the fury of Jeevan's village stickfighter's instincts and silence fell among them as the consequences of the sailor's death became evident.

As for Jeevan, the man who had performed the gatka feat, he stood, unflinching, over the man he had killed, waiting for the inevitable. Gainder, blinded by fear and terror, flung herself at her rescuer, holding his feet and sobbing uncontrollably. Minutes later crew members arrived and tore her from him, beating and kicking Jeevan down to the floor of the deck. By the time the captain appeared, they had bound his hands and feet and were carting him off, like so much cargo, to the damp little place in the hold reserved for such emergencies. For the rest of the journey he stayed there, wearing leg irons, one hand manacled to a rusting hook on the wall of the tiny cell. Gainder visited him twice, aided by an Indian nurse and a topaz who spied and helped her when the captain and crew were at dinner. She was beside herself with gratitude and sorrow, and on both occasions she offered herself to him. Jeevan held her child's hands and kissed them over and over, but he would do nothing more.

At St. Helena he is led off, formally charged with the crime of murder, and jailed. The ship leaves; his fate is unknown.

EIGHT

Any minute now. That curve of road bordering the land, the house sloping down from it, any minute now along this winding road, bounded by chataigne, mango, and pawpaw trees, with patches of siquier and gros michel figs at the side, any minute now our curve will come into view on Manahambre Road.

So many, many years have passed and yet I know it well, the rise of land from Cedar Hill curving upwards to Hope Road and then down the hill again, bending twice into looping hairpin curves before stretching out to a semicircle around our land, then rising up again, gently now, to Pierre Street, once a boundary before Da-Da's family had begun to own houses and shacks out on that tiny street, the land where Da-Da had brought Muddie as a bride.

Any minute now—but no, here is a Coca-Cola plastic logo nailed up on the door of a cheap-looking café, next to a poster of the Carib girl, lush and full-bottomed in her yellow bathing suit, a blank and broken street sign dangling loosely from a lamppost, a little knot of limers around it.

We stop, and without waiting for Bess I jump out of the car—I hold on to the vanity that I am exactly like them, nothing has changed, even if Pierre Street has turned itself inside out in the middle of the night and now sits flat and dull, even if a little red and green café full of plastic tables stands directly opposite to where the celamen tree once was.

I ask them, "This is Pierre Street?"

"Is Pierre Street, yes," one sharply dressed limer says. "Where you from? You from away?"

I nod. Without speaking I walk down the hill, chastised, and decide to leave the rest to Bess.

The hill at the top of the land is broad and wide, just as it always was, but now spreading below is a forested wilderness, unfamiliar in shape, thick with unknown shrubs and trees. I wonder about snakes as I work my way through the bush, but Pappy's voice is loud and clear rising from the pit where he used to roast sweet potatoes for us: "It ain't have no poisonous snakes around here. All the mapipire snakes does live in the North. Don't frighten, child."

In my memory the chenette tree comes first, then the chataigne tree at the side, and the giant breadfruit tree just beyond. Finally the zaboca tree and the cluster of three mammy-sepote trees, close to the sweet potato pit. Pappy would dig the red sweet potatoes out of the fresh dirt and scrub them clean, then pierce them with an iron stake he rotated for hours above the fire. It was an ingenious little contraption, like the others he made, my old grandfather: the file for his papers and bills, which was the end of an old coat hanger mounted on a block of wood; the hanging wire stand for squares of old newspaper that he cut and hung in the latrine.

But the land had changed and I recognized nothing. I walked around trying to imagine the house through the many times over the years that the land had changed form, slipping and sloughing off posts and trees and memories to end up as this wilderness.

Still, there was a zaboca tree and a mammy-sepote tree, though nothing like the shaggy, comforting shapes of my childhood. And fixed firmly under the zaboca tree a set of steps rose up into nowhere: six concrete steps still holding fragments of red paint. A little farther down, near a patch of gros michel banana plants curving towards each other like a storybook grove, I saw a pilotrie of the house, the one that had supported the lower left side where the land first showed its weakness. The pilotrie stood erect, two or three posts still hanging from its sides like bits of tinder, brittle like tinder.

Leaning against that old pilotrie and waiting for Bess to come down the hill, I was assailed by an unimaginable sense of desolation. When she reached me, tears were flowing freely down my cheeks. There were no words. She gathered me up against her solid bosom and held me until the weeping stopped. When we gained the top of the hill again, the limers took no notice of us, and I was glad that my distress had escaped their commentary.

Bess, my cousin. She is a beautiful, vital woman. There is serenity in her short, stocky frame, her hair pulled back into a loose chignon or a French braid, her strong limbs, her taut breasts. Her skin is exceptionally fair; her eyes the green-blue of the Caribbean Sea. She is a woman of the world who exudes no particular age but she is ten years younger than Kello, and eight years younger than me. That made her only thirty-four when we met again after so many years, a young age to have achieved such completion. There is nothing of the outside child in Bess, nothing tiptoeing and apologetic. She is exquisitely at home in her own skin.

Bess was six before we knew she existed, and then we found out only because Auntie Vannie had decided abruptly that the child should not have to pay for my Uncle Sweetieboy's prevarication. Grandma Lil welcomed Bess with warmth, and used all her wiles and skills to persuade the child's mother to give her up, which in the end she did. And now it was Bess's fierce determination that had got us back that Manahambre land for a song. There was some justice there, I thought, because we had sold far below its worth during that time of crisis when Da-Da could see no way out of the mortgage that was strangling his very substance. And in any case, that first mortgage, taken out in a panic by Pappy to pay the money-lender, should never have been the family's burden of debt.

I stayed with Bess at Iere Village for two more days. She was shocked to hear about Kello's illness. She had known only that he could not come to Trinidad and that I would act on his behalf. But when I told her that he was seriously ill, she never asked why he wanted to buy back the land. I discovered that Bess had a notion of family that transcended the immediate: she dealt in lineage and posterity and generations and descendants. Family was not just breeding and reproducing—it was a work of art in itself, as carved and sculpted as any other legacy that one could leave behind.

We had tea in the dining room of Grandma Lil's house in Iere Village, now Bess's home. Bess had won the legal battle to get herself declared Uncle Sweetieboy's only heir, no easy task in Trinidad, where legislation about inheriting property was still colonial to its core, ignoring illegitimacy and the straying habits of ordinary people. That Uncle Sweetie remained unmarried and rakish forever, that he had an outside child, that he never took the trouble to provide for her except occasionally and even then with useless extravagant gestures such as an expensive watch or brooch: these were actions that passed without comment in the unwritten codes that bound us to the life we knew.

We sat together, Bess and I, at one corner of the dark mahogany dining table, its leaves never folded down just as in my grandmother's time, having tea out of an antique amber tea service I remembered well. It had been Muddie's favourite piece of china and she had hoped to inherit it after Grandma Lily died. But life had looped and turned by then; we lived far away and my mother returned only briefly for the funeral, leaving Uncle Sweetie and his women to the house. Many items, lovingly collected by Grandma Lil over the years, had disappeared, but Bess regarded everything that remained as her personal heirlooms.

"I hope Kello thinks it's okay. You took pictures? No pictures?"

I had forgotten all about the camera in my handbag. Bess decided that she would return that evening and take photographs of the property. I was relieved. She would know the exact angles to take the pictures from, a real estate perspective that would not focus on old steps rising into the air or lost pilotries.

We ate sponge cake and drank tea and talked about old times, the bonds of family deepening as Kello's impending death cast its pall over us. Acquiring the land was my most immediate task, but Kello had also asked Bess to oversee the planning for the building project. I had been unaware of this development until she mentioned it, but Bess was serene: "Mona, Kello's efforts will pass on to his son, his daughter, to you and the others. His efforts will not be wasted. The property has possibilities if it is terraced and retaining walls are put in properly. It is a beautiful sweep of land, and Kello will be very proud of developing it, even if it's his last act."

His last act. I felt very bitter at that.

Kello was dying, not of lymphoma, but of another, more unmentionable illness, his fingers raised to his lips in a warning silence. I reached out for Bess's hands and broke the lie apart sitting there with her, her ordinary acceptance of things as they were the wedge that did it for me.

My voice was flat and heavy. "It's not cancer, Bessie. Not lymphoma. Something else, something not talked about in our family."

To my relief her eyes signalled recognition and my mind strayed to the headline of the newspaper that morning: TRINIDAD RANKS THIRD IN AIDS CAPITALS OF THE WORLD.

"AIDS. He's had it for years. It's at an advanced stage and he's in a hospice where he gets palliative care."

Bess's deep sigh of sympathy was comforting. She was taking in the whole picture at once, I thought. She saw it all—Muddie, Da-Da, the whole extended family, the ole talk, the shooshooing in corners. She stroked my hand.

"Kello is right, Mona. It's nobody's business but his own. And you and Babs have been privileged to share his journey. Think of how tragic it would be if you didn't know at all, if he trusted no one. Sometimes the bare truth is the biggest lie. You know that, right?"

I stared at Bess, trying to decipher some meaning here that eluded me. She pressed on relentlessly, "How can we explain what really happens, why people do things, all the tiny pieces that get rubbed out, leaving big actions so easy to condemn? Too easy." She shook her head, her mouth curved down, her chin set. She got up and poured more coffee for us both, leaning on the table and looking at me squarely in the face.

"Mona, don't make the mistake of going against Kello's wishes about this. You're tempted to talk to your parents, right?"

I nodded; she had taken my measure precisely.

"No, it's not your call. What you are doing now is all you can do. Leave it to Kello, Mona."

The conversation drifted back to the everyday as I tried to quell the turbulence inside me that always rose at the thought of the hypocrisy, the web of deceit that held families like ours together.

"Are you ever lonely here, Bess? Or afraid? We read in the papers about all the crime in Trinidad these days, all the drugs. Isn't the place now being used as a transshipment point from Colombia? I hear that the links are really sophisticated."

Bess snorted her disapproval. "And Canada is not a transshipment point too? Canada don't have plenty drugs in the streets too? Trinidad is just like anywhere else. The transshipment point don't come into your dining room. You think you safe there, right? Well"—she paused for dramatic effect—"I think I safe here too."

We laughed together then and seemed to reach some kind of understanding.

It was so comfortable being in Bess's house. I felt as if I was journeying backwards, sleeping like a child again in the bedroom our grandparents had always kept for us children, the one that had held two big beds and two extra fold-up cots in the cupboard. With her old-world taste, Bess had transformed this semi-dorm into a Creole nineteenth-century bedroom, complete with a washstand holding a patterned basin and jug, a chamber pot and spittoon to the side, a deep armchair for reading with lace antimacassars covering the arms and back, all of it done in deep rose tones. Under the pillows she had tucked a fragrant sachet of vetiver, its name embroidered on the outside.

When Bess returned that night with several rolls of film and a few instant snapshots, I was surprised. She had walked to the boundary lines and taken panoramic shots, and later when I saw the photographs, the place looked even more remote and harshly beautiful than I myself had observed. The instant snapshots had captured the sudden raw beauty of the land, dropping steeply from the top of Pierre Street, giving itself up to natural terraces and rises. She saw within its contours a housing complex, buttressed and landscaped, using the features of the land itself, its unexpected twists and turns offering more than an illusion of privacy to the modern townhouses it would sustain. Through her eyes I saw the property's possibilities and knew that Kello would be pleased.

I fell asleep that evening thinking of the wilderness that the land had become, this place where I had first breathed life, where all that was to shape me took root within my first seven years, opening inside me with perfect timing, and only threatening to disintegrate now that so much time had passed and so much had been left to chance.

That night I dreamed of the old house. At first it was exactly as I remembered it. It stood with two or three unevenly spaced hillocks surrounding it, its boards dark grey and weathered, as solid a shelter against rain and blast as I would ever have. The little garden,

Muddie's creation, was in full bloom: a riot of multicoloured zinnias and sunflowers, and at one end an array of crotons edged by white tuberoses.

I walked to the side and discovered a fresh bed of anthuriums in full bloom underneath the back stairs; she had planted those just before Da-Da decided to sell the house and I had never seen them flower. But something had changed. Those stairs were no longer at the back of the house but had moved up to the side. Up those stairs was the outdoor bathroom, the one whose flimsy walls had sheltered us during Da-Da's madness after Mama's death, now elevated and nestling right under the chataigne tree at the side.

Kello was waiting at the top of the stairs and greeted me kindly. He was unperturbed by the surroundings, he who among us all had felt the deepest need to forget the past, to banish uncertainty, to reinvent himself in comfort and financial security. I was shaken by the stark poverty—the smallness, the rough tin walls of the bathing place, the galvanized iron tub full of water, the makeshift tin can dipper, everything. Kello seemed to understand my shock, and gave off an air of being in charge, while remaining unapologetic.

Inside I found that the house had changed into another, more haphazard place—the one we had inhabited for two months at Ramgoolie Trace in Penal. In that house we always had trouble with the keys for the front door. Now I looked and noticed an outsized key locking the door firmly in place. All of the windows, though, a whole wall full of windows, were flung open to the night. The room was dark except for a small lamp on the big dining room table. It was the kind of lamp I remembered with "Home Sweet Home" embossed on its shade. I sat in the middle of the darkened room, alone in the house, feeling great gusts of wind rushing through from the night outside. I sat for hours, it seemed. I felt no fear, no pain, nothing.

The house changed again, and I was back in the kitchen near

where the altered back steps seemed to disappear into the over-hanging chataigne tree. I heard a sound from the far bedroom and hurried in to investigate, but not before checking all the doors to make sure that they were secure. It occurred to me then that I was alone, locked in with those strange sounds from the far bedroom. I flung open the bedroom door—better to be bold than to tiptoe in. It was Da-Da crouched in one corner of the bed dressed in an old maroon bathrobe that I remembered well. I knew it was him, yet at first all I saw was an indistinguishable heap emitting those sounds. There were several versions of him lying there. His eyes were in great pain.

I woke up suddenly. It was the middle of the night and pitch black.

I blinked several times, but not a crack of light entered my field of vision. It was then that I became aware of a terrible, terrible sound. Someone was crying, making gurgling noises that came from the bottom of a well. The cries ricocheted throughout the small board house, circling between the front door and the overhanging chataigne tree. They drew me to the edge of the well, left me staring down into the depths of well water, then all was quiet until another more anguished sound rent the night air, this time a high squeal. Exactly like the time my black pig had had her throat cut just before Christmas.

A voice broke through. It was not possible and I had to be dreaming, but somehow I was awake. Something had woken me up. The voice, thick and muffled, was Da-Da's voice.

"Mudds," he said hoarsely, "tell me where I went wrong. I ain't tief, I don't lie, don't mind how late it is, I does kneel down and pray to mih God. Tell me, what I do? I strangling, I really strangling here, and I can't take it again. I can't take it. I tell you I really can't take it. Don't be surprised if I do something drastic, you hear? This is too much pressure for one man to take, you hear me? I refuse to take it . . ."

His scream this time was piercing; it was followed by explosive sobs. The whole neighbourhood would be woken up, everyone would hear, the others—my brothers, the baby. But nothing moved; the whole world remained still, listening without response. Another low series of sounds joined the sobs. I could not recognize them at all but imagined it was Muddie speaking softly. Who else could it be? I lay still on my pillow, staring straight up into black night. There was no one in the world but me and what was going on in that far bedroom.

Then, without warning, the sound changed. It was clear and precise and measured, like the beat of the big drum at the Hosay festival.

Tummm-tum-tee-tum-tum-tum-tee-tum. At first I could only discern a beat. *Tummm-tee-tum-tum-tum-tum* . . . Then words: "Yuh mudder cunt, God de father, you could kiss my arse you hear me? You hear me, God, you could kiss my royal arse, when you have some time, you old bitch, you . . . Yuh backside, God, and Jesus Christ causing man to catch hell here, causing me to suck salt day in, day out, and what crime I do? I ain't worship mih God enough? I ain't bow down and kiss you arse enough for you? I don't kneel down every night and pray and tell you bout all the hell I catching? All yuh Holy Ghost and God de fadder and Jesus Christ have allyuh hands on mih throat, yuh hear me? Like I is allyuh stepchild! Allyuh must be think I is a outside child!"

The scream began again and changed to the howl of a wild animal.

Then the voice returned. "From now on is a different story. All yuh refuse to help me so ah go help mihself. Is clear as day that ah on mih own and ah cyah depend on no kiss-me-arse spirit whether allyuh call yuhself God de fadder or Jesus Christ or de Holy Trinity or any fucking name allyuh want to give yuhself. Ah on mih own now and you go see how ah go prosper. All yuh can't kill me, don't mind how allyuh try. Is mano a mano now and none ah all yuh fuckers ain't go kill me." Loud sobs.

Another voice, one that I had never heard before, a girl's soft voice, said gently, "Stop now. Hush. You tired. Hush now." The voice continued, making velvety soothing sounds—the water in the well was swishing in the bucket, cool and sweet, swishing in the bucket . . .

In the dark I began to pray. Something bad would happen to all of us. "In my little bed I lie / Heavenly Father, hear my cry / God protect me through the night / Keep me safe till morning light." God would punish us, all of us, no one would escape his wrath. "Our Father who art in Heaven, hallowed be thy name, thy kingdom come . . . Merciful Father, help my family, bless Muddie and Da-Da and Kello and Johnnie and Babsie and me and all our family, forgive us and don't turn us out into the world naked and full of shame, spare us from becoming wanderers on the face of the earth forever like Meg Merilees in the poem, help us to move and find a safe house."

In the morning I woke up with the brightness of daylight flooding the room, banishing all reverberations of those strange sounds I had heard in the night. Daylight meant hustling, dressing, making sandwiches, getting ready for school; and Muddie and Da-Da sitting down, eating breakfast together at one end of the big table.

I put out my arm and touched the pillows, the matching rose-toned sheets, the embroidered spread. It took me several minutes to reorient myself. Everything was so near, so vivid—the decades between then and now had fallen away in the middle of the night. It was morning, promising a day of brilliant sunshine, but I was in my cousin Bess's house. And suddenly I knew that it was in this house that I had first heard those night sounds. I heard them when we were pitching about from pillar to post, when Muddie and Uncle Baddall had the fight in the kitchen, when I really began to hate Uncle Baddall.

The thought of those old times filled me with uncertainty. Anything can happen to us, I used to think then, and scenes of possible disasters would fill my mind. Now I rose from the bed and started my day, wryly considering how no imagined disaster could prepare us for the blows that life delivered, blows that, without reserve, will come when they will come.

NINE

I spent the next two days suspended in time, fitting more easily than I had expected into this world that had remained itself, regulated by a distinct rhythm of its own, rough to my ears, now grown metropolitan, but immensely comfortable. The sound of the fish and shrimp van slowly cruising the narrow one-lane road, its crier intoning in the early morning "Fish, ancho, jashwar, strimps . . ." over and over until his plaintive voice faded in the distance. The man who came early in the morning to cut down the back bush near the fence stood at the creaking iron gate and shouted, "Morning, Miss Bess! Ooo-oooh, Miss Bessie! Oi, Miss Bess!" The dogs in the yard were locked up and he entered, nodded at me in greeting, went down to the back, and began to swing his brushing cutlass with a vengeance. A tiny girl came and shook the gate with vigour, shrieking as if from a script, "Miss Bessie! Mammy say if yuh want any dasheen bush or ochro today?" These voices, these lives, intersected easily, unlike the discordant notes of my distant Canadian world.

Bess showed me some boxes in the storeroom that we had left behind when we moved to Canada. I was startled and curious to see the several stacks that had been labelled neatly with the names of everyone who had moved—Vannie, Alice, Myrtle. Their past lives, boxed and ready to go. To my surprise, Uncle Tristram's matched Muddie's in volume. I knew why our pile was so big since it had been my job to sort our belongings and decide what to save, but I had never thought of Uncle Tristram, locked in his prairie whiteness with his ultra-Canadian family, as a hoarder like myself.

The place was dusty; and I wandered instead into Grandpa Jamesie's old study with its glass-lined bookcases.

Bess had transformed this clumsy add-on into her special place, and I was lost there for several hours, admiring her books—wonderful pictorial records of Trinidad that she had amassed over the years, a book of Cazabon prints, Boscoe Holder's works, old Codallo prints, an M.P. Alladin book of reproductions. An entire history that we had never been taught at school. Living in Montreal for as long as I had, I was completely unaware of these marvellous books, some new and others recently reprinted, in spite of all the research that I did. Bess had made an entire wall into a collage of family photographs—where on earth had she found them? Probably in Grandma Lil's belongings. There was the young Grandma Lil, Lily Evangeline Sarah herself, her flashing eyes, her proud chin; my mother Myrtle, quiet and defiant; Auntie Vannie extravagantly embracing Uncle Baddall in his star-boy days; Kello in England, head held erect against a hard wind, complete with duffle coat and backpack; and the young Mona accepting a prize on Speech Day, curtseying and presenting a bouquet as a child of five, then another bouquet presentation much later that showed a thick layer of hair on her arms, a visible pelt covering her wiry forelimbs. I looked down at my now smooth arms. Those hairs must have fallen off over time. When did my rough, tough hairiness disappear? I felt a pang of regret as I looked at the steady arms of that young girl, so sure of herself, so different from the older woman on the other side of the family wall.

Bess had mounted an array of silkscreen prints at the side, sketches of La Pastora, the girls' high school in San Fernando that she and I had both attended. All the girls in our family had attended La Pastora; Grandma Lil was one of its earliest students. The prints brought back memories, whispers, and secrets. The image of the big oven was particularly striking, a series of bold geometric lines the colour of baked earth. The oven had been used at La Pastora's dorm in the early days. It was made of clay and beautifully plastered with mud, lepayed, all around; the non-paying students took turns doing the early morning baking every day for the more fortunate girls who could sleep through such chores.

I heard the story about this oven from one of the oldest teachers at the school. She was our oral historian and knew every fact concerning La Pastora's establishment in 1912 by some progressive Canadian missionary women. She had started her education there in 1925 and never spoke of it without using the word *privilege*. We were fortunate to be continuing in the line of privilege, she always said, and should ensure that we remained worthy of our selection into the top ranks. She had never married. She taught us deportment and etiquette in the first form, and in the higher forms she taught mathematics to the level of advanced calculus. She taught me to love the logic of algebra with a passion equal to my hatred of arithmetic. Her name was Miss Annabella Bowen; her family had been early Presbyterians and had taken the missionary's own name after their conversion, discarding their Indian name of Sankar in the process. Miss Bowen also lectured us on how to conduct ourselves as proper young ladies, using moral tales of those who had been ruined to drive home her point.

During one of her lectures we heard the tale of Kowsilia, the unfortunate. This had happened a long time ago, when Miss Annabella herself was a student. Kowsilia had been doing the baking for two weeks after the students had returned from the August holidays, and no one even suspected that anything was wrong until the morning they smelled the bread burning.

The smell of fresh bread baking had wafted over the girls, homey and comforting, while they snuggled deeper under their blankets, anticipating the first morning bell. Then when the smell changed to something acrid, bursting into their lungs and causing fits of coughing, the matron awoke and ran, following the smell to the outdoor kitchen with its big oven, gathering a small crowd of wide-eyed students in her wake. They found Kowsilia hanging from one of the beams in the oven's shed. Her body was still warm, twisting and turning in the black clouds of smoke sweeping out of the oven door. It was discovered that she was pregnant. Who was the boy?

"They say it was the father and the brothers."

Miss Annabella Bowen always shook her head tragically when she said these words, but she would answer no more questions, not even about what had happened to the girl's body or to the father and the brothers. We all looked at each other in silence. We never discussed it; better to forget such a tale and get on with our own, more modern lives. But there was no denying the powerful sense of menace in the air.

I never saw the oven or the inside of the dorm. We moved to the new house in La Plata the year before I started at La Pastora. I recalled my anxiety as I waited through the long vacation for the results of the government exhibition examination. Every time I bumped into school friends we had one topic of conversation: "You think you pass?" We were only eleven but our whole lives were to be decided by those examination results. Every school on the island had an exhibition class, but out of five thousand students only the first five hundred were picked for high school. The competition was steep, especially for prestige schools such as La Pastora. To us, failure meant early marriage and a life bound to a washtub, scrubbing dirty clothes and smelly diapers.

The day the results were published Uncle Sweetieboy brought the papers to our house in the early morning while it was still dark. He stood there pounding down the door, the paper opened to the page where the results were printed, my name outlined with a thick black crayon. Uncle Sweetie was grinning and chuckling and slapping tears off his face. Muddie and Da-Da, Kello and the whole household woke up, and when I came out Uncle Sweetie lifted me high above his head and danced around with me. Kello was jumping up and down shouting, "Two in and two to go!" He had passed for the boys' college two years before. Da-Da held me close, tears in his eyes, and said softly, "Aim for the stars, Mona. Always aim for the stars."

We had a breakfast party on the spot with oranges and buljol and bake. I even got some sweet milky coffee to drink. Da-Da celebrated with his friends for days. Muddie was so proud that she took to boofing me regularly for feeling too great and getting a big head because of my success.

A chance. I had a chance, but I saw around me many who didn't. For a few years I would call out to them when we saw each other on the streets until we faded out of each other's lives. I knew what their lives would be—selling cloth in Syrian stores for low wages, taking typing courses that would end nowhere, getting married to their young, poor boyfriends or being married to men their families chose. Lives stripped of love maybe, or lives of poverty and hope, always on the lookout for a chance. Or maybe just ordinary, reasonably happy lives.

For all the chances and opportunities it offered, high school was full of false promises. But on that first morning when I walked up the steep hill to La Pastora as one of its crowd of schoolgirls, supremely comfortable in my uncomfortable new uniform, I took strong, certain steps, knowing what was expected of me.

Walking as if you know where you're going. Walking without a slip, without a blemish, without a flaw to ruin your character. Walking and holding up your good name, your family's good name. Walking with your back straight, your posture taken from imprinting yourself against a wall (but one day maybe, walking right out of those classes in deportment and needlework and cookery).

Walking with a tempo moving between thinking out what steps to make, carefully now, and thinking out what false steps not to make because you could lose everything, thinking how not to shame everybody, how not to stand at a street corner and talk to a boy, especially a boy out of a school uniform, a big boy already working, a big man.

Being careful. Walking and hustling: so much to do before life passes you by and one false step could mean that you lose it all. You lose and get left out of the whole thing and you sink behind a tub of dirty clothes, your raw knuckles endlessly wiping a procession of babies' dirty bottoms. Washing, bleaching, scrubbing dirty diapers. Scrubbing heavy gaberdine pants; khaki pants. Becoming a wife, with a husband, drunk maybe, after a night out with his friends in the rumshop, a boy out with the boys, now drunk, falling on you late at night, his mouth reeking of stale rum and the remnants of cutters lodged between his teeth, tugging and pulling at your underwear, intent on one objective—the release of his tension, aroused by the boys on his boys' night out. Tiptoeing through life, frightened, following rules and laws that hold down your skirt, your hair, your mind, serving all the men in the family, "Make a cup of coffee for me nah," "Bring some water for me, girl," "You eh cook yet? Cook, yuh hear, cook," or, more cajolingly, "Girl, cook something to eat, nah, something nice like how only you could make it." Yeah, careful. Better be careful.

Careless is being on the swing at school, the one at the very top of the small hillside with the park benches, the one fixed to the highest branches of the tamarind tree, and flying as high as possible, dangerously, dangerously high, only a few feet away from the top of the tennis court, hair flying, wind rushing, flying free of all the little rules and laws that entrap. Swinging at the top of the world, past the treetops; swinging and never falling.

Careless is sitting in class freely, relaxed, thinking about the teacher's words, learning about logarithms and simultaneous equations and knowing the periodic table by heart, not wanting to stop doing algebra or chemistry problems, reading, learning, thinking about the world, a big big world, bigger than home and school and back again. Careless is not worrying about when your father comes home late at night, drunk too, like the men in rumshops, and begins another row. Careless is not worrying about whether he will drag you out of bed and beat you again because of some little thing that you did or did not do. Careless is not worrying about being put out of the house and having to sleep all night on the back stairs, hiding at the bottom of the steps so people on the road will not notice, like what happened to Savi when somebody reported that she was talking to a taxi driver.

At school we heard stories about what fathers or brothers or uncles would do if they caught wayward girls in slackness. When I thought back to those times, it seemed obvious that other girls— black, Chinese, mixed, the few white girls in the school—did not live with the same threats. Or did they? I never knew. There must have been some reason why the stories circulated only among the Indian girls, though we never admitted it, so strong was the habit of denial. I know that we felt our separate sense of embarrassment sharply. But the whole school joined in the talk about Rosanna when her family found her boyfriend in her bedroom after he had climbed in through the window. She was an only child and lived in a big house with her parents and grandmother. She had a whole room to herself. For one term we had sat together in class, and she told me her parents were planning to send her to Scotland or Ireland to study medicine. Rosanna had failed one year and was repeating; she was older than we were, already fifteen, and not interested in school at all.

One day during algebra class she told me her dreams of having a husband and having him come home for dinner. They would have a little meal of crisply fried fish—two whole redfish, one each—and afterwards they would go and lie down together. A sweetness came over her plain round face when she whispered the word *husband*. "Nobody in the house, just the two ah we," she whispered, "for the whole night."

Our school was secluded on its own grounds and there were rules about not leaving unless you had permission to go home for lunch. Rosanna broke the rules and met her boyfriend every day at the bottom of the hill. They would sit on high stools, stare at each other, and drink sweet drinks in a little parlour. He was a young taxi driver of nineteen. My friends and I patrolled the beat a couple of times after learning of these meetings, breaking the rules as well in our curiosity, and established that he was indeed cute. When her family found him in her bedroom one night, they chopped him up fine fine. It was the father and the uncles, Rosanna's cousin Rohini told us. Chopped him up fine? How fine? Like mincemeat and minced-up fruit for Christmas cake, Rohini said. The scandal lasted for weeks, and Rosanna was taken out of school and out of our lives.

One false move could cost everything—my whole life. No time for carelessness, for slackness. Slackness was talking to boys, writing letters to boys, having sex, doing the thing. We knew the thing was on their minds all the time. Big people were never careless, and all they ever thought of doing was the thing.

My friends and I talked about *the thing* every single lunchtime when we sat together after eating. We limed on the grass outside and began simply by trading basic information. Everybody in the group had two straps showing through their blouses—a bra strap and a camisole strap—except Susie, who had only one because she wore an all-in-one. It sounded impressive but no one believed her. Our questioning revealed that she had sewn two sponge falsies on to her camisole because she was as flat as a bake.

We were searching for something in those intense conversations every day as we refined the skimpy stock of knowledge that we had, but what? Who could lead us through the minefield of liking boys, having crushes, holding hands, kissing—and keep us from the shame and scandal and ruination and stinking washtubs and babyshit and drunken cursing men? All any of us wanted was a little breath of sweetness, of niceness. All Rosanna had wanted was two crisp fried redfish, a dark night, and a safe bed to lie in.

There was no talk at home of boys except Da-Da's sudden outbursts when he was drunk. He would use phrases such as "looking for man" and "taking man on the sly" in a general way, referring to some instance of low-down womanhood at his job or in the newspapers, but I knew that he was really talking about me. I was always surprised when he acted normally the next day. After a while I could tell, just from the rattle of the gate latch, whether it was Da-Da or the drunken stranger who would walk through the door.

Around this time Kello left home. Pappy begged him to hold on a little longer, but Kello had made up his mind. He got a transfer to a northern school and went to live with Auntie Alice. He wanted to do a more intense science program than the San Fernando school offered, so it was said. I knew differently. He had escaped. That was the beginning of Pappy's decline. He was eighty years old and strong as an ox until Kello left. I remember the desolation of my brother's leaving, the smell of a cloying wetness in the air, an ugly in-between light shrouding the entire day.

Muddie had told me everything about my body in a clinical way, even drawing a little horseshoe-shaped diagram to explain. I shared this diagram with the other girls but it was useless information. A map of the body's inside organs could not tell us how to find our way through the minefield. It could not show us how to swing carelessly, high over the trees and not get the violent push from behind that would pitch you off your perch and down into the bush. Once you fall into the bush that's the end of you.

There were six of us in our little group. We worked out an equation to explain sexual matters, and never told anyone outside what it meant. Each letter in the equation stood for something connected with intercourse and reproduction. We formed a secret club so that we could talk dirty in peace after lunch. Aided by brown paper packets of achar—mango or pomme-cythère or chalta—we heated up our tongues and our wicked imaginations.

We called our secret meetings the Dirty Skirts Club. The day we hit on the name we knew it was exactly right. We thought of it because one weekend Susie and I had decided not to clean our skirts. Some of the neater girls in the class never had a crease in their blouses and their skirts remained immaculate all day long. We decided to do the opposite. That Monday morning we arrived at school defiant, prepared. "Leh we see what they go do," we whispered to each other. We lined up as usual for inspection. The class prefect checked us for forbidden jewellery, nail polish, and stand-up badjohn collars. Then the form mistress double-checked us again before we marched into the auditorium for morning worship. But nobody noticed the sorry state of our skirts. The second week we waited and again nothing happened.

After we formed the club, all six of us began to concentrate on our skirts, deliberately letting food fall on them, wiping our hands boldly on them after drinking water, doing our best to abuse them. But these were not ordinary skirts and they stood up to our punishment without flinching. They were made of navy blue woollen serge straight from the mills of England, as our geography teacher never wearied of pointing out.

They were also a "lifetime investment," Auntie Vannie said, her mouth full of pins as she pinned up a deep hem that would be let down as I grew. Her skirt had lasted for her whole high school career. The placement of the box pleat at the front and the inverted pleat at the back was obscene, we decided, as we speculated rudely upon the wisdom of a closed box at the front and an open vee at the back. In Form I we learned a specific method for cleaning our skirts, and we were expected to apply it forever after. Every Sunday each girl used a wet rag to slough off any stray residue of soil, then steam pressed her skirt with a damp cloth. The skirts always looked clean and new. Very smart, our form mistress would say.

Our guerrilla efforts yielded little result, and after a while we had to concede that our Dirty Skirts Club was a good idea but could not work. The skirts didn't take naturally to soiling and didn't seem to notice a lack of steam pressing. They sloughed off the stray specks of dirt on their own. The woollen serge knew what it was about and eventually we had to declare in its favour. However, we realized at least that the Sunday cleaning ritual was unnecessary and we stopped doing it.

In the club book we wrote this down as a rule: "Never clean your skirt if you want to be a member of this club." We kept a record of the daily lunchtime sessions under the heading HTs for Hot Things. It was lucky that we wrote everything in code because one day we lost the club book. If anyone had cracked the code, we surely would have been expelled from school, and we lived in a state of terror for about a week until the book was returned by Shameela, who demanded to be included in the club. We agreed but her addition broke it up, especially when she kept calling it the Dirty Dogs Club. Her curiosity had been aroused because she thought that we took turns meeting boys in secret and sharing the spoils the next day. We listened avidly to her account of kissing for hours with her cousin, but she was not one of us and the mystery had vanished.

What got us into big trouble was love comics. Some girls had them and we would exchange them like crazy. The comics came from America and had graphic black-and-white pictures of men passionately kissing girls with long hair that hung down just so. I never got to buy one of these because the day I showed them to Muddie in a store, she nearly slapped me in public even though I was big and in my high school uniform. She bent and whispered savagely, "Don't let me catch you in this kinda slackness, you hear? This kinda thing is not for girls like you."

The comics were about romances between doctors and nurses, successful businessmen and temps, or injured explorers with ravaged faces and ardent, caring girl-women. The men were wealthy, and after much trial and heartbreak the faithful girls were rewarded with marriage and happy, prosperous lives. We found temps exciting too. We fancied that *temps* meant temporary lovers and would whisper clever, worldly remarks such as "the more the merrier" or, in calypso mode, "man gone, man dey." The best of these comics were those romances where tomboys were turned into loving, caring women nursing their men back to health. Nursing and serving, leaving tomboy ways behind—love comics taught us the ways of good women. Good women were trained to serve; even our school motto reinforced this: Not for ourselves only, but for others.

Our form mistress, Miss Camilla Lee, was incensed when she found out about the love comics. She dragged three girls up to the front of the class and raged about the comics for a good fifteen minutes. Miss Lee was just twenty and had only recently left school herself. We knew that she was very religious and was a member of one of the new fundamentalist churches being established in Trinidad. She was not Indian herself; many of the newer teachers were not because all teachers were now hired from a common national pool. She was a "red" girl of mixed African/Chinese ancestry. Our school was still Presbyterian but now financed largely by the government, like other denominational schools. Everything was changing around us since we had won independence from Britain. The new government banned both "Rule Britannia" and "Land of Hope and Glory." It was an exciting time, everybody was saying so, building a new nation in which "all ah we is one" was the new catchphrase.

For Miss Camilla Lee, however, that day was still to come. All of the girls caught with the love comics were Indian. She brought us up to the front of the class. "My mother wouldn't even let me read these," she stormed. "Why would you girls, with your whole future ahead of you, want to read this trash? Why fill your heads up with vice like this? Why not concentrate on your studies? Some of you could win scholarships. Why look for men and marriage so early?" She gave out a loud steups and continued more quietly, "I say allyuh lef dat kinda ting behind on the estate long time! Why all yuh so hot up? What these little taxi-driving boys could give you all in life?"

She confiscated the comics. We were deeply embarrassed, especially as Miss Lee was young and good-looking and dressed very well. We all looked up to her. The worst of it was that we had thought the love comics were modern romances—nowhere did they include poverty and hiding and peeping in order to see boys. The women were free to do as they pleased. When Miss Lee reported the matter to the principal, our detention lasted for a week, and many girls cried because they had never had a bad mark against their name. Susie and I and the other members of the Dirty Skirts Club defiantly shouldered our bad marks as honourable stripes for our rebellion, but we talked about that episode for a long time. The depth of Miss Camilla Lee's anger and disapproval stayed with me, with all of us.

I realized later, long after La Pastora, that racial differences probably led Miss Lee to view our behaviour as predictable and deplorable. There was talk about how Indian girls were hot hot from small—no wonder they had to marry them off as children, and no wonder wife beating and chopping was so common among those people. They were not civilized or "creolized" enough. They did not reach the approved standard of proper Trinidad society. We were hot coolie girls who had to be brought in line and who, at twelve or thirteen, were already showing signs of wantonness. As a young girl I had always admired Miss Lee, though even then I sensed an undercurrent that disturbed me.

A few years later, as a senior girl, I joined a group from the school that was accompanying the choir to Port of Spain for the island-wide high school music festival. The town girls walked carelessly along the street with no teacher in sight, black girls, whitish girls, red girls like Miss Lee, and a few Indians in between who accidentally or not never looked at us as we filed past in a straight line into the great festival hall. "Now, girls, be on your best behaviour, you hear?" our form mistress instructed us. "Let's show those town girls a thing or two." Walking past, we heard a giggling group of these town girls talking about a "busload of country bookies," and one of them exclaimed, loudly and hysterically, "You mean a busload of country coolies!" Most of us were Indian, though our group included a few black girls and some mixed girls too. Everyone pretended not to hear the comments and we never discussed them. We had an animated discussion, though, about the town girls' stylish uniforms, which we preferred by far to our own accursed serge skirts.

But if race was not part of our exploration, sex certainly was. Harlequin romances came next, and we forgot about the humiliation of Miss Lee and the love comics. Harlequin novels were what we craved. *Pride and Prejudice*, *Jane Eyre*, and *The Tempest* made fine reading but they could not tell us what we wanted to know about being free and careless and safe all at the same time. In the Dirty Skirts club book we listed what we wanted out of life: Glamour, Travel, Money, Love, a Career. The careers were law, medicine, and teaching. Marriage we considered only vaguely, although falling in love was high on the list.

It was then that the wars about appropriateness began. Some girls were so certain about what could and could not be done. Susie and I were always incensed at their certainty and would demand, "Why? Who say so?"

I will marry a gravedigger if I fall in love with him.

But you wouldn't fall in love with a gravedigger.

Who say so? A gravedigger is just another person. Suppose a good-looking young boy can't get work and start to dig graves. Why I wouldn't fall in love with somebody so?

Well he would have to be a dunce if that is his job. You want to marry a dunce?

But what if your parents approve of somebody and he turn out to be a wife-beater?

Well, if that is your luck, then that is your luck. Gopaul luck is not Seepaul luck. Everything is a chance. But at least your parents would be trying their best. If you pick a gravedigger then you not even trying. You aiming down there.

And Susie, dearest Susie, my best friend, she of the dark skin, the high cheekbones, the willowy frame, Susie wanted it all—a travelling career, falling in love with a wealthy Arab sheik, and living between Cairo, Paris, and Rome. Glamour and adventure non-stop. And happiness too, she always added.

How precarious our lives were—Rosanna, Susie, and the other Dirty Skirts, brave and bold, wanting it all, recklessly inventing our own world. It wasn't so long ago that they would have married us off before we reached the age of danger. Now they could only warn us to be careful and accuse us of not being careful enough long before we had even figured out what careful was. I thought sadly of how we never knew that it was okay to be like Rosanna, wanting nothing but her own warm bed, her husband, her fried redfish, that it was okay to be like Susie with her desire to ride the whirlwind into glamour and adventure non-stop, okay to be like me too, the young Mona, her tough hairy forearms ready for anything, swinging and never falling, swinging beyond the tamarind tree, at the very top of the world.

TEN

I returned to Toronto. Even though I had been away for such a short time, I felt myself landing with a thump into an almost alien landscape. Reorienting myself in the taxi to my parents' home was strange, and I wondered about the unexpected homecoming that I had experienced in Trinidad. The smells, the familiar lilt of voices, the uneven mix of hustle and neglect, even decay, that characterized the island, seemed suddenly more real than the predictable order of the cityscape before me. It was a cold afternoon, the wind brisk and uncompromising.

The next day Babsie brought Kello home for a few hours and we made like old times again, cooking callaloo and stewed chicken and macaroni pie. Da-Da offered the quickly seared chicken liver, his special treat, as if we were children, almost forgetting about Kello's illness. And Kello's euphoria was infectious. He examined and re-examined the deed, the photographs, asking endless questions about the property. I suspected that he had never believed he would regain possession of the land. Nor had I, and I was sure that Da-Da had kissed it goodbye forever. As for Muddie, I was uncertain. She believed Kello could move mountains, and once he had floated the idea, perhaps she knew it would come to be. But her excitement was kept in check by Da-Da's feelings that even the repurchase of the land was a direct comment on him and his own inability to hold on to it. After a while, though, we all began speculating about how the townhouse development would look, how we would manage it, how we would keep one unit as home base, returning to Trinidad and Tobago regularly from now on.

We talked too about old times. Kello's picture of those times was deadly accurate; I knew this in my bones even though our memories differed. I mourned our lost youth but Kello took it in stride. There was a hard line in his life between childhood and manhood and the only softening that would ever occur was his reclaiming of Pappy's land. In leaving as early as he had, only a few years after the big row, Kello had succeeded in removing our father from his life. Not like me, still struggling with the burden of understanding, often finding myself examining the past from this angle and that, the light streaking or glimmering and changing without warning to shadows. Why, Da-Da, why, why? The unasked question never left my mind.

Babsie remembered nothing of the old house, but she was moved to tears at the sight of the place where she was born, the landscape that had no presence in her memories. Muddie and Da-Da had kept their doubts to themselves throughout all of the earlier fuss, the phone calls with Bess, the decision-making, though once when we were at the hospice together I caught my father fixing Kello with an astonished look, his eyebrows raised quizzically, as if about to launch into a speech to bring his son to his senses, his illness, the present. But he kept his silence and Kello, if he noticed, gave no sign.

Now, overcome by the general babble of excitement, Da-Da got up and embraced Kello, dissolving into sobs, mumbling about how proud he was that his son had reclaimed the family property and how this could be a new start for everybody. Our father, the optimist, still the most innocent, the most idealistic of all of us, always ready for a new start. Kello held him easily but his eyes remained dry. Da-Da went on and on, as if unconscious of the absurdity of his words, until with unexpected directness Kello called him to account. "What made you sell the property even after you were told not to?"

Startled, Da-Da cleared his throat and paused for a full minute or more. Then he responded to his son as to an inquisitor:

"I was at the lowest point in my life. The old people sweat blood to buy that land and to keep it through thick and thin. For me, for us, for all of you." He opened his arms to embrace us. No one moved. "But God turn his back on me, he turn me into his stepchild. Ah feel"—looking up to the heavens—"like I was God outside child. I was in a don't-care-damn state of mind. You see, all you don't really know hard times. I was sucking salt day and night for so long I forget any other way to live. The old lady was dead already and the old man couldn't do much. It was up to me. Everything was up to me.

"When they made the offer—because don't think the house was free, you know, it had a big mortgage and the mortgage was sucking all the money—when the offer came, the old lady visit the house in a dream. She came from the other side to warn me; she warn the old man. She say, 'Dear, don't let Mackie sell the house.' And don't think for a minute, not for a minute"—here his voice rose to a wail—"don't think that I didn't understand. My old lady band her belly and work like a horse to keep that house and land. In the old days they would call your mother your queen. She could do no wrong. Well, that old lady is my queen, you hear? Even if she still punishing me, she can't do no wrong."

Da-Da's voice broke, and without a word Muddie walked over and sat beside him on the big couch. Their legs touched.

"Whatever else they did, those two old people knew that they had to keep the land. I knew that too—I always knew that. And I try, I really try, but the time was different. They had their foot in the past and I was in the modern world. I thought I was doing the right thing."

Muddie and I exchanged glances as we looked at Kello and Da-Da facing each other down, one dying, the other grown old. I felt that we were thinking the same incongruous thought about how no way could two boar-rats live in the same hole.

Then, as she always managed to, my mother steered us out of trouble and drew everyone around the table, saying grace and starting the meal. I opened my eyes, caught Kello's wicked grimace, and stuck my tongue out at him. Babsie watched us, trying to control a smile. Children, we were children again that day, perhaps for the last time.

For generations the members of our family had all come to consciousness in the same place, rooted to the same spot on the island, seeing the same trees and streams and beaches, bound by the same laws. Then, in my generation, everything had changed. Now Kello lay dying among strangers, with only a few family members around him. He had been best friends with our cousin Esau once; now Esau lived in an English suburb and they had not seen each other for years. Sonia and I had lost touch except for Christmas cards. The smell of ylang-ylang, the recipe for drunk pies, the sawmill burning at the end of our childhood—when I replayed those memories in my mind, I wondered, did they really happen that way?

As my stay in Toronto lengthened, my life in Montreal seemed to recede. Roddy called frequently, but he was beginning to complain about my distance. I was sure that our relationship would be okay when we were together again, but a worry was beginning to nag me at the back of my mind. Maybe being surrounded by family made me long for a shared past with another person, a shared history. Roddy's understanding of my life had the stamp of a Third World studies or poli-sci course about it. I hated myself for thinking these ungenerous thoughts but couldn't help wondering whether, in the end, I would turn my back upon the settled life he offered and become once more my true nowarian self. I found myself smiling at this idea; the *nowarian* game was so silly, and I could not imagine why it gave Sonia and me such delight for hours on end.

We made up the game in Grandma Lil's yard. I would always play the part of the road-weary wanderer landing upon this welcoming house at evening. I would stand at the gate and appraise it, wondering if it would take me in. I would rattle the gate until an old woman with a stick—Sonia shrouded from head to toe in Grandma Lil's cast-offs—would emerge from the depths of the yard shouting encouragement and abuse. "Ah coming. Hold on, ah coming. All yuh can't wait for nothing these days. All ah allyuh so damn hurry!"

"Good evening, madam. I is a traveller. A nowarian. I could get a room for the night?"

In the game the house was an inn like the English ones we had read about, with fireplaces and hat racks, where a weary traveller could rest in comfort for the night.

But perhaps my pleasure in the game was no riddle. Even now I sometimes found myself entertaining the fancy of walking away from my own flat, leaving it open and ready for whatever chance occupant fate might send its way. A homeless person would be walking into an ordered shelter while I would be walking away and becoming a nowarian.

One Sunday morning I went to church with Muddie and Da-Da. Kello had persuaded me to go and take communion on his behalf, but this was to be our secret; he did not want them to think that he had recanted his conviction that the church was full of Pharisees and hypocrites. In church the service began with one of my favourite hymns:

Part Two: Manahambre Road

Where cross the crowded paths of life,
Where sound the cries of race and clan,
Above the sound of endless strife,
We hear thy voice, o son of man.

And sitting again with my parents in a selected pew at their church, a little country-looking church at the northern end of the city set in wide fields now covered with snow, I felt a powerful sense of belonging. Around me was a congregation that could be found as easily in San Fernando as here, give or take a dozen white faces. Singing the hymns, I felt myself small again, and ached to have Kello and Johnnie swinging their legs on either side of me. In Trinidad Da-Da's churchgoing had been intermittent, but in Toronto he attended regularly, led by Muddie's unswerving faith.

On the way home they talked of how many former Presbyterian missionaries, from other parts of Canada originally, had retired in Toronto where their "old flock" had dispersed. These old missionaries reached out to their Trini friends, and sometimes showed up at dances and boat cruises just to keep in touch. Funny how I had never imagined that they could be marked by us as well. After years in Trinidad they must have found it difficult to fit once more into the Canadian mould.

Da-Da mentioned that Miss Lotte had invited them to a garden party a few months before she died, and said that the place was full of old-time church people and their children. Her lady friend from Europe was visiting—here his eyebrows arched skywards but he made no other comment—and she had wanted her friend to meet everybody. Miss Lotte had asked after me and had even asked for my address in Montreal.

I had not thought of Miss Lotte in years and now I felt real sadness at her passing. I remembered with gratitude how she had opened up her rambling, eclectic library and let me run loose in it.

Her lack of censorship was a gift. Her sadness, deep and resonant within her tall, slender frame, was almost palpable. Miss Lotte was of German background. She had come straight out of the Canadian prairies at a young age—she could hardly have been more than twenty-two when she appeared one morning with Reverend Marks at church. She was introduced to us as a deaconess, a church worker for women.

Lotte was a great organizer and set up classes in crafts, nature study, and cooking and knitting for girls and women. She lived in a low building on the church compound called The Teacherage and held all the classes in her gigantic drawing room. The landscaping around these buildings was exquisite: fuchsia and gold bougainvillea entwined with frangipani and oleander, setting off each building separately. Almost from the first Miss Lotte showed great interest in me, and Muddie was pleased. In one of her craft classes I made a sand-coloured plaster of Paris plaque with a Bible verse on it: "Do unto others as you would have them do unto you." For years afterwards this was my mantra. Miss Lotte was so different from anybody I had ever met. She would open up her storage box full of paints, clay, charcoal, paper, wire, paste, and invite us to work. She never kept track of who helped themselves to what, and the first few times we attempted to report that others were taking too much of this or that, she would look at the news-carrier vaguely and then resume her task without comment. This generosity was part of the appeal and novelty of her classes, a kind of freedom with valuable supplies we had never known.

Around the time of Miss Lotte's arrival we heard the Squires estate was to be sold. I remember Da-Da cursing savagely at the news. San Fernando was ringed by large plantations known as estates, some of them already being phased out of sugar cane and diversified. For those estates nearer the town diversification readily took the form of property sales. Our new house at La Plata was in one of these newly created suburbs. The Squires estate was to be deeded to the church because Old Lady Squires was a staunch Presbyterian. All the arrangements had been made. The Board of Men had laid out tentative plans for the land—a boys' camp, a retreat, an acreage for model gardening. But at the last minute she got a better offer, so the church arrangement fell through.

Then word came that Reverend William Marks himself, our minister, was the secret buyer. His name had leaked out because one member of the Board of Men was a clerk in a lawyer's office. Mrs. Squires was moving to Port of Spain to live with her daughter and family; her daughter's husband was a "local white," it was whispered, and had sold the property for cheap to Reverend Marks. "Blood thicker than water" and "all them bakra does stick together like laglee," Da-Da sneered, between curses. Now all the lands along Grand Trace, Corliss Hill, and Rodriguez Street were being cut up into lots and sold. People were buying the lots really fast. Da-Da was raging.

"Like they train that old hypocrite, that so-called reverend, in real estate or what? When he join the priesthood was to thief other people money or to convert the heathen? Eh? Them damn hypocrites! You think I going back to that church again? Not me! Not if you kill me! Them hypocrites could kiss my arse!"

All the same he never dissuaded Muddie or any of us from attending. On this issue Kello agreed with Da-Da and contrived to avoid church altogether, but Muddie and I always dressed up and went. In spite of his hot mouth Da-Da continued to go irregularly and always at Christmas and Easter.

Once I heard a dark rumour about Miss Lotte and another lady minister from one of the new fundamentalist churches. It was after Sunday School one day and I was hanging around, waiting for church to begin, when a car drove up and I saw Miss Lotte getting into it. A plump white lady was driving. A big girl whispered to her friend that they were going to make zami and that it was a good match because one was tall and thin and the other was short and fat. I had heard the expression *making zami* several times before this and I had some idea what it meant, but I could not associate Miss Lotte, with her gentle manner and her slow way of talking, with sex.

I had forgotten all about the girls' gossip until I heard Muddie and Da-Da talking in lowered voices about Lotte and Lorna a few nights later: the two Ls, they called them. I couldn't hear much of what they were saying because only occasional words filtered out of the far bedroom, but the tone of their conversation confirmed the girls' whispering. Muddie spoke very low but Da-Da sounded irritated. He steupsed a couple of times before breaking out in anger, saying that people like Lotte and Lorna always came to backward places like here to do what they couldn't do at home.

"You think they could make zami open so in de Prairies where Lotte come from? Them reckless prairie men wouldn't stand for it. They would beat them like snake, yuh hear? But here they could come brazen so and do anything just because they white. And everybody here fraid to say a blasted thing. If they wasn't white, it woulda be licks sharing down the line."

He steupsed again.

Those words filled me with fear and curiosity and excitement all at once. There were zami rumours at school about two older girls and two teachers, and sometimes during our HT lunchtime sessions my friends and I would speculate on what they would do and how they would do it. Someone suggested that zamis would have twinthings, an interesting little word that we quickly shortened to twins, and that they could take turns playing man or woman. We decided that tryouts did not qualify as making zami, and I was relieved because I had wondered nervously if my experiments years before with Sonia counted for anything. Whenever I wondered about Miss Lotte and what she did with Miss Lorna, I felt vaguely uncomfortable, but her library compensated for everything. She had books such as *Sex and Temperament* by Margaret Mead and also a new book called *Trinidad Village* written by Herskovits, a world-famous anthropologist, she informed me. She had a corner labelled "West Indian Books." All three of V.S. Naipaul's books were there and I borrowed these first. She lent me anything I wanted to read and never asked any questions, not even when I borrowed her battered paperback copy of *Desire in the Dust*.

Uncle Baddall was visiting with Auntie Vannie one day and he saw me reading this book. He pointed an accusing finger at Muddie.

"That is the kinda book you letting the child read?" he demanded angrily.

Muddie had never censored my reading and I couldn't understand why she did not say so. She only sighed and said nothing. I was bringing Uncle Baddall a cup of coffee from the kitchen when I heard his remark and saw him leafing through the book that I had laid face down on the arm of a chair. I had the wildest urge to dash the coffee into his face, scalding him and bringing shame and scandal into the family. I glared at him instead and Auntie Vannie's eyes opened wide. Muddie rebuked me in a vague, abstracted way. "Don't be so rude and puffed up, child," she said. I thought to myself viciously that whether life was fair or not fair, I knew for sure that Uncle Baddall was its fool. "Life's fool," I whispered to myself as I snatched up the tattered book and left the dining room. *Life's fool*. The phrase sounded exactly right and I took great comfort in it.

ELEVEN

Throughout those months while Kello was dying I felt a wild, unassailable sense of grief. Yet it was unnerving how calmly I joined everybody else in accepting the fact that he was leaving us. We acted as if we were helping him prepare for a long journey, preparing ourselves too for a farewell, knowing that we would not be seeing him for a long time. It's death, I had to keep reminding myself. I would never see Kello again, and there was still so much to be said and understood between us. Muddie clung to the lymphoma lie, but I knew Da-Da better than that. He had wordlessly refused it. His eyes were pools of knowing, his sorrow bitter as gall and wormwood and other biblical images that I imagined floating unbidden to the top of his mind, such as Sodom and Gomorrah, the pillar of salt, or a deluge that might come and wash everything away in the blood of the lamb and make it white as driven snow.

When we were alone now, Kello took to hugging me often. His newly acquired softness, his longing for reminders of that early time in our life, its different rhythms, its soft Trini-Creole phrases and intimacies, often brought tears to my eyes.

"Mona," he said one day, "you're so close to my heart. We're so close we could be twins. Except that you were born after me, you're a girl, and we grew up so different. You took the brunt of it for all of us—my leaving, Da-Da's rage, the hard times. Mona, I know your cross, I know it, doudou."

The impact of that last word, its old-timeness, a sweetness flowing out of Kello's hard brown face, his tightened lips, was overwhelming. I burst into tears. He stretched out an arm and drew me close.

"Come, hug me. It's not infectious, not in this way. But it has advanced and I know I won't last too long."

Another day he gave me his pocket watch, an antique-looking piece. He wanted to have it cleaned and serviced because his children were coming to visit him that Sunday. He had thought of giving it to ten-year-old Joey as a present.

"This pocket watch saw me through some really raw times, I tell you. I bought it in the early days in England because it looked like Pappy's. I found it in a junky little shop in Camden Town. The way I left Trinidad with Uncle Samuel and Auntie Alice, Mona, sometimes I think it all happened in a dream. I was living with them up north, remember? A few days before we left I came back home and told Pappy goodbye cheerfully, as if I would come back soon—in a year or something. And I never saw him again. I have nothing of his, Mona, not a single thing. What happened to Pappy's pocket watch, the one he used to wear with his waistcoat and watch-chain? Did you all throw it out?"

I nodded. "Maybe. Lots of things were thrown out without too much thought. I was in charge of packing up our belongings for the storeroom in Grandma Lil's house, and there wasn't too much space. But everybody acted as if we had to jettison everything. We felt a sense of desperation, of panic even, and yet we had no real reason. We felt as if we had so little time."

So little time. I told Kello that the pocket watch or the watch-chain might turn up in the attic. I also made a mental note to search the boxes I had shipped from Bess's storeroom. At the dinner table that night I mentioned the boxes, thinking that Muddie would be interested in sorting them with me, but no, she wasn't at all. Da-Da asked how I would know what to throw out and what to keep, and

Muddie waved her hand grandly in my direction. "Leave it to Mona," she said. "She'll know."

Leave it to Mona, of course, the one she had made to be her own right hand, the one whose mind was supposed to keep the details of family life together while she dealt with her task of the moment. Muddie had an uncanny ability to focus on an immediate need and ignore everything else. Kello had inherited this trait. In whatever game he was playing, however silly or casual, he always had only one thought: winning. And why shouldn't they? I told myself with anger. There I was, always nearby when Muddie called, born a fool, ever-willing to please people—to curtsey and smile and present a bouquet because I was asked, to cook and clean because I was asked, to sort and pack up the jumbled bric-a-brac of our lives in Trinidad, and now to unpack those same boxes. My unexpected bitterness, so deep and unfocused, surprised me.

Kello had taken what he wanted from the world. He had wanted to change his fate; he had wanted to unyoke his destiny from Da-Da's. He wanted money and had found it; he had closed his hand. He wanted love and freedom in love, and in meeting Matthew I guessed that he had finally found it. He had lived his life quietly, outside the gay community. I could not know what he thought of the politics of being gay. Had he come out to his wife? Was that why their marriage had broken up? Her distance still kept that secret. Irene was a Canadian girl—bright, reserved, from an Italian background that she had left behind her. Their children, Joey and Linda, were generic Canadian kids.

But I began to see Kello as a drifter through life and relationships, in spite of his accomplishments. He had been married, he had worked as an engineer, he still played the stock market. Kello was a money hound. Even from his sickbed he spent part of every day counting money on his laptop and making notes in a ledger that he kept near him at all times. A "money peong," Da-Da would often say, somewhat ruefully. Da-Da loved money too but thought that if he concentrated on going for broke, and watching each roll of the dice, each play of numbers as they threw themselves into the world in a certain sequence, his luck would one day change. Da-Da would always be watching and waiting for the big kill. Not my brother Kello; the big kill was already his.

I was certain that earlier in life, Kello had not set himself the task of buying back the land in Manahambre Road. After he left home at fifteen to attend school with Esau in the North, he wrote and passed his senior Cambridge exams, then worked and saved his money. As soon as Kello left La Plata, the full blast of Da-Da's rage turned on me. When Uncle Samuel and Aunt Alice travelled to England on long leave, taking along Bella and Sonia, Kello went with them. Before I could properly assess his moves, he had removed himself from Trinidad.

We did not see Kello for many years afterwards. He wrote letters, excitable ones at first, telling Muddie his every move. But when I wrote him about her distress because of the menial jobs he was doing to fund his studies—sweeping up the floor in a factory, working in a bakery, delivering messages for a financial house—the letters changed. He told us less about how he was making it, although we were never in doubt that he was. By the time he had got his engineering degree, we were already in Canada. He had hoped that Muddie could attend his graduation, but they couldn't afford the airfare to England and he received his honours alone. After he reunited with the family in Toronto, he stayed at home only a few months. He and Da-Da still couldn't live in the same house. Neither could I at that time. Kello left first and got married; after a year I left as well to attend university in Montreal. Now we were all back in the same house, the ancestral lands reclaimed. I was sure a deeper meaning would unravel in time, but for now I felt as if our history was like a spider's web in which we were all caught fast.

Muddie had kept in touch with her family through the years, scattered as her siblings were all over North America. When Uncle Tristram heard about Kello's illness, he and his son Jason stopped in Toronto on their way back from a skiing expedition in the Laurentians. Muddie was serenely in command of the situation. "He's in a hospice, you see, because the staff offer the best palliative care we could find for him. Lymphoma mimics many of the symptoms of AIDS and most of the patients there have AIDS. Not all, though." She paused reflectively. "And anyhow, it's not catching, not in that way."

Uncle Tristram was having dinner with us after visiting Kello; Jason had stayed at the hotel to meet some college friends. He nodded sombrely now at Muddie's remark. "A big strong man like Kelvin getting lymphoma! Boy, this cancer is a hell of a thing, yes! It could strike anybody at any time."

Uncle Tristram had left Trinidad for the prairies over thirty years ago, yet his subversive Trini accent was as rich as ever. I wondered whether he was turning it on for us, and became convinced that he probably tried to be fluently Anglo-Canadian in other settings. He talked about how cold the winters in Saskatchewan were. He said, "When that cold hold you so, boy, is only a puncheon rum could move you!"

We all laughed together. But Da-Da kept his eyes averted. Uncle Tristram pressed a wad of bills into Muddie's hands before he left; his contribution, he said, because he might not be able to come back. I didn't want her to accept the money. Kello's care and medication were paid for. I was tempted to interfere, but one look at Da-Da, sunk now in the sports section, changed my mind.

Muddie took the money, embraced her brother, and the visit ended. I was suddenly enraged by the charade, and I wanted to tell my mother that Kello didn't need help from Uncle Tristram in Saskatchewan, his ultra-blonde wife Kathy, and their two ultra-pale children Jason and Kirsten, who live on another planet. But instead I left the room quickly, knowing my place.

Kello told us that the early evening was the worst time of day for him, but I showed up one day after supper even though he had asked us to leave him alone then. In one of the Trinidad boxes I had found Pappy's old pocket watch, its watch-chain broken in two places but the timepiece otherwise intact. That was the night I met Matthew, and finally I understood everything. He was only slightly younger than Kello, and I was struck by the unabashed openness of his face. You grow used in life to closed faces, shut from the world by those masks that we construct for different uses—the family mask, the subway mask, the workplace mask, the one for friends, the ugly shut-in one for cocktail parties and events needing mindless small talk . . . but this Matthew had a maskless face. The whole person looked at me and smiled, and I smiled back. I suppose Matthew's face was nothing special—light grey-blue eyes, blond hair with a touch of red, a pointed chin. Just another pleasant-looking white boy. I hugged him deeply, trying not to cry, seeing only that Kello had found someone who really mattered.

I looked up at my brother, propped high on his pillows, his breathing laboured, and noticed that he was staring at me grimly, waiting for something. I moved to the doorway and he made no attempt to stop me. Matthew walked me out, and when I reached the car he held me close, burying his head into my shoulder for many minutes while I stroked his back awkwardly and murmured as though to a child. He turned his face away as he walked back into the hospice, back into Kello's room.

I wanted to tell Kello that I knew something about love, that I too had risked much to understand it. I knew that loving brought us fully to life, forced us to risk ourselves, and I was so happy for him and Matthew. One afternoon when I was alone with my brother, I began talking about how I found Matt to be a beautiful person. But

Kello only stared at me in silence. He was intent on shutting me out—me, Muddie, the whole sinuous Indian family that wound itself into every crevice of each other's lives, like miles and miles of lovevine. He would not allow us into this one place of his own.

My thoughts drifted into my own relationship with Roddy. The peace that I had found with him was something of a moveable shack, always ready to provide a shelter, and I was grateful. I missed him, I missed my house, I missed my work. The film would be launched in late summer. I had given up on Cecile Fatiman. At the vodou exhibit where I had first seen her name, I had been intrigued as well by the vévés, also new to me. They filled a whole wall, their symbolic markings complex, secret, each sign signifying its own deity. But of the several altars displayed, it was the one to Baron Samedi that held me—its intimations of a heedless, immensely compelling masculinity, unbound by rule or convention. This was a maleness that propelled itself into the world purely on its own terms. It seized on the wickedness of the grimy city as its launching pad, all of its seizure signalled on that altar by its offerings: the metal contents of a scrapyard, a cigarette lying at the edge, evoking the lips from which it would hang down carelessly, a flask of rum, a hat, shoes. That altar was a praise song to a sweet city lover, a typical West Indian sweetman, but also the harbinger of death, also the Grim Reaper in his Caribbean incarnation as Basil the cricketer, bowling spin balls until a wicket was stumped. This Baron Samedi had visited us and was now taking Kello.

TWELVE

It was late March, the days drab and grey, piling on in never-ending sequence. Intermittent snow, freezing rain, misery, and no sign of spring buds. I was sitting in the wicker armchair in Kello's room, looking out the window into the boxy little garden below, wondering whether he would see it in full bloom. In the middle of our conversation he had fallen asleep. He had been talking about how important it was to balance a load. Any load, he was insisting, any load could be carried for long periods once the balance was correct. He recalled women from our childhood, such as Grandma Lil's washer and ironer, who could carry enormous bundles of soiled clothes on her head, or women in the country districts of Trinidad, who would walk for miles with a bucket of water perfectly balanced, the metal resting on a cloth pad.

At La Pastora we had learned that erect posture. Our form mistresses would say, "Girls, always take your walk from a wall. Flatten your backs against a wall as far as possible. Hold it—relax now, it must look natural—and keep the posture." A straight back had been one of the goals I had set myself in those early days.

We also talked of the land. The speed at which development took place in Bess's Trinidad was remarkable. The island was in another of its booms (for the past century it had moved from boom to bust to boom again with astounding rapidity) and the townhouse project looked good. She was sending the building plans by courier. It was the hot dry season, a good time to start laying the foundation. Kello hoped that, in time, Joey and Linda would come to understand the value of the land in Manahambre Road.

"Though I can't be sure that they'll even think of me when they grow up. Or Pappy either. But it doesn't matter. My seed—it exists. It'll surface in time. Nothing perishes."

Nothing perishes. I would believe that if I could. But I knew better. Some events should disappear entirely, banished forever from one's mind. Events, memories that still seeped through, uninvited, and stalked my dreams. Like fierce swarthy men wielding brushing cutlasses. Like my hatred of Uncle Baddall. Nothing could dissolve my hatred of Uncle Baddall.

Baddall had left Auntie Vannie unexpectedly. The year I turned sixteen we spent a day at Aunt Vannie's house so that she could sew a new dress for me to wear to the school bazaar. Even though my mother could run up little dresses or dolls' clothes if pressed, the big sewing jobs always went to my aunt. Vannie lived in a tall rented house near the Usine Ste. Madeleine estate, the same one that had fired Pappy once upon a time. She knew everything about everybody and didn't mind at all being the village seamstress even· though people said she should go back into teaching. But she was adamant—she hated teaching and loved sewing. And that was that.

The canes would be burning at this time of year; the smell would be everywhere, sharp and sweet. Some of the fires would be legitimate, with men of skill directing the flames quickly through the underbrush to clear snakes and razor-sharp cane straw while leaving the cane stalks intact, but many fires would be acts of sabotage to settle matters with errant estate managers. Burned cane ferments on the stalk if not harvested quickly, and the timing of cutting cycles is crucial. Men with grievances used to quarrel with the crop when they had no chance of having it out with a white overseer. The complaints would be diverse—cruelty, poor wages, unsettled scores over the year.

The canes were burning the day Muddie and I went to Auntie

Vannie's house to sew my bazaar dress. Auntie Vannie was talking about how Seeram, who sometimes did work around the house for her, had to let his wife go to the overseer's quarters three nights a week for a whole month. Seeram was the driver of a cane truck, but Dularie was a weeder and in plain sight of all the estate men every day. She was a damn good-looking woman, everybody agreed, and Seeram said that she was a good woman. A good wife and good mother. She was own-way about one thing only, and that was working. A few times when the crop was good and his bonus more generous than usual, Seeram would come home drunk and beg her to stop working. "We eh need it," he would cry sometimes after vainly pleading with her. "Me eh want everybody to see yuh every day. Some man go bring he farseness to you and ah go have to chop him, and then what go happen to we?"

Auntie Vannie, from her sewing machine, would give wise counsel on both sides. Dularie would come to help her sometimes with heavy cleaning or a big kitchen job such as making achar or kuchela with mangoes or pommes-cythères in season. Dularie was tall and slender with green cat's eyes and a light complexion. That she would probably meet her own mother's fate, producing an even lighter-skinned child for Seeram, Auntie Vannie understood, but she also knew that the few dollars Dularie hoarded every payday were her meagre insurance against adversity. The new overseer was flagrantly indiscreet, wanting Dularie to visit by night. "Mark my words," Auntie Vannie prophesied darkly, "Seeram set one of those fires. I only hope that they don't catch him. At least he had the sense to leave Dularie alone and punish the estate instead."

A fine black ash was settling on everything in Auntie Vannie's house. In this season she would take down her fancy lace curtains and use plain brown cotton on the windows, on the furniture, on the beds. The cane ash would contaminate the air until June, when the crop season ended. Even in La Plata where we lived, far from any neighbouring sugar estate, the wind would carry the black ash into our house. Muddie ignored it; housekeeping had never been important to her.

Muddie sat on a low stool near the sewing machine, exchanging gossip while Auntie Vannie stitched away at minor alterations and mending for us—hemlines and darts—before starting on the big job, my dress. My mother listened to the tale of Seeram and Dularie and sighed. Myrtle and Evangeline, two sisters, so different yet so alike. They came from a big family but now everybody had separated into their own lives. There was Alice, who lived in the North and was married to Uncle Samuel, Tristram (Tristy), who had migrated to western Canada, and William, whom everyone called Sweetieboy. Muddie and Aunt Vannie were the closest to each other. When they agreed on something, nothing could change their minds. In their presence I became invisible, blending into the walls and floor and furniture, deep in a book, while they conducted their half-whispered exchanges about life.

During one visit, about a year before the day of the bazaar dress, I had heard my mother and aunt talk about Uncle Baddall's accusations—how he suspected that Auntie Vannie had not been "untouched" before their marriage. Baddall's suspicions had arisen when he and my aunt had run into an old family friend, someone they had not seen in years because he had gone abroad. They met by chance at a party and the man, nicknamed Joker, walked over to where Auntie Vannie was seated, clapped her on the shoulder in a familiar way, and exclaimed in a hearty voice, "What happening, girl? Like you eh change at all! You eh close dem legs yet?"

Someone nearby rebuffed the man for his boorishness, but the damage had been done. Baddall had thought Joker's question was much more than a joke. After Auntie Vannie told my mother about my uncle's accusations, Muddie whispered, "How he find out?"

Auntie Vannie shook her head. "Maybe he was told much more than that," she said.

My mother answered gloomily, "The less he know, the worse it will be. He will think all kinda thing."

They had both forgotten that I was sitting at the other end of the room, my elbows on my knees, my head propped up by my hands, my face buried in the book I was reading. Vannie said in a slow, flat voice, "He took advantage of me. Joker took advantage of me. I was studying when he walk in the room. He really came to see Sweetie-boy and was going to the back of the house to look for him when he spot me. My back was to the door and I didn't see him right away. He walk in the room, and next thing he lift me off the chair and kiss me. Then it happen. Just so. Quick quick, I didn't even realize . . ." She stopped, silent and thoughtful. That was when she had made the fateful decision to tell Baddall everything.

Now, a year later, she was whispering about something else. Uncle Baddall had been in Montreal for six months and had suddenly stopped writing.

"How long since you hear last?" Muddie asked.

"Three and a half months. But that is not the worst thing. Myrtle, he take almost all the gold I owned. I realize it only last week because you know how I don't like to wear gold. I always keep it locked up. I went to look at it, just so, no reason, and found all of it gone. All the chains, churia, bera, rings, my butterfly necklace, everything. The one thing he leave was the thin gold chain that he buy for me when we got engaged."

"You sure that is Baddall who take it?"

"Who else? The drawer had two keys and we had one each. Nobody didn't break into the drawer. It was him, I don't have a doubt. I just wish I had realized sooner."

Then their voices dropped further. They were talking a secret language, but I knew the sound of it. The sound was full of danger.

And all such talk ceased when Jenny ran in crying for her mother from the yard outside, where she had been playing with a child from next door.

I studied Auntie Vannie carefully from behind my book. Her eyes looked anxious, yet her face remained as smooth and uncrumpled as the piece of sateen cotton that she worked on as she spoke. My aunt's face was not striking in any way, although everybody agreed that she was pretty. Her speech was clear, deliberate, and modulated, lacking any obvious accent. Sometimes Muddie could sound like that too, but she couldn't keep it up for long. Trouble would break up her vowels into hissing sibilants, and once I heard Da-Da exclaiming in mock wonder, "Well, ah never know ah get married to a cussbud. Whey you learn all that kinda talk? You wasn't brought up so."

She had seized the opportunity to turn on him fiercely. "Is true. I wasn't brought up so. Is the life you bring me here to live, catching mih arse every blessed day."

My aunt should have been beside herself with worry, but here she was calmly measuring and cutting and sewing a fashionable dress for me to wear to the bazaar at our high school. The way she handled the cloth, turning it this way and that, positioning it just so and then cutting it effortlessly, was a real pleasure to see. The cloth itself was a heavy sateen cotton with a soft sheen. The background was a pale Egyptian blue covered with night flowers—indigo, forest green, navy, and black. She was making me a plain, straight shift, sleeveless, curving at the hemline as was the style, with a small round neck. A nice cool dress for a nice cool girl of sixteen. The shift involved a straight piece of stitching, and though Aunt Vannie possessed lightning speed as a seamstress, even her sister could hardly believe how quickly the job was finished.

Of all the bazaars and fairs that schools in San Fernando held for their annual fundraising, La Pastora's was the most popular. Our school was sculpted into a hillside, its lavish grounds housing several small buildings containing labs and temporary classrooms, all ranged around the grand main building with its formal auditorium. Every inch of this sprawling space was used for the bazaar. School alumni, businessmen, and well-wishers pitched in to set up booths selling everything from homemade jams to a royal high tea served on borrowed tea services. The bazaar was a fashion parade for old and young, and schoolboys and young men gathered to gape and admire. Later in the evening there would be dancing, and I passionately wanted to stay this time because the Hillside Boys' Combo, our own band from the South, was just beginning to hit it big. They were playing for free because they had had their start at La Pastora only a couple of years before. But nobody from the family was going to the bazaar this year. Auntie Vannie did not want to go alone, Muddie would not go without Vannie, and Grandma Lil was "some days up and some days down."

I was allowed to go alone, but before leaving I had to sit down and pay attention to Muddie's strict instructions. She told me to take a taxi back home because walking alone on the road to La Plata would be too dangerous after six o'clock. She told me to make sure that the round-de-town taxi had at least three passengers in it before I got in. For safety, she said.

When I flagged the taxi down on my way back home, the required three passengers were all cramped up in the back seat. I got into the front next to the driver. The front seat could hold three, but I hoped that he would not pick up a fifth person because I had no desire to make the return trip tucked under the driver's armpit. He was chatty, constantly turning his head around to look at the passengers in the back seat as he delivered what was obviously a well-practised monologue. Every now and then he would hit a particularly apt phrase, incline his head sideways, and give me a hard look.

"Indian boy go ketch hell jes now. Nowadays all de girls going in for Creole boy. Watch dem nuh, in dey tight tight skirt and tight pants, looking for Creole boy. Indian boy eh good enough for dem. Indian boy go see real trouble jes now, yuh go see."

The passengers in the back seat, all Indian people themselves, made murmuring sounds of assent.

The hemline of the shift was just above my knees; when I sat, it rode up even higher and the slight curve at the side of the dress made an even wider sweep of leg visible to the driver. When I had tried on the finished shift at Auntie Vannie's, everyone had exclaimed at how nice it looked, and little Jenny had clapped her hands, jumping up and down and hugging my legs. Auntie Vannie had even asked whether I was wearing stockings because my legs looked so smooth and pretty. Now in the taxi, with this man staring sideways at me, his malevolent disapproval almost palpable between us while he raged against the fallen state of young Indian girls and the resulting deprivation of Indian boys, I felt almost naked in the shift dress. My bare legs were exposed; I wished now that I had not shaved them.

At the school bazaar everyone had worn shifts, teachers and students alike, and many dresses were much shorter than mine. But how many of the girls and women would have had to find their way back home by taxi alone? I was sure that I was the only one.

When I left the bazaar, the dancing had just started. It would have ended at ten o'clock and Susie had urged me to stay because I could get a ride back later in her father's car. No matter how she and the others tried to persuade me, though, I knew that I had to leave at six because Muddie had told me to do so. We had no telephone at home; I couldn't call to renegotiate and I couldn't risk staying later.

When I got out of the taxi, I walked to the house slowly, kicking stones along the way even though I looked like a young lady and was wearing my one good pair of pointed tipped leather shoes. I felt subdued and full of a trepidation that was hard to place. I fixed my face before entering the house though. Muddie was pleased that everybody had liked my dress. Those of us formerly of the Dirty Skirts Club had stayed together all afternoon, moving from stall to stall, having tea like grown-up young ladies in the tea stall, gathering in a circle underneath the tamarind tree with the high swings attached to its branches, and appraising each other critically. Mona was the prettiest, my friends had agreed, and my heart filled my chest with so much pride and pleasure that I thought it would break through. But Susie was the most beautiful, with her classic features. Other flattering adjectives were hauled out: statuesque, well-proportioned though small, perfect Coca-Cola bottle figure. All of these descriptions we took from the annual Carnival Queen contests and from the Hollywood gossip columns. Beauty contests were held frequently and everybody seemed to agree that Trini women were the most beautiful in the world. "Is the mixture of races; is our cosmopolitan population," the papers would boast. There was a beauty contest at the bazaar, and as we had expected, the winner was a lovely red girl, mixed-up-just-like-callaloo, I told Muddie. She listened, hands clasped in her lap, eyes shining. We sat there in the kitchen like sisters, sharing the spoils of success.

But I did not tell her about my ride in the taxi and the anger the driver had shown at young Indian girls. His words had frightened me in a way I could not explain. And I understood now why Muddie had warned me to choose a taxi with two or three people already in it.

The next time I wore my new shift was on a family excursion to Mayaro. The beach was a good hour and a half away, and after driving for a while we were all thirsty. We pulled into the paved yard of a country shop where Da-Da knew the shopkeeper. They made jokes with each other and Da-Da was expansive. He ordered sweet drinks for us and asked for some cutters—shop cheese and salami cut into cubes and doused with pepper sauce. The shop was empty at that hour, mid-morning on a Sunday: people were either in church or relaxing at home. We piled out of the car and sat on barstools on the rumshop side of the shop while we ate our snacks. I began to notice that the shopkeeper's glances kept straying back to me again and again as he pottered around. I felt a bit uncomfortable at first, but then I just decided to ignore the idiot. When I turned suddenly to ask Da-Da something, I found my father staring hard at me, a tight frown knotting his brow. I raised my eyebrows at him in an unspoken question, almost jokingly. He rose abruptly from his barstool, ducked outside, and motioned me to follow. No one else noticed; the others probably thought that we were just going to the car for something. Once we were out of sight, Da-Da turned and stared fully at me. His face was livid; he had become a cold-eyed stranger, full of hatred. He spoke then in a voice I had never heard before, even when he was drunk and cursing, yet it was a voice that I knew well, it was the voice of the stranger: "Move, quick sharp! Get in de car and stay there, you little bitch. Flaunting yuhself up and down looking for man. All yuh lil girl so damn ting with all yuh-self. Stay dey and keep yuh lil tail quiet, yuh hear?"

Somebody sent Johnnie to the car with my red sweet drink and I sat there alone, staring at the cars whizzing past on the main road-way, sipping the warmish liquid and thinking nothing. Nothing at all except how Kello had fled and how I missed him.

As Da-Da drove away and we continued our journey to Mayaro Beach, I realized that he was still vexed because of the way he mashed his brakes and cussed other drivers. Muddie said nothing, but I thought she avoided looking at me. I wondered what Babs and Johnnie were thinking and suddenly felt a deep wave of shame, remembering how the shopman had looked at me. Near Mayaro Da-Da flagged down an old truck, laden with watermelons, that was having trouble climbing the last steep hill. He laughed then, joking with the men as he selected a choice melon.

As soon as we got to the beach Da-Da carved up the watermelon. He was in a good mood again, offering the fruit to us as "the pause that refreshes" in an echo of a silly commercial jingle we all knew. He broke off an old coconut branch, stripped it down, and made a bat. We all played beach cricket, and after a while I forgot the shopkeeper and concentrated on my spin-bowler's art of delivering the ball. It was the style I admired most: the long, loping movement up from the field, the beautiful turn of the arm, and the unexpectedness of the exact moment when the bowler would let the ball fly. The batsman would be on the alert the whole time, and yet the ball would come spinning out of nowhere with a life and timing of its own. Not that I ever managed to execute a perfect spin myself—I could only imagine my arm arriving at this moment of perfect pitch. But Muddie could hit a mean six with a consistency that defied logic. She would hardly even be concentrating on the game, giving directions about serving a snack or throwing a quick warning to some straying child, when out of nowhere a ball would come flying, and nine times out of ten she connected with her bat. She scored often on that Sunday, much more than Da-Da or any of us.

Details about that day at the beach still lie quivering in my memory. The unusually thin white strip separating the red of the watermelon from the striated skin; purple jellyfish washed up on the sand; the echo of the bat dully whacking the cork ball we had brought with us; the thin film of dust and debris floating back to land on the surface of the brown lagoon. I know the colour of that day—its strange luminescence as if the events were taking place within separate frames. I was Mona, the helper, the organizer, the sister in charge, Muddie's right hand; I was Mona, numbed and suspended in a glass orb somewhere between the fine dry sand and the cliff at the far end of the bay. I was safe, suspended, while the sun gave off a white white light, free of glare, while the batty-mamselles ducked and played without fear, their gossamer wings shimmering above the water, while far out at sea the outlines of a pirogue crested the breakers. We stayed later than usual, driving back in pitch darkness along the winding road, with no dwellings for miles, cocoa and coffee trees swooping with long tentacles onto the roadway.

The next day Muddie gathered up our beach clothes and washed them. She washed my shift with two of my white school blouses, and the night flowers on the dress ran over everything with a green-blue inky colour. She tried various remedies but they were useless; the staining was permanent. This laundry disaster reduced me to one school blouse a couple of weeks before the end of the term. I had to wash that blouse every evening and iron it the next morning. But not only were my blouses ruined; it seemed that everything had changed all at once.

At school we had to get serious about our studies because the big exams were looming. We had already been streamed into either the arts or the sciences because a mixed program was not toler-ated. I loved both but I had chosen the sciences because the bright girls picked that stream. A couple of years earlier I had petitioned first the vice-principal and then the principal to do history as well as science. "That Mona again?" Miss Boodram, the principal, said in exasperation one morning to the school secretary as I waited on a bench outside her office. "Why she feel she so special? Why she can't do what the other girls doing? In life you have to choose. You can't have everything." That was the day I stopped petitioning. My future depended on choosing well and I chose the sciences. Secretly I thought that I could still have everything by doing history and drama on my own.

Part Two: Manahambre Road

I remembered how pleased Da-Da was at my choice. Da-Da and Muddie had such modern ideas about their daughters' education. They had known about my efforts to create a mixed program but had never tried to influence me in either direction. At the time, I believed I had made the decision myself, but later I realized that I had had no choice. It was science or bust. Da-Da would boast to his drinking friends about me when they came to our house, sometimes in the middle of the night for a reviver. He would wake up Muddie, and I would get up as well to help her fix snacks and coffee for them. Da-Da would jerk his head in my direction and say, "Yuh see mih big daughter there? She bright too bad. She go end up in a big old lab coat and some goggles like Madame Curie, watch and see. All kinda experiment she go end up doing in some lab, wait and see."

Da-Da was in awe of my love for science. My prizes in chemistry and biology impressed him more than anything I ever achieved in literature or language. He wanted me to have a career and to grow into an independent woman; he repeated this wish constantly. To him, a scientist would be an ideal profession for me because I would be hidden from everyday contact with the world, pottering around in a hidden lab, emerging on occasion to astound the world with a remarkable discovery, then retreating to safety again.

I loved science, but the stodginess of the image gave me trouble. I much preferred the glitter and glamour of life as a career girl, dressed up in high heels, make-up, and earrings, swinging my hips with a real leather handbag across my shoulder. Auntie Vannie had one of these; Uncle Baddall had given it to her as a wedding present, and after all these years it still looked new. My handbag would be dark burgundy with deep pockets. Auntie Vannie's was black so that it could match anything she wore, but my independent life would provide different accessories for each outfit.

All these choices and so much to learn. Every day our form mistress would say, "Girls, remember that you can be anything—I repeat *anything*——you want to be. Just aim at the stars and study like hell." We would always giggle at that little impropriety. Some of my friends did not yet know what they wanted to be, but I had made up my mind. I would be a career girl, working in the city, enjoying a big complicated life, not caring about what others thought. All my decisions would be mine and I would not get into trouble; after all, everybody said how grown up I was for my age, how wise, how mature. Around that time I began to keep a journal in the unused pages of an old copybook, although I was always in a hurry and never managed to do more than write rough notes. I would keep a journal from then on.

One night in my parents' attic I found one of these rough journal pages stuffed into a file box. It told what had happened to the beautiful night-flowered shift: *Cannes brulées. Shift. Kneeling on gravel. Hot sun. Cars on the road. The public yard.*

It had happened about two years later. The fabric of the shift was old and faded, the design distorted, but the dress itself still kept its lovely clean shape. I had taken to wearing it occasionally as a home dress. On a Saturday afternoon Da-Da arrived back early after drinking with his friends and noticed that I was wearing the shift. There was no preamble or ranting explanation. He lunged at me and tore the back of the shift off my shoulder. "You little bitch. You ho." He spat the words out. "What the hell you doing again in that ho dress? You ain't find you attracting enough man already?"

It all happened in a rush like those absurd scenes in a silent movie. Muddie advanced from the kitchen towards Da-Da, bearing in her hand a metal pot spoon still dripping gravy. Now it was she who spoke in the stranger's voice: "If you strip that dress off that child, is me and you here today. Yuh hear me? Is me and you here today."

Part Two: Manahambre Road

I saw my mother clearly for the first time. As long as I live I will never forget her face. Her eyes were balls of fire. Da-Da's hand dropped slackly to my shoulder and for a moment he did not know what to do. His rage was real though, a vast rage that could not be contained. He slapped me, and the back of his hand sent me spinning towards the open door of the bedroom. "Get that thing off now and bring it for me. Quick sharp."

Quick sharp. Quick sharp I stepped out of the torn shift and put on another home dress with a flared skirt. When I handed the shift to Da-Da he stormed outside, flung the garment onto the small concrete landing near the washtub, and poured gasoline on it from a small container we kept nearby for treating the dog's fleas. Then he lit a match. At the same time he grabbed me by the shoulders and forced me down on my knees facing the fire.

"Now turn around and walk," he commanded.

I stayed still, kneeling on the gravel that was already cutting into my flesh.

"Walk!" the voice barked. He turned me around by the shoulders and pushed me roughly forwards. Rage flashed up my spine like lightning and at that moment my rage was equal to his. If I could fling myself around quickly enough, I could catch him off guard and push his face into the flames. Or I could jump up and cuff him hard in his belly. Then he would fall into the fire. Behind me I heard his voice again, the stranger's voice: "Little ho."

I walked on my knees across the yard. "Now turn around and come back," the voice barked. Tears blinded me, and when he told me to stop, I couldn't at first. Moving fast hurt less than kneeling on thousands of little knives. I had reached the fire again. I looked up at the open doorway of the kitchen, but Muddie was nowhere in sight. Where was everybody? Where was Johnnie? Was Babsie hiding? Pappy had gone to his lodge meeting, I knew that. I faced the flames, near enough to feel the heat on my skin. The night flowers on my burning dress blazed through and were restored momentarily to their original inky beauty. Da-Da turned abruptly and went into the house, but I stayed there, clamped to the ground. The afternoon sun beat down on the gravelled yard. I was clearly visible from the road. Cars passed by and a big-mouth boy shouted, "Ay, girl! Whey you do? You take man or what?"

The gasoline was efficient. The night flowers burned until nothing remained but a fine blackish-brown pile of ashes. Muddie must have waited until Da-Da was asleep or had passed out in the bedroom. I heard her voice from far in the distance, calling me in from the yard. I dropped onto the gravel heavily then and examined my knees. The gravel cuts were arrayed in neat lines, the blood running in a patterned flow down my legs. I felt no pain, no shame, nothing. I was wandering alone in a land without water or light, with little air to breathe. I was strangling and beginning to gasp when I felt strong arms closing around me. The sharp hot fragrance of ashes cut the evening air. Muddie was helping me up now, holding me close to her and sobbing. "What we going to do? What we going to do?" I held on to her and rubbed my stinging eyes against her shoulders. I opened my mouth to speak but my lips were dry as sand. I knew, though, what I was going to do. I would pass my exams, leave school, and begin to live my own life. It would not be long now. I would live my own life. I would escape the way Kello had.

THIRTEEN

 It is Saturday night across the land and the sounds of husbands at it again fill the air. Husbands and wives engaged in their favourite pastime. Not making love but making body music anyway, screaming out the end of one more despairing week—work, drudgery, washing wares, washing clothes, work, a desk, a field, a garden, a little task-work, work, grief, no change. The silt of a procession of sad, bad, boring times backing up and overflowing down their grimy corridors . . .

Reading my own words in a teenage journal startled me. Could I have changed so little? Did life harden in me at such an early age? The thought of marriage or domestic life still filled me with irrational feelings of dread, even towards Roddy with whom I was deeply involved.

I had always refused the idea of marriage. Not love, never that. But marriage with its eternal domestic trappings seemed like certain death, even in that far-off time with Bree when he wanted to come home and talk to Da-Da.

I first met Bree during the long August holidays at a practice soccer match between the team from King's College, the boys' counterpart to La Pastora, and the crack team from the Catholic Boys' College in San Fernando. King's was trying hard, as usual, but we were sure to be whipped, sure at the end of the college tournament later that year to resort to singing with more energy than the occasion warranted, "We go win next year!" Susie and I joined our friends in the stands, and everybody talked and laughed at once, glad to be together again after several weeks apart, looking forward to the game. I noticed one of the King's College players talking ani-matedly to Kemal, Susie's boyfriend, at the side of the crowd. Kemal waved us over and introduced me to Bree, his best friend.

Bree smiled, then mumbled shyly, "Real name Carlos Antonio Gonzales."

We all laughed. "Heavy Spanish blood," Kemal joked, "from Columbus time, right?"

More laughter. Bree was a red boy, an obvious mixture of African and other races, medium height, medium muscular build, medium good looks. I liked him at once but was unprepared for the rush of feelings that overwhelmed me when I saw his action on the field. The game transformed him. He was a natural leader, his eyes saw everything at once and anticipated movement before a player had even begun to move in that direction. From the start I could see that the game was his, yet his manner was so unobtrusive, I found his skill difficult to pinpoint. I knew the game of soccer well enough, but I had never given much thought to the intricate mathe-matics of setting up the field for the shot to come. I saw now that the set-up absorbed Bree most—the actual scoring was almost an afterthought. Even though he was team captain and a forward, he gave away many of his own chances for glory during that practice game. Kemal watched intently, nodding. "Team building," he mur-mured to himself, "sharing the spoils. Good, good."

After the match the four of us went to a little café near the playing field and drank sweet drinks and talked and talked. I listened avidly; Bree and Kemal spoke a different language as they analysed the game with scientific precision, planning strategies for the rounds to come. "We go win this year!" His sudden smile and wink threw me into utter confusion. After that day I saw Bree accidentally a few times on the street, in a store, and at a concert one evening. Every time we met the same rush of feelings came over me, though our meetings remained casual. I noticed little things about him. He had a deep dimple on one cheek and long curling eyelashes. A wistfulness about his smile would turn him for a few seconds into a little boy before the careless, laughing adult rose in his face again.

The buildup to the college tournament later that year was intense. The King's College team was showing great promise because of Bree, Carlos Gonzales—"A Red Boy With Heart" as one cheeky headline put it. But the King's players were inconsistent, the papers said, were not welded together as a team, unlike the Catholic Boys' College players, whose movement was almost symphonic in its coordination.

"Indians can't play soccer. Is the few Indians on the team that throwing off the whole side. Yuh see any Indian on the Catholic team? Is one set ah people and they moving as one. They go buss we ass in the tournament, watch and see." The speaker was one of the Indian team members himself, a sour-looking boy named Mansingh. We were all drinking cokes at the café after a practice; I had fallen into the habit of walking with Susie to meet Kemal afterwards.

Bree turned now to his teammate and spoke in a low voice. "That is the kind of talk that go sink we for sure. How the hell we could ever win if everybody thinking like you, eh? The only way we could have a team is if we believe we have a team! So believe it, yuh hear me, Mansingh? Yuh better believe it!" He turned away, his face troubled. Impulsively I put my hand over his and squeezed it. In an instant he had turned his palm upwards and was holding my hand tightly, right there on the tabletop, fixing it firmly in his, keeping it there. And I wanted him to. We left soon afterwards and I walked home with Susie, never mentioning Bree.

The day of the big tournament came and we were in a state of high expectancy. For the first time in years King's had a chance at the trophy. Susie and I joined our group in the King's stands.

Teachers and students alike were beating tin cans and bottles, blowing whistles, and singing the school soccer chants. I noticed Da-Da's drinking friend, Mr. Cornelius Gosine, among the bunch of teachers clumped together at the front and said a polite good afternoon to him as I passed by. He had a news-carrying mouth— people said that about him behind his back. I loved the precision of the word they used to describe him: a *chugulchor patarki*, a thin news-carrier.

Then the game started and the other team scored first. The tension built as King's matched that goal and then a second by the Catholic boys. The score was 2–2 with only minutes to go. On our side of the concrete stands the hysteria was uncontrollable. To draw would be a disgrace when we had come so close for the first time in six years. Bree was in command, a whirling dervish around the field, kicking the ball backwards, forwards, sideways, dribbling like crazy, setting up shots for the forwards who had already missed two. The whole stand began to shout in unison, "Bree! Bree! Bree!" And some magical movement in the air caught Bree, flying down the field at the side, about to send the ball to the centre, and pro- pelled him, ball and all, just short of the waiting forwards. From the most unlikely angle on earth, and with a ferocity of speed faster than the eye could witness, he delivered. The goal was scored and King's had won. An unbelievable victory.

The team lifted him high. Horns and whistles and even a trumpet kept the tempo going as they paraded around the field. Afterwards, drenched with sweat, Bree walked straight up to where I was cheering with Susie and the others and gave me a big hug. He was the most beautiful sight on earth, and forgetting about home and family and propriety we held each other tightly and kissed. That was all. But it was enough.

I got home later than promised but my excuse of going out with "Susie and the others" would have held except that I saw Mr.

Gosine's car parked in our yard. He was at the door, about to leave, but as he squeezed past me in the narrow doorway he spat the words "red nigger" into my face with such venom that I drew back in shock. No one heard him but me; we were locked in a secret moment. Da-Da said nothing at first, but later that evening his rage was triggered by a small incident and he lashed out at me, a "lil girl pretending to study but only studying man." I waited for the words "red nigger" to follow but they never came. Those hateful words, spat out into my face, became Cornelius Gosine's special connection with me. I would see him at church every Sunday. Several times, catching me when no one else was within earshot, he would hiss at me, "Red nigger!"

For weeks after Mr. Gosine's visit Da-Da seemed to be in a rage. He arrived home late each night, "drunk as a lord," as he would declare though no one had asked, and Muddie would set out his dinner. I would be awake still, studying in my room. He found fault with every little thing, the food or some chance comment of Muddie's, often loaded with acid, it was true, and in no time at all a row would break out. I was terrified for my mother and planned ways to help her if he should attack. One time I even picked up a pair of scissors and held it at the ready, but he never did strike her. His mouth, though, was as nasty as it could get. I feared that Da-Da was angry about Bree, about Cornelius Gosine's news, but he never mentioned it. I was sick with apprehension those nights as I wondered if it would be Da-Da or the drunken stranger who would open the outer gate. From the clang of the gate bar I could tell.

I remember the concrete floor of the kitchen, the window held open with a long wooden window-stick, the open back door on one side, the small hallway leading to the side door and then the dining room. One night Johnnie dropped a heavy glass water bottle and damaged the sink near the dining room. Da-Da turned ugly the moment he walked through the door, spotting the hole in the porcelain at once. He cursed all of us for our backwardness, our coolie habits. Were we so unaccustomed to the good things in life that we couldn't even take care of a stupid little thing like a sink? No, we had to go and break it. He turned the tap on full blast and let the water run. Petrified, we stood on the spot and watched while the water poured through the hole, gathered momentum, and ran in a stream through the hallway and out into the kitchen, which was not level, so it began to pool and run back into the dining room. When Muddie saw the flood moving rapidly towards the bedroom, she stood up. Da-Da growled, "Anybody who touch that pipe go get dey hand break. Today, today, ah go break dey hand." Nobody moved.

The tap ran full blast for a few more minutes and then he shut it off. His hand stayed at the sink and he kept his back to us for much longer than necessary. When he turned, he did not look at Muddie. To my amazement he caught my eye, his expression almost guilty, and then gave a loud steups and stamped off to the bedroom. I leapt from my post, got the mop and bucket, and started cleaning. Muddie did not help me. I don't know where she disappeared to. I never spoke to her about the incident. I never spoke to anyone. The sink was fixed a few days later.

Susie's family was as rigid as mine about allowing her to go to parties and public fetes. Most of my Indian friends had the same problem, but we suffered in silence. It was yet another shameful Indian secret to be kept from our Creole friends and those of other races who would hold us up to ridicule for being backward. Only those girls lucky enough to have brothers and a family car at their disposal were spared the indignity of concocting stories. When we went out, I always told my parents that I was spending time with "Susie and the others." Surprisingly, they let me go without too much questioning, but when I came back suspicions would overpower Da-Da. I was always enraged by his accusations but never once answered him back—in our family that was unthinkable.

Part Two: Manahambre Road

For Indians, life in Trinidad at that time was a mess of contradictions. Even in urban San Fernando we heard of girls being cursed and even beaten by family members for so much as looking at "man." And husbands too, beating and kicking wives, except not in our family, never in our family, although Da-Da's cursing and threats began to take a different note after Kello left. A note of rawness.

It was a puzzle, the sheer violence of that time. Perhaps our parents were convinced that in this newer, freer world, with new rules being invented overnight, safeguarding their daughters' honour had become much more complicated. Now I can see that not the least of the complications would have been the new freedoms being sought by those same betraying daughters, especially those like me and Susie and the other Dirty Skirts, wanting all, determined to assert our rights.

In the attic one day I found a dusty parcel, my own, well hidden because it was wrapped in several layers of newspaper, then brown paper, then tissue paper. The objects inside were intact: two more gushing copybook journals, school badges and tie pins, a few love letters, a handwritten copy of Yeats's poem "When you are old and gray and full of sleep." An old red sweatshirt. I must have put these items together after Brooklyn, after that one time Bree and I met again, years after we had both left Trinidad, packing away in so many layers the two different times of my loving him.

The walks, the long talks, the current that flowed between us. The explorations of sex—how tentative they were. And the funny times too. Once he cupped my small breast and said daringly, like a seasoned lover, "I like. It have shape, it have size, it have weight." We giggled for hours over such silliness.

Later, when we met in Brooklyn, in between his wife and his outside woman, when he had established himself solidly as a West Indian man in New York, it was as if nothing had changed. I had gone to a film festival in Manhattan. He was easy to find—Flatbush Avenue in Brooklyn curving like a stretch of Piccadilly Street in Trinidad, and peopled by so many of our mutual friends and acquaintances. Before I left Montreal, I wasn't sure whether I would try to make contact. We had parted on such bad terms. He answered the phone himself, flipping into a soccer-practice camouflage so automatically on the telephone as soon as he recognized my voice that I felt uneasy, almost alarmed. I had not known what to expect or even what to hope for from this encounter. I fancied that if his wife answered, I would be friendly and casual, perhaps invite them out for a drink. Trinis laughing and talking about home—I imagined his wife to be a homegirl. His was a practised deception; I heard it clearly.

We lay together in the college dorm room I had got cheaply and made love on a thin iron bed. Afterwards I put his red soccer sweat-shirt next to my cheek and slept through the late afternoon. He slept with me. I awoke remembering how we had never slept together in Trinidad, had never reached for the comfort of each other's presence in sleep, had only had the quick times that we stole. Late that night he put his clothes on and talked about how sleepy he was, but said that he had to go home, living as he did between his wife and his outside woman. I begged him to stay—even then I wanted nothing more than to lie down and sleep fully with him—but he could not do it.

"It's New York," he said. "But I'll be safe on the subway because I'm black."

His words, casual, unthinking, disturbed me. He was black, yes, and I was not. Would I be safe on the subway too? I was Indian, an Indian from the Caribbean, an Indian long out of India, for genera-

tions now—did that count? For how much? Mixed-race black people could look like me; in New York, most people thought I was
black too. But between us lay the place Bree and I had come from,
where our racial difference was solid, immense, never leaving us.
We never spoke of it directly, even on that one day we met again,
although race was clearly the great wedge that had driven us apart
when we were young.

If I had married Bree, he would have been my eternal love while I
turned slowly into a wife and mother, forever coping, forever
keeping everything in balance, managing everybody's lives, living
in the real time between his hardness, his hard decisions, his hard
eyes, his hard body that I would never forget. The real time would
be made up of his young man's longing, his sweetness, his beautiful
corded body lying easily on mine, his strength to meet the world
head-on flexing its way through every sinew of his athlete's frame, a
strength that would have been part of my own as we met the world
together.

Another journal entry: *Bree made me love him in the way that melts a
woman down to that original place of want, smelling of molasses and the sea
and fresh grass and sweat and the odour of sex, a good clean place of fresh
sheets, smells of homemade bread baking and children's solemn questions*. I
recognized my unmistakable crapaud foot handwriting, but the
words made me shake my head in disbelief.

Bree and me. Who knows but that it might have been splendid,
watching each other's face change over the years and still seeing
only the same beloved face. Open skies, a clear sun, a clear day for
our love. And how much clearer and shapelier our love has become
with time now that we have not made it happen.

There was a day when, standing in a piece of swampland near the
sea, mangrove flies buzzing at our feet half-sunk into the squelching
mud, we loved each other standing there for hours. We held each
other close, standing deep in the muck, hidden from the world by

mangrove bush, looking out to the far end of the Gulf of Paria where the sun was sinking in a bloodied heap. We held hands, we pressed our bodies together, our heartbeats drummed past our ears and created the cacophony of evening birds flying in to nest for the night. The birds—scarlet ibises and white egrets—perched around us where we stood, welded into one flesh, becoming just one more solid mangrove trunk with twining branches. We whispered that this was where the world should end, slowly freezing in time, that love lasts, a love like this, forever cast into relief against a dimming sky, shielded by armies of nesting birds inside a mangrove marsh.

Love lasts. For Da-Da and Muddie it was everlasting love. I believed that on the day they met fidelity sprang to life between them.

"My wealth," Da-Da would always declare grandly at moments of heightened emotion, "my wealth is my children."

How their meeting and courtship and love and marriage had proceeded with the civility they often described, I could not understand. Within their lifetime the world had changed to a nasty, suspicious place where survival was possible only if you stood on guard. Muddie and Da-Da would still tell stories of their storybook courtship, the dances, the choir practices and church teas and picnics they had attended. A scant fifteen years later life became very different for us. For us, my parents had to stand on guard all the time against the outside. And what the outside was, I was then just beginning to understand.

With Bree I grew bolder, as most of my friends did with their boyfriends. Hollywood movies such as *Where the Boys Are* and *A Summer Place* gave us half-baked scripts about dating and petting. We were nothing like these wild, rich American teens in convertibles, yet it hardly mattered to us. Movies starred white people and that was that. The stories, the ways of life, we could always adapt to our own lives.

Whenever Bree and I got the chance, we used to sit in cafés, holding hands and talking for hours. New cafés were springing up all over the city. There was a feeling in the air of more money and lots of talk about how the island was really floating on a lake of oil, the same oil that had oozed up to form our natural wonder, the Pitch Lake.

Once we were sitting in Cedars of Lebanon, a new café that a wealthy Syrian family had just opened, when in walked Grandma Lil with her friend Mrs. Joseph. Grandma Lil would always try out the new places as soon as they opened if she happened to be in San Fernando for any reason. Bree and I were huddled close together in a booth. She glanced casually our way as she passed with Mrs. Joseph, quickly hiding her double take and continuing to chat with her friend. I drew my hand away quickly from Bree's, in spite of his surprise at the sudden move, and pretended that I needed to search for something in my bag. How could I let him know that my grandmother and her friend were at a table behind us? I knew Grandma Lil's habits well. She liked ice cream sodas, and I knew they would relax in the café until Mrs. Joseph's son finished work and came to pick them up. I sat there miserably until we left.

Grandma Lil came to our house a few days later and in casual conversation with Muddie remarked that Mrs. Joseph's daughter was getting married next month.

"A nice boy, Spanish-looking, but a little darker than the Creole boy Mona was in the café with."

"Mona?" Muddie was puzzled.

"Yes, Mona was sitting down in the new Cedars of Lebanon café drinking cokes with a Creole boy."

I heard this exchange from the next room and waited apprehensively, but "Huh!" was all Muddie said.

I was eighteen already. It was the month before the big exams and I was studying day and night. That night while everyone was asleep and I was poring over my textbooks Muddie suddenly appeared, standing over my desk like an avenging angel and glowering fiercely at me. "You make me shame today, making your grandmother bring news on you. I don't know when I ever feel so shame. What the hell is wrong with you? You want a next incident?"

She was referring to the burned dress, I knew, and I shuddered inwardly at the thought.

"Before you study your books, you studying boy. And a Creole boy too! What will happen to you?"

Nothing will happen to me, I thought, but was silent. I no longer wanted to tell her anything. When I was younger, she would set up her ironing table in the room where I studied late at night. She would wait until I took a break, and then we would have long conversations about life and the future. She would listen without interruption to how I planned never to marry and always to live a free life. I didn't want any husband telling me what to do. Why was it that everybody had to have a husband? What was so great about that? As far as I could see, men had all the benefits of marriage and women had all the work, all the washing of pots and diapers and stinky babies' bottoms. She would listen with great sympathy but always ended up saying that men could do things that girls could not and I always had to be careful. But everything had changed and she no longer ironed at night. Her tone too was different. The sympathy had vanished.

I wanted nothing more than to have Muddie hug me so that I could explain to her that I still felt as I always had, that my studies had not suffered, that I loved Bree but would not turn overnight into a girl with no ambition. I started to tell her, but when I looked up, I saw the naked pain on her face. Pain and utter bewilderment. My helplessness at that moment was uncontrollable, and I held on to her and wept. She stroked my hair and even rocked me a little in silence. Then she spoke hesitatingly, almost formally. "Mona, you are a big girl now. You will leave home soon. I trust you to do the right thing. You mustn't lose your head and do anything you will regret later. Remember to be careful."

With these stilted words Muddie tried to tread the narrow ground between my passion for Bree and her own sense of what was right, wrong, or even possible in our world. She was trying to protect me. But my sense of desolation was complete. I sat back on the chair and said nothing as she turned and left the room.

After that night I lived in a state of continued apprehension. I was afraid of being seen with Bree but didn't want to give him up. When we went to cafés, I always made certain that we were sitting in groups with other friends. One day we sat at a booth in Blizzards drinking ice cream sodas and eating hot dogs. Typical teenagers, we thought ourselves, as advanced and free as anybody in America. Susie and Kemal were seated opposite us. Susie needed me for a cover too; her parents disliked Kemal because he was Muslim, even though they were Presbyterians themselves. She argued with them, and she and Kemal got engaged although they broke up after a while. But Kemal was Indian and Bree was not: that was the difference.

That day in Blizzards we were talking about the last days of our school life and the big end-of-term dance La Pastora was holding. The Stones were singing *I can't get no satisfaction* and the words made me feel abandoned, as if I had been cast out of everything familiar to me. Bree was talking about coming to my house to pick me up on the night of the dance and I knew that he couldn't. When

I didn't answer at first, he persisted, and I was forced to say that he couldn't. That was when he declared his intention to come home and "talk to my old man" about what was between us. I was alarmed.

"No, you can't do that! Is impossible!"

"But why not, is ah ordinary thing to do. Everybody does visit their girlfriend house. Is better than sneaking around here, there, and everywhere."

Susie and I exchanged glances. Everybody but us.

Then Susie changed the subject and started talking about the new programs that the prime minister was instituting. One was the "grow local, buy local" campaign, intended to persuade people that our fresh mangoes and pawpaws were nutritionally superior to expensive tinned goods such as fruit cocktail that came from England and America. The other big program was the change in curriculum, which would be local too; we would learn about slavery, our own history and geography, and the names of our own flora and fauna.

Objections to the new curriculum had sprung up everywhere—from teachers, lawyers, highly placed civil servants, and all who valued the superior education that the mother country offered. Our GCE examinations were marked in England at Cambridge University. Every year there was a story of how a student from a country like ours had topped the whole field, whipping the English at their own game. Everyone knew that our system in Trinidad was superior to the one in America or Canada; the proof was that students who left here for universities overseas found the work extra easy and became overnight successes.

The newspapers joined the debate. Colonial to the core, owned by foreign houses, they carried front page stories about the decline of education under De Doctah. They predicted that soon everybody would be forced to eat bodi and bhaji and pone and bluefood.

Even for Christmas, one writer lamented, there would be no nice things in the grocery like apples and grapes. One editorial raged about how the classics would be replaced by local writers who couldn't even write proper English, and how poetry and the finer things in life would disappear altogether. The poetry issue got me hot, and I let off steam about the new government's ignorance and insensitivity. Kemal was in the pure science stream, so he sat observing us complacently as a passionate argument erupted.

Bree hated poetry, but he was forced to study Shakespeare and the Romantics together with economics and accounting. He had a special hatred for T.S. Eliot and the Moderns, whom he felt were sheer frauds.

"Anybody could write that shit," he said. "You just have to let your mind wander. And to beside," he added, using the catchphrase of the moment, "if De Doctah say so, is so!"

I believed that all of the threats to replace this and replace that were sacrilege, but I especially hated the threat to abolish poetry. I loved poetry and considered it my personal place of refuge. I had read everything I could find by and about the Moderns and had even written out love poems by Yeats for Bree. I felt a sharp pang of betrayal at his words and exploded at once. "How you could say that? Why we have to be so limited? Local this and local that? Why we can't have everything? De Doctah could haul his tail, you hear?

And Susie, ever ready for a fight, continued aggressively. "Who say De Doctah is God, eh? Who say so? De Doctah say pay as yuh earn, De Doctah say learn dis, learn dat, so yuh have to do it. Who de hell is De Doctah to tell me what to do? Who?"

I kept it up then, tapping Bree on the hand playfully and continuing Susie's tirade. "Who? Who de hell is De Doctah to tell me what to do? Who?"

But Bree wasn't playful. He rapped me sharply on my hand, and out of surprise at the sudden sting of what was obviously a slap, I hit him back, really furious now. Susie and Kemal said nothing but watched uneasily.

Without warning Bree's hand moved to my face and laid the next slap on my cheek. Nothing was clear after that. I returned the blow across his jawbone, and as if a dam had broken its ramparts, his hand struck my left cheek over and over. Once started he did not stop, could not stop, maybe. I was too stunned to react—here was Bree, my best friend, my heart's own, slapping me repeatedly in public. Finally Kemal grabbed Bree's hand and wrestled his arm down to the table, saying to his friend in a soothing voice, "Awright, nah, take it easy, man. Control yourself. Take it easy."

It was over. One side of my face stung as if bitten by a thousand Jack Spaniards. I looked at Susie seated across from me and a high trembling voice that was not my own squeaked, "Is swollen?" And because she did not answer, I repeated the question more emphatically: "Is it swollen? My face?" It was then that I realized she was glaring angrily at me.

I couldn't sit in the booth any longer. I got up abruptly and walked out of Blizzards, leaving Bree with his face in his hands. The slaps had echoed like gunshots through the small café; it seemed that everyone had stopped talking or serving drinks or laughing just to listen, but now no one paid the slightest attention as I walked quickly to the door, wondering if my burning cheek looked the way it felt.

Only when I reached home did I look into the mirror. But no, there were no bruises at all, not the slightest trace of Bree's hand moving back, connecting, and moving back again. My skin remained unmarked. But the incident marked the end of our relationship. I refused to meet with him in spite of the many messages he sent through Susie. Susie delivered all his notes but she could not forgive me for letting it happen. I should have done something, anything, bawled for help, screamed. Instead I just froze there like an idiot and let him slap me.

"Why, though?" she kept insisting. "Why, Mona, you with all your courage, your argument, what happened to you?"

Da-Da, and now Bree, I thought numbly.

Years later, when Bree and I met again in New York, we talked of neither the future nor the past. We listened to jazz in a juke joint, pressing our legs together, held hands, laughed, and talked. The musicians nodded and smiled at us. Walking back to our small room, I brushed against his body, feeling its muscular contours, wanting him so much that I felt my knees wobbling. It was like that time in the mangrove when we loved each other standing up for hours. We reached the small room of our tryst and I jammed him against the door, forcing his head back with the bluntness of my lips. This time we made love on the floor, briefly, absolutely.

We spent hours on the small iron-railed bed, talking and simply looking at each other. He could not hide from me and I watched the small boy in his eyes, still reaching for something that would be his entirely. A shadow fell between us, that shadow that streaked through his days remorselessly, the shadow of the cursing man with whom his mother lived, the man who never relented in his curses of the boy who was not his son. Once long ago Bree had told me about the day the cursing man tore a board from the rotting edge of their front verandah and flung it after him, a small boy crouching in the mud, the board flying across his legs and stopping there, the man flying after it and spitting, spitting, spitting on the board, cursing without stopping. I had loved him then like nothing else in the world. He had made me enter everything that had made him, even that.

But I was wiser when we met again. I still ached to love him in his way. The way of the suburbs, the trees, the garden, the children, the two-car garage. A part of me really wanted the foreverness of it, the depth of its lies. I wanted the turn-on of his need for it, his belief in its power to make him whole again. Bree and me. But my own rockiness would not let it happen. Vast and shifting was the sea of desire we had generated between ourselves, vast it would remain, but without motion.

FOURTEEN

 Only three and a half months had passed, but Kello had changed entirely from the person I had known all my life. His ruddy dark brown skin had taken on a translucent pallor, and every day he inspected his arms and legs for sores but never found any. Not yet, he would say. His hands trembled, and on the days when he could not eat Muddie stayed at his side for long hours, coaxing him with a spoonful of Jell-O or a sip of an energy drink.

On his good days we talked together with an intensity that often left me exhausted. Time was precious and so little of it was left. How much time? We probed events in our earlier lives, small, forgotten incidents. He seemed to be overpowered by a need to have everything resolved.

"Mona," he said to me one morning, catching me off guard, "remember the time you almost scalded me to death in Manahambre Road?"

I was indignant at his version of this event. I would never have done anything like that, never.

"Yeah, but you thought about doing it, huh?" He was smiling, teasing.

I got into his mood. "Yes," I admitted readily enough, "I thought about it."

We had never discussed this incident before. Could Kello have read me so accurately, even as a young boy of nine? I had picked up the heavy enamel teapot and banged it down so hard that it crashed right through Mama's marble-topped little table in the kitchen.

Kello remembered the event vividly. "It was your rage, Mona. I couldn't understand it. All I did was come in and ask if dinner was ready. That was the only thing I said."

The only thing he had said. My brothers and I had been playing outside at dusk, a wild game of whoop, running through the yard, hiding behind trees, tripping up each other. The boys had continued to play but Muddie had called me in to help with dinner preparations. As usual. Set the table, mix the cocoa, put the food out, call everybody to the table . . . and during these chores Kello had galloped in gaily, still playing whoop, and in a perfect imitation of the big men in his world had yelled out, "Dinner ready?"

My rage had been vast and blinding, the first real rage I remember. "You must be think you have a servant in here," I shouted back, "coming in here and just bawling dinner ready?"

That was when I lifted the kettle of boiling water off the stove and put it down again quickly, before anger could get the better of me. That was when I banged the tall blue teapot right through the marble. "But Mona,"—Kello's touch was light—"I've thought about it since. All the work always fell on you. It just wasn't fair."

Another morning, about a week later, he wondered what was pressing down on me and strangling me. "Are you okay? Sure? It isn't Roddy, is it?"

I avoided saying that I hadn't seen Roddy for over a month and hadn't heard from him either. I said that everything was fine with Roddy, but Kello persisted.

"What's holding you back, Mona? Tell me. Tell me, please." He was very serious, and against my better judgement I ranted on about how I was never free to do what I really wanted. Something always got in my way, somebody else's agenda, some course of action that had to be taken, some call of duty.

Instantly I was sorry I had spoken, but he remained undisturbed. He touched my arm and said gently, "But you are free, Mona. You can do anything you want to. Just do it, that's all."

I said nothing, thinking about how I had always insisted on my freedom to do whatever I chose and had ended up doing so little. What was my explanation? What was the hidden obstacle that I simply could not get beyond?

That day we talked a lot about our family, Grandma Lil and the old house, about Bess and how beautifully she kept the place now. Kello was nostalgic about old times, about Esau and how close they had become in England. Esau was older than Kello and was already halfway through university when Kello arrived. For a time they had shared digs, but after Esau's marriage they drifted apart. It was Esau, Kello said, who had brought him the news of Pappy's death. They were living in a rooming house and Esau's room was near the telephone in the hallway. When Kello heard the knock on the door very early in the morning, he knew what it was at once. He had just woken up and was sitting on the edge of the bed, thinking about his dream. He had dreamed of Pappy walking through the doors and into the hallway, carrying under his arm an unusual-looking scroll. It was the Trinidad newspaper, rolled up the long way, the wrong way. "The news," Kello said to me now. "Pappy came to bring me the death news, Mona." His eyes were bright and hard like diamonds.

I told him about Sonia, also in England but trapped in an unhappy marriage, the mother of two teenagers. I recalled the swingbridge incident with Kenny La Fortune and Kello remembered him at once; they had also fought each other as youngsters, especially when he lived at Aunt Alice's house. "'The country girl!' What he really meant was 'the coolie girl.' You know that, right?" Yes, I knew that. "I hear that the race business is different in Trinidad these days, Mona. Open competition seems to be the new style and that may not be such a bad thing. I don't know if I could live there again, though. Of course it doesn't matter, not to me. But when the townhouses go up, we'll keep one for the family. You should go there for a while if you want to."

I didn't know if I wanted to go anywhere. My thoughts were scattered. While Kello went on talking about how Trinidad had changed, my thoughts drifted off to the film and my dissatisfaction with Carene's decision to omit Cecile Fatiman. If her sacrifice of the black pig had been crucial to the Haitian Revolution, how could we leave her out?

I thought of Majie, my own pet black pig. We had kept pigpens behind the house on Manahambre Road, and one Christmas the family had killed my black pig. That morning I was feeding her when they told me that she was the one they had picked. I tied her out in the usual spot near the zaboca tree and played happily all day, silly four-year-old games, never thinking to ask what she had been picked for. Towards evening I heard a terrible squealing rising from the valley at the back of the house. It cut my heart into ribbons, and I stood petrified for a minute before I began screaming at the top of my lungs. "Don't mind, don't mind," Mama said, and bathed and fed me and put me to bed. But I developed a high fever in the night, woke up, and started screaming again in the pitch dark. Mama never left my side, and it took two days of rubbing me down with camphor oil and candle grease melted over a flame to bring down the fever. That Christmas when they killed Majie, she weighed ninety-eight pounds.

Uncle Sweetie had brought me a replacement pig, a cute pink and white creature from a new litter in his experimental pen behind Grandma Lil's house. These pigs had concrete troughs, with separate compartments for feed and water. They ate only imported feed. Ours were local slop-eating pigs, much taller than these short-legged white ones. Majie had even eaten pawpaws and zabocas that had fallen off the trees. When Uncle Sweetie brought the piglet, I refused to touch it. Pappy took it to the pigpen and put it in with the others, but they attacked it savagely and in two days it was dead.

To my surprise Kello had no recollection of Majie. Instead, he began to talk about Pappy again. One day he had accompanied Pappy to his "lodge," an institution called a Friendly Society where members paid dues every month. These societies or lodges were a community enterprise providing services, small loans, and death benefits largely to the black population. Not many Indians belonged, but after Mama and Pappy nearly lost their land to a moneylender, they were determined never to trust one of those sharks again. Instead, Pappy joined the society. Kello's visit to the lodge took place shortly before he left home, and Pappy was already walking with a stick, too shaky to go any distance alone. The people at the society were friendly and courteous, but one lady had pointed them out to others, exclaiming loudly, "Yuh see how the Indian children and them does treat their old people? You think I could get my grandson to bring me here if I couldn't come on mih own? Never!" The others had nodded and agreed, and Pappy had smiled.

"Mona, I felt like a freak show, a real pappyshow," Kello said. That was the day race hit me straight between the eyes. When I walked in with Pappy, I didn't feel odd or anything. But after the lady spoke, I just wanted to clear out of the place. I didn't like them talking about us as 'the Indian people,' as if we weren't even present."

Race had hit me between the eyes much earlier than it had Kello. The first time I was called a coolie I was only about five years old. I remember that I was just going into Muddie's zinnia and sunflower garden to hide when a bus passed on the road in front of our house. Some girls stuck their necks out and shouted, "Coolie, coolie, coolie!"

I'm in motion. I'm walking on the grass verge near my home on Manahambre Road, as quickly as my short legs can carry me, walking away from the traffic as I've been instructed. I have broken loose from the big girls who are in charge of walking me home on the evenings when Kello stays at school for sports. I have run ahead of them because I know the way. This has been going on for weeks; it is a secret from my mother because the girls do not want to lose the shilling they collect every Friday. I work out a system. I hide in the little garden and play with my transparent friend Elladora until the big girls round the corner at the top of the hill. Then I burst into the house, shouting to announce my return from school.

Until the moment I heard the words "Coolie, coolie, coolie!" I had been just a girl. The big girls who took me to school every day were not coolies, I knew that. Yula was half-Chinese and Yvette was mixed. A coolie was a nasty ugly thing. I hated coolies. My transparent friend Elladora who lived between the zinnias and sun-flowers was not a coolie either. I had never told anyone about this incident before. Now I turned to tell Kello but he had fallen asleep.

I sat and read as he slept. When he awoke, the burning question was still in his mind. "Mona, you can tell me. Something is holding you back. What is it? What is keeping you stuck in neutral, Mon? Your life, your talents, the films you want to make, what's stop-ping you?"

His eyes glinted. "It's not Da-Da, is it?"

I was distraught at the events swirling around me, and his insis-tent questions only added to my sense of being caught in a vortex. But I struggled to appear composed and only said, "No, not really. It was our pitching about from place to place, Kello. I never put down roots again after Manahambre Road."

He reminded me that the La Plata house had been ours until we left Trinidad and I said nothing. Was it possible that he had forgotten how we nearly lost that house, the hard times we experienced then? Da-Da worked by day and gambled by night, praying to Lady Luck for a windfall to redeem his debts. He had mortgaged the land to a British insurance company, and was still paying off loans for building supplies, labour, and a watchman at night. Then the British company declared bankruptcy, fired all its staff, packed up, and left. Those with mortgages had to pay the whole sum overnight or forfeit their property. That was when Da-Da really felt like God's outside child, and his despair never lifted except for brief bursts of humour.

"Who is me not to have bad luck, eh? I mean I ain't bar round. Anything flying could hit me just like everybody else!"

Or, "What ain't miss you ain't pass you."

Or, "When yuh unlucky, even brown paper could cut you."

His gambling ate up all the money we had, even money for daily necessities. How Da-Da pulled it off, by hook or by crook, I could only guess at. But he kept the house even though it was mortgaged to the hilt again when we left. Did Kello know that after the sale, buying tickets and necessities gobbled up most of the money? That there was precious little left for starting up in Canada? That for Muddie and Da-Da, a barrelful of hope was all they had brought to their new life? Obviously not.

A settled life we had never had. How to begin to compare that precariousness with the settled lives of people we encounter in North America or Europe? What must it be like to take for granted a place for everything and everything in its place?

For us, every scrap of the surrounding chaos had to be weighed, judged and set into place before we could even begin to approach an elementary idea of order. Peace in Europe indeed, Roddy my love, and no peace at all beyond the line.

The next morning I went jogging and then decided to visit Kello before returning to my parents'. I was walking up the stairs to his room when I heard my father's voice: ". . . and it was all for Mona. You don't know the dreams, the hopes I had for Mona, she was so smart, such a bright bright child, so much spirit. And all I could see was if we didn't take sufficient care, she would run wild, she would turn into some slack woman, drinking in clubs, smoking cigarettes, and hugging up all kinda man. But it wasn't even that, it was the dress she was wearing that day, a slack kind of dress . . ." Da-Da's voice trailed off.

I froze on the stairway. What were they saying about me?

Then he continued more strongly. "Kello, I was a strict father. Perhaps too strict. But I never punish my children like on the estate, you understand? You don't know, boy. On the estate they use to beat children with rope, thick thick rope tied up in knots. They would make them kneel down on a grater or stand up in the hot sun holding up big big stones in their hand. And it wasn't only Indians on the estate—black people too would beat their children worse than that. And don't think we so stupid that we don't know what cause it. What cause it was slavery days when them bakra would find sport in thinking up all kinda punishment for the slaves. That is what cause it. I try never to ill-treat my children, Kello, I always try to be fair. But what I do to Mona I can't believe even now." His voice broke, but he recovered and went on. "I want to forget it, Kello, but I can't forget it. How I could do that to Mona?"

Abrupt silence. I was about to rush in when I heard another voice. A hard voice, unrecognizable to me, the voice of a judge. "Mona *and* Kello. You tried to kill me too, Da-Da. It was only because of Pappy that you didn't choke me to death that day. It was Pappy's stick that saved me. I couldn't breathe; you would have killed me. And you tried to kill Mona."

I remained where I stood. The hard voice went on: "I don't know why you wanted to kill me. But I can tell you that right now the reason is not important. And I understand some of it, your grief at Mama's death, the responsibility, the land. I want to forget. I want peace between us. But it's Mona I'm really worried about. She is drifting too much. Help her to tie herself down to something, any-thing. Ask Mona to forgive you, Da-Da. Tell her why it really hap-pened—you know why it happened. It wasn't about any old dress, it was about her black boyfriend. The red boy she was in love with. I wasn't at home but I heard. If I had been there . . ."

Kello began coughing. I wanted to go in then but found myself still standing on the stairs, eavesdropping. He pressed on, his voice flat. "You are a racist, Da-Da. You with all your high talk about equality for everybody. Ask her to forgive you. You did this to a girl who showed the kind of courage that our pissy little Presbyterian world wouldn't allow. Stinking prissy little hypocrites. Creeping and crawling, yes, ma'am, yes, sir, to the white racist missionary, the white man. You did that, you with all your scorn for the whole pack of hypocrites. You tried to kill Mona because she had a Creole boyfriend. Ask Mona to forgive you. You have to do it. The last thing I'm asking you for, you must do it, Da-Da."

I found myself in the room then, holding Kello, stroking his frag-ile hands, kissing his cheeks, this thin brown skin that would disap-pear soon, turned to dust, this bravery. When I looked at Da-Da, his face was ashen, a grey mass of flesh without shape or direction. I stretched out my arm and he moved closer to us, groping like a blind man. Kello nudged me hard. "Tell him you forgive him, Mona. Tell him. He needs those words."

My mind was whirling, a magic net full of desert creatures, danc-ing centipedes, blue and yellow snakes, huge cacti covered with needles, spinning round and round with me in the middle, held securely. Kello had said the unsayable. Da-Da had never directly punished me about Bree. The kneeling on gravel, the burning of the shift dress, all of it was about Bree, we both knew that, Da-Da and I, but we had remained locked in silent complicity. Kello had smashed open that locked box.

Out of nowhere that I knew, from underneath a mangrove

swamp, from the place of the poisonous manchineel, came a voice mouthing these artificial words: "I forgive you, Da-Da, I forgive you." The voice was breathless, high-pitched, and not mine at all.

After that, we stayed in the room for a while. Then Kello said abruptly that he wanted to sleep and we left, Da-Da leaning heavily on his cane as we walked out. There was a brightness to the April air, a yellow-white shimmer like that of daffodils and forsythia and poui trees. I held my father's arm. I said, the words spilling out with rapid fire, "Da-Da, you remember poui trees at home in the dry season? Lines of poui against the sky for miles and miles, especially up in the hills? Remember the day we drove through Moruga, through the forest to La Lune, how we sat on the beach and watched the hills behind us blazing with yellow poui trees? Remember, Da-Da?"

I clutched his hand and he squeezed mine in return. "Yes, Mona, I remember. That was real beauty. Nothing up here could touch it, nothing."

On the way home Da-Da remarked that Kello was looking weaker and I agreed. Kello was eating with difficulty now—ulcers had taken over his mouth and throat in spite of the drug cocktails—and he could only manage food like Jell-O and custards and, surprisingly, mangoes. He always had a mango, green or ripe, and a tiny paring knife on his bedside table, though I saw him wincing in pain one day as he tried to eat a sliver.

Then as I turned the car into my parents' street, Da-Da cleared his throat and began to talk, almost as if giving a speech. "Mona, Kello was telling the truth. I was frightened for you, I didn't know what would happen if you went with that Creole boy. And people were talking, the place was small, people would spot you with him and then tell me. I had to do something. But I was wrong to get on like that. I mean, I never even met the boy. But I couldn't bear the talk, the disgrace to the family. It was a racial attitude, I admit that.

That 'one nation' idea the new government was pushing was a direct attack on Indians. You remember how it was when we left home?"

I nodded and Da-Da continued. "Yet I believed, I always believed, that racial attitudes were wrong. You know how I used to mix with everybody."

He shook his head as if the whole situation was still a puzzle. "Up here, my life suddenly take a different turn. After the first or second week I realize that to the white man, to these people, black was black and everybody was in the same boat. I tried my best not to restrict Babs. But I didn't worry about Babs the way I worried about you. You were always so own-way, I thought it was so easy for you to get on the wrong track. And then what would happen to you? You know? I mean Trinidad then was a dog-eat-dog place—people used to say, 'What on de ground is dog own.' You couldn't see it then, maybe you still can't see it, but Mona, it was dangerous for you. Plenty women just went to the dogs. That was my real fear. I used to see it happening in front my eyes day after day."

Da-Da's words terrified me. All my fears about drunkenness and cussing and beatings and brushing cutlasses wielded by overpoweringly strong men rushed over me. And Da-Da was one of them.

"Mona." I had stopped the car in the driveway now, and Da-Da grasped both my hands, turning me to look directly at him. "What happen happen. I feel a lot of shame for making a big girl like you kneel down and walk across the yard, cutting up your knees on the gravel. I mean, is hard even now to believe I could do a thing like that. If I could turn back the clock, so help my living God I would turn it back. Mona, I am so sorry, you have to believe me, you have to believe how sorry I feel. I can't change what happened then, but we must cross that bridge. For Kello's sake, but for our sake too. For your sake, Mona."

Da-Da paused. He let go of my hands and looked outside the car.

He was waiting for something. As he silently shook his bent head, I saw tears falling on his hands. Poor, poor Da-Da, I thought. Poor Mona.

I hugged him and closed my eyes. At Kello's bedside he had heard my artificial words. I was sure that he was waiting for me to really forgive him, to make the words real. But no words could get past my closed-up throat and after a few minutes he touched me gently. "Let's go in, Mona. It's getting chilly out here."

FIFTEEN

As Kello had predicted, his illness did not last long. He died of a pneumonia that could not be brought under control, just three months and eighteen days after he had collapsed in his apartment. It was late at night and Babs had just left. Matthew was with him and they must have said their farewells because when we arrived Kello was alone, his face uncovered on the small bed. I embraced him, kissed his cheeks, his eyelids, feeling him still there in his body, which remained warm. Muddie lay beside him on the bed, put her head on his shoulder, and wept like a little girl. When Babs arrived, Muddie stood and led us in prayer. Then she recited her favourite psalm and we accompanied her: "God is our refuge and strength, a very present help in trouble. Therefore will not we fear, though the earth be removed."

We said our own words spontaneously, each of us needing to say something to Kello's spirit, still hovering in the room. Babsie said the Lord's Prayer. Da-Da's words were formal, almost an address: "Father, I am laying down my son before I myself am called to rest. To bury a child is a bitter thing. I never thought it would be like this. Lord, take him into your bosom, salute his courage in the face of life, salute his strength to dream, to follow his dreams to the end, to create a life for himself, for all of us. Thank you for his life, Lord. My own fatherhood might have often been at fault, but Kelvin's filial duty and loyalty never were. Receive him, O Lord, and may he continue his journey secure in the knowledge that he walked his road on earth well. Amen."

It was my turn. I stood at the foot of the bed. My brother's feet stuck out from the bedclothes. I held those strongly moulded feet in my hands and rubbed them; they were cold. "Dearest Kello, we love you, we stand by you, we stand together forever. May your journey out be safe, may your feet be warm and dry as you walk from this place to another, may the stones on the road be not sharp enough to cut you. Kell, we love you, we miss you already, may you find shelter from the wind and storm, may you find your home. In our journey we will always remember you. In yours please remember us. We love you."

We held hands around the bed and joined our lives together, as imperilled as any small family could possibly feel. Kello was gone. My brother was dead, my love, my second self, the bravest of us rushing headlong to meet an indifferent world, my brother without whom I was left uncovered in a place where nothing could be the same again.

I called Roddy when we got home but heard only the drone of his answering machine. Phone calls were made to the other members of the family, scattered in different places. Babs and I poured a shot of Scotch on the kitchen floor for the spirit and then had our own dose of spirits, giggling helplessly at the silliness of the pun. I had bonded more with Babs in this period than we ever had in our lives, and I was truly humbled by my new awareness of her. A butterfly in a house of sex and indulgence had been my arrogant take on her life, and now my own simple-mindedness and conceit shamed me. Her life was fuller by far than my own, a fact that showed in the friends we called to share the news. I talked to Carene, who said she would come the next afternoon. Roddy I hadn't yet made contact with while Babsie was going through her phone book, making up a list for the next morning.

By the time Roddy returned my call, the bottle of Scotch was low and Babsie and I were deep in our own private wake. We were talking and laughing and crying, remembering Kello. I told Roddy the news. He was flying to London in a day but asked if I needed him to come. He sounded brusque, businesslike.

"It's an important interview with a Middle Eastern hotshot. I've spent a while setting this meeting up. But I'll come if you want me to, though I must say that funerals are not my thing."

"Not your thing?" I heard the ugly rasp in my voice but could not stop it. "What's your thing then? People die and they have to be buried. Why does it have to be anybody's thing? Is every fucking thing a matter of choice?"

Babs, hearing my sodden tones, rushed over to me in alarm. She grabbed the phone from my hand, but Roddy had already hung up.

He called again the next morning, but by then I was in command of the situation. I urged him to go to his interview and not to worry about the funeral.

"You'll be missed," I said, "but everyone will understand, I'm sure. You can't help it, can you?"

Even then I hoped that he would drop everything and fly to me, hold me close, and take away some of the chilling emptiness, but I knew he would not. I couldn't bring myself to tell him how much I needed him and now it was probably too late.

Muddie filled the funeral chapel with wild bush for her son. She bought all that she could find in the shops at the end of a Toronto winter. There were climbing orchids, white with purple centres, red and white anthurium lilies that Bess had brought from Trinidad, and heliconia, standing stiffly, like sentries. Spring was late that year but the funeral day blazed with sunlight and I was glad as well for the hymns from an older time. They took me back to childhood, when my brothers and I would swing our legs over church pews in the old Savana Grande church, its bells tolling. *Time like an ever-rolling stream / Bears all its sons away / They fly forgotten as a dream / Dies at the break of day.*

Johnnie and his wife Caitlin, a quiet, earnest woman who wore her red hair in a French braid cascading down her back, came from Vancouver. He was greying at the temples and had the dignified exterior of a man who was set in his ways. He kept his reserve intact throughout his visit, but Muddie took comfort in his presence. Sometimes they sat together for long periods, he with his newspaper and she with her crossword puzzles, saying little to each other. Uncle Tristram, as he had warned us, could not make it. The extended family was together again briefly: Bella from Orlando, Auntie Vannie and Jenny from Texas. Aunt Alice was now too frail to accompany Bella. Sonia, caught in messy divorce proceedings, was on the phone every day from England. Esau, now a self-made man of means, remained deathly afraid of flying and would not make the trip. Muddie wept as she talked to him on the telephone, and I knew that at the other end Esau was crying too. And Bess was an angel, overseeing flowers and arrangements at the church, the reception, refreshments, cards. It was Da-Da who chose the hymns, and when we sang "Shall We Gather at the River" as we had done at Mama's funeral, he couldn't go on, and Babs and I had to support him.

Muddie had insisted on banning alcohol from the wake. She was convinced that the big row would never have happened after Mama's death if liquor had not contaminated the events, and for once Da-Da could summon no argument to counter that opinion. I understood Muddie's position but couldn't bear the thought of sobriety and hymn singing and Canadian Mission piety as the centre of Kello's send-off. My madvex impulses got the better of me. I could not, I ranted to Babsie, I would not let Kello go without a real old-time send-off—rum, cheese and biscuits, black coffee, card playing, and ole talk. A real Baron Samedi send-off. I had not been to a Trini wake for years, but then I lived in Montreal. In Toronto these wakes were more common. Babs was distraught.

She dreaded a family bust-up at the funeral, and she knew that Muddie and I were equally matched in stubbornness. Without further discussion she enlisted Auntie Vannie and the cousins and they worked on Muddie together while we were making piles of cheese sandwiches in the kitchen. It was Bella's cuatro, though, that finally persuaded Muddie.

Everyone chattered on about Grandma Lil and family gatherings in Iere Village as the refreshments for the evening piled up around us. Bella confessed how much she missed all of us. Orlando was often lonely, and even though Florida had a lot of Caribbean people, they were mostly Cuban. "Is sad that we only get together for occasions like this. We should visit more often."

Muddie agreed and Bella continued her wheedling. "Auntie Myrts, you know how lively Kello always was. You don't think he would like a little lime with friends and family to send him off? I mean a real all-night wake, with the prayers and hymn singing, of course, but after that, bottle and spoon, a cuatro maybe, some ole time kaiso, and maybe a little something to wash it down? Something light, you know?"

Muddie had no defence. She smiled for the first time in days. As a child, Bella was the calypsonian among us and could play the cuatro. She and Uncle Tristy—The Buccaneers—would team up and entertain us at Grandma Lil's family gatherings while Uncle Sweetie played bottle and spoon in the background.

"You bring your cuatro?"

Bella nodded.

Once Muddie relented, Auntie Vannie swept in and directed the action. The garage was converted into an outdoor room, cars put out on the street, tables set up for cards and drinks. The Canadian minister from my parents' church conducted the wake service, and after politely sampling the refreshments he looked around with interest at the second phase of activity. One of the elders in the church mentioned this to Da-Da afterwards but none of us thought of inviting him to stay. The West Indian crowd—some of Babs's Caribana friends, church members, some of Da-Da's friends, old-timers I had last seen in Trinidad a hundred years ago—stayed until the early hours of the morning. Singing broke out when Bella began to strum her cuatro, and the sweetness of the moment was almost too much for me. The rum had gone to my head and I joined in:

> It was de night Mozambo dead
> it had a wake in San Fernando
> the people outside was drinking rum
> and the people inside was having fun
> and de dead man get up and start to walk about
> Sans Humanité.

I leaned over and whispered to Babsie that we should invite Matthew over. I was drunk enough to ignore her hard look and continued arguing about how it would do him good seeing so many people celebrating Mozambo Kello's life and how our kind of burial is the most civilized in the world.

"His place is here," I insisted, "here with us, not in some dingy room by himself. This is Kello's farewell."

"Shut up, Mona," she hissed at me. "Leave it alone. It's done."

Bess, sensing trouble, came over and suggested that we take some air because she wanted to smoke. I walked out with her, stood against the stand of pine trees facing the house, and wept. Carene joined us outside and stood close, rubbing my back and murmuring soothing words. A great weight of sadness threatened to press me into the ground.

But I was calm the next morning, calm as I dressed and walked downstairs, joining the others for coffee before we left for the funeral chapel. Johnnie and Caitlin both wore houndstooth jackets and plain trousers. The rest of us were dressed in solid black, Muddie sombre, Da-Da elegant in his well-cut suit.

"But you and Babs," Bess said admiringly, "you look stunning. Kello would be pleased."

It was important to send him off well, and Babs and I had shopped for our dresses together at an off-season sale earlier in the year. At the time we had taken a ghoulish delight in buying these vampire dresses, but our choices had paid off. In the pictures afterwards we all stood together like a handsome flock of corbeaux, Da-Da standing slightly off to the side, like the King Cobo that he was.

In the end Kello was right; I could see that clearly. His departure was as it should have been, his death from lymphoma, a galloping form of it, the only possibility. Matthew brought a spray of three brilliant tropicals—birds of paradise—that Bess took wordlessly and placed in the coffin before it was sealed. He sat inconspicuously in the congregation; Kello's wife Irene sat with us at the front, Joey and Linda at her side. Two funerals were simultaneously in progress—the public one, and the private one that was between Matthew, Babs, Bess, and me.

SIXTEEN

I hung around after the funeral. Roddy was still in England and, in any case, we had not managed to bridge the rift created by my attack on him after Kello's death. All of the leftover activity of family talk and relatives lingering for the next few days, the hashing and rehashing of events—Muddie could hardly bear it. But I loved being in the kind of old-time family setting we used to have in Trinidad when the world was new and so much more spacious. Auntie Vannie boasted about Jenny's career as a travel agent specializing in cruises and about all the trips her daughter had won because of her glibness at sales talk. "Takes after her father," Auntie Vannie confided, making a wry face. The gossip about Esau was that he had even shredded his passport, just to be absolutely sure that he stayed grounded. Bess left two days after the funeral with the understanding that we would see each other soon. The land was my charge; everyone now took that for granted.

I settled into a hostess role that was curiously like play-acting. It filled up my days and held at bay the anxiety that had gripped me throughout the previous months every time I imagined Kello dead. I received the stream of friends and well-wishers, offering them tea and snacks, accepting their condolences graciously, and listened to them chatting with Da-Da about home, the politics then and now, and, inevitably, the questions about whether leaving had been the best decision for them. I got tired of the sameness of their conversations. Prevarication was their nature, and few were as outspoken as Da-Da. But I grew interested in their language and how the years in Canada had made little impact on the West Indianness of their speech. The odd time that I heard any of them in a conversation with white Canadians, the register seemed to shift into a stilted classroom English with which the speaker was distinctly uncomfortable. Not Da-Da, however, who could skip faultlessly from Creole to the Queen's English without a beat.

Da-Da and Babs were both glad that I had decided to stay because a few days after the funeral Muddie contracted a viral infection. My father took practical steps to cope with the situation; he handled the shopping and most of the cooking too. But he had always been first in Muddie's life and seemed unprepared for being shut out. Grief wore her down, wore him down, and even in the days after her symptoms abated she would hardly leave her room, sitting in one spot for hours, quietly knitting and humming to herself. There seemed to be a vacancy inside her that no ordinary distraction could dispel.

Late one evening I was setting a tray down with the tea and biscuits she had every night when one of her low tunes caught my ear. I began to sing it: "Begone dull care, I prithee begone from me / Begone dull care, thyself and I will never agree." Muddie joined me then, her voice as tremulous as water lapping over tiny pebbles in a pond, breaking and catching again, as we sang one of the songs that Grandpa Jamesie had taught his children and later his grandchildren. Other songs followed, all drawn from the British Isles: "Oh the days of the Kerry dancing" and "Flow gently sweet Afton." Muddie's voice was light and sweet as she sang these refrains that had haunted her childhood in the Caribbean. I touched her hand and she held on to mine, stroking it gently.

After she fell asleep, I lingered in her darkened room, relieved at the sound of her regular breathing and thinking of how her even, ordered spirit had presided over our lives' disorder—mine, Da-Da's, and Babsie's. Kello had inherited her capacity for balancing the load while Johnnie had retreated into a space as placid as the pond at Usine Ste. Madeleine, its surface oblivious to the squalor and grief of its surroundings. Muddie's practical streak ensured that she was never at a loss for a solution. In all our lives she had smoothed over the rough patches, lifted us out of the mud, had plotted and planned for our escape from God only knows what forces. To see her lying in bed, sick with grief, helpless, had filled me with a quivering sense of dread. Now I felt a great weight being lifted. My mother, Kello's Muddie, she whom I have never known the way he did, as simply and directly.

When Muddie and Da-Da jettisoned everything they had built in Trinidad and set out on that journey to Canada, this was not the way they thought our lives would turn out. The day we left Trinidad we took a family photo in the newly constructed waving gallery at Piarco Airport. The photograph hangs on Babs's bedroom wall, handsomely encased in antique copper. Muddie, Babs, and I look like sisters, Da-Da is smiling in a reserved sort of way, his apprehension only just hidden underneath, Johnnie looks wide-eyed and frightened. Kello has already left. Our fragile hopes are captured in that snapshot. But it is Muddie's face that anchors the frame—eyes unflinching, she stares ahead into the unknown.

Muddie never wooed and won my love as she did with Kello. She didn't have to; she simply fashioned me with her hands and sent me out into the world. Escape was my goal; the means, her eloquent gift to me. And daily I witness how deeply my mother's signature is written on my life. She signs herself in my walks through roads without end, through lengths of time longer than twine, in the click of a pot spoon, in the winding and knotting of silver threads around a too-fast bobbin, in the creation of a whole meal, a dress, a life, out of scraps of nothing.

* * *

It was the month of May. Muddie and I took pleasure in watching tiny crocuses and irises poke their heads out in her front garden. One day we received a call from someone who introduced himself as Horatio, Uncle Baddall's son. He was passing through and wanted to visit. I was startled, having heard about this cousin only once or twice over the years, but Da-Da and Muddie took Horatio's desire to pay his respects in stride, inviting him for a meal the following evening.

He had received the news about Kello from Uncle Tristram, with whom he maintained a surprising contact. More surprising was the news that Baddall had also kept in touch with Uncle Tristy. But then, as Da-Da remarked wryly to Muddie, Tristram was always a master of indecision. For Uncle Tristram to cut off Baddall, he would have had to declare in favour of Aunt Vannie, and "for your brother Tristram, making that choice would be impossible." They had laughed heartily together, while the prospect of meeting Horatio unsettled me. I considered going out for the evening, but as Babs was working late, I stayed to help.

The mismatched meal Muddie planned suggested that my mother was also ambivalent about inviting this person with the unlikely name of Horatio. She prepared French Canadian pea soup and a pork tourtière, jerk chicken, a real Trini pelau, avocados, and plantains. When I was checking the rice, I absent-mindedly caused the congo pepper to burst in the pot of pelau, intensifying the deep musky flavour but also the heat. Muddie was distressed.

"I don't know what you was thinking," she snapped. "Since when we start cooking with pepper, eh? You know I always put pepper sauce on the side."

"But Muddie, they have chilies in every cuisine these days. Surely Horatio is not as delicate as all that." I tried to make light of my mistake but she kept steupsing and sighing.

"I don't know." She shook her head, upset at how her dinner was turning out.

"Remember how when we first came, every Trini would have a story about some Canadian friend and pepper sauce? Remember the time Da-Da's friend came for dinner and insisted on eating a whole teaspoon of lime pepper sauce? I thought he was going to die of apoplexy or something, his face turned so red and he was choking and coughing . . ."

She laughed at the memory, but continued her vain attempt at picking out the offending bits of yellow pepper.

Horatio arrived punctually, armed with a convenience store clutch of flowers. He sported a preppy look, open-necked checkered shirt, slightly baggy pants, neatly pleated, incongruously small, slim shoes. A dapper little man, I thought, observing his narrow shoulders, his skinny frame, the clothes well-chosen to enhance his smallness.

He settled easily into the living room and into calling my parents Uncle Mac and Aunt Myrtle. He kissed my hand gallantly and complimented Muddie on her decor, her furniture and plants. He was especially taken with the small heap of calabash gourds—plain, carved, and varied in shape—that she had collected over the years. And he did suffer visibly through the pelau, sweating and drinking so much water that Muddie finally said, "Here, take a clean plate, Horatio. Forget about the rice and just eat what you feel comfortable with."

All the same, he let us know how much he was enjoying the meal, the first home-cooked one he had had in months. I felt sure that his effusive, customer-oriented manner, so like his father's, had come from training in public relations work. I could see Da-Da and Muddie exchanging sceptical glances when they thought no one was looking. They were underestimating him, I thought, because Horatio missed nothing.

He said the right words about Kello and regretted not having had the opportunity to meet him. And he talked without reserve about his father, Ralph (Baddall to you folks, right?), and the circumstances of his death the previous year. He said that Ralph had all of our family's names and addresses stored in a binder marked Family, so it was easy to send out the death notices. Wow, I thought, such organization. But the very opposite was the case.

"You know, Uncle Mac, my father was dead for nearly two weeks before anyone knew about it. Not even the mail piled up in the lobby, not even his welfare cheque lying there, alerted the other roomers. It was the smell that finally did it, but when the police broke the door down, they couldn't find him. The room was a complete mess. Clothes and books and old newspapers everywhere. Ralph had fallen back half-sitting in a busted-up armchair, off to one side. Maybe he was trying to get up. The chair was behind an overflowing shelf of books, with notebooks and folders scattered on the floor."

Horatio was eager to talk about family connections as well. His mother was French Canadian, and she and Uncle Baddall had never married. Their contact had been a short and intense one; it became sporadic over the years as his support of the boy grew less and less, eventually stopping altogether. He spoke without bitterness. His mother Catherine lived in a little house in Quebec, in Ste. Anne de Bellevue, and was quite okay, he said. Now in his late twenties, he wished to find out more about his family. He was astonishingly brown-skinned, I thought, darker-skinned than I was in spite of his French mother.

"The funeral," he was saying now, "was put together in a day by some West Indian friends. They pooled the money for burial."

He had contributed nothing and displayed no trace of embarrassment in telling us. He had appeared at the funeral, shaking everyone's hand and thanking people for their kindness to his late father. He heard one of the wives whispering about the "pick-up side" that had come together to bury Baddall, a fact he now related without rancour. He stood aside politely while the pick-up side searched the pews, trying to replace two pallbearers who had not shown up. He did not offer himself as a replacement and no one asked. I could see that Da-Da's opinion of Horatio was going through some revision, and that my father was now appraising him with something bordering on respect.

Da-Da spoke then about Uncle Baddall's style, his good looks and his way with women. He spared no detail, telling Horatio about his father's marriage to Auntie Vannie and his desertion of the family when their daughter Jenny was only eight years old.

"When Baddall decided to migrate to Canada," Da-Da continued, "he warned everybody that Indians would eat grass in Trinidad, that everything was going to the dogs, and he promised to open the way for the whole family to follow. Instead, he just disappeared completely, you hear me? Completely. He stopped writing to Evangeline, and eventually she had to believe that when he left, he left for good."

We expected that Horatio would be eager to find out about his sister Jenny, but he gave away nothing, waiting for more. By now Da-Da had changed to his main subject these days, his early days in Canada and how hard it was for him to make the decision to leave Trinidad. His was a completely Trinidad story and I wondered how much Horatio, listening attentively, understood of it.

"Listen to me, Horatio. Back then it was like spinning top in mud. Every day you seeing yourself getting pass over for promotion, for housing, for government loans, everything. You had to wake up and see that it wasn't Indian time. And I decide there and then that I wasn't going to stay and kiss nobody arse. And my children wouldn't stay and do it either. Not as long as I name man."

The old fire and brimstone Da-Da. He did not kiss arses in Canada either, I thought. And here the kiss demanded was a more thorough one. The land of missionaries and snow and Wabun the wolf dog had fangs, deep and sudden.

"Once," he continued to Horatio, "when I was selling insurance, I was all over the country—Montreal, even Nova Scotia and New-foundland. Once I was walking with my briefcase in Old Montreal, you know it, right? Not like it is now, so touristy. Then it was still full of pawnshop and tavern and bruck-down buildings. Just so a man standing in the doorway of a tavern crook his finger at me. I point to my briefcase and the man nod a few times. For emphasis, you know what I mean?"

Horatio's eager eyes had never left Da-Da's face, and now he nodded assent.

"I say to mihself, 'What! Dey does buy insurance right off the street so?' But I went—after all, a sale is a sale. I follow that man inside the tavern, through a long corridor into what look like a dark hallway at the end of it. Then we start to climb up some stairs. Halfway up the stairs the man turn and look directly at me. And so help my living God, I never see a face, before or since then, so full of naked cunning and slyness. I stop walking on the spot. The man was wearing shades covering a whole half of his face and even then the slyness couldn't hide.

"I tell you, all them words like cement shoes, hitman, Mafia, kneecapping, all them words start tumbling down the stairs and hitting me left, right, and centre. Something just turn me around and I start walking brisk brisk back down them stairs and all the way to the end of that long long corridor with my back to the man. Fright? When I tell yuh, fright! But I couldn't do nothing else, I had to get out.

"I reach the corner sweating and is only then I realize that the man didn't even bother to follow me. Well, sales trip finish long time! I get in my car and drive all the way to Toronto. And you know, Horatio, is only when I reach home and start talking to your aunt here"——he pointed his chin towards Muddie——"that I figure the whole thing out. The man motion me over and I gone. I show him the briefcase and he nod. I think they had a new hitman in town or something. A darkish Sicilian type maybe, and he thought it was me. And I like a fool following the man up the stairs to God knows where or what. I don't know nah, boy." He shook his head. "This place full of surprises."

The laughter at Da-Da's story thawed us out. Horatio had a businesslike air about him that contrasted with his ready enjoyment of our company and his easy laugh. In a way he was the best of Baddall, I thought.

He told us that he was preparing for a trip to Trinidad and wanted to find tombstones, family sites, any kind of history that he could. He had all of Baddall's papers retrieved from his room, but none of them made much sense, not even the fifteen notebooks covered with spidery writing. Ralph wrote weird stuff about reincarnation and karma and Indian philosophy, Horatio told us. He also asked us about when the family had converted to Christianity, and other, absurd questions about whether there were buses and cars where we came from. "My father often spoke of the family land near a place called Jerningham Junction. A town like an extended bazaar, with a train station. Do you know it?"

"Jerningham Junction," Muddie exclaimed with enthusiasm, and I rose at once and went into the kitchen to check the pelau. I knew she was about to launch into the apocryphal tale of how we rode the last train from San Fernando to Jerningham Junction and back. When I returned, Horatio was talking again about his father's inheritance.

"You see, I don't have all the clues yet, but I know I'm on to something big. I feel it in my bones, Uncle Mac. And I was hoping you could help me. I have the facts, all the facts about our origins from ancient times." He leaned forward now, his eyes bright and demanding. His idea of *ancient* was amazing. Centuries, decades, his father's lifetime, all tumbled together into the story he related to us.

"My father Ralph descended from a line of Rajput princes who had moved their whole dynasty to the West Indies in the nineteenth century to escape the British Raj. Then a black African government came into power in Trinidad suddenly. No one was expecting it. Overnight my father had to pack up and leave because government officials threatened to confiscate the Rajput fortune. The family scattered in all directions and lost touch with one another. But before they left, wily members of the clan used their wits once more. Now all that fabulous wealth—gold jewellery, nuggets, diamonds, precious stones—lies buried in the hills of Whiteland. Have you heard of the place called Whiteland, Uncle Mac? What's it like? I want to travel there soon. I expect that I'll need a guide and a donkey too, I think. Do you know of any?" He turned eagerly to Da-Da, who was glancing quizzically at him.

"Which one, the guide or the donkey?" Da-Da's deadpan reply caught us off guard for a second before Muddie and I broke into laughter. Horatio smiled but was back on track in an instant.

"It only sounds far-fetched because we live in the middle of a modern city. But buried treasure is a fact of life in the Third World. Buccaneers, sunken galleons, the looting on the Spanish Main, the plunder of India by the British Empire—all that raw wealth is not locked up in banks. Some people were smarter than that. I believe that my father's family treasure lies intact in Whiteland."

My father's narrowed eyes registered puzzlement. I too felt puzzled. *Wily members of the clan used their wits once more.* Which family? Weren't we discussing our family? Uncle Baddall's one brother, whom he hardly ever visited while he lived in Trinidad, was a simple market gardener living in the heart of Piparo. "Wily" would not describe his personality. But in the geography itself there was a hard kernel of truth; Piparo and Whiteland were neighbouring villages, both nestled within the low-slung Central Range of Trinidad.

Da-Da's tone was measured and thoughtful when he replied. "Whiteland? You mean Whiteland, near Mayo, just on the east of Talparo?" He paused, considering. "I know Whiteland, yes."

I knew Whiteland too. You passed through it in a flash driving on the new highway that jackknifed through the low Central Range. The stretch called Whiteland was a lovely shadowed piece of road, bordered by cocoa trees. Its real treasure was that cocoa: jewels of golden and ruby pods hanging suspended along the roadside as you sped by. You could hardly say the name Whiteland before you had already passed it and had reached Mayo or Flanagin Town or even Gran Couva itself.

For a few moments an uncomfortable silence filled the dining room. Then Da-Da broke it up by saying reassuringly, "Horatio, listen to me. You must consult a map before you go, you hear? Buy a map of Trinidad and you just study that. Get a good idea of the extent of the island. Then I will send you to a feller I know in Gran Couva. His name is Louis Cardinez and he is one man who really know that bush. He will take you anywhere you want to go. You say Baddall leave a little map of the place? Well, if anybody could find that site, is Cardinez. You just have to tell him that is I who send you. He will carry you to Whiteland and you could do the rest yourself."

I noticed Da-Da exchanging further glances with Muddie. Her face was still; only a quivering at the corners of her lips betrayed a suppressed smile. It must have been the grandeur of Horatio's picture that confounded us all. He wanted ancestral sites, buried treasure, a kingdom, while the whole acreage of the island of Trinidad was just over two thousand square miles. What could the shapely map of Trinidad tell him about a story without a beginning, a middle, and an end? Muddie bit her lip, but in the end the strain was too much. Without warning she collapsed into helpless laughter, and in spite of myself I too began to giggle. Within seconds, though, I composed myself and turned quickly to Horatio to explain, but his hurt expression stopped me. Instead, I got up abruptly and began to clear the table. Just then we heard sounds in the hallway and Babs walked in, to my great relief.

The evening turned lighter after that. Babs was her usual flirtatious self and she charmed Horatio absolutely. Muddie apologized to him, explaining that she hadn't been laughing at anything he had said, really. It was just that Trinidad was a small place, and buried treasure was not something she associated with the island. Besides, it was her general state of mind, nothing to do with him. He nodded; he too had recovered, but he declined the dessert she offered. He had to leave because he had an early start the next day.

Babs and I walked down the street to the bus stop with him, chatting about nothing. He never took cabs, he said. Why should he when public transportation was so efficient? He took out his bus tickets with care and tore one off neatly, resting it between his teeth while he tucked the unused strip away in his wallet. I noticed his nice even teeth. When the bus arrived, he kissed Babs and turned to me. He kissed me on the face and then, in an unexpected gesture of tenderness, laid his smooth brown cheek against mine, lingering there for a few seconds. Then, saying goodbye in a too cheerful voice, he climbed into the bus and waved as it drove off.

Babs was full of curiosity about the evening, Muddie's odd laughing fit, the tension in the air. I explained the awkwardness of the situation she had walked in upon and she laughed as well. But then she shook her head sadly. "Poor guy, poor poor guy. Whiteland and buried Rajput treasure. It's all he has, Mona. What did Uncle Baddall leave him but this idea of a royal past in some place called the Third World? In a way I understand his obsession fully because I too feel a sense of not being grounded anywhere. I can't remember a time when I belonged some place, when I was not an outsider. You're grounded, Mona—you and Kello came from somewhere, but I had to start from scratch like Horatio. Imagine growing up in a French city with his dark skin." Babs shuddered as she thought of it.

I understood, but nothing about Baddall—neither his death nor his offspring—provoked my sympathy. His life had come to a fitting conclusion, I thought. I turned to Babs and said calmly, "I hated Baddall. I still hate him."

"God, Mona, I had no idea. Why on earth?"

"He walked out on Auntie Vannie and stole all her jewellery. He attacked Muddie once but she fended him off."

Babs was staring at me, wide-eyed. "This same Baddall, Ralph?"

I nodded. "Oh." Babs was at a loss for words. Her expression was questioning, but we walked back to the house in silence. I was thinking of the softness of Horatio's cheek against mine, of the longing in his eyes as he left us.

SEVENTEEN

 I lay in bed for a long time afterwards, thinking about the ever-unfolding map of our lives. About Uncle Baddall's tortured life, his elegant brown fingers, his hands always reaching out for something forbidden. The theft of the jewellery meant that he could never return to Vannie; he must have decided upon a final severance from the whole winding, untidy family that had enmeshed him. A severance too from Catherine, Horatio's mother, and from the Canadian home they offered. Yet why did he keep a binder marked Family with all our names and addresses? What was he trying to write in those fifteen notebooks with their tight, spidery writing?

Jerningham Junction. Horatio had asked about it. The name intrigued him and he wanted to know more.

The last train journey before the railway closed for good was to be a historic one, and the whole of Trinidad wanted to be on the last train. Muddie had looked forward to the event for weeks, but we were struggling through our hard times in La Plata and there was no possibility of making the trip. Listening to her voice rising and falling lightly in the dining room had given me a pang, and I realized that missing the last train must have been another of her deep disappointments with Da-Da, the man she had stood by defiantly. Over the years, however, she had imagined the trip so often that her dream had hardened into reality. She talked of the journey as if we had taken it.

When Muddie first told this tale at Christmas a few years ago, I was adamant that we had never made that trip, citing my own memory as proof. But Kello sided with Muddie and tried to shore her up by denying other events that I and no one else remembered. "You making it up," he jeered mockingly. "You can't fool me. You go all over the place and do research on Trini stuff, and then you say you remember. But you can't fool me, you little scamp, you!" His whole face broke into that old laughter, teasing and cajoling, until I understood that he was goading me into indulging Muddie.

"The fact is," Muddie had told Horatio, "when the railway was being scrapped, the children were taken on a train ride through the country. We were living in La Plata already, so we took a taxi into San Fernando, met the train at the wharf, and took it all the way around the island, stopping at Jerningham Junction, and then back home again." The route would have been to Rio Claro, through Tabaquite, then to Jerningham Junction; proceeding north-northwest, it would have stopped at Curepe, twisted around, and then turned southwards to San Fernando. I knew that the journey would have taken a full day.

"On the way back," she continued serenely, "everybody broke into the old-time calypso—*Las train to San Fernando / Las train to San Fernando / And if yuh miss dîs one / yuh'll never ketch anudder one . . . Is de las' train to San Fernando . . .*"

Muddie's story was a giveaway because it lacked details. When pressed, she simply retreated without a fuss. My questions used to be ruthless: Was it a fine day? Did we pack a picnic lunch? In a basket? What basket? We never owned a market basket—where would we have found a picnic basket? But we might have had tins of sandwiches. For school excursions my mother would make wonderful beef sandwiches, the beef stewed, then ground finely in an old hand-turned mill and mixed into a spread with mustard. A fabulous beef sandwich. And she would make a chequered cake with an orange-flavoured icing; when cut, the slices would actually form a checkerboard pattern. If we had made that trip, we would have packed those two excursion staples and would have bought drinks on the way.

I would have sat on a window seat, staring out at the cane fields whizzing past, at the rolling hills of central Trinidad, then the excitement of Jerningham Junction——the intersection of North and South. On the platform, women with baskets and trays would sell sugar cakes, sweet and salt paimie, pone and sweetbread, and several varieties of Indian delicacies: phoulouries, saheenas and bara and channa with chutney and achar on the side. What would we have bought at Jerningham Junction during the long stopover? Would we have gone outside and stretched our legs, explored the surroundings, and managed to get back to the train just in time?

Here the Indian, rural South collided with the urban North. Bright orange and gold saris, shimmering orhnis, women walking barefoot or in flimsy chappals but with thick silver churias and bera on arms and ankles, men in dhotis and turbans; and laughing African women in brightly patterned skirts and madras head ties, Creole men in careless shirts and pants, cigarettes dangling from their lips.

That night I drifted off to sleep but sat up twice in panic, feeling my foot slipping off some steps and my body beginning to fall steadily downwards. I awoke a third time later, shaking and whimpering. I was covered in sweat, terrified. I sat up in bed and switched on the lamp. The dream had receded, but it began to return in a rush and I became aware of its nauseating familiarity.

I was running through the dark, through thick forests with trees so tall I couldn't even see their tops, running, running . . . while a terrible danger pursued me. The dream began with a family gathering in a wide windswept house with cavernous windows cut into the walls from floor to ceiling. The table was laid as for a New Year's Day feast, and everyone was there, talking and laughing in groups. I saw Horatio as well. Then something suddenly changed. In no time I was running for my life, running powerfully through a forest stripped of underbrush and weeds. I ran unhindered along the even, clear ground, and my legs would stretch sometimes until the trees and I were almost the same height. I felt no fear, no hesitation, only motion, smooth and free. Then I left the forest abruptly, rushing out into a busy junction filled with people—many, many people going about their business. It was their cry that struck terror into my heart: "Oh God, is a lil child!"

I sat in bed, not moving until my heart stopped pounding through my chest, listening, but the house was silent as a house of the dead. I had not had this bad dream for years. It had begun the year I started at La Pastora, and I remember how glad I had always been to hear Babs's light snore regulating the darkness, to see the few cracks of light from outside illuminating our bedroom's familiar contours. After a few minutes I would fall asleep again and forget about the dream until the next time.

It was Horatio's visit that had brought that terrifying dream back, I was certain. His visit had reminded me about Ralph, Uncle Baddall, the coward, the loser who had died like that unfortunate bird, the semp, both feet stuck in the air.

It was during the August holidays, and Uncle Baddall had picked me up at the end of my holiday with Sonia at Auntie Alice's house.

". . . and it was here, at Jerningham Junction, that the rural South met the urban North." His voice droned on while his hand found its way past the thin cotton of my panties, pushing my legs apart in a practised movement. "The urban North," he said, recently back from attending a university in Canada, and wearing his sophistication carelessly, handsomely. He and my aunt had just married.

"Don't you wear any panties?"

"Yes!" I answered indignantly, not wanting to be thought stupid and backward.

"They must be very shor-r-r-t then," he said in a drawling kind of American accent.

"No, they no-t-t-t," I responded quickly, in imitation.

His skin was dark mahogany, his hair fell over his forehead like Elvis's, he looked like a boy sometimes, yet he was confident, like a man. Sonia and I never grew tired of talking about Baddall and Vannie. They were the most romantic couple we had ever seen, Uncle Baddall with his dark, flashy good looks and Auntie Vannie with her girlish prettiness.

The car sped through the night, the forest encroached upon the road, but there was no train station anywhere in sight, nothing but the darkness, his hand, and his Hollywood voice describing the urban North clashing with the rural South.

They say that memory protects us by burying terrible events, yet I remembered it vividly and without fear. I remembered it all. I had felt no sense of danger that night, but I had known something was wrong, something I could not stop, a secret part of life revealing itself while I sat there helpless, acquiescent, unwilling. I was eight years old, going to spend some of my holidays with Uncle Baddall and Auntie Vannie, being driven in his car late at night.

We reached their house. The time in between had vanished—the forest, the dark night, everything had vanished into Jerningham Junction.

Auntie Vannie opened the door for us and stood for a moment framed in the high arched doorway, beautiful, soft, welcoming, waiting for us dressed in a soft rose-coloured housecoat. She had made peanut butter cookies. The whole house was full of the smell, warm and sweet. The house was brightly lit; the room they gave me was over the steps facing the northern mountain range so that I could stare for hours in perfect safety at the darkness outside. Auntie Vannie was just beginning to show signs of pregnancy. She was radiant, a newlywed, in love.

I lived inside the glass panels of their large bookcase for the week that I spent with them. I read all about what Katy did, Paul Revere's famous ride, and American Indians in a story called "Wabun the Wolf-Dog" from a Canadian compendium of tales. Auntie Vannie invited me to help with her baking or with the meals she was making out of a cookbook, but I didn't want to. I preferred to read and imagine what it would be like at the top of that green and blue mountain in the distance. One day I would explore the heights of the Northern Range and reach the topmost peak, El Tucuche.

When they drove me home at the end of the week, they took a shortcut through the cane fields for part of the way. We didn't drive through the intersection at Jerningham Junction, and I never saw it. Not even on the last train to San Fernando.

As I grew older, Uncle Baddall's menace increased. I took care never to find myself alone with him. If I happened to be at their house, he did not miss the opportunity to stalk me. I told no one, not Sonia, not Susie. And definitely not Muddie, who had no secrets from her sister Evangeline. The sight of Uncle Baddall gave me a nauseated feeling inside. But I also felt a murderous rage towards him and hated the idea of being marked. I was sure that this nastiness had not happened to anyone else in my family or to any of my friends. Everyone else looked so clean and ordinary.

I grew my fingernails long until they curved downwards like pincers, even though I sometimes collected bad marks at school for them. My nails, hard as iron picks, were my personal arsenal. Baddall and I remained bound in the deep complicity of warfare. Yet how did he explain the raw scratch marks on his neck to Auntie Vannie time and time again as I managed to get out of his grip, struggling away from the slippery heaviness of the tongue that forced its way between my lips.

The year I turned fifteen, the same year that Baddall deserted my aunt, his proposition was more direct. At church a young minister, a fundamentalist zealot, freshly trained and brimming with ideas, had just delivered his first sermon. The government in Trinidad had recently launched a birth control campaign, and diaphragms were being given away for free. Condoms were also recommended, of course, as well as older practices such as premature ejaculation. The young minister made this campaign the subject of his sermon, saying that God created us to be fruitful and multiply, warning about hellfire and the evils of onanism.

Back at Grandma Lil's house after church, on a brief visit with the rest of the family, I came out of the bathroom and found Uncle Baddall lurking in the corridor. He caught me, and this time I was terror-struck by the tone of his voice. He was begging and pleading for something. His voice was low and desperate. "It'll be like Onan," he was whispering. "Nobody will know, nothing will show." He would scatter his seed, he said. As usual I scratched my way out of his grip, but as I hurried into the adjoining room I saw a long shadow on the corridor floor, an elongated shadow with a thin hooked nose. In a second the hook had become a hump, and I glimpsed someone at the far end of the hallway—Auntie Vannie, both hands flying up and covering her mouth and nose. I stopped, turned fully around, and looked, but the corridor was empty.

I escaped. As usual, I told nobody. Baddall left Trinidad not long afterwards. The last time he grabbed me, he must have already made his plans.

I remembered too how much comfort I used to get thinking of Uncle Baddall as "life's fool." The scene of his death, as described by Horatio, was as vivid as if I had been there myself. I could see his corpse leaning halfway out of an old armchair, the fifteen notebooks piled around him like a spiderweb.

It must have been towards morning that I had the funeral dream. The funeral was in a tropical country, in an official setting, with long avenues bordered by royal palm trees. The buildings reflected a gracious colonial-style architecture, the kind that hides the misery just beyond its palatial arches. It was a military funeral with full honours, the coffin draped with the red, the white, and the black of the Trinidad flag, the trumpets, the twenty-one gun salute. No pick-up affair now, and at the centre of this spectacle was a solid wooden coffin. The coffin, though, was ridiculously small, holding a tiny brown man laid out in a dark pin-striped suit. Baddall—I saw his face. There was a solemnity to that procession of strangers as they bore him to the graveyard.

EIGHTEEN

I returned to Montreal. I had to pick up my everyday life again, but in spite of my efforts I fell into a funk, a misery I could not seem to shake. A numbness possessed me, but it was my loss of equilibrium that distressed me most. These last few months had taken all my certainties about life and flung them into the air, letting them land, like dice, in disarray.

Unexpectedly, my thoughts ran to Pappy and his rapid decline after Kello had left for England. It was a rainy dank day, just like these dreary days of early summer. I had just come back from the docks after Kello had left with Aunt Alice and Uncle Samuel. Pappy hadn't gone; Kello had already told him goodbye a few days earlier, and although Pappy looked sombre, no one had noticed any change in him. When I came back that day, ahead of the others, I picked up the mail and sat at the table opening the one letter addressed to me. Pappy came and sat at the table, watching me companionably, I thought. I was halfway through the letter when Pappy said, polite but chiding, "Excuse me, Miss, but that is Mona letter. You ain't have no right to be reading Mona business." I stared at Pappy, amazed, as he repeated his words.

"Is me, Pappy, is me, Mona!" I cried, but he continued to look at me reprovingly, shaking his head.

I ran over to him and grabbed his shoulders. "Pappy! Pappy!" I shrieked, shaking him. But then I saw the vacancy in his aged face and gathered him close and hugged him. He held me tightly and his whole body began to tremble. When at last he released me, I saw that his eyes were bright with tears. After that it seemed that his memory came and went and time passed through his head in a seamless and continuous stream, as he summoned up whatever he wished. A revision of his life was taking place, I thought, sometimes pleasant, but mostly disturbing, requiring decisive action. One day when he was home alone, the neighbours found him in pyjamas and slippers waiting to catch a taxi to Princes Town. He wept and pleaded when they tried to convince him to return, and they had to lift him bodily while he struggled. Now, as I sat there at my kitchen table, I understood how it had been for Pappy, a sudden emptying out of life.

Roddy had left for the Middle East on a year's assignment. It was a posting he had craved and for which he had competed fiercely. We had talked about my visiting him as soon as I had calmed down a bit. But two days after I returned, I received a letter clotted with evasions and half-truths. Roddy had disappeared into another place altogether; even his handwriting spoke lies. His familiar scrawl had been replaced by careful semi-printing, as if to make sure that nothing could be misunderstood. He was sorry that things between us were still so unsettled, but suggested that we should use the time apart to think over our relationship and see where we wanted to go. He had left; deep down I knew it. In anger I tore up the letter and threw the pieces in the air. Late that night I called him and accused him of hiding behind hypocritical Anglo-Saxon attitudes, of running away, and we had a prolonged and nasty row. I hung up the phone in fury but found myself weeping bitterly.

After that conversation I felt tired beyond anything I had ever imagined. For days I did nothing but sleep. Carene called often and I was grateful for the sound of her familiar voice, talking non-stop about the film, about her plans for the launch. After a week, I was able to hobble out again. I met Carene for dinner and caught up on the latest about *Ou bwa seche?* You give up? Still my title, though the film was now called *Les Mesdames Saras*. We ordered a bottle of wine and I listened to newsy gossip about people we knew. I told her about Roddy and she reached across the tabletop and patted my hand. I knew that she would listen, but I couldn't talk about it. We drank more wine and listened to the jazz band. I left her long before midnight and made my way back to the empty flat.

I stared at the blue painted kitchen table and against all possibility I longed for Roddy to be there, sitting in his casual half-crouching way, smoking a cigarette, waiting for me, but the flat was as emptied out of life as before, and as disordered.

I hadn't said goodbye to Roddy. I was the one who had wanted to keep our love loose, but all the same I couldn't swallow it. I fall in love. I'm not an arm's length person, though I often fool myself into thinking I am. Kello was, I think, for most of his life, but that must have changed with Matt. And in the end, for all of his tenderness, Roddy had chosen to leave. All men are probably cowardly bitches, afraid to stay close, I thought savagely, bolting myself in against the night.

I went to the launch of Carene's film in the heart of the Haitian community in Montreal. Her excitement was infectious, even though I still mourned the absence of Cecile Fatiman. I remained convinced of a symbolic connection between her sacrifice of the black pig on that lightning-struck night at Bois Caiman in 1791 and the mass slaughter of the black Creole pig in this century and the ensuing ruin of the Haitian peasant.

The slaughter of the Creole pig in Haiti reminded me of the destruction of the mule train in Princes Town by the local elites from Port of Spain. Like those mules, the pigs were suddenly diagnosed with a deadly virus and had to be exterminated. Peasants were paid a few dollars for their pigs and then ordered to kill them. It seemed that the virus did not render the meat inedible, however, and in Carene's film the aroma of roast pork and crackling pervades the air. The air is filled as well with the wailing of those who grieved for their family pigs night after night. The Creole pigs were replaced by a dainty pink breed from the United States, for whom packaged feed had to be imported. No more slop pails. No more black pigs.

The loss of the Creole pig was vital to the story of these brave women of Haiti, ebony against the dirty white of the Montreal snowscape, trudging through the drudgery of their lives. The pig was in the film; the manbo Cecile Fatiman was not. And Carene and I, Caribbean women, had taken her out. The room suddenly felt close.

I left and walked along Sherbrooke Street, making my way home slowly. Something had cracked inside me. I felt it, although I had no ready explanation. Something had brought my drifting lifestyle to an end. But I resisted it. Montreal had provided me with a charmed space where I could live free of commitment. I was neither Québécoise nor Anglo; I had felt no passion about Quebec's future in Canada. Nothing, when I thought about it, brought out strong feelings in me anymore. I walked through those streets I had grown to love, thinking of my early years here, of the friends and lovers of that time, the nights spent drinking and arguing at the Swiss Hut. I remembered a time when, as a student, I was walking with some friends in the park at Mount Royal and an old man had stepped up to us. Bowing, he presented me with a rose. "Voilà! Mademoiselle, pour toi, ma chérie!" Did he think I was more in need of a rose than the others? Was he struck by something, the naked want on my face maybe? And what was it that I wanted? Yet my very anonymity offered a kind of freedom difficult to imagine anywhere else. If I left Montreal, I feared that my shell would dissolve, leaving me naked, bare for all the world to see.

When I arrived in the early seventies, Canada was a white country. If multiculturalism was an idea, it never touched me. For

Part Two: Manahambre Road

Da-Da, the moment of truth came when he saw a wall covered with graffiti that read Keep Canada White. As if it ever was. That first year winter piled up in huge drifts around me. I wrote in my journal that I had come to the edges of the First World and had been set adrift. I swore now that before another winter set in, I had to get myself back on course, but there was no course mapped out for me.

PART THREE

*CARONI
DUB*

Gainder, the girl who had escaped an unwanted marriage, is thirteen years old when she arrives at the island of Trinidad. She had been a happy child, living at home with her widowed father and her older brother. Her father was a learned man, a poor Brahmin who taught both his children to read and write and to compose poetry, but it was Gainder who showed an early talent for dancing and for singing her own songs. Her father had talked of taking her in a few years to the temple of the Vaishnavites. But tragedy intervened when her father died suddenly of cholera, and her brother took the advice of village elders and arranged a marriage for her. The bridegroom was a much older man, a widower with two grown children. Gainder escaped. She ran away after stealing the money her father had hidden away for them in a hole dug into the floor of their hut. She made her way on foot and by rail, trying to find the temple of the Vaishnavites, and travelled mostly at night when fewer people were about.

When she reached Benares, she found the ghats at the side of the river Ganges and picked her way through until she found the one with almost perpendicular steps at the side, leading to a temple of Shiva at the top. She had been told that many women gathered at this temple from early in the morning, walking round and round the sacred shrine, praying to Shiva for guidance. Vaishnavites and widows were among them: in Benares everybody called them rands. Gainder joined these women and prayed with them, still hoping to reach the temple of the Vaishnavites. During the day other temple worshippers gave the women alms, but at night men would come to the shrine looking for them. Some women went willingly; others were taken.

Gainder was more frightened at the temple than she had been throughout the whole overland journey. Even on the train to Benares she had not been so frightened, although she had never travelled alone before. She hid herself night after night. She heard some of the women talking about leaving with an arkatiya who was looking for people to work in Demerara and Chinidad. The arkatiya had been recruiting among these women, wanderers all, unhampered by ties to family and kin. They were ideal for his purpose. The shortage of women on Caribbean plantations of indenture was already leading to severe problems—wife-murder, choppings, beatings, serious crime. There was a drive to recruit more women, and this enterprising arkatiya had hit his mark. Some of these women, especially the younger ones, formed a band and travelled by train to Calcutta. Gainder was among them. She went with many others to the depot at Garden Reach and was registered there. Her journey across the kala pani had begun.

Arriving at Trinidad the labourers are quarantined at Nelson, one of the five small islands off its northwestern tip. Gainder is a strong young woman and is soon transported to the plantation where she will work first as a weeder and then as a full-fledged cane-cutter, wielding her cutlass like any man for one-third of a man's wages. She is sent to Petit Morne estate near the little town called The Mission in the South of the island, the very heartland of sugar cane production. Her talent for singing and composing soon becomes known, and she begins to earn extra money as a performer. She is very popular and often procures a free paper on weekends to journey to nearby estates for special celebrations such as weddings or kathas. Without this pass Indians can be jailed under the newly legislated Vagrancy Act for leaving their estate of indenture. Gainder saves the extra money she earns for the time when her five-year contract would be completed. She tries to get the land allocation promised in her contract, but the estate refuses to encourage single women to live alone and will not give it to her, even though it is her due. She continues to stay in the estate barracks and to work in the fields, living with her barracks family. After Jeevan killed the sailor on the Artist, a young couple took her under their protection on board the ship. Like others on the journey who formed these special bonds, they are her jahaji bhai and bahin, her shipmates, the only family she has.

A young Indian man, one of the few beginning to be educated through the missionary enterprise of the Presbyterian Church of Canada, is already establishing himself as a moneylender in Iere Village. His Christian name is Joshua; he is a bania, from the trading and moneylending caste in India. He sees Gainder singing and dancing at a wedding and inquires about her. When he hears her story, he sends an older man from the village to make her an offer of marriage. Joshua was born in Trinidad; his mother, an earlier indenture, had died the year before. He had never worked in the fields but had been one of the missionaries' earliest and proudest converts. Yet he keeps his marriage from the missionaries, instinctively knowing that they would disapprove and would try to make him a better match with a Christian girl.

Gainder's jahaji family hold a small wedding for her under bamboo because even though her husband-to-be could have paid for a bigger one, it is customary for the bride's family to stand the wedding costs. Her earnings are worn on her person, the silver coins melted into ornately wrought jewellery made in the style of villages in India, where the goldsmiths in the southern towns had learned their craft. She refuses to pawn her jewellery for a wedding. This is the dowry she brings to her husband and to her new life in his mother's small hut near the teak forest in Iere Village. The village is halfway between The Mission and another little town called Petitbourg, which is growing rapidly. Once the whole island of Trinidad was called Iere, land of the hummingbird; now the Amerindian name survives only in a small village where no Amerindians are left. She settles down well at first, listening to her husband's plans for building a high house and planting coconuts and citrus in the lands that he is acquiring. Joshua waits a full month after the wedding to tell Gainder that she must never sing or dance in public again. Her heart turns to stone when she hears these words.

NINETEEN

I took the idea of going back to Trinidad seriously. Bess was more than pleased; the townhouse development had been proceeding apace and she was eager for me to see it, to assure her that Kello would have approved. Making the decision helped. I felt brisker, stronger, more in touch with the world. I spent a weekend in Toronto with Da-Da and Muddie. Babsie, amazingly, was thinking of marriage to one of the men she had been dating for the past year, a computer wizard by her description. He was from Sri Lanka. She looked happy and relaxed, but was full of concern for me.

"You look like hell. What's the matter, Mona?" Her tone was brusque, aggressive. "I suppose you haven't patched up your quarrel yet. You should call him. You were the one who raved at Roddy, you know." Babs was partial to Roddy and had not seen his evasive letter, which I had torn up. For the time being I decided to say nothing.

Horatio called to say that he had enlisted the aid of the embassy in Ottawa and ordered topographical maps of the Central Range of Trinidad. We made jokes about his determination to excavate the treasure buried by his father's dynasty in Whiteland, while feeling sorry for him at the same time. "But," added Da-Da, with a flash of his old impishness, "look at how things could turn out in the end, eh? Above all places to hide buried treasure, Baddall had to go and hide it in Whiteland!"

I talked about my anxiety to Muddie. Her unaccustomed gentleness was disquieting. She urged me to drop everything and take a good rest. "You must give this to yourself, Mona. You need it now."

She embraced me and pushed the hair back from my forehead. The concern and affection were so unlike her usual reserve that I felt the panic rising in my chest. She was obviously worried about me and this fact, more than anything else, gave me a real fright.

I found myself ranting to her about the film and how much it vexed me that women's actions were so often erased. Muddie was trying to soothe me with her usual advice about the ways of the world when something struck me. In all of Muddie's stories about Grandma Lil's life, Muddie had never mentioned Lily's mother. Indeed, nobody in the family had ever mentioned her, and I did not even know her name. I asked and was surprised at my mother's sharply dismissive tone. "She was a woman they called Gainder. She took on the name Beharry, but it wasn't her real name."

"What was her real name?"

Muddie gave me a hard stare. "She didn't have a real name. I don't even know whether Gainder was her first name. We don't know too much about her. She was a low-class kind of person, you know, something like the old beggar woman in Ramgoolie Trace. You remember her?"

Baboonie? My heart was pounding now. "Yes, I remember Baboonie, I remember her very well."

"She couldn't be a Beharry. We are not related to any of the Beharrys in Trinidad. I don't know too much about her. She died when your grandmother was born."

She knew little and was uninterested in pursuing the conversation, but when I persisted she sat down and tried hard to recall what she did know. All she remembered were bits and pieces of gossip and hearsay. Joshua, Grandma Lil's father, was suspicious of Gainder all the time and used to accuse her of giving signals from the house to the men in the village. "She used to sing Ramayana before they married—not the real Ramayana you know. She used to sing the kind that village women would sing. Actually"—Muddie lowered her voice—"we learned some of the songs when we were small. From Nani. I think I still remember the tunes."

"Who is Nani again?" I asked, vaguely remembering the name.

Muddie talked with more warmth about Nani, Gainder's bahin, who had brought up Grandma Lil. She was still alive when Muddie was a child. Sometimes when Nani visited, she would summon the children and teach them old-time songs. Now Muddie could recall only fragments of the songs, but I listened eagerly. The melodies were haunting, plaintive. Muddie didn't know what the Hindi meant, but she thought some of the words might be questionable because Grandpa Jamesie had forbidden them in his house.

"That and calypso. You couldn't sing a calypso in the house. You know all that singing and cuatro playing that Bella and Sweetie and Tristy used to do on New Year's Day? Well, Pa couldn't say a thing then, but when we were small calypso was the work of Satan! He wouldn't allow it. Not at all, at all. One day we had a concert outside under the sapodilla tree, and Tristy was playing calypsonian. He dress up with a cigarette and a felt hat and everything. He was singing away when Alice warn us that Pa was running down the steps with a belt in his hand." She was laughing uncontrollably now. "Tristy just keep on dodging him behind the guava tree and the fence, and your grandfather keep on shuffling in his bedroom slippers, trying to catch him. But," she continued, "nobody could ever catch Tristy. His nickname at school was Dodger, you know." She paused, frowning.

"Dickens?" I ventured.

"Right. After the Artful Dodger in *Oliver Twist*. We laugh so much that day, nobody even worry about the licks Pa share out in the end."

Muddie and I talked a lot that weekend. I felt her closeness and warmth again as on those ironing nights so many years ago. I wondered why it had taken me so long to come back to her. So much had happened in between then and now. She confessed how much she missed Vannie, who had been telephoning twice a week since she had returned home. She reminisced fondly about Grandma Lil and her own early life with her sisters, then said with undisguised bitterness in her voice, "I didn't grow up like you all, you know, pitching around here, there, and everywhere. I came from some-where." I knew these were dry words of rebuke about Da-Da, but as usual she did not continue in this line.

The house in Iere Village where Bess lived now was where Grandma Lil had grown up, cemented there for her whole life. But that house was only one of her father Joshua's properties. Muddie had told me long ago about how he had made good on other peo-ple's little acres and half-acres of land when their debts ran into for-feiture. My great-grandfather, a newly educated Presbyterian product, had never bought into the gospel of considering the lilies of the field who toiled not, neither did they spin; in direct contra-diction he had emulated the merchants of the church, such as the one who had the lucrative chocolate directorship in England or the one who had later cut up the Squires estate. Joshua's literacy had made him a moneylender. Poor people—newly arrived indentures and lifetime estate workers—contracted debts to purchase cattle and seeds for their acreages, but more often their monetary needs were for celebrations like weddings and barahis, funerals, kathas, and pujas. Officiating pundits would collect a good sum of this bor-rowed money. People blamed the moneylender, Muddie said with a sigh, but was that fair? Money was needed and banks were for white people, for the local whites and high-browns. "Not for poor people, coolie people and black people. You could run a sou-sou and get an early hand, but for big money that wasn't enough. Black people had their Friendly Societies—all Indians had was their moneylenders."

I grew interested in Joshua, about whom I knew little except that he was an early convert, had received an education, and became a teacher—one of the first locals to do so. He had become a wealthy man, but by the time the second generation came along a lot of the wealth had evaporated. Grandma Lil, however, never relinquished her high-style living. In a jiffy she would make beignets dusted with icing sugar, pink and white sugar cakes, and fudge. If she had visitors for tea, she would whip up a cake, make dainty cheese sandwiches, and bring out a fresh tablecloth. I had always taken Grandma Lil's high style for granted, but suddenly the incongruity of her habits struck me. My own family always lived in a catch-ass zone; in the barracks in Iere Village women crouched in hooded piles like dogs fending off kicks and blows, while Grandma Lil lived as if in a Victorian novel. She lived a mannered life, Indian style though. She would make massive jars of pickles every year when tamarinds and mangoes were in season. Rows of pepper sauce bottles would be ripening green and golden in the sun beating down on her windowsill. She had style, this statuesque woman—a striking beauty in her early photos, a handsome woman to the end. Babs is the one who inherited her good looks, her taste for glamour.

Grandma Lil's height and her well-formed physique were those of her father. When I asked why we had no pictures of Joshua, Muddie reminded me of one yellowing portrait buried at the bottom of the wardrobe in her photo box. It was the only picture of him that anyone had ever seen. A studio shot of a man with distinctive features, stout, well dressed, complete with waistcoat and watch-chain. Maybe, I suggested, we could enlarge it and mount it. But Muddie would have none of it—out of respect for Grandma Lil, she said. "You ever see a picture of him in her house? Why not, eh?" There was a dark secret, all right, but not what I had concluded with my North American mindset, seeing incest in a situation ripe for it, no mother and a young girl growing up.

Lily never forgave him for the beating he inflicted on her. It was because of a boyfriend from the village, in time a lover, a half-white bastard, Muddie said, living on the edge of the cane fields with his cane-cutter mother, while his white father lived in the overseer's quarters on the hill. His name was Devindra, but his white father used to call him Davy. He was a good-looking boy, very fair and nice, although he had cat's eyes and a big hawk nose.

"Your grandmother," said Muddie, "was in love with this boy to the point where she forget herself. She would sneak out early in the morning to meet him in the teak forest over the road from their house. When she find out she was pregnant, the same Nani who mind her from small after Gainder died tried to boil bitter-leaf and carilee bush to throw away the child. But before that could happen Joshua get to find out because some news-carrier in the village observe everything. The boy used to bring some sugar bags tie up in a bundle so they could lie down on the grass. Well, this man notice him going with the bundle inside the teak morning after morning. So he follow them and see everything. He tell the father, and the beating that Lily get was the talk of the village for months.

"You know," Muddie continued, her voice softening at the thought, "I think she had an idea that she could talk Joshua into accepting the boy, although he was poor. But that talk didn't take place because all Joshua could see was his one daughter's life going down the drain. His one daughter, who had so much schooling and could do so much. After she finished school he sent her to Fanny's Place, you know, where the missionaries used to train young Indian girls to be good wives for the boys being educated. She could cook and bake and sew and do embroidery. And to throw everything away for somebody in the gutter!

"They say Joshua nearly kill her but Nani jump in between them and take the blows herself. He didn't want to kill Nani—he himself was with Nani. He didn't kill your grandmother, but she knew it was the beating that killed the baby. Even though she tried to throw away the baby before, she still held Joshua in mind for that and for forcing her to marry your grandfather. Jamesie was a shy chupidy young man, just starting to teach, and the missionaries had high hopes for him. He was a bright boy. And after that merciless beating, I tell you, Joshua had more guts than a calabash. He had Grandma Lil married in church, and gave her away, staring everybody in their face as if he couldn't mash ants. They had a big wedding, the biggest Iere Village ever see yet. A real pappyshow wedding. It was Alice," Muddie said, "who tell us all this when we were growing up. Alice was the one who could tell you everything about everybody in the family. No, my dear. Even though he was my grandfather, I prefer to respect my mother's wishes. I wouldn't put up a picture of him in my house."

Surely Grandma Lil had grown to love Grandpa Jamesie, I protested. She had made sure that he had the best piece of chicken at meals always, that his juice was squeezed just so, and that the slice of lemon in warm water that he drank every morning as a cleanser was ready and waiting. But Muddie didn't agree. She believed that Lily had simply been doing her duty, fufilling the ideas she had of being a good wife. In that, my grandmother was proud to be above reproach. But he couldn't keep her spirit down. Grandpa Jamesie never took Grandma Lil's advice about business matters and it was a pity, my mother said, sighing deeply, because she had inherited Joshua's shrewd head for business. She saw that Petit-bourg was growing rapidly and wanted to buy the cheap land that was available. "If she had done that, if we had owned property in San Fernando, we would be well off today. Who knows . . ." Muddie's voice trailed off. But I was sure that any wealth we had would have sifted through Da-Da's wide open fingers like sand on the seashore. Muddie explained that when Lily married Jamesie, everything that was hers became his. James, the poor boy just beginning to make good in the world of missionaries and education and Indian high society, took the advice of everybody over hers. He bought worthless country land full of cocoa and coffee saying, as everybody else did, that cocoa was king. But cocoa did not remain king for long, and Grandma Lil watched her fortune dwindle, her sharp tongue the lone weapon against his foolishness.

For his part, Jamesie tried in vain to turn her flamboyance into something more modest and becoming to a young teacher's wife, a man soon to be a respected head teacher. Lily seemed to acquiesce at first, Muddie thought, but once her father Joshua was dead, nothing could stop her from cussing like a market vendor. She would curse and scandalize Grandpa James before the listening village with such ferocity that he would cringe in shame for weeks afterwards. She was a confident woman, steadfastly refusing to be held in check by this quiet, scholarly man, fluent in Hindi and English, trying to keep his footing in both worlds while missionaries laid down the law on one side and a virago tormented him on the other. No wonder, I realized, that Grandpa Jamesie had retreated to the comfort of his library.

It was in this library too that Grandpa committed the one error Lily never forgave him for. Muddie thought that it was loss of face and not real jealousy that ate into her, but even so nothing could temper her fury. Muddie and Vannie had heard the whole story from Aunt Alice, the irrepressible, and now my mother erupted into the kind of laughter the sisters must have shared as rude little girls, rolling around on the floor at what they saw as the absurdity of their parents' predicament. The thought of them sharing secrets and giggling at their parents' sex lives brought back memories of me and Sonia, always on the lookout for sexual evidence of one kind or another. What we all had in common was the certainty that sex was a crime, and bad things like wrongdoing and cussing had to be a part of it. It was good to hear Muddie laughing like a girl, but I felt sorry for poor Grandpa Jamesie, always in over his head except with his books. And not even his little book-lined room was inviolate.

The incident that caused so much ruckus coincided with Muddie's birth. A girl of fourteen or so, being trained in the domestic arts at Fanny's Place, was sent to help Grandma Lil. One night Lily was walking the baby, trying to burp her, when from Grandpa Jamesie's study she heard his pained voice remonstrating with someone and saying, "No, no, no . . ." more and more weakly. Astonished, she stopped walking and listened. There was only one voice coming from the study, so she tiptoed up to the door and saw the Fanny's Place girl writhing on Grandpa Jamesie's lap while he lay back in his comfortable chair, eyes half-closed, no longer protesting. Sensing a presence he opened his eyes and saw Grandma Lil in the doorway. The startled Jamesie jumped up, throwing off the suddenly offensive girl and revealing everything. Lily was beside herself with rage.

"You is a fool, a damn blasted fool, you is such a stupid, stupid man! A real coonoomoonoo from behind God back! So help me, God, I never see a fool like you! You ain't have the sense yuh was born with self! Taking woman and yuh can't even take yuhself! You is a blasted whitewash sepulchre. You nasty old hypocrite, you!"

Throughout the night Lily's loud denunciation of his stupidity and his damn hypocrisy echoed through the darkened village. She would have pitched the girl out of doors that night, but a neighbour intervened and took her in. When they heard the story from Alice so many years later, Muddie and Vannie thought their father had acted like an idiot and that Lily would have respected him more if he had not panicked like some guilty schoolboy. But brazening and bluffing his way out of things was not for my grandfather, who was likely experiencing the first and only fling of his life.

I myself didn't find the story that funny, but I imagined that it was

Grandpa Jamesie's concern for propriety in everything that gave Muddie and the others such amusement at the thought of his unwilling seduction by a wild young thing. Irrationally, my grandfather blamed Muddie's birth for the incident, and my mother believed that this notion explained his lack of closeness to her. The moment that Da-Da, the young rebel, appeared in her sights, love sprang up between them. In defying her parents and marrying him, he of no firm prospects, she had declared her independence from her father and sealed her fate.

But where Muddie was calm, Grandma Lil was explosive. She had her own strong views about everything; I knew that from my own experiences with her. In life, she would say, you had to pick sense out of nonsense. No matter what anyone told her about anything, she would find the hidden clues in a casually averted glance, a strand of hair pushed back at a certain moment, or a slight variation in the pitch of the voice. She could always work backwards and piece together the real story. The pre-ordained shape, the beginning, middle, and end, she dismissed as nonsense.

Once I was at her house cramming for a Shakespeare test. I put the diagram for the rise and fall of a tragic play on the little blackboard in the room they kept for us children and went through the schema of the five acts. I noticed her at the door looking on with interest, but she didn't say anything as I continued my hectic memorizing. After I had recited it verbatim, she clapped her hands and beamed at me. Then she said quietly, "So that is how it is, eh? Rising, climax, and falling action, eh? Huh!" I knew enough by then to understand that she didn't believe life was like that at all. Not at all. Her favourite book was *The Basket of Flowers*, a nineteenth-century romance novel about a lost ring, thieving magpies, and the heavy hand of fate. Her favourite song was "Que sera, sera."

Down the long driveway as we approached the house, the sounds of her singing would greet us. Sonia and I would spend holidays there together. We loved to help her with the big jobs of shelling tamarinds or cutting up green mangoes for making achar. One time a young village girl was helping us. Her major task was to pick up the mangoes that were drying in the sun if a rain shower threatened. She was idle most of the time but loved to talk, and we became avid listeners to all the juicy gossip in Iere Village.

One tale I heard filled me with dread. The girl told us about her aunt, who had run away and "married Creole." Nobody in the family ever visited this aunt and "they forget she," the girl said. She had moved up north to a little village somewhere near D'Abadie.

"If they see she anywhere, they would say how yuh do and walk on. Some of them would even pass she straight. What they want to talk to she for? She make she choice and just as how yuh make up yuh bed, just so yuh go lie down, yuh hear?" The aunt became sick, "and when ah tell yuh sick, not joke sick yuh know, but sick up here," the girl said, pointing to her head. "She start catching fits and everything. She used to walk about and talk to sheself and bawl out the names of all she brothers and sisters." In her distress she would often journey the considerable distance to her family's village to try to reconnect with her relatives and neighbours. But no one there welcomed her. They would warn her that if she did not return to her husband at once, they themselves would hire a car and send her back at her own expense. So she would leave house after house, disconsolate, and make the long trip back to D'Abadie by route taxis and buses. Three whole hours the trip would take. The girl had stopped then, for dramatic impact, and concluded in the voice of a prophetess, "It good for she! Who tell she to marry Creole?"

Who tell she to marry Creole? The words rang in my ears. I thought of how I did not marry Bree. I thought of Grandma Lil who did not marry the boy she had loved.

* * *

Part Three: Caroni Dub

Mornings find Grandma Lil lifting her skirts carefully as she tiptoes through the back door to meet him in the farthest corner of the teak forest. They lie on burlap bags that he brings tied in a tight bundle. He unties and spreads them on the grass, where she lies and stretches her arms, her legs, arching up to meet the sky in him, the horizon at their back measuring the slow beat of sunlight rising over the cane fields below. Is this what she yearns for? she wonders, while she watches his cat's eyes burning into hers, his hawk's nose cutting into her shoulder at times, his strangely burnished hair, not black or brown but the colour called auburn that she had read about in books. A boy without a past, looking towards no future. His mother's hut poised at the very edge of the cane far back from the road, away from the whole village. His father's house, on the hilltop, surveying the cane field, surveying the village, his father safe with his own little brood, surveying the hut of mud and grass he visits at night.

Lily, my Grandma Lil, yearning to rise over rooftops and kitchens and dirty washtubs, rising in rebellion against the marriage they would make for her, against Aunt Alice, Myrtle, Sweetie, and all the other children to come. Lily, sixteen years old, burned into burlap, rising to meet a desire no one before or since would ever know, desire for a boy with no world to live in, hard as nails, possessing her softness as he lashes and lashes at the hand of fate. Lily, lying still afterwards, morning after morning, asking him for nothing.

And later, the strange stirrings inside her. Nani's questions, her whispers, the bush tea she makes Lily drink. The bush baths too, in the backyard in the sun, the kneading and probing and waiting. How her father finds out every-thing and she is shamed in front of the whole village. And the pappyshow wedding not long after. The infant Daisy is stillborn. Her first. Buried with her tiny hands holding some black beads for maljo, protected even in death from the curse of bad-eye. Wrapped in burlap and buried with her navel string under the caimite tree near the far boundary. Grandma Lil, whose erect bearing never faltered in all the time I knew her, whose voice never lost its edge of command. Lily, standing erect, rising to meet a boy's vast unspoken love, hidden with him in a stand of teak trees.

. . .

But what about Grandma Lil's own mother, Gainder? Her songs, banned from the house when the children were growing up, rude songs sung in Hindi, intrigued me. Muddie thought that maybe I could find something in Bess's house, in the storeroom or in Grandpa Jamesie's old bookcases. Alice had drawn up a family history once, and Muddie was sure that some of the songs Gainder sang were included. Grandpa James had objected, but there was nothing else, not even a picture, so in the end he had to give in.

He gave in and had to include Gainder in our family history, my great-grandmother who bore Grandma Lil, who in turn produced five children, not counting the stillborn Daisy. Grandma Lil, who bore Muddie, who bore me and Babsie and Kello and Johnnie . . . I made up my mind that when I went to Trinidad I would search for her songs until I found them. Gainder, the name of the humble yellow marigold, used in Hindu rituals of worship.

TWENTY

The place had changed but not around Grandma Lil's house, now Bess's house. On one side of the main road, still called Main Road, there were houses, parlours, shops. On the other side for several miles, sloping downhill and back up again, there was still a magnificent stand of teak trees, a continuing experiment in forestry.

Bess had changed little of the exterior of the house. Its colour was still creamy yellow. Its outside was made of shapely large bricks, fashioned by hand, one by one. The sapodilla tree leaned gently towards the house, its bats shrieking high and sweet in the gathering darkness. When I am old I know I'll still remember the shrieking of fruit bats at twilight.

The outer stairs were painted red, edged by the yellow brick wall; sturdy rails protected the sides and an asparagus fern climbed all the way to the top. Sometimes there were tiny buds on the fern. Asparagus, asparagrass—asparagus that people ate in England and America, paragrass that we used to feed donkeys and cows. A filigreed evergreen fern, sometimes used in bridal bouquets. Underneath those steps there had been a sandbox. Uncle Sweetie had made it for us out of old boards and sand left over from a renovation. That was where Sonia and I had started making drunk pies and cursing.

It was dark by the time Bess and I crossed the stretch of teak trees and turned into the driveway at Iere Village. The house was as welcoming as it had always been to its nowarian of old, and Bess's nineteenth-century Creole bedroom with its rose-toned antimacassars and vetiver sachets was mine again.

That first night I slept with a soundness that I had not known for weeks. My dreams were mapped by a spotlight moving backwards rapidly, leafing through stacked papyrus folios half-lying in the shallows near the shoreline of a turquoise sea.

I am driving on the well-cut new highway that joins the two cities of my life, Port of Spain and San Fernando. I apprehend a newly prescribed order. Here on this highway is the place where the urban North meets the rural South. The bridge across the Caroni River is splendid and wide; small boats are anchored at the edge where the river road at the mouth of the swamp leads into a bird sanctuary for scarlet ibises and white egrets.

And along the highway a dog is running at the side. The day is hot, a hot dry Sunday afternoon, and she is in panic. She runs steadily at the side, dugs loose and flapping, tongue hanging and dry, skin slack. She is a short brown dog. Around her the cane fields stretch for miles, green and limitless, their silver arrows shooting to the sky. She belongs to no one; she is going nowhere. The cars speed by going north; she is headed south. I read the panic in that dog's eyes.

She has that sense of being alive common to all living things— have mercy on us, mercy—caught in the dread game called life. Death runs up and down that highway, stalking the little bitch or indifferently cutting her down. Death doesn't really care; neither does she.

Later, I return as evening is shifting through the canes. There is a restlessness in the air. The light is that marvellous tropical amber we get in the early months of the year. The frogs are settling down for the evening, the wind is cool. There is a small dead dog in a heap at the side of the road. It might be her. I don't know.

Part Three: Caroni Dub

The death of a small brown dog is not inconsequential. I am over-whelmed by an unassailable grief.

I awoke to find myself in tears. It was morning in Bess's bedroom. I had slept deeply, dreaming and grieving. The restlessness had shifted through the canes in the night and into my mind.

The dreams I had were of life breaking apart, of not caring any-more. There must be a breaking point in every life—animal, veg-etable, or mineral—after which nothing was of consequence anymore and acquiescence set in. No exact formula existed for cal-culating when this giving up started, and I had heard theories about its origins in the womb. Every living thing had to have an internal code for determining the exact moment when stress became insup-portable and death the only release.

Then I recalled another dream that I had that night about a man from Iere Village. He is a close relative, but I have no idea what his connections are. I cannot make out his face. He is bewildered; he walks or, rather, his feet flap about a large flat terrain, as unmarked as a concrete carpark. He seems to be looking for a signal from a guide who is not yet a part of the dream, but no cue comes and he is forced to meander, feet flapping helplessly, until he is erased. It is evening when he wanders in again. Evidently he has been exposed during the day to some kind of experience—a devastating experience.

Time is important in the dream, and there is no time left. The ear-lier time is morning—clear and luminous. The evening is character-ized by red, manic and desperate, ticking in short rapid breaths.

The man moves uncertainly on flat concrete, but the surface changes and he begins to ascend a small hill. As he rises to the top, I see his full form and it stabs me to the heart. One arm is broken and hangs limply down the side of his brown, angled body. The man's shirt still winds around his torso, ill-fitting and too long, but it cannot conceal the fact that he has lost his pants and now wears a pair of cheap, flimsy, whitish drawers completely ruined on the behind. The crotch seams have separated from each other and drift down loosely. There are large splotches of blood, and, wet, wet, human wreckage. But worst of all is the helpless, half-apologetic look on his face.

That body, once sinuous, had perhaps lain fully upon another body. Once, perhaps, a woman might have spent time touching his lank discoloured hair, teasing the nervous muscle at the side of his mouth. That hair, now long and unkempt, falls down the side of his face, masking his beautiful cat's eyes, his hawk's nose.

And suddenly I sat up in bed. The cat's eyes, the hawk's nose—those were not my words. They were words from Muddie's story of Grandma Lil's first love, the boy Devindra, whom everyone knew as Davy.

At the breakfast table I talked to Bess about my troubled dreams. When I mentioned the man with the cat's eyes and hawk's nose, Bess was at the kitchen counter, fiddling with the toaster. She swivelled slowly around and glanced my way, the movement of her body veiling a threat. "Cat-eye?" She spoke softly. "Like mine?"

I said nothing in response, wondering about her touchiness. But my discomfort was too deep and I had to ask what she meant. Bess looked me fully in the eyes this time, shaking her head in amazement.

"Mona, I can't believe that you described him so fully and you still don't know who he is. The man from Iere Village with the cat-eye and hawk-nose was my grandfather. You didn't know that? You know who Daisy is? Grandma Lil's first child? The one who everybody remembers by the navel string buried under the yellow croton bush near the caimite tree? Well, Daisy is that cat-eye man's daughter. Our grandmother's daughter. My grandfather's daughter."

I stared at Bess blankly, trying to follow her words. I knew from Muddie that the stillborn baby was Davy's child, I knew that Bess was Sweetieboy's outside child, but I had never heard that Davy was also Bess's grandfather. Did Muddie know? So many secrets in such a tiny place.

"That hawk-nosed boy, Mona, became my grandfather. His name was Devindra but his white father always called him Davy. After Grandma Lil married Grandpa Jamesie, Davy was married to Samdaye, a shopkeeper's daughter in a village not too far from here. A village called Hardbargain—you know it? He was a nice fair boy and the shopkeeper himself came to ask his mother for him. The day he got married, Davy promised himself that he would never cut another cane in his life." Bess paused dramatically.

"And you know what? He never picked up a cutlass again. He never did a scrap of work outside the rumshop. Morning and evening he would be there, drinking non-stop and selling rum. His father-in-law would curse him and quarrel about how he would drink them out and turn them into paupers, but Davy never paid him no mind. The old man used to complain too about how Davy was such a nice fairskin boy, nobody would ever suspect that he could drink so."

Bess was a great storyteller, and I could see that she relished the unlikely chain of events that had brought her into the family. No denial in her; no dressing up of the dirt; nothing of the hypocrite. She went on.

"But this Mr. Davy had a magnet for attracting people. That was what he did the whole day long, just drinking and carrying on with ole talk. He took his revenge on Grandma Lil by talking about how sweet she was and about the sugar bags and everything. At least he lived in another village. Samdaye didn't like how Davy was carrying on. But what she could never forgive, the turning point between them, was the naming of their baby. Right after my mother

Doudou was born, Davy went and registered the birth, calling her Daisy. Then Samdaye found out about Grandma Lil's baby, who was called Daisy too. I suppose she felt as if he was punishing her for something that wasn't her fault, and after that she would have nothing to do with him. She started calling the baby Doudou, and that was that.

"And from early on Doudou was wild and rebellious and wouldn't do any work in the house. Samdaye used to cuss her and Davy would shield her. Samdaye was a short dark woman. She hated Doudou's cat-eye and her fair skin. She used to say that Doudou thought she was too great just because she looked half-white. And you know, Mona, I don't know how that one white man blood so strong because look at my cat-eye and fair skin too!" She laughed wryly. "With parents named Doudou and Sweetieboy, no wonder I have such a sweet disposition!"

I laughed too, having witnessed her keen negotiation for Pappy's land.

We made plans for the day. The first thing I wanted to do was to visit the land. Kello had been right, I thought. Buying the land had brought him and Pappy together again. Pappy had been right too, holding on to the land and warning Da-Da not to throw it away.

We drove to the site, and even though I expected change, it was astounding to think that this had once been the place where we had lived, where we ran freely through the trees, rolled down hills, and lay in the grass. The place had been levelled, graded, and terraced. The buildings were taking shape. Masses of stone—blue metal, marl, striated stones on a white ground—lay in heaps all over the site. Bess was pleased at the pace of construction. She was not satisfied, however, with the retaining walls and the terracing. She insisted that more reinforcement was necessary to prevent any more landslips.

I got out of the car and walked in and around the fallen acreage, down to the hollow near where the mammy-sepote trees used to be. They had not started the terracing yet at that end. I thought of Pappy and Mama making a decision to borrow from Peter to pay Paul, not knowing whether the gamble would work. I imagined Pappy setting out alone in the cool of the night, the high white moon riding in the western sky, directly over the Gulf of Paria, pointing its crooked finger to the place he would reach by morning. Pappy picking his way through Corinth, Cocoyea, and down the cane road that would become The Coffee, already smelling of coffee boiling in coal pots at the roadside by the time he reached Petitbourg. Pappy walking alone through the night on the road with tall canes on both sides.

The moneylender coming to their door clutching in his hand the fistful of papers. A vulgar little man, imagining himself well dressed, with an oversized watch-chain and a ring on every finger. The overseer spitting and calling Pappy a bong-coolie, hearing from Pappy those curses from the back of his throat—old Hindi curses that nobody in the factory had ever heard before, and bad curses in patois. And the moonlight bright as day on the white gravel, no dust, nothing on the road but a small man dressed neatly in grey crash pants and two old shirts for the night cold.

And the next day, after securing the mortgage, when he rounded the corner at Hope Road in the evening, and saw his breadfruit tree towering over all the others in the neighbourhood, the money for buying the donkey safely in his pocket, Pappy's joy must have hit the top of the breadfruit tree, standing like a sentry on the land that was his again.

I walk around the land, remembering what it had looked like before, recalling where the chenette and celamen and breadfruit trees had stood. I imagine that something of me, and of all our lives here, lies buried in it. I sit on the ground and then lie flat. I press my face into the earth and search for my scent. A musky, wild scent like that of a young child, running all day through the land, between trees and bushes, lying on dirt, hiding between tree stumps and old boards while playing whoop, and then, close to evening, just before darkness hits and they call her inside to bathe quickly, washing the dirt off her feet at the standpipe outside before she enters the house, before they soap the smell off her and put her into clean pyjamas.

And I was not disappointed. The smell I had then rose up into my nostrils from the land, up from long ago. The land, the land had remembered. I lay face down on the earth, my first earth, breathing it.

TWENTY-ONE

 I stayed in the next day to search for Aunt Alice's book on the history of the family. Bess was sure that she had seen a copy somewhere in Grandpa Jamesie's bookcase, but she herself showed little interest. My search did not take long. The well-thumbed cyclostyled folder had lost its front cover but was otherwise intact, its pages held together with metal clips on the inside. Thumbing through these pages I read the official story of the family. There was a family tree at the very front with no mention of Bess. And at the end of the final page was a three-sentence history of Gainder: *Lily's mother was named Gainder. She came from India in the nineteenth century. She died in childbirth.*

That was all. I looked underneath the metal holders and saw the telltale marks of pages torn out. Were they the pages with the songs? Perhaps Grandpa Jamesie had taken his private revenge. This copy was the only one that I could find and he had ripped out the songs. I found myself overcome by anger that felt like a personal violation.

I went down to the storeroom next. There I found some boxes that Bess had labelled G.L. Grandma Lil was a pack rat and all kinds of junk fell out of those boxes. Old recipe books put together by ladies of the church, programs for concerts and Speech Days, some letters. My eye fell upon one box filled to the brim with black soft-covered notebooks, all the same size. Her shop books! I leafed through these with pleasure, remembering our countless errands to the village shop with these books. "Message" was the catch-all word for the items we purchased. The shopkeeper gave Grandma Lil

unlimited credit, and all of the lists were dated, signed by him, and
initialled by her after she had checked off the goods.

> *1 lb cheese*
>
> *2 boxes cockset*
>
> *1 lb brown sugar*
>
> *5 lb flour (the good one)*
>
> *1 lb saltbeef*
>
> *1 Guinness stout*

I smiled at the mention of cockset—one of those words from an
older time. How did coils of mosquito destroyer come to be called
cockset? At the end of each shop book were blank pages with scrib-
bled notes. I checked the dates. It seemed that Grandma Lil deliberately left a few pages blank at the end and used these for a journal of
sorts after starting a new shop book. I smiled again at some of these
rough sentences, obviously made for her own private consumption.

> *Went by Alice to spend the day. Nice time. She gave me a big set of dried
> flower-seeds. Double zinnias, margarets and flocks.*
>
> *Sweetie is so wild. He wouldn't settle down at all. He was owing money
> again and I had to give him 20 dollars. I can't tell Jamesie.*
>
> *Went to town to shop for Xmas. Apples and thing so expensive nowadays.
> I bought a big hat with hanging rosebuds. The dress is pink and it will
> match well.*

The entries continued in this vein and I amused myself skimming
until I saw a scribble about "my mother." I scrutinized the pages
carefully and saw that some of the shop books had whole passages
about Gainder Beharry. Facts about her—the ship *Artist* was the one
in which she had left India, in 1879. I went through the shop books
madly after that, searching and searching. The ones at the very bot-

tom of the box were beginning to be gnawed by mice and bugs, and I jumped back as a few insects scuttled away. But in these books I found words at the back, Hindi-sounding words in verse form, like the bhajans that were sung as hymns in the early days. I knew the word Esu, meaning Jesus, and I searched through the songs hoping not to see it, hoping that these songs or poems would be Gainder's songs, and not bhajans.

Finally, by combining Lily's jottings in several of her books, I was able to piece together the story of my great-grandmother.

My mother name was Gainder Beharry. They say she was a rand. She had thirteen years when her father die. Her father teach her to read and write. She used to sing and make up her own songs too. Her brother was Prabhu, a good boy, nice and quiet. The brother marry off Gainder to a man in the village when the father die. The village was in Beehar. The man was old and she run away in the night. She thief a little money to help with the trip. She was trying to find the Vashnava. She hear how they used to sing and dance for money, and how all of them could read and write too. But she find the arkatya instead and he carry her to the depot. The depot was full of people going to Trinidad for work, she hear them calling it Chinidad. To the end she used to say she was in Chinidad. She was in a place where they had a lot of other rands in Benares. It was up some steep steps and they would climb up early in the morning and walk round and round the Shiva statue whole day, praying and chanting. People used to give them money in the day but in the night, men would come and take them. She used to hide in the night. When the arkatya came, bands of them went with him because he explain that they would go to a place call Chinidad and get plenty money for easy work. The white sailors used to trouble them a lot on the ship. They used to call them the band of rands. A man on the ship kill a sailor because one night he try to feel up Gainder. A gatka man name Jeevan. They leave him in jail on a island name The Rock. The rands cling together till they reach Trinidad and then they separate them. They send them all over the island. Gainder went to Petimon with her jahaji bhai and bahin. My father marry her from Petimon. When her jahajis move from the estate, they come and settle right here in Iere Village. My father help them. The lady name was Sumintra. She was only a little older but she was like a mother to Gainder. This is the lady I grow with and still call Nani. She bring me up like her own. She was a mother to me and a companion to Pa. After her husband die, we beg her but she still wouldn't come and live with me and Pa. She had her own house. She teach me all Gainder songs. Nani tell me that Gainder couldn't get over how they leave Jeevan so far away on The Rock. He used to come to her in dreams. She never love Pa. All her songs had Jeevan in them. If Pa didn't stop Gainder from singing and dancing, she would still be alive, so Nani used to say. But Nani say she was too too sad, only singing when Pa leave the house. Is a good thing Nani listen because she knew all the songs even though she couldn't really sing. Nani say that she and Gainder used to go and see a rand in St. Julien and another one on Bonaventure estate. Both of them was jahaji bahins from the same ship. The ship was the Artist. It leave India in 1879. Gainder was my mother. I wish she didn't die and I could know her.

The songs followed in Hindi.

All of it was there. Everything about us, where we came from, our connection to despised women like Gainder Beharry, like Baboonie, the journey on those ships of indenture in the nineteenth century. I put the books down and sat there in the dusty storeroom, my brain filled up with images of ships, ocean waves, an island called The Rock, veiled women, bold and frightened at the same time, fearless men whose powerful arms could kill a sailor with a single blow. This was the most exciting research I had ever done and it had happened in a rush. An island called The Rock? Some of the words were unfamiliar, like rand, arkatya, and gatka, and the songs themselves were puzzles that I somehow had to decode.

Back in Bess's study I opened up the glass doors of the bookcases and examined my cousin's books, looking for some clue to the word *rand*. In a book about Christian converts in India I saw that *rand* meant widow, but also harlot. The author explained that widows were often abandoned by in-laws and driven to prostitution as a result. The journey from India involved a stop at St. Helena, a small rocky island off the coast of West Africa; this must be The Rock.

A runaway woman from a village, a journey by night, a decision to leave India. A woman alone. A story waiting to be told—my own story. I waited impatiently for Bess to return. There must be a way to decipher the Hindi. Eight of the shop books had words that looked like Gainder's songs. The sentences about Gainder herself were contained in ten other shop books scattered in the boxes. Grandma Lil had hidden the books, of that I was convinced. They were her domain; Jamesie would not have come near her household records. And I wondered how much of my grandmother's life had been conducted in secrecy while she struggled to hold the pieces that she had lost, her mother Gainder and the songs she sang, the hawk-boy Davy, her own considerable wealth. Grandma Lil, her flamboyance flying in the face of all these setbacks, meeting everything with her own grand style.

Grandpa Jamesie had struggled too, even while he directed his energies towards keeping his house safe from scandal and looseness and calypsos, the work of Satan himself. He lived in blissful ignorance of the seamier side of life, studiously protected from the world, translating this and that, preaching on weekends, encouraging the use of Indian instruments for worship, continuing his Sanskrit studies. I felt certain that his calling was to be a pundit, but after his early conversion, that route was blocked, so he deployed his passion in other ways. He knew whole sections of Tagore's *Gitanjali* by heart.

Bess had preserved his section of the study intact. Her bookcases were constructed of local woods that she had chosen with care; her books were beautifully shelved. I browsed through the newer books, noticing a few on indentureship that had been published recently. And for the first time in my life the absence of the subject of indentureship from our history texts at school hit me with force. History was the study of English kings and queens and brave explorers, Mary Queen of Scots, Sir Walter Raleigh, Hawkins, and Drake. We had been taught about slavery but almost nothing about indentureship. What were the actual dates for the beginning and end of the system? I was embarrassed to realize that I did not know. The indentures must have begun arriving in Trinidad after the emancipation of slaves in 1838, but I was unsure about the details. My ignorance was distressing.

Bess was delighted by my find of the shop books and made plans to take me to a rand nearby who sang Ramayana and might be able to decipher the songs. A *rand*? I asked Bess about the word but she was off-hand. "Oh, just a lady living alone down the road."

We went to visit the rand, a big talkative woman in her seventies, still robust and strong. She still performed on wedding nights, she said. She sang for us, beating her little drum and belting out the words with power. There was nothing retiring about her. We showed her the books and she read the songs easily, explaining their meaning. One she actually knew; it had become a popular love song for festive occasions. In the lyrics a woman sings to her lover, a man who has never touched her and to whom she swears everlasting fidelity in her dreams at night. He is abandoned on a rock. This one had a haunting melody that stayed with me for days. I asked the woman, Chandroutie, if I could tape these songs, and she invited us to a wedding night where she was performing.

Part Three: Caroni Dub

I was alive again. In the excitement of discovering all this information about the woman Gainder I forgot my earlier anxiety. I
woke up early and dug through the new books on indentureship.
And we decided to go to the wedding night in Debe, in the "deep
South." Bess laughed as she said the words but became serious as we
talked about the two Trinidads that still existed. "We are just
beginning to be known to the general population, Mona. So much
about us is unknown to them." And to us as well, I thought, so
much about us is unknown to us, but kept the words to myself. She
seemed to be moving in tune with a process of change, while I could
only observe from a distance.

Bess was familiar with the ritual, but I had never seen the Matikor
before. It took place the night before the wedding when only
women gathered, and through bawdy songs and lewd dances, love
songs and open talk, the bride was instructed into the mysteries that
awaited her in marriage.

We arrived at dusk. The drummers, all women, had already
started. Not a man was in sight. Two older women crouched at the
side of the house where the soil had been freshly dug. They mixed
together ghee, earth, sugar, salt, and some petals on a broad leaf,
wrapped it tightly and buried it. Bess whispered that this signified
the start of another household. The women formed a circle, taking
turns to dance to the centre of the ring, simulating the sex act in
various ways, angry, fierce, tender. There were games as well,
older women knotting their skirts into phallic forms, running races
while holding eggplants clamped firmly between their legs, frolick-
ing and teasing the younger women. The songs were wonderful,
varied in rhythm and so unlike the lushly arranged Bombay film
songs that blared out in the markets and maxi-taxis. The wedding
night songs were held fast by their own beat, an underbeat it
seemed to me, nasal and piercing at times, yet whispering, as if
secrets were being passed from woman to woman. An ancient aura

surrounded these women, a oneness with their past and present that showed in every ripple of bare flesh, every beat of their bare feet against the mud-daubed earth.

On the way home Bess and I talked about the new Trinidad that was coming into being. It was 1995, she reminded me, one hundred and fifty years since the first indentures had left India for Trinidad. Major celebrations had already taken place and many more were planned. The country had a general air of prosperity; oil revenues had made the island an entirely different place from the one I had left over twenty years earlier. But violence had increased, Bess said, sighing deeply, especially domestic violence. I kept my own counsel, remembering my own experiences and those of the women I knew about—the schoolgirl at La Pastora, Baboonie, Grandma Lil herself. Was Joshua abusive to Gainder? I wondered.

Grandma Lil's need for secrecy still puzzled me. I had always thought of my grandmother as a woman in control of everything, and especially of my quiet, scholarly grandfather. But Bess had lived with my grandparents since childhood and I became convinced that her reading was far more accurate.

"She wore the pants inside the house. She managed everyday life, her children, the running of the household. But anything to do with the outside world was in Grandpa Jamesie's control. He was the boss of all her money because she was his wife. Even though he didn't know what to do with it, he was still the boss.

"You know, Mona, when Sweetie died I had hell to get this house declared as mine because I was illegitimate. Grandma Lil saw this problem coming and wanted to deed the house to me and Sweetie together, but Grandpa said no. He insisted that the house belonged to Sweetie and that it was up to him to do whatever he wanted with it. Grandma Lil cautioned my father about making a will and I'm sure he meant to—he did want me to have the house—but he never got around to it, his usual style, you know. Well, he couldn't have known that he would die so young. It was your mom and Auntie Vannie who came and swore affidavits to the lawyers about Sweetie's intention. I don't know if their statements helped really, I might have got the house anyway, but there were lots of claims." She laughed. "Sweetie had so many women, different races, sizes, and ages. I myself was surprised at his 'collection of dames,' as your mom and Vannie called it. I loved meeting my aunts again, Mona. They were so warm and loving, and treated me as family in a way that I badly needed then. They were fun to have around too. They joked about things and did not hide what they thought about Sweetie's slack ways, but I could see they really loved him. I really loved him too. He was what his name said he was, a real sweetie-boy. You know how he got his name?"

I shook my head. "When I was growing up, I used to hear that nicknames were created to hide the real names from spirits who might want to do us bad."

Bess looked thoughtful. "I never heard that but it's probably true. Sounds like an African thing. My God, Mona, so much crossover in this place, and still so much war about two nations this and that.

"Anyhow, Sweetie's baptismal name was William Theodore Chesterton. Amazing, eh, those names that they would pluck straight out of novels or history? And Tristy, remember his name?" We laughed together. Tristy's name was Tristram Julius Abraham. "Grandpa Jamesie picked everyone's names, and it was Lil who found ways of shortening them, I think. Well, when William was born, one of the ladies' clubs in church received a whole set of seeds from Canada for the school garden. Plants they had never even heard of before like cosmos and nasturtium. Even some bulbs." Bess giggled at this. "Not a tropical in the bunch. Anyhow, Grandpa brought home some of the seeds. The school garden perished in no time but Grandma Lil's green thumb did wonders. The cosmos and the gladioli are still there, hale and strong, but the nasturtiums died after flowering only once. And one of those plants was dianthus, Sweet William. She potted those seeds and once she had transplanted them, you couldn't hold them back. They went wild on the ground and she had to keep thinning them out. She thought their growth was a good sign, so she blessed my father with the name."

Bess, like Muddie, was convinced that Grandma Lil was never happy with Grandpa. But I felt that they were both being too hard on Grandpa. "It wasn't his fault, Bess, I mean that's how life was then, it's not fair that he should be blamed, maybe he wasn't happy either."

Bess had seen them close up and Grandma Lil had been her mother for most of her life. Her grandfather Davy was Grandma Lil's lost first love. God, the tragedy and melodrama of it all, I thought to myself. When Grandma was dying she had called for Bess, kissed her and stroked her hair, and right there in the room in front of all the others, she had held her and said, "My daughter. My own daughter." I knew this, we all knew it, but Bess repeated it now with tears in her eyes.

"It's not fair? Life is not fair, Mona, we know that. When Grandma was dying, she refused to hold it in anymore. If Grandpa Jamesie even appeared in the doorway to her room, she would scream loudly, 'Get that man outa here! Get him to hell out!' She didn't care who was around, church people, family, neighbours, she didn't give a damn. He would shuffle out quietly in his bedroom slippers, looking hurt and puzzled. I felt sorry for Grandpa, even though he never accepted me as a true member of his household. For a few years after I came here to live, he would only refer to me as 'the girl.'"

When Grandma Lil died, we were already in Canada. The other deaths followed in quick succession. Grandpa died within a year, and two years later Uncle Sweetie dropped dead of a heart attack. Bess was in her early twenties when her father died and she waged the inheritance war with his collection of dames. All of Grandma Lil's daughters were at her deathbed and she died happy, Bess felt certain.

"She had a smile on her face when she died, Mona. Sweetie had gone to the airport to meet Tristy, but the flight from the Prairies was delayed and only got in one hour after she had passed. Grandpa Jamesie was sitting in the rocker on the front porch. When Grandma's breath got raspy, Auntie Alice made a move to go and fetch him, but Lily reached out and held her hand. Alice called out to her father, but by the time he heard her voice and came into the room Grandma Lil was dead."

TWENTY-TWO

Two weeks passed. At night my sleep was deep and uneventful. On mornings in Iere Village I would awaken and lie in bed, listening with pleasure to the low singing of Girlie, Bess's helper from the village. I had never heard these songs before—country songs that had somehow persisted in spite of the rap and hip-hop and Jamaican reggae and calypso played on the radio all day.

> *If you love me*
> *Do not rough me*
> *Sweet soap and powder*
> *You must gie me*
> *If you love me*
> *Do not rough me*

Girlie was young and shy. The plaintive cadences of her song flowed effortlessly from her throat, but she was not one for conversation. Bess didn't mind; Girlie would arrive early and by midmorning would have finished her work and moved on to another house. The country's prosperity had reached Iere Village too.

Bess had dedicated herself to the making of a museum of Indian heritage. One day she took me to the makeshift warehouse that the Indian Heritage Committee had set up only a short time before. The plans had been drawn up and the committee members were engaged in massive fundraising to make the museum a reality. In the meantime artifacts, objects, and precious mementoes from the Indian past were pouring in and they needed to store them. Bess disappeared into a small meeting room to the side with the other committee members while I toured the collection of objects labelled with rough tags. So much work to be done! There were chuntas, calchuls, a whole clay chulhah, peerhas, pooknis, belnas, tawas, lotas, tarias, hammocks—objects brought from India once or made here out of skills that had survived the crossing.

Items such as these had made our lives possible in times when a life could barely be imagined. Like the *chardon bene* plant with its distinct coriander smell and strong taste. Its Creole name was *shado-beni* but for us it had become *bhandhania*; not *dhania*, but its wild cousin. On my last visit here Bess had taken a short cut through the back roads of Malgretoute. She had stopped to offer a lift to three women who appeared out of the cane fields suddenly, each with her skirt rolled up into a bundle at the front. As we drew nearer I noticed that these were outer skirts and two or three other skirts showed underneath. The women were market vendors and had been walking through the cane fields in the early morning, harvesting the wild herb. They gave us a generous heap, advising Bess on how to blend it with garlic and vinegar. *Every time ah passing by yuh grinding massala* . . . I had started to hum the tune and Bess tapped her fingers in recognition. Blending bhandhania seemed incongruous to me, out of step as I was with the changing times. What a pleasure it must have been for those early labourers, with their meagre estate rations, to come upon this redolent herb, fresh and abundant between the stalks of cane they were cutting.

My thoughts were interrupted by a door creaking open as four men walked out of the meeting room, deep in conversation. They passed by, not seeing me behind the piles of stacked objects, and I heard one saying, "If woman is trouble! All ah them feel they too damn great now they forming they own association and thing. Getting vex because we ask them to do the Indian delicacies. Since when Indian woman can't cook, eh? Tell me that! I can't understand why they get so vex about a lil thing so. A real tempest in a teapot, if yuh ask me."

Another voice said, "I think is the girl who put them up. Long time I telling allyuh that girl is trouble. I mean, she good with organizing and thing, but what kinda example she is for Indian girls, eh? She ain't no Sita, let me tell you."

The rejoinder from another was equally dismaying. "And ah hear she have a Rasta man up north she dey with. I ain't know, nah. We go have to look at she sharp. Just let this Divali thing pass off and then we go see. This museum too important for some strayway girl to spoil the whole thing. You know how important this is to de politics! Hah, Lord!"

A youngish voice, quiet and conciliatory, raised a weak protest. "But Mr. Narine, I hear he is ah Indian Rasta. We can't be too hard on the girls nowadays, man."

But the first voice shot back with venom, "You stay dey, yuh hear! Rasta is Rasta, and what right ah Indian have to turn Rasta, eh?"

It hit me then that Bess was the only woman I had seen among the committee members for the museum. In the car she had been chatting excitedly about the upcoming Divali celebration. It was to be a big community event in an open car park that she had already secured for free, and any money made would go to the museum fund.

Just then Bess rushed out of the room, calling to Mr. Rattansingh. Through the stacks I saw the shortest of the group turning, smiling and courteous, as they quickly discussed something. Bess looked thoughtful and they all returned to the meeting room. When they re-emerged after a few minutes, they had the air of a solution hanging over their heads as they made their way out of the building.

In the car I began to tell Bess about what I had heard, but she dismissed my concern with a shrug.

"That's how they are. So they stop. They can't help it. I can't bother with that, Mona. If I were to bother, I wouldn't do a damn thing. In any case, I, me one, can't change the situation. We have to build something new, and if we have to build it from the ground up, then we have to, that's all. What I hate is denial. Denial is a cop-out and it does not change a damn thing."

Da-Da used to make this point when I was growing up. "Look," he would say, whenever he was rebuked by Muddie or someone else for ranting about an act of hypocrisy or false pride, "if is so, is so. I didn't make it so. I find it so. But I ain't going to lie and say is not so, yuh hear?"

"I don't expect it to be easy, Mona. But this place will change—it has to change. Backward men like Mr. Rattansingh will help it to change in spite of their backwardness. What they could do to me, eh? They not putting bread in my mouth and they can't take it away. They are not the biggest problem. The real problem is how we fit into life here. You know people talk about Trinidadian culture and another culture called Indian culture? So Trinidadian culture don't have place for Indians too? And you know, is not only the prejudice against Indians by Creole people and white people and red people and Chinee people I talking about. Is the way Indians hate their own background. People like our family, Presbyterian people and middle-class people, they hate the history that marks them as coolies. And why? Coolie people wasn't people too? It's so ridiculous."

Bess steupsed loudly and we drove on in silence. I wanted to tell her more but hesitated to introduce anything personal. She swerved suddenly to avoid a pot-hound crossing the highway and cursed to herself. Then she turned her anger back on Mr. Rattansingh. "That man is not only ah ass," she raged, "he is a damn mischief maker too. Imagine him going behind our back and asking a women's organization in Central to provide the Indian delicacies for the Divali reception. The chair of the organization call me up right after and say in a real nasty voice that I could tell Rattansingh that none of the women and them could cook. That if we want a cook, we should hire one. I tried to find out what was happening, but she slammed the phone down on me. The whole story finally came out at the meeting. Rattansingh said he was only trying to include them. Now I have to find a way to patch up the rift because I want them to be part of the organizing team. Mona, you know how hard I tried to get these women to join the committee? But I kept hearing the same thing: 'We can't deal with the man and them.' So where to start now? I don't know, but there must be a way."

There must be a way and if there were, Bess would find it. If she couldn't find it, she would create it. We were driving to Mt. Hololo poised at the northwestern edge of the Northern Range, outside of Port of Spain. I was looking forward to meeting Rajesh, Bess's boyfriend, and Bess hoped that his mother would be there too, coming in from Cunupia for the weekend.

I asked Bess to tell me more about her grandfather Davy, still intrigued by what I was beginning to see as the deeply erotic connection between him and Grandma Lil, and how their bloodlines had entwined themselves, *malgré tout*, after every possible event had thwarted their love.

Bess told me that she would have died when she was an infant if it had not been for the intervention of Ma Toussaint, an obeah woman in Caigual Trace where her mother Doudou lived. Doudou was a nympho, Bess stated flatly. She believed that Davy had had an incestuous relationship with Doudou and that this probably explained the origin of her wild ways. Davy was always drunk. He did not seek village women and Samdaye did not disguise her hatred of her husband and her daughter. As a young woman, Doudou had lots of men friends. The family was scandalized but would not throw her out. They exiled her to a small hut behind the main house and turned a blind eye to her doings, making sure to send her a plate of food morning and evening.

"Very tolerant of them," I remarked.

"No, Mona." Bess's tone was sharp. "Not tolerant, just very Indian." Doudou was part of Samdaye's bad karma, tied in with Davy. She believed that she had to do her duty so she wouldn't keep carrying around the bad stuff. Whatever the reason, she took care of Doudou like a dog or a beggar. By then Davy was dead of rum and ole talk. Only Samdaye was left.

Why did Uncle Sweetieboy go after Doudou? Bess had a theory about her father's instincts. Like Grandma Lily he had rebelled against the prissiness of Indian Presbyterian life with its hundreds of rules and restrictions handed down by foreign missionaries, but like her too he could only manage his rebellion in secret. He visited Doudou by night and ordered her to keep herself only for him.

"He was a coward and a sadist." Bess's voice faltered briefly. "At first he wanted to dominate her completely and even used to bring bunches of lovevine to bind her hands and feet. The lovevine was strong, but one day she managed to undo the knots and gave him the beating of his life—using the vines and a bullpistle that she kept under her bed. Grandma Lil knew about the beating because she had to dress the cuts he got from that dried bull's penis." Bess laughed dryly. "He refused to go to the hospital. I suspect he had something going on with a nurse there." Bess was describing her parents but her detachment from the situation seemed absolute.

"From that day on Sweetie was Doudou's slave. He did whatever she asked, and she asked for things outside of his experience. I heard this from Ma Toussaint herself. Doudou would boast about it. She was kinky as hell, I bet. He was adamant in one way, however. He swore that he would never bring down his family by having any outside children. When Doudou got pregnant, he moved her to Caigual Trace, way in the heart of Moruga. Very few Indian people lived there and she was completely isolated."

Bess paused, observing my incredulous expression. Uncle Sweetie had been my favourite uncle; he had been everyone's friend, mischievous, laughing, always full of fun. This account of lovevines and bondage and willing enslavement had me shocked into silence. "Hard to believe, right, Mona?" She shrugged. "But the truth is the truth, and who the hell are we to judge them anyway?"

Bess was born at home, delivered by Ma Toussaint, who claimed a direct line of descent from free Africans who had been brought as indentures themselves, after the abolition of slavery. When Ma Toussaint lifted Bess up, she told Doudou, "This child will take her own road. She is not for this kinda life. Let this child make her own way."

"You see, Mona, I have come to see who my mother Daisy really was. I spent a lot of my life hating her, being bitterly ashamed of her. I hated her, I hated Davy, I hated the white man. Now I know that I, Bess, Elizabeth Daisy Ann, am a full human being. Not an accident, not an apology, not a creature born of a white man's need to put his waste somewhere. I am not rapeseed. And that white raper-man who took advantage of my great-grandmother, who caused my grandfather Davy to drink himself to death because that overseer, the white coward, would not smile on him, I curse him and all his generations. I am not of that line.

"I heard that Mai, Davy's mother, cursed the white man's line after her son died. She was old then and half-crazy, but she sharpened her cutlass so that more than half of it was pure blade—you could see your face in it—and she waited at her door mouth night after night. If he only set foot in her yard . . . but the white man, the overseer, had gone back to England by then with his little white family. Mai drank gramoxone one night and they found her days later when the cobos started circling over her hut.

"My mother Doudou was wild but not in the slightest way independent. She never had to fend for herself, and once she was locked away in Caigual Trace, she had no idea what to do with herself. How Sweetie persuaded her to move I don't really know, but I think he let her believe that he would be living with her. She would never have left Samdaye's house, I can't see it. But you know how these families are. Once she was out, she was out. She could never go back. Sweetieboy hardly came to see her then though he paid the few dollars rent.

"It was Ma Toussaint who saved the day. One day she dropped in and found Doudou sick and crying. The village women would send food for her sometimes, but nothing had come for days. It was Ma Toussaint who organized a kind of village brigade for food, for the sake of the child, she said. When Doudou's time came, she delivered me and it was she who registered the birth, naming me after the queen, my mother Daisy, and herself. Her own name was Ann. She put down my parents' names as Doudou and Sweetieboy, but she knew his last name so that was how it was recorded on the birth certificate. This was unusual for an illegitimate birth, but she was well known and I suppose the registrar trusted her. You know, Mona, Sweetie had 'thrown' quite a few children, people said, but not one of them had his name, so there was no proof. That birth certificate helped me win the court battle for the house." Bess shook her head. "My two parents. Sweetieboy and Doudou. Two useless sweetie pies."

But the story had even more twists and turns. A few days after the birth Ma Toussaint gave the child a cleansing bush bath and journeyed with her to Hardbargain. She went directly to the rumshop.

"Call Samdaye," she said to the boy behind the counter.

Samdaye came out, took one look at the baby, and began to curse Ma Toussaint. "Take this rakshas child outa here. Mih daughter is a ho and a nemakaram, and now yuh bring she devil child inside mih house! Take she from here before I mihself throw she in the road."

Ma Toussaint pleaded and begged in vain. She left the shop and was walking with the baby along the main road when Sweetie passed by in a car and stopped. He was aghast at the events and embarrassed by Ma Toussaint's loud accusations, promising to bring money and goods more regularly to Doudou. He heard about the registration and steupsed threateningly, but he was no match for Ma Toussaint. He liked the names, though, and it was he who started calling the baby Bessie, later shortening it to Bess. And so Bess lived a catch-ass, dependent life until she was six.

At that time Auntie Vannie, who was the best seamstress around for miles, grew tired of the pressure put on her by her teacher clients from Princes Town, who always made it their business to tell her about her brother Sweetieboy's outside child—bright bright and pretty, running around barefoot and coming to school in old clothes. Vannie brought Bess to live at Grandma Lil's house, over the objections of Grandpa Jamesie.

"Did Doudou object?"

Bess grinned at the thought. "I think she was relieved. I know I was relieved."

Bess's composure was hard-won. She was very clear about the fact that life was not fair. No revisionist history for her. She was Grandma Lil's natural inheritor.

I had never been to Mt. Hololo before and marvelled at the wild tawniness of the vegetation, the mountain's rugged contours, its sense of impermeability. The land here in the North differed completely from that in the South. Bess's boyfriend, Rajesh, a Rasta-farian with almost floor-length dreadlocks, lived in a wonderful ramshackle wooden building. His canvases were everywhere. He painted vast landscapes and was beginning to attract a lot of attention among art circles in the Caribbean. He had started by using house paint and had made it his medium. His work was astonishing, I thought, *les Fauves* rising out of the Caribbean Sea. He was easy, relaxed about his work, talking about his plans for the future. He was leaning towards abstraction, he said, but first he wanted to finish a huge mosaic he was working on. He invited me to a shed outside to look at it.

The mosaic consisted of a huge wooden slab divided into small asymmetrical shapes. In each of these "tiles" Rajesh was inscribing a miniature portrait of Trinidad—he had got the idea, he said, from the miniatures done in India on grains of rice. The tiny scenes were intricate, marked by a sense of collision, fruit and vegetables, landscape and people of all races clashing in minuscule spaces. He had just started, but the intricately wrought effect of the work was already visible. Bess pulled me aside and confided that Rajesh clearly liked me because he never showed unfinished work to strangers and only rarely to her.

I met his mother too, a small, dark Indian woman with a comfortable frame. She hugged me warmly, held me at arm's length to appraise me directly, and then, satisfied, folded me into her arms again. "Call me Soomin," she crooned, and her voice was immeasurably soothing to me. Bess had told me that Rajesh was her only surviving child. Soomin talked about her husband, a Creole man tall tall just like Raj, who was too sick now to travel any distance. "Both a we use to sell in the market. I use to sell tomato and he use to sell crab. So when we meet and thing start up, I leave the tomato and come to sell crab with he. Was mangrove crab we use to sell and you know how they hairy. He use to sell and I use to charge extra to clean the crab. People use to leave everybody and come to buy from we. That was before it catch on. Now everybody paying to clean crab."

Rajesh was a fine cook. He had made us an oil-down with bread-fruit and fish and a trace of callaloo bush, everything in perfect balance. His mother had cooked the superb curried crabs. We dawdled at the table, she and I, eating crab long after Bess and Rajesh had gone out to the verandah to smoke. She still grieved for her dead children. "I mind all my baby," she said softly. "But the only one lucky to live is Raj. And now I get back a daughter. I so glad for Raj that he find Bessie. She is a good good woman."

Yes, she was, I thought, they were good for each other. Their sensual connection seemed real, unhurried, completely without reserve. The way she listened to him talking about his painting, the way his hand around her waist dropped naturally to the rise of her buttocks—I loved their grace with each other, and thought with a pang of how simply and freely they belonged inside each other's world.

For the time being they lived separate lives, but they were planning to have a child. Bess's life was serene, completely suited to her balanced disposition. For the first time I understood how necessary this order was to her and how much she had invented herself, out of virtually nothing.

TWENTY-THREE

 I visited the rand several times after our first visit and wrote down her explanations of Gainder's songs. I taped her singing the one that had come into common usage, the popular chutney love song whose composer was long forgotten. These songs were my bounty, swinging open a doorway into another world, returning across the *kala pani* to the India the girl Gainder had left, alone. They told a tale of love and loss, distance, journeying, hope, hardship piled upon hardship, and, in the end, the triumph of fidelity. I began to piece together an English translation of them, with more difficulty than I had anticipated because of the *nagara* beat that informed their distinctive rhythmic structure, so unlike any poetic form that I knew. And in Bess's study I started to make my own notes from the new books about indentureship and the old Trinidad that was hardly visible these days.

Our great-grandmother's name was Gainder, just that, and she had named herself Beharry afterwards. Muddie had said that we were not related to any other Beharrys in Trinidad, and nobody knew where Gainder had picked up the name. Only my own digging yielded the information that indentured immigrants were registered under one name, and that many of them came from Bihar in India— hence the anglicized spelling of Beharry. The register of indentureship included columns for father's name and next of kin, village, zillah, and pergunnah, but she must have left all of these blank.

And like an image developing slowly on photo-sensitive paper a picture of the woman Gainder began to appear. I connected the dots with a sense of relief that was indescribable. My research was yielding real gold this time, gold that would make sense of my own life. The outlines of my own film began to form themselves in my mind—a film about the crossing of the *kala pani*. Gainder's crossing.

I discovered that *gatka* referred to an Indian martial arts tradition, involving stick fighting. Grandma Lil had misspelled the word, but *arkatiya* simply meant a recruiter for indentured labour. Sugar plantations in the late nineteenth century had a recurring problem that British administrators bluntly referred to as the "coolie-woman problem," but it was wife-murder, uxoricide, plain and simple. The causes were infidelity, jealousy, the scarcity of Indian women, and, startlingly, as the records indicated, a stubborn belief in "the low quality of the coolie-women" themselves. For the administrators the solution was simple: more Indian women. But where in India could be found young labouring women, as yet unmarried, whose families would readily allow them to cross the Atlantic to find work on a sugar plantation? An administrator's paper dream was an impossibility in the Indian social structure.

The solution, when it did appear, presented itself from an unexpected source, the outlawing of sati in 1829. Now, instead of being immolated on their husbands' pyres, thousands of young widows were regularly turned out of doors by their in-laws and could be found wandering in the cities, seeking a living by various means, singing and dancing, begging for alms, often prostituting themselves. Large numbers of these widows proved to be ripe for persuasion by recruiters for the ships of indenture. Rands. Grandpa Jamesie read and spoke Hindi. He had been taught Sanskrit. He would have known the meaning of the word rand, widow, but also harlot. And the three meagre sentences given to Gainder in the family history I found in Grandpa's bookcase, the torn pages where the songs had been ripped out, suddenly fell into place.

I finished the translation of Gainder's songs into English and printed the words side by side with the Hindi versions found in the shop books. My first act was to replace the pages torn out from the family history. I faxed a copy to Babs, and she and Muddie telephoned that night. I was both overjoyed and relieved to hear the excitement in their voices, especially Muddie's. Her earlier reluctance had been replaced by curiosity at first, and now this enthusiasm. Bess was pleased, especially with the Divali celebration drawing near. She got Rajesh to design individual boards for displaying the songs. The popular one was the last of the trilogy; the fact of its survival testified to the indomitable spirit of Gainder herself, the woman who had found the Vaishnavites and crossed the *kala pani* alone.

Gainder's Songs

I

Free as the birds up singing high
Free as the wind up in the sky
Free as the world that is my home
Free anywhere that I might roam
Free when I laugh and when I sing
Free in my way with everything
Freer than wind and stars and rain
Free in this land, free from stain
Free as a little child
Free as a little child
Free, free again

II

Your hands that burn me
Touch me, touch me again
Your eyes that see through me

The Swinging Bridge

Turn to me, turn again
Your lips I never knew
Press me, kiss me again
On the rock, black against the sky
On the rock, there until you die
Touch me, burn me
Press me again
Your hair so black
Your skin so dark, my lord
Your touch like fire and salt
Your eyes that burn, my lord
I reach the black rock in my dreams
Sweet sleep take me away
On the rock, black against the sky
On the rock, my love until I die
Touch me, burn me
Burn me, burn me again

III

Faithful like Sita
Virtuous like Lakshmi
All the gods and goddesses
Will light our house, my lord
You will swim through sea
You will walk through fire
Throw away your ball and chain
Walk, walk to me
I will be your household light
I will offer flowers, my lord
I will kiss your feet, offer water
Take you from the black rock, my lord
Sweet sleep take me

To the rock where I will find you
In my dreams I will find you
Burn me, burn me again

I had suggested a short history of Gainder's life to accompany the display, but Bess decided against it.

"You see, Mona, the grand picture is still what everybody wants. The righteous Indian family, intact, coming across the *kala pani* together. Like the way the migration is presented today. Not this story. Not a journey of young widows looking for a new life. Wife-murder? Beatings? You must be mad, they would say."

That's what they would say. Yet I believed there had to be a way, some other way, to tell this story of the courage and endurance of these forgotten women, even though, for Bess, it was too near, too risky altogether. I thought of how the first glimmerings of that perilous journey had come to me as a child, listening to the beggar woman, Baboonie, singing her grief on nights when it rained so heavily that the culvert near our house swelled to a river, sweeping everything in its path out to the open sea. It was Baboonie's hooded figure, her music beaten out of nothing but pain, that shadowed this tale that Grandma Lil had struggled to keep alive.

The rand, casting her vivid shadow upon the face of indenture, obscured for more than one century, shook her defiant, dancing body in the faces of those closed knots of jahaji bhais, boys all, who clung together for solace in rumshops and gayaps, canepiece marajs among them, laying down the codes for holding brave women in their places. They clung together, these shipmates, boiling with anger and shame at having to settle for other men's leavings, having to take for their wives rands, own-way women who had tasted freedom and refused to bargain for less. Banding together for strength, these jahaji bhais devised new codes that would force women down on their knees, back into countless acts of self-immolation.

And in the face of renewed opposition to their freedom, women like Baboonie, like my great-grandmother Gainder, sang songs, stringing together with bawdy humour, tenderness, pain, and honesty the scattered beads of their new lives. "Singing Ramayana" they called these nights of singing, when women would get together to listen. Like the Vaishnavite women of Bengal they sang the words of love and loss, they sang moral tales and stories of surviving their new life. Gainder sang these songs and Grandma Lil hid them for safekeeping in the back of her shop books. Lily recorded them for her daughters, for my cousin Bess, for my sister Babsie, for me, for all the women to come, for my film that would tell Gainder's story.

TWENTY-FOUR

Lakhs of light. Divali Night was splendid beyond belief. A night bazaar in a huge public space, the grandeur of arcs and bowers and pillars of lit deyas contrasting with the simplicity of older women who had brought their coal pots and tawas, filling the air with the smell of home cooking. Sada rotis, bhaigans and tomatoes roasting for chokhas, pepper, bhandhania leaves, ochroes, bhaji, curried mango, and carilees. All that simple peasant food from the great Indo-Gangetic plain had crossed the *kala pani* and nourished us during a passage into death and sickness and unending labour, and into a light that was the present. The entranceway was flanked by two huge coppers filled to the brim with water, hundreds of lighted deyas floating on their surface.

In a small, well-guarded enclosure, Bess had set up an exhibit displaying some of the early artifacts of indenture. Gainder's songs were mounted on Raj's panels; many visitors recognized the popular chutney love song instantly. There were everyday cooking utensils, a chulhah on a high table, lotahs, tarias, and other brassware. It was Bess's jewellery display, though, that drew the crowds. On several tiers of a plain wooden structure multicoloured silk and velvet cascaded in a stream of red and gold and jade, and anchored upon this exquisite burst of colour was Bess's collection of the jewellery of indenture. There were nakphuls, chakapajee and chandahar necklaces, beras, churias, armbands, and ankle bracelets— ornately worked pieces that had to be priceless, now that they had disappeared from modern life. All in silver, all made by the hands of

artisans who had melted down the silver shillings given to indentured workers on payday into these filigreed works of art.
Women's bodies, covered with thick silver from wrist to elbow,
ankle to mid-calf, would become walking banks, repositories of
their families' wealth. The metal carapace served another purpose
too, that of a weapon that could crush the head of an unwary
attacker when wielded by an arm unafraid of the swing of its power.
The arm of a rand maybe.

The high excitement of the bazaar was infectious, the wares, the
camaraderie; in the mixture of races and faces and smiles, I saw the
country that Bess was dreaming about.

Later that night she considered the success of the Divali celebrations as we sat on her enclosed back porch, the land sloping down to
what was left of the little stream at the back, bars of moonlight cutting through the burglar-proofed latticework, her deep rattan
chairs an enfolding shelter. The frogs occasionally punctured the air
with their soft croaking; sometimes a bat would shriek its high-
pitched whistle from somewhere in the branches of the sapodilla
tree. The night, full of light and shadow, high bush, hibiscus shrubs,
clumps of bougainvillea, and a spreading frangipani tree shaking its
heavy scent around us, could be threatening, visible as we were to
the outside. I was uneasy until Bess blew out the lantern and we sat
in the dark with our nightcaps. It was then that she confessed some
of her fears and discomforts about the project.

"It's Indian time now, Mona, everybody says that. Every time I
go to an Indian celebration and I see who we are, hundreds of thousands of us, dressed in shimmering clothing, in the reds and yellows
and shocking pinks that we brought to this land, I feel a sense of
pride. And power too. But nights like this I am filled with fear about
what might go wrong, terribly wrong. Indian pride is commend-
able, but hatred of others is not. I feel a rigid kind of thinking com-

ing through—I heard a lot of it tonight, just listening to people who visited the exhibit."

I talked about my own doubts that life was changing for women. Bess held the firm position that she had to work within the organizations that already existed. She had no urge to reinvent the wheel, she said. The attempts to marginalize her in the museum project she considered petty, even though the official pamphlet for the exhibit that night had made no mention of her name. "I've got work to do, Mona, and I'm doing it. That's what counts. The rest will take care of itself. I don't want my name on a plaque. I want the museum to happen, that's all, and I'll stick with the project to make it happen." I felt bad that she was still in the dark about the true intent of her fellow committee members, whose conversation I had overheard that day in the warehouse, and I repeated it to her, holding nothing back. She was quiet when I had finished. The implications for her were vast, I knew that. She had set up a happy, satisfying life here. She loved Rajesh, she loved the work she was doing on the museum, and more to the point, she felt entitled to her fulfilling life.

She seemed to understand the long-term political consequences. Her decision not to tell the story of Gainder's life at the bazaar had shown her awareness clearly. Not now, she had said, maybe later. It would be impolitic for anybody now to suggest that most Indians had not migrated as families, or that once they had arrived, they had not set up families post-haste. To Indian men and others too, the idea of unattached women, especially in those early days, would conjure up one image—that of the whore. I remembered Da-Da's fears for me when I began to show my wilful ways. "What on de ground is dog own" was still true, I thought.

. . .

One Saturday night Bess and I returned late from the beach at Mayaro. During our long, relaxing outing we had talked again of many things, appreciating our deepening friendship. I was getting ready for bed when I heard sounds whacking through the night, dull thuds at the front gate mixed with yelling, cursing, and wild screams punctuated by a high whistling.

I ran downstairs to see Bess already at the front door, holding it ajar. A few minutes later Girlie, Bess's village helper, ran in. She was gasping and wheezing—the whistling sounds came from her constricted throat. She leaned heavily against the wall as Bess held her, spoke comforting words, and rubbed her back. "Now, slow down, breathe, Girlie, breathe slowly." Girlie's face was bloody; one eye was blackened and already swelling.

After a few minutes she pulled off her top dress and unwound several layers of old clothes from around her body, eventually revealing her slight frame in a thin cotton shift. Then, bending briskly, she picked up the pile from the floor and went straight to the back of the house, where she started the washing machine. By the time she came back Bess was making tea and had a cold rag ready for her face. These actions took place with a wordless symmetry. I was the odd one out, and realizing Girlie's appearance at night had to be a frequent occurrence, I left the room. I thought of all the scenes of violence and pain those kitchen walls had witnessed—Uncle Baddall's attempts to assault Muddie, his attacks on me, Da-Da's rages—and all the other scenes in countless homes across the island, scenes that I would never know. As I climbed into bed the sinking feeling in my stomach would not go away.

The Mayaro sea entered my head, its stretch of sand winding far into the distance, its brown lagoon water unchanged from when I was a child. This sea, this cerulean sky remained unchanged from what I had known all my life. Girlie's blows, Bess's enfolding house were part of a pattern that I knew by heart, that I would have been a part of if I had stayed. If we had stayed here, anchored on the ground that made us, Kello might have been alive—who knows? Johnnie would have been nearer, Babs might have found a serenity like Bess's, Muddie's garden would have been glorious, and Da-Da—dearest Da-Da, now grown old—might have been more at ease. And me? Would I have had a real life here, a real love, like Bessie's? Would I have found a place of repose with someone like Bree? Could I have lived here with Roddy, whom I missed more than I cared to admit? But I knew the answers now. I would still have left and become a wanderer, a nowarian.

I thought of Kello again and wished that I had just one photograph of him that captured exactly who he was—his shirt collar turned up at a rakish angle, his head flung back in abandoned laughter, his whole face open to the world around him. If I had only one such photo! But there were none. All the pictures of him alone were formal and meaningless, and the two or three in which he looked natural were group shots. No photographs of Kello on his own, the man alive, the man fully himself.

At elementary school we would always play picture-no-picture at the beginning of the school year when our textbooks were brand new. We had to open the book at random and scored points if we hit a different picture each time. The pictures were mostly historical, Napoleon exiled on St. Helena, Elizabeth I, Sir Francis Drake. All the images were of the people who had shaped our lives—shoving, herding, transporting us from one end of the earth to another for their own gain. They were bent on creating fortunes out of nothing—that was what they considered their genius. That nothing was us, flung by one turn of the wheel of fortune into a place entirely unknown, where we built our lives not out of nothing, but out of the back-breaking work of reinvention.

The Swinging Bridge

Later, almost overpowered by sleep, I sink below the surface. Underneath the mask of everyday life lies the swirling sea of memory and desire, of dreams and mythmaking. In the separation of these two worlds we perish. The bridge between them arches high above a raging river, held in place by silken ropes, ropes strong as gossamer.

Morning comes. Every single day has its peculiar colour, taste, and smell. The day decides its texture in the early morning. I wake to a day of light and radiance, a day for unravelling a too tightly wound cocoon.

I left Trinidad in the afternoon with a mixture of sadness and excitement. In a strange way, I felt as if I was leaving home for the first time.

TWENTY-FIVE

 It is late November and the Montreal city streets are slick with freezing rain when I return. I hunch my shoulders and walk faster. My walk is purposeful and strong. The chill in the air is pungent, the leaves have fallen, the year is coming to a close. I am part of this city I live in, and right now I want no other place. Like any other migrant navigating new terrain, I bring my own beat to the land around me.

The beat I sensed early, but where it started exactly and when I cannot now say. It must have been one day when I was very young, living in that small island at the bottom of the Caribbean Sea, that I first heard that beat, never to lose it. It was made of itself, a sound not yet in its present form because even as I spoke the beat was just coming into existence. Any new beat is like that: parts of it at war with itself until the separate parts recognize the point of fusion and merge seamlessly. When the rhythm becomes right, everyone forgets the time when cacophony threatened to drown the whole enterprise.

I heard the beat of the hosay drum inside the steelband, heard chac-chac and dholak, dhantal, cuatro, and iron, coming to me in a rhythm that had me transfixed for hours. A dub rhythm, the Caroni Dub.

Sometimes, in the middle of my hustling city life, I pause just long enough to hear the edges of that beat pulsating at the outer corners of my mind. When I do, I know that I'm safe, memory intact, body alive, heart still felled by pain.

The Swinging Bridge

Caroni Dub is the beat I hear, behind the songs my great-grandmother Gainder wrote, telling the story of her secret life, her life, her love, locked in a cell carved out of a rocky outcropping on the island of St. Helena, off the coast of Africa.

ACKNOWLEDGEMENTS

Thanks to:

Phyllis Bruce, my editor, for her work on this book and for her incredible combination of perspicacity, skill, and stubbornness

Denise Bukowski, my agent, for believing in this book long before it attained full form

Austin Clarke, for his encouragement and support

Manshad Mohammed, for his assistance with the use of Hindi words

Mom, for all her stories; Dad, for his ole talk

My family, for unstinting support and love

Vincenzo, friend and foe

and finally, to the San Fernando posse at large, for inspiring this work.

Ramabai Espinet was born in Trinidad and has lived in Canada for 25 years. She is a poet, a writer of fiction and essays, a critic, and an academic. Her published works include the poetry collection *Nuclear Seasons* and two children's books, *The Princess of Spadina* and *Ninja's Carnival*, in addition to the performance piece *Indian Robber Talk*, which has been staged in Toronto. Ramabai Espinet lives in Toronto.

To receive notice of author events and new books by
Ramabai Espinet, sign up at www.authortracker.ca.